ABOUT THE AUTHOR

Sherlin Henderson Lewis is a debut novelist. Born and raised in the Ninth Ward of New Orleans, Lewis was formally educated at Newcomb College of Tulane University. As is her writing, Lewis' formative years were shaped strongly by her various experiences within the Christian faith and colored by a myriad of experiences throughout the Ninth Ward, French Quarter & Uptown New Orleans. Lewis and her husband make their home in Louisiana with their children.

Printed In the United States of America
First Printing: 2011
ISBN-13: 978-0-983-5097-0-7 (paperback)
ISBN-10: 0983509700 (paperback)

Sherlin Henderson Lewis

Birthing Pangs

ENOUGH GRACE PUBLISHING

Acknowledgements

I am running over with thankfulness towards God for giving me the opportunity to write this work of fiction. Words alone will never express my full gratitude.

To Kevin, my leading man, who has worked with me to build the sanctuary that is our love; I say thank you for our family's special resting place, your deliberate love, self-possessed strength and tender guidance. You are truly my brother, best friend and hero.

To my wonderfully precious children, I want to say thank you for your refreshing honesty and contagious joy throughout the process of completing this project. It is a joy to be your mom.

To my dearly loved mother, Theresa, who while working for years as a highschool English teacher determinedly taught me to care for reading and writing, and my beloved father, Verlin, who as an unprofessed folk teller sat beside me at a young age, telling me tales and nourishing the storyteller in me, I say thank you for your devotion and tender loving acts.

To Rev. Eric Rhodes & Mrs. Jonell Rhodes, two of the remarkable souls in this world who for the sake of the cross have taken it upon themselves to care for the lost, orphaned and injured birds of this world, I say thank you for lovingly embracing one little bird in particular. Thank you for sheltering her, feeding her and tending to her wounds until she was able to resume flying.

To each and every one of the faithful and remarkable men and women in the ministry who have taught and/or supported me in my walk and in my coming to trust and know God as father, I say thank you. I want to give thanks especially for my dear sweet grandmothers, Celestine Singleton Ashford and the late Willistine Montgomery Powell, also, the late Minister Alex Anderson, Rev. Charles W. Duplessis, Rev. Dr. Walsdorf H. Jenneford, Rev. Raymond A. Jetson, Clarence Moran III, Janice D. Moran and Dawn J. Roussel. As it regards your gifts of charity, yours have been priceless and life-saving contributions that will echo throughout all of eternity.

To my former English professors at Tulane University, an exceptional bunch, mainly those scholarly instructors who made it their business to encourage me to think and formulate sentences at the expense of losing face with those who might object to my breaking rinks with their particular manner of conformity, I say thank you.

To neo-griot, Kalamu Ya Salaam, one of my most appreciated and compelling writing mentors, I say thank you for unselfishly planting seed with no intention of controlling or benefitting personally from the harvest. Your investment in the NOMMO Literary Society has meant a great deal to this world.

Last but certainly not least, to my impressive and creative brothers and sisters in the NOMMO Literary Society, I say thank you for opening up the doorway to your souls and pouring out your gift. Working with you in NOMMO was a rare and special treat.

CONTENTS

As a women with child is in pain and cries out in her pangs, when she draws near the time of her delivery, SO have we been in Your sight Oh Lord. We have been with child; we have been in pain. . .

Isaiah 26:17-18A   KJV

PART ONE

BIRTH

ANNOUNCEMENT

1

Birth brings to life that veiled formation and then deliverance of a baby from the body of the mother, the one who conceives. While it is designed that women exclusively give birth to humanity, it is still undeniably true that both men and women give birth to the things in their lives. The multidimensionality that exists in the process of the birth of life has been underestimated. It is next to impossible for a person to live without being impregnated with something.

For there will forever be etched in history the record of Moses, the Hebrew who was raised in the house of the Egyptian Pharaoh, whom God impregnated with a vision to lead his people, the Israelites, out of their slavery in Egypt. Did Moses experience his own birthing pangs? He most certainly did. Moses travailed amidst hardship and pushed to see his people delivered. Moses was inspired by God to write in Genesis chapter three and verse sixteen that women will bring forth their physical children through sorrow. The spiritual principle that we are introduced to here is that when a man or woman bears the very pressure of their own life there will be a certain degree of pain and laboring involved in their birthing process.

2

In physical labor, when a baby is about to be delivered into this life, our pain can be an indication that a baby is on its way. In everyday life, the same principle can be applied. Not only can women experience pain and sorrow when giving birth to their children, but also both men and women experience pain and sorrow when bearing the very weight that embodies their lives.

What then, do we humans do?

Do we jump from life's delivery tables, biting off the heads of those closest to us and blocking off our passageways, hollering, "Nothing and nobody is getting in or out of me. No babies, no love, no faith, no joy and no mercy". Without exception, do we refuse to make room for life? Because of pain and sorrow, do we decide that we no longer want to continue being the vessels of life that we were created to be? By ceasing to recognize who we are, do we become assassins, misunderstanding and destroying the life that has been placed within us?

Or do we continue on? Do we continue to pray and live through our tears, smiling even in the midst of our pain and embracing our opportunities to participate in God's magnificent plan for life?

Do we dare?

If we do dare continue, do we press? Do we push forward through our painful labors, refusing to shut up our wombs and kill our babies and refusing to be misled into mistaking our passing sorrows for the full extent of our actual lives?

I believe we must! We must push on through our pain, refusing to shut up our wombs and kill our babies and refusing to be misled into mistaking our passing sorrows for the full extent of our actual lives. Even as we work through this world's pressures, struggles and deceptions, we must live.

I understand that it gets hard sometimes, but we must. We must! We must live! We must breathe deliberate breaths of life and in the midst of our living; we will give birth to new life!

PART TWO

OVULATION

1

Matia was conceived in the bed of my belief that birthing pangs are an inevitable part of both spiritual and physical life. Her birth and life lay bare how our troubles in this life mark periods of increase that are intended to bring about advancement and maturation in our development. Without stomaching these difficult periods of preparation there can never be the full maturation or realization of our babies.

Now ovulation is that veiled process that must occur prior to both conception and maturation. From a biological perspective, ovulation is simply the releasing of a woman's eggs for fertilization. While from a spiritual perspective, ovulation can be seen as the ripening and releasing of the fruit of one's non-physical womb.

2

Before the enchanting Matia experienced the flow of the dark blue Nile, she had already been familiar with the light golden Candy. Before there had ever even been the chance of the charming young woman loving a Nile, she had already possessed an involuntary kind of love for a Candy. Loving Candy was something that was so accidental for her because it had occurred quite naturally and without any force. Although she had already conceived some things in her twenty-one years, she had never before held an amorous kind of love for a male, at least not before finding herself carrying the idea of love that she bore for Candy.

She had suspected her love for him at the exact moment that she had seen him for her very first time. She was home alone, sitting on her front porch, staring into an eternal lavender sky, chatting with God in a matter-of-fact sort of way and awaiting the twilight hour. She was sitting, when Candy, both a glorified Mulatto and confused Black boy, gallantly strolled by with another schoolgirl at his side. As glorious as Candy was to behold he was still searching for his true self, determined to find it somewhere between his fiery haired Irish mother and Black Choctaw father. The word in the neighborhood was that the young woman accompanying Candy, a milk chocolate colored, pleasingly plump and lovely red head, was Candy's co-ed at New Orleans' Southern University. She was new to Matia's neighborhood, but then so was Candy. There he was, the Opelousas born golden boy that the neighborhood girls had dubbed a precious new commodity, carrying the delicious red head's books.

Then he discovered the beautiful Matia for his very first time. As a result, he most ungraciously handed the red head her own books to bear, almost dropping them. As the lovely red head cursed Candy with death, he stopped and stared at his newest discovery. In the middle of New Orleans' Charbonnet Street, Candy stopped and stared at Matia, noticing her alluring exquisiteness. Something quite divine, her beauty demanded his attention. The scrumptious, yet poor and neglected red head had to walk on without Candy, grieving and leaving him alone with his newest preoccupation, which was Matia.

After several moments of enduring his silent study of her, Matia grew tired of it and returned to her own familiar niche within the walls that made up her home. But she did not neglect to take the time to get one last glance of the delectable Candy on that first afternoon. From her father's home office window, she stared at him through her mother's cameo ivory lace curtains. As she peeked, he slipped his hands into his front pockets and strolled down her street with a proud and knowing grin.

Matia was looking again on the very afternoon that Candy returned to her street. She studied him from a distance as he walked past her house until he noticed her. His noticing her caused her to abandon her post at the office window. Before leaving the window, she noticed that Candy was alone this time. Before she left the curtains, Candy noticed that she had noticed him and before she could decide whether she should go out onto her front porch or just stay hidden within the Southern Yellow Pine wood framed walls of her home, Candy had already taken matters into his own hands and made a significant decision. Matia cracked her front door open just in time to see him sitting down on her front porch in the exact same spot that he'd first seen her sitting in.

Did she mind?

She did not mind really. And though she knew that if her much esteemed father were home he might have had an infinite number of problems with Candy's presence on the porch, she was more than pleased to see the golden stranger who had made himself quite at home on her father's property as though it were his own.

A few moments after Candy had sat on her porch, Matia joined him, giving up her seat without a fuss; there agreement was made, but unspoken. He would take whatever she was willing to allow him. She would let him have whatever he

was able to take. This arrangement worked well and without
failure for twelve weekday afternoons. For twelve weekday
afternoons, the two of them sat on her front porch, staring
at and talking to each other.

But on the twelfth afternoon as they sat hungrily gobbling each other up with glance after glance and answered
question after answered question. On the twelfth afternoon,
as they sat awaiting the twilight hour: the hour that the sunset began and that her father left his South Claiborne Avenue
office. Candy seized her rather roughly by her shoulders and
aimed his mouth for hers, pulling her towards him and pro-
ceeding to attempt to steal a kiss from her.

Oh, yes! He most certainly did.

First, he asked, looking at her with a starved expression,
"Can I taste you?"

She, clueless fully of what it was that he had meant was
unable to supply a fitting verbal response. Candy mistook
her hazy look for one of passion and he flattered himself
with the thought that she was overtaken with anticipation.
Plus, he thought that she was speechless and finding her that
more irresistible because of it, he decided that he could wait
no longer. He must indeed know what it was like to savor
her.

Matia watched as the whole dramatic affair began to
unfold before her very eyes. It was as if she had seen his
hungry mouth and covetous hands coming several moments
before they had arrived. Consequently, she became resolute
on vacating the premises. She jumped to her feet whilst he
snatched violently at the hem of her patchwork midi skirt,
ripping it at its delicate hem. At first, she was temporarily im-
paired both mentally and verbally. So, she was unable to find

the right words to say. Consequently, she settled for action and quickly stood to her feet. As her verbal speech returned, she spoke scornfully to Candy, retreating from the concrete seat that they once had shared.

"You want somethin' that's not for you," she said, the tone of her voice harsh.

On her way through her front door, she dug deep within herself and found additional words for Candy, deserving words. She suggested to Candy that perhaps it would be best if he just left.

Did he leave?

He did. Candy left, never returning.

3

The next two weeks were long. Matia made herself sick with anxiety, trying to figure out if he had misunderstood her. She had only instructed him to leave. He had not heard her say never return.

Would she ever see him again?

Seated on an aged oak saddle stool with her elbows resting on the living room's front windowsill, she searched up and down Charbonnet Street. Distressing inside of herself, she anticipated what she would say the next time that she saw Candy, if that time ever came. She agonized over his audacity. For him to handle her in such a way as though he was entitled to her. She agonized over his protocol. Exactly, what kind of a young woman did he take her for?

What did it all mean?

Matia would not accept the thought of Candy having only befriended her for the sake of seducing her. She rejected realism, turning it away at every turn. Instead, she obsessed over Candy's redeeming qualities. The few that he possessed, being his striking good looks, silky voice and his beguiling charm. While thinking, she wondered if on that faithful day when he might return. She wondered if on that day things could ever go back to the way that they had begun. Back to when he and she had sat. Two seemingly innocent young adults exploring the possibility of courtship and making dreams come true.

Would Matia be happy or sad if he were to return?

This was her question. She decided after very little deliberation what she would be. She would be glad, of course. A little stiff necked, but delighted still the same.

After all, she found it too hard to remain angry with Candy. The anger that she had felt towards him for his last actions had turned quickly to a double-minded kind of remorse. Her remorse turned to sorrow. The sorrow turned to a sweet melancholia. This melancholia became a deep pool of sadness. Consequently, she had a fleeting case of emotional emptiness.

After the arrival of the melancholia, Matia's nights were difficult. She could no longer talk to God or even search for her laughter without considering Candy. Still, she did manage to go on dreaming. Yes, she did. She dreamed of Candy's hazel eyes, sun soaked golden skin and loosely curled and golden locks. Denying the obvious, that she had lost whatever it was that she had thought she had with him, Matia bothered herself, by playing their first and last meetings repeatedly on her mind's screen. Each new day she awoke, breathed and awaited his next chanced coming.

4

Only, Candy never came.

Instead, on the third afternoon he sent a messenger with a handwritten note that was quite simple and to the point. It was a very curt message, but a message still the same. It read:

> Matia,
>
> From what I can tell, you would make me an alright friend, but I already have enough friends. When I am ready for the one that I want to grow old with, I will look you up again. I promise.
>
> Candy

Spontaneously aborting Matia's dream of what their relationship could be, Candy pushed on in another direction with little to say about his ever returning. Still, Matia foolishly held onto yet another vision, just the same. She soothed her heart by preparing herself for his next chanced coming. She prepared for the time when he might have decided to make good on the potential of his promise, the time when he would be ready for her friendship and perhaps courtship.

Only, Candy never had the opportunity to make good on his promise. At least his time to work his way back to Matia happened to be cut short. You see on the very afternoon that she received his brief note and sat reading it on her front porch, his life was terminated or let us say spontaneously aborted.

While she sat, brand new visions of their potential future forming within her, he was in a rather compromising position with a married and quite undeniably creamy white blonde. By the twilight hour, the hour that Candy would have normally just been pushing off from Matia's porch, he lay bleeding in Uptown New Orleans. By the twilight hour, the pretty blonde's wealthy, German and much older husband had walked into the master bedroom of his prominent Victorian Colonial-Revival Mansion, catching Candy and the young housewife in the act of adultery. By the twilight hour, the said husband had pulled his revolver from his dresser drawer and shot a hole straight through the essence of what Matia had seen as a possible component to her future, terminating the chance of Candy ever working his way back to her.

To terminate the development of a birth is to perform the action of bringing the pregnancy to its end. Furthermore, the termination of a baby whilst it is still within the womb is definitively identified as an abortion. Abortions end growth before full development or maturation can be achieved. As such was the case with Candy's death. Candy's life was ended prior to Candy reaching full maturation.

5

Many gloomy skeptics believe that the miraculous event of birth is merely death's doorway. That life is all downhill after our mother's courageous labor and delivery of us. Some go even a step further as early as the day of our birth, digging our graves and preparing coffins for us.

Are they right?

Let us consider!

Paul of the Mediterranean city of Tarsus, what we presently know as South-Central Turkey, was born centuries ago. Employed by God as an apostle of Jesus Christ, Paul had been moved by God to make a different assertion. In Chapter six of the book of Romans, Paul explained that by their faith Christians are crucified with Christ, dying to their old lives and being resurrected with Christ to live sacrificially new lives in which Christ lives through them. After their spiritual death to sin comes new life. The Christian is born again.

So, in the spirit of what Paul was inspired to maintain as regards Christianity, let me suggest the very opposite of what the cynics have said regarding life's commencement being a doorway to death. Let us consider that in theory the non-physical deaths or endings that occur in the lives of all of humanity can be indirectly, new births. Then, these deaths or endings in premise would by their very nature usher in the conception or beginning of new life.

6

Two years after Matia learned of Candy's murder, she had the following dream:

She dreamed that she had just learned that she was pregnant with twelve babies. Suddenly, she was in a bright pristine delivery room, where she had given birth to twelve babies. Pronounced dead at birth, five of them were stillborn. The remaining seven babies survived.

Once, she was home with her babies, she became aware of the fact that she was not alone. A young man, the epitome of tall, dark and handsome, was at her side. She did not know him and had never seen him before. Still, he acted very much as if he might be her husband, showering her with the kind of support that most women long for. The striking young man poured her a large glass of water from a crystal pitcher. He fussed over both her and the babies, tenderly massaging her shoulders, fluffing her pillows and working hard to assist her in meeting the babies' needs. She drank from the glass of water that the good-looking guy had given her and labored to relax.

Then, she struggled with great difficulty, attempting to nurse all seven of the new babes at her breasts. She felt overwhelmed and upset. Still, she was resolute in her effort to feed all seven of her children, alternating one baby after another.

7

It was December 1976, New Years Eve and two years after Candy had killed himself, by confusing what he wanted with what was his. It was two years after the pretty blonde's husband had killed Candy because of what he had coveted. It was two years after Matia had killed Candy, as she sometimes guiltily worried, by not giving him what he had desired. And there Matia stood in a friend's yard on a muggy street corner on a Friday night. She was about to meet Nile for her very first time. Only, she did not know it. She could not begin to perceive what she was about to conceive. In her mind, she was simply making a mad get away.

How do they say it?

She was indeed out of one man's arms and straightaway into another's.

At any rate, the spirited Matia had barely made it out of her father, Franklin Singleton's, house.

Earlier Franklin, a deacon of integrity, civil rights activist, modest philanthropist and accomplished contractor, had been quite unhappy with her drafting her own plans for the evening. He, a skilled draftsman, had objected to her leaving, laboring to protect both her and her soul.

Was it this simple?

No, a more candid take on the earlier scene would require my saying that what Franklin had done was more like trying his hand at convincing her that she really did not want to go.

Though, he did take the time to explain that he was afraid for her: afraid of what she did not know and how it might hurt her.

But wait!

In no way am I implying that you should believe that his intentions were solely upright. For while the efforts of a man endeavoring to keep his adult daughter safe are totally honorable, this man had added intentions. Matia's father was under the influence of an agenda that was not altogether good, though he would have had Matia believe so. No, there were components of it that were quite problematic. Mostly because Matia's father was as afraid of what could happen to his heart, as he was afraid of what could happen to his daughter's heart.

He was not at all, what one could honestly call a bad father. No, such a description of him simply would not do. Matia's father only had lost too much to entertain the idea of losing Matia too. He loved her, but even more, he loved what she gave him. He had made the critical mistake of coveting what was hers instead of recognizing and embracing what was his. He thought that he needed her to provide him with the gift of something to live for, during a seasonal drought that he believed had left him little else. Even more, he had managed to misplace his much-needed faith in God.

His need to have Matia depend upon him more than God or anyone else for that matter. This need, an ungodly clinging to her, created somewhat of a burden for her to bear.

Frankly speaking, she did not need him. She was fortunate to have her father, but she did not need him to provide her with a life's purpose. She had God. Whom she felt had brought her through more than she had ever imagined possible. Yet, she had begun to try to live for her father. She loved him far too much to watch him drown in the disappointment that she feared would come with her ever choosing to live outside of his jurisdiction. She had decided that she would try to be his savior, bearing out her love for him.

So, up until the moment that I just spoke of (that is the exact moment that she had made her way out of her father's house), she had been trying to play the part of the quintessential martyr. Yet, she knew that she was fashioned to be so much more.

Actually, she was already. Already, Matia was so much more. Her parents had trained her well. Still, now her father, Franklin, was determined to undermine his life's work in her in order to insure that he would not have to endure loneliness.

Translated into a language that Franklin was unwilling to admit that he spoke; this meant that he simply did not want to lose his illusory dependence on her. He was unable to live with the thought of allowing himself to lose it. Bent on making Matia unable to live with the thought of his losing it, he was.

Now, here she had been, his not so little girl. She was long waisted and tall. She was unapologetically Black, beautiful and gifted. All grown up, she was a force to be reckoned with.

Yes, she was a woman. Here she had stood holding her hands at one side and with her head cocked towards the other. She had expressed her intentions to begin living on her own terms. Just one friend's birthday party around the corner on Alabo Street, was all she intended. She would be gone only a couple of hours. Whatever her outing would cost her, she was both willing and prepared to pay.

Still, Franklin was determined to stop her from going. He was determined to stop her from rejoining the living. He could not afford to just sit by and watch this happen. He might lose her to life or to death. It did not matter which. He might lose her! So, he turned his face from Matia's face, hiding his signs of contempt for her unusual and startling plans.

He managed to focus his attention on a new episode of his favorite television show, *Sanford and Son*. Since Franklin found it too difficult to attempt to undermine Matia's plans, while looking her dead in her longing eyes, he stared stoically at his television.

Showing disdain for his own adult child's liberty, Franklin said, "Now you know you don't have no business at no birthday party, Matia."

"No?" Matia asked.

"No," Franklin said, "our books could use a good tightenin' up. And nothin' out there in those streets for a young lady at night."

"Singleton & Co.'s books look fine daddy," Matia said. "I worked late all week, seein' to it."

"What about completin' the application for those night classes I suggested?" Franklin asked, contradicting his concerns about the hours of darkness. "A masters in business will help you, when you're runnin' Singleton & Co. one day."

"I don't need the classes."

"But you can't get your masters degree without the classes."

"Don't need a masters degree," said Matia.

They avoided the obvious elephant that was sitting in the living room with them. Neither of them wanted to address the fact that Matia had never agreed to run Singleton & Company. This was a nauseating fact that needed to be addressed, but Franklin pretended that he could not see Matia's lack of devotion for the family business. Instead, he knelt beside his bed each night chanting desperate prayers in hopes that God might see his side of the story and move Matia to have a change of heart.

"Havin' your accountin' degree and CPA license are a good start," said Franklin, "but a master's degree in business will put the icin' on the cake."

"I need to start gettin' ready to go, daddy."

"You don't listen," shouted Franklin, angrily. "A lovin' daughter would listen."

"I love you daddy," said Matia, worked up.

"Then why are you dead set on goin' to this party? Young women these days runnin' up and down the streets of America like they lost and you itchin' to join em nonetheless."

"Do I run the streets like I'm lost? Really, daddy, do I even run the streets?"

"No," said Franklin, "you don't. But if you go to this party tonight you'll be sorry."

"Daddy, please don't give me a hard time. I was lookin' forward to seein' some of my old friends tonight. It has been a long time since almost everybody from the neighborhood was back home at the same time. It'll be good for me."

"No, it won't."

"Why?"

"I don't want you to go."

"Daddy, please! Can I go anywhere without havin' to repent?"

"Go then," said Franklin angrily. "Go on and go to hell in a handbasket if you want to."

"You're makin' my head hurt," said Matia.

"You're makin' your own head hurt," said Franklin.

"Oh, daddy," Matia cried. "Why must my not agree-in' with you about this birthday party be considered disloyalty?"

"It is disloyalty. You never did appreciate me, Matia."

"You're spoilin' the evenin' for me," said Matia. "I'm too stressed to bother with even goin', now."

"You're spoilin' it for yourself," said Franklin. "It's not my fault you don't have your priorities straight."

"You want me to stay," said a frazzled and dejected Matia. "I'll stay. I'll stay, if you just stop with the condemnation. I'll stay."

"You will?" said Franklin, his voice dripping with both pleasure and satisfaction. "You'll tell those two friends of yours to carry on without you, then?"

"I will," conceded Matia unhappily.

So, the case seemed settled. Since, Matia did not have an appetite for discord between her and her father. Franklin had disapproved of her wish to attend the party and she had abandoned her right to protest.

Then Franklin made a mistake. He made the mistake of taking his eyes off the television screen. He looked up at his daughter as she turned to walk out of the living room and into the dining room.

"Alright then," Matia said reluctantly, wearing her dis-appointment like a comfortable sweater. "I'll call Binta and tell her to tell Shallow I'm not meetin' em on the corner."

Franklin saw Matia's head and shoulders collapse and suddenly his victory was not so sweet. Matia's sudden disap-pointment reminded him too much of his own defeat in life.

This realization, seeing that his only living child was overly familiar with loss, shook him to his very core.

"Matia," Franklin heard himself saying, as though asking her a question.

"Yes."

"Who is it?" he asked. "That's throwin' this here party?"

"Mr. Johnny and Ms. Annie," Matia said with shock. "They use to be in that couple's group down at the church with you and mama."

"I can recall my own life, thank you," said Franklin gruffly.

Matia went red in the face.

"Well," he said, "tell Johnny and Annie I said hi!"

"What?"

"You heard me," Franklin said. "You have my blessin'."

"Oh, daddy," Matia said as she realized her father's change of heart. "Thank you for not holdin' it against me."

She wrapped her arms around her father giving him a kind hug.

Franklin cleared his throat and gently moved his daughter's arms from around him.

"Alright, alright," mumbled Franklin. "You are makin' me miss my show."

8

When Matia arrived to Binta's house on the corner, a gust of wind blew past her as she approached Binta's front porch. No, I will not tell you that she arrived to meet her friends alone. To do so would be a deliberate act of deception. Hence, I must tell you that she was not at all alone. She brought with her Jesus. She believed that He was in heart, saving her from all of the iniquity that she had done and would do. She had brought with her Candy. He was in the pit of her stomach, refusing to go away and making her sick about what she would not do. She had brought with her Franklin and Safiya, her parents. They were in her head, reminding her of all that she should do. Finally yet importantly, she had brought with her Sadiki, her older and mostly dead sister. Sadiki lived on within the very depths of Matia's consciousness, encouraging her to dream. Sadiki encouraged Matia to dream even of that, which seemed impossible. Sadiki's presence was never ending. It was perpetual. It just went on and on ad infinitum. Like time refusing to stand still, it was continuous, conjuring up both the vital and abortive junk that survived at the core of Matia's being. Sadiki was a part of Matia.

Actually, Shallow Flowers and Binta Baptiste, Matia's two closest friends, reminded Matia of Sadiki, but in unrelated ways. However, a little known fact was that Matia's unconscious reasons for being drawn to them was initially due to their reminding her of her sister.

A descendant of Haitian Creoles and West Africans, Binta was short, thick and possessed a sweet and hypnotizing indigo black hue. It was the very same blue-black hue that the beautiful Sadiki had had. Binta's face was that of a full-lipped China doll that had been dipped in rich dark chocolate. Her smile flawless, eyes big and bright, Binta was alluring innocence. Her head full of voluminous hair; she adorned it with two beautiful afro puffs of lustrously coiled corkscrew curls. Shallow was a blend of caramel redbone beauty. Her somewhat Roman nose prominent, she possessed high cheekbones, full pouty lips and dark brown almond shaped eyes that her maternal grandfather said spoke to her father's dearly esteemed Black heritage and her mother's maternal Creole ancestry, a treasured blending of African, French, Spanish and Chitimacha Native American. It was Shallow's naturally straight, course and waist long hair that reminded Matia of Sadiki whose long locks had been much the same as Shallow's hair.

Matia stood before her two quarrelling friends as they sat on Binta's porch swing, rocking it bit by bit. It was Matia's initial intent to stay out of the spat, since she was not particularly interested in playing mediator this night. She endeavored to keep quiet, since she was certain that, her two friends, having always been predictable, would eventually grow tired of picking away at each other.

"Happy New Years, Matia," sang Binta. "You ready for 1977?"

"Happy New Years, y'all," said Matia. "Yeah, I'm ready."

"Aw *'sha'*, I can't believe this," said Shallow, as she transferred some of her body weight from her left foot to her right. "This cow goin' come strollin' up twenty minutes late with a smile on her face and struttin' too. Struttin' just like she thinks she God's gift to men."

Matia winked at Shallow, ignoring the intended injury that she might have sustained from the blow of Shallow's cool and impulsive words. Instead of nurturing feelings of offense, Matia spent several seconds entertaining wondrous thoughts of what it would actually feel like to strut like one thinks that their God's gift to men. She found the thought of one woman being given as a gift to all men impossibly overbearing. She found the desire of any woman to be so mindboggling. She determined that the movement of a woman who had been burdened with the reality of belonging to all men would not at all be a strut. She was certain that this woman's motion would be more like a lifeless crawl. There would be no being God's gift to men for Matia. Being God's gift to one man was almost too much for Matia to believe in. The closest she had ever been to any male besides her father was Candy. She questioned whether she was prepared to bear the weight of any man's love. And her father, Franklin, could not conceive the very idea of it.

So, what man, if any would ever be hers?

She wondered, privately.

"Now, come on Shallow," Interjected Binta, jolting Matia back into the present moment. "Your behind was runnin' late too. If I wouldn't have showed up early to help you get ready, you would still be draggin' your butt around your room, tryin' to find the perfect outfit to wear. Besides, you wasn't studin' bout Matia. You been too busy tryin' to talk me into comin' to one of your women's lib meetings."

Rolling her eyes and placing her hands on her hips, Shallow said, "Well, nobody asked you to help me. As for my suggestin' that you come to one of Dr. Stark's meetings, it just might help you get your priorities straight."

"You sound like my daddy," said Matia to Shallow. "Always tellin' somebody else what their priorities ought to be."

"What's wrong with my priorities, anyway?" asked Binta.

"Binta Baptiste," said Shallow, "you really don't know do you?"

"No," said Binta, "I don't."

"Why won't you come to at least one of our meetings?" asked Shallow. "Then you'll know."

"Why would I?" asked Binta. "I'm just an average woman. I'm not book smart like y'all. And besides that Dr. Stark don't have nothin' to say to me that I want to hear."

"Binta," said Matia, annoyed, "why you always have to say you not smart?"

"I'm not," said Binta. "And besides mama's always sayin' there's no sense in me gettin' conceited and thinkin' more of myself than I am. Pride come before the fall."

"Yeah, you're right, pride does come before the fall, but there's a difference between a humble woman and an insecure one," said Matia.

"Matia Singleton are you sayin' I'm a coward?" Binta said. "Because I'm a lot of things, but I'm nobody's chicken."

"No, no," said Matia, "I'm just sayin' it seems like you're scared of your gift. Besides, we all have our fears."

"Yeah," said Shallow, talking to Binta, "if I could do what you do with a piece of material, I'd be as conceited as they come. In my opinion, today's top designers can't touch the stuff you come up with, Ms. Baptiste."

"Today's top designers," said Binta, "girl please, I'm just a seamstress and in mama's opinion just barely that. She says the clothes I make look like a bunch of raggedy scraps that somebody ought to throw out with the trash. She says I might be able to sew a little bit, but what I do is nothin' to admire."

"Well, no disrespect to ya mama, Binta, but I disagree," said Shallow. "I'd be happy to buy your fashion label."

"My label?" Binta said in disbelief.

"Sometimes, Binta," said Matia, shaking her head in disagreement.

"What?" Binta said.

"Sometimes," said Matia, arching her eyebrows, "I wonder if you know what you're worth."

Binta shrugged her shoulders with indifference.

The three friends were both still and quiet for a few seconds.

"Matia?" said Binta.

"Huh?" said Matia.

"You ever wonder if God love women as much as he does men?" asked Binta uneasily.

"I wonder sometimes if God love," said Shallow.

"Ya'll can't possibly know how much God love y'all talkin' like that," said Matia. "God is love and he loves us all no matter who we are."

"How can you be so sure?" Shallow said.

"Because I know Him for myself, that's how," said Matia. "When mama and Sadiki died, I didn't feel like goin' on, but I'm still here tonight because God loves me. I know He loves me."

The young women were silent. They stood deep in thought for several seconds.

"You see, 'sha'," said Shallow to Matia. "Dr. Stark is only tryin' to liberate women like Binta from that backward way of thinkin' she has."

"Maybe, I don't need to be liberated," said Binta.

"Everybody needs to be liberated," said Shallow. "Don't you think, Matia?"

"I guess everybody does need to be liberated from something or somebody," said Matia, thinking of the conversation she'd had earlier with her father.

"The only liberatin' I need I got from Jesus," said Binta.

"What about your rights," Shallow insisted. "At the meet-in' this week Dr. Stark was explainin' how women's rights are always at stake."

"Black folks are the ones whose rights are always at stake," said Binta. "You can correct me if I'm wrong, but I never heard of nobody bein' hung from a tree simply for bein' a woman."

"Listen Binta," said Shallow. "Dr. Stark's mission is to free women from those who make it their business to tell us what it means for us to be women."

"But isn't that what she's doin'?" Binta asked.

"What?" Shallow sighed.

"Isn't she usin' her meetings and rallies to convince you of what a woman should or should not be?" asked Binta.

"You just don't like her," said Shallow defensively, "be-cause she's not the kind of woman who'd let a man take care of her."

Matia shook her head, frowning. "Here y'all go again," she said. "Can't we ever do anything without the two of y'all fussin'?"

"I don't think your Dr. Stark is in danger of any man tryin' to care for her," said Binta, paying no attention to Matia. "She don't have that to worry about."

"What about you?" Shallow said as a criticism. "I bet you are that kind of woman."

"Yeah, you right," said Binta. "I am just that kind of wom-an that would let her man take care of her, but I'm also the kind of woman who understands that a man needs somebody to take care of him. And I'm woman enough to do it!"

"Not me," said Shallow. "I could never be that kind of woman."

"Last time I checked the jury was still out on whether or not you even want to be a woman," said Binta, snickering.

"You're so passé," said Shallow. "Even your ideas on womanhood are out of date."

"Am I less than a woman than you and your Dr. Stark because my ambition rest in havin' a family."

"You really have to ask?" Shallow asked in disbelief.

"But you'd say I was wrong if I said that you were less of a woman for not wantin' a family," said Binta.

"I'll see y'all at the party," said Matia, having finally grown tired of listening to her two friends picking at each other.

Leaving Binta and Shallow behind, Matia walked out of the corner yard with a vision of her mother, Safiya, running clear through her mind. Her mother's investment in home had been of such great consequence that Safiya herself had come to signify home for her family. For months, after Matia had become motherless she had also felt quite homeless. The cedar shingled roof, Southern Yellow Pine wooden frame, sheetrock and hardwood floors of their house had not been enough to provide a home for Matia or her father. Without Safiya, they felt dispossessed.

It was out of necessity that Matia had recognized the need to begin again the young life that had been stalled by untimely death. It was in response to basic need that Matia had resumed living. Thus, she gave birth to the marked genesis of her adult life, helping to create a new home for both her father and herself.

As Matia turned the corner, off Charbonnet and onto North Prieur, her two friends caught up with her.

"Shallow," said Binta, as she and Shallow joined Matia. "I know I'm not perfect, but you can't get mad at me cuz I want a family. God created family. So, your problem is with Him, not me."

"Doctor Stark says that God is a flawed rationalization to an enigma that can't be grasped," said Shallow.

"What?" Binta and Matia said in unison.

"God's just your crutch," said Shallow.

"Yeah, you right," said Binta, smiling. "He's my crutch, emergency room doctor and heart surgeon too. Everybody needs somethin' or somebody to depend on."

"So, now you don't believe in God no more?" Matia asked.

"I still believe," said Shallow, slowing down her pace. "I was just sayin' what Doctor Stark says."

"Doctor Stark says this and Doctor Stark says that," said Binta, comin' to a dead stop. "I'm so sick of hearin' about that woman."

"Keep walkin' y'all," said Matia, leaving her friends behind again.

"I'm comin'," said Binta, catching up to Matia. "She workin' on my nerves."

"Wait Matia," said Shallow, catching up to her two friends. "You don't agree with Binta do you?"

"Who you agree with, Matia?" Binta said.

"Do I have to agree with somebody?" Matia asked. "Can't I just stay out of this?"

"Yeah," said Shallow, "you've got to agree with someone."

"And no," said Binta, "you can't just stay out of this. You're smack dead in the middle."

"Alright," said Matia, hesitantly.

"Alright," said Binta and Shallow in unison, while walking on opposing sides of Matia.

"To tell the truth," said Matia. "I don't really agree with either one of y'all."

"What?" Shallow asked, frowning.

"Why not?" asked Binta.

"The Bible says it's foolish to compare ourselves with ourselves," said Matia.

"What?" Shallow said. "Who else can we compare ourselves with?"

Binta was silent and thoughtful.

"That's just it," said Matia. "It's not good to compare yourself with anybody."

"Yeah," said Binta, "but what exactly does that have to do with what we're talkin' about."

"Y'all wanted me to say somethin'," said Matia.

"Yeah, we did," said Shallow.

"Alright then," said Matia.

"I'm with Binta," said Shallow. "I don't see what that has to do with what we're talkin' about."

"It don't make sense for us to be patting our own selves on the back about how right we are in what we're doin'," said Matia. "Then critiquin' each other based on our own accomplishments. What does any of us have that God has not given us?"

"That's comes from a scripture doesn't it?" asked Binta. "It's somewhere in second Corinthians."

"Second Corinthians ten and twelve," said Matia.

"Alright, Minister Singleton" said Shallow, teasing Matia.

"I'm not studin' bout you, Shallow," said Matia.

It was quiet for a few moments before Binta broke the silence.

"So," said Binta, "you sayin' I'm wrong, Matia?"

"Only if it's wrong to condemn a woman for wantin' to become accomplished academically or professionally," said Matia.

"What ya tryin' to say?" asked Binta, defensively.

"No, what are you tryin' to say?" said Matia. "You're gifted, but you're always exaggeratin' about what you don't know and about what you can't do. Like God is lookin' over you smilin' and sayin', there's my dumb baby, Binta. She so stupid, she make me proud! I don't think He's happy one bit with you doubtin' what He's put in you or what He can do with your life. Besides God doesn't value a fearful woman who prides herself in bein' a fool anymore than He does a stiff-necked smart woman."

"I knew she'd agree with me," said Shallow, poking her tongue out at Binta and laughing."

"Nobody's agreein' with you," said Matia to Shallow. "My mama use to say that people hear the word marriage and they get scared because it means so many different things to so many different people. Like you Shallow, you're determined that you will never try to please a husband in a marriage, but you don't have a problem with the idea of a woman bendin' over backwards to please her male boss at work."

"That's for money, honey," said Shallow, singing. "I don't think it's funny when you messin' with my money. Oh, what I wouldn't do for money!"

"Not much," said Binta, fuming. "You sound just like a hooker. Why is your respect for your career more bona fide than my respect for marriage?"

"Ladies, we're all created to serve," said Matia. "Servin' is just another way of sayin' helpin'. My bible teaches me that in marriage both the husband and the wife have to learn and be willin' to serve each other in order for marriage to stay alive."

"I will not," screeched Shallow. "I will never serve some Negro in a kitchen or a bedroom. He better look like findin' a million ways to serve me."

Matia laughed and shook her head in disbelief.

"Shallow," said Binta, "if everybody thought like you, the nuclear family would become prehistoric. Divorce would sweep the country, if anyone even bothered to get married. Women would be too busy tryin' to prove that they could be men to enjoy bein' women and men would not know who to be. Women everywhere would be askin' themselves, 'Where are the true men?'"

"Now, that's the question." Shallow said, bitterly. "Where are they?"

"Hidin' from you," said Binta, snickering. "That was too easy. You left yourself wide open for that one."

"She did," said Matia, laughing.

"Seriously," said Shallow, "Binta your kind are causin' women everywhere to take giant leaps backward. If it weren't for women like us, Matia, I just don't know where the future of this country would stand."

"Women like us?" Matia asked, laughing nervously. "I'm not a fellow recruit of the school of Dr. Stark or her goofy war against men. If man is the enemy to destroy, where does that leave women? Sex wars like race wars will be the death of us all."

"Tell her, Matia," Shouted Binta, "besides I believe a good man should be loved and not defeated."

"Now, you know that's the truth," said Matia high fiving Binta.

"Like you know somethin' about lovin' a man," said Shallow. "Your behind is as green as they come with the way Mr. Franklin watches over you. You know you've never had a dude lay one finger on you."

"Excuse me," said Matia. "You're confusin' love with sex. Lovin' does not require touchin'. Besides, the man that truly wants the privilege of touchin' me will be willin' to wait until I'm his wife."

"Besides," Binta chimed in, "I thought we were all green, since we all promised God and each other that we would wait till marriage. Is there somethin' you need to tell us Shallow?"

"No, nothin' to tell," said Shallow, looking away uneasily and quickly turning the subject. "What about Bill and you? Anything you need to confess?"

"Now, I love Bill," Said Binta, "but he has to walk me down that aisle before I give him a full understandin' of all of my wonderfulness. I'm not goin' lie, though. It's hard, but that's why we do a lot of double datin'. Don't fool around with my sweet and chocolate-coated Bill, girl! Don't mess with my Mr. Washington!"

"Binta," said Shallow, "I know you're excited about your man and y'all weddin' next Winter, but please don't start singin' that song."

"She changed the subject on you, Binta," said Matia, raising a suspicious eyebrow.

"Oh yeah," said Binta, "she did. She never told us whether or not she was still as green as she said we were."

"I'm still green," said Shallow, biting her tongue, "but not for a lack of many guys tryin' to change my mind about it. "

"Some will try," said Binta, "but it's your job to cut them off at the impasse."

"Well," said Shallow, "Lexy has tried, but I'm not havin' it. I think he'd love to get me pregnant, just so that I'll marry him. He's tryin' to keep a sister down, but I'm no fool."

"But didn't Lexington's uncle hire you to work at his drugstore and practically guarantee you a pharmacist position at his pharmacy?" Matia asked.

"That's right," said Binta, "I forgot she told us that. His uncle, Amedee, owns Savoies pharmacy."

"Yeah," Said Shallow, rolling her eyes, "what about it? Mr. Savoie will be lucky to get me. My hard work at Xavier has earned me any opportunity I get."

"How much longer before you finish pharmacy school?" Matia asked. "You should be finishin' up soon, huh?"

"Yeah," said Binta, "you been in school a while."

"This is my last year," said Shallow.

"Pharmacist Shallow Flowers," said Matia, winking her eye at Shallow.

"Yeah, *'sha'*," said Shallow, "I like the sound of that."

"I wouldn't want you for no pharmacist of mine," said Binta.

"Why?" asked Shallow. "Knowin' you it's probably because I'm a woman?"

Binta was quiet and rolled her eyes at Shallow.

"Must be nice to not only have a guy who is interested in helpin' you with your goals, but to have his family in your corner too," said Matia, elbowing Shallow.

"Yeah," said Binta, "it don't sound like he tryin' to keep a sister down to me."

"Well, I'm here to tell y'all, Lexington Marcellus Savoie is! He's always tryin' to distract me with talk of marriage."

"When you're old, ugly, and alone," said Binta, "don't come knockin' on my door beggin' for a ray of my sunshine."

"Shut up, cow," said Shallow.

Matia shook her head disapprovingly.

"I expect a little bit more understandin' from you, Matia. You attended a prestigious university where you were twice the minority, bein' both Black and female. You're in this fight to win it!"

"Shallow please," said Matia. "I do support you, but I didn't go to Tulane to compete with anybody."

"That's right," said Binta, laughing and elbowing Shallow. "She went because Mr. Franklin told her to."

Shallow joined in the laughter with Binta.

"What?" Matia said, shaking her head in disbelief. "You two are a trip. Yeah, okay. So, daddy wanted me to go to college, but I prayed about my decision. I chose to further my education. I've always enjoyed havin' success in the academic world and enjoyin' the rewards that academic success brings."

"I don't know why you wasted your time prayin' about it, said Shallow. "It's not like God is watchin' and waitin' to tell you what college to choose. He don't care about that!"

"Shallow," said Matia as they turned onto Charbonnet Street. "That's not true! God does care."

"Dr. Stark says," started Shallow.

"Dr. Stark says this," interrupted Binta, "and Dr. Stark says that. Is that why your grandparents payin' for you to go to pharmacy school? So, you can walk around, spoutin' the rhetoric of some retired English woman from Uptown who holds meetings for angry women in her poisonous den of women scorned. Don't sound like you learnin' anything, but the ABC's of Dr. Empty's indoctrination."

"Me, bein' indoctrinated," said Shallow, "the way you go on about God and marriage."

"Hey," said Binta, confidently, "like I said people have to believe in something. I'll take God over your Dr. Empty anytime."

"Her name is Dr. Stark," said Shallow.

"Uh-huh, boo," said Binta, "that's what I said, Dr. Empty and Unfulfilled."

"You see," said Shallow. "That's the attitude that I'm talkin' about. Just because a woman is unmarried and child-less doesn't mean that she's unfulfilled."

"I agree," said Binta. "I know plenty of successful and amazin' women who are both unmarried and childless. What makes your Professor Stark empty is the fact that she can't stomach the thought of the love of a man dwellin' in-side of her or any other woman. I can't understand."

"What are you talkin' about?" said Shallow.

"I think I understand what Binta's sayin'," said Matia as they arrived at the house party.

"You do?" Shallow asked, staring at a small crowd of peo-ple, standing on Patricia's front lawn.

"Yeah," said Matia, "she's sayin' your Dr. Stark hates bein' a woman and hates men because they're not women."

"Huh," said Shallow and Binta in unison.

"Think about it," said Matia. "Dr. Stark argues that women don't get enough attention, but spends all of her time talkin' about men. She's clearly confused."

"That's ridiculous, "argued Shallow. "Doctor Stark only wants to make women see the error in allowin' themselves to be burdened with marriage and childbearin'."

"Well," laughed Binta, opening the wrought iron gate to the front yard, "how nice of you and the good doctor to try to save me from what my soul longs for. While you and Professor Stark are fightin' for a woman's right to do what you want her to, you might want to remember to fight for a woman's right to do what she was born to do."

"And what might that be," asked Shallow, sincerely.

"To love her man," said Binta, unapologetically.

"You can't be serious," said Shallow. "Surely you don't believe that a woman's existence could be so pointless."

"Well," said Binta, placing her hands at her hips, "I can guarantee you this, honey. I was made to love Bill T. Washington and I'm not apologizin' to anybody for it."

"There she go," said Binta's fiancé, Bill, as he swaggered down the concrete steps of Pat's front porch.

His chestnut brown hue stood out in contrast against his plum polyester shirt.

"I was just sayin' to one of my boys that I shouldn't have let you talk me into lettin' you walk to this party." Bill said, as he lifted Binta into the air, squeezing her tenderly. "I was worried sick about my baby."

"I barely made it here without you," said Binta, smiling at Bill.

"I don't see any infants around here," said Shallow, sarcastically. "Surely Binta's capable of walkin' around a corner or two without your help."

"I see despite my steady prayers you are still with us," scoffed Bill.

"Oh, shut up," shouted Shallow.

"Be thankful I'm a perfect gentleman," said Bill, taunting.

"I'm gone ya'll," said Binta, giggling as Bill put her feet back down on the ground. He took Binta by her right hand and gently kissed it.

"My queen," Bill whispered, bowing before Binta.

"Uh, yuck," said Shallow, swinging around to face Matia, "they make me so sick."

"Go to the hospital then," said Binta as she and Bill strode off, disappearing into a mass of people."

Matia looked distracted by the other party guest as she fidgeted with her clothes, while looking around at a myriad of faces both known and unknown to her.

"What's on your mind, Sweet T," said Shallow, tugging on Matia's arm playfully.

"Shallow," said Matia, wistfully.

"Huh," said Shallow, distracted by a tall dark sophisticated young man who was staring at her.

"I sound pretty sure of myself," said Matia. "Don't I?"

"You always do, 'sha'," said Shallow.

"You too, Shallow," said Matia. "You do too."

"Thank you, thank you," said Shallow. "I'll take that as a compliment. A woman is supposed to know what she wants."

"Is she?"

"Of course she is," said Shallow.

"Sometimes, knowin' is only half the battle," whispered Matia.

"What?" Shallow asked, refocusing her attention back onto Matia.

"Yeah," said Matia, shrugging her shoulders, "people always want you to be who they imagine you should be."

"You think so?" said Shallow.

"I do," said Matia, "and when I'm not workin' at Singleton & Co., helping daddy with what he wants, I dream of what I want."

"And what's that," said Shallow, suspiciously.

"The joys of experiencin' love, marriage, motherhood and success in fulfillin' my dreams," said Matia.

"Oh, no," said Shallow, gasping, "not you too. Wantin' success in your professional dreams, now I can understand that, but marriage. For what? A man and children will just complicate matters."

Matia was quiet for a moment and shook her head in disappointment.

"You haven't been listenin' to a word I've said," said Matia. "Have you?"

"What?" Shallow said. "I hear you, but you shouldn't be thinkin' about wastin' your time with marriage. Wives and mothers come a dime a dozen, Matia."

"Do they?" said Matia.

"Yeah," said Shallow, "and if you're goin' to have an effect on the world it won't be from home."

"Shallow," said Matia, leaning up against the gatepost of the birthday girl's wrought iron fence. "Who says? My mother did. Always loving, giving and helping people, she was a beacon of light in our community and you know it."

"She was," said Shallow, nodding her head in agreement. "She really was, but don't you want to be more? I mean don't you want to change the world?"

"That's just it, Shallow," said Matia. "I want to do all kinds of things, but what I want to do most in this world is what I was created to do."

"Aw *'sha',*" said Shallow. "There you go again, with that God stuff."

"Well, it's true," said Matia, exhaling. "I can't tell you what to want, but I know what I want. I want to know for myself that I've done the things He created me to do. I've been prayin' about it and I'm becomin' more convinced everyday that this desire that I have for marriage and children comes from Him. I've searched my bible several times over and nowhere does it suggest that it is wrong for me to want these things. In preparin' myself for the future, shouldn't I be preparin' myself to be a wife and mother too? Why do my desires for entrepreneurship have to conflict with my desire for family? I mean isn't there a place for success in both in my life?"

"I don't know what God has to do with any of this," said Shallow. "I mean you can't really be naive enough to keep insistin' that something as outdated as the bible has any relevance in today's world."

"Shallow," said Matia, "times change, but God's principles don't."

"Hey there y'all," shouted Ms. Dot, Pat's grandmother, standing at a distance and brushing her long thick silver hair out of her face.

"Hey, Ms. Dot!" the young women shouted.

"How y'all two doin'?" Ms. Dot said as she toddled over to where Shallow and Matia were standing. "Everything alright over here? I see you two standin' over here by the gate. Y'all not goin' inside the party? I made pecan pie, okra gumbo, fried catfish, fried shrimp, fried chicken and potato salad tonight."

"Fried catfish and shrimp," said Shallow, placing her hand on her lower stomach.

"Uh-huh," said Ms. Dot, laughing, "yeah baby."

"I can hear that okra gumbo callin' my name," said Matia, smiling at Shallow.

"Last one in is a rotten egg, 'sha'," shouted Shallow as she rushed into the house party."

9

That night's house party was Matia's first, since tragedy had consumed her life. She had had a heart filled with a delicious hope and she was anxious for what the evening might bring. Her primary concentration had been on a thought that Sadiki had given their mother, the notion that life is a string of new births. Perhaps, this night would give birth to a new beginning for her. Maybe this would be the genesis of the rest of Matia's life.

There was a force. No, it was more like a momentum that was pushing Matia forward. She felt a gap widening between her and her past.

She was about to give birth to a new beginning.

Had her new beginning already begun?

Her father had broken from his usual habit of swaying her into seeing things his way. He had given her his blessing and sent her own her way to a neighborhood house party. Here she was amidst this vibrant lively celebration: A place were young people, veterans and rookies alike, met and joined each other in a dance that turned into a rainbow colored parade of spirits.

PART THREE

CONCEPTION

1

Biological conception is the fertilization of a woman's egg by a male's sperm. It is a baby at its start. While spiritual conception, an intangible beginning, happens when a seed is implanted, causing the development of a baby that grows into a plan, vision or thought.

How then should I say that this tale, a tested romance, was conceived?

Should I say that it was with Matia's relishing Candy? Should I say that it was with Candy being terminated? Or should I say that it was with Matia making a mad get away from her father's shotgun?

Let me say that the start can be found most definitely, but not solely in all three incidents. Yes, there is more. Still yet, another beginning occurs during the initial conception of this story. It is indirect. It is a beginning focused primarily on Abecca and her passion, which unfortunately for her was Nile. This was a passion that she unwittingly passed on to Matia prior to Matia's even having met Nile.

So, yes it is true. Matia had fancied a very real passion for Nile long before she actually met him. In her was born the ambiguous craving for her own knowledge of Nile.

Abecca Rosengarten, the Parisian daughter of a Jewish and Black father and Haitian French mother, had been sent from Paris to live with her paternal grandmother whilst attending Tulane University. Abecca's grandmother, a native Black New Orleanian, happen to live on Milan Street in Uptown New Orleans.

As fellow members of Tulane University's class of 1975, Abecca and Matia had both been a part of the body of students who could claim some African ancestry. Consequently, this had provided the two young women with the opportunity to meet and meet they did. They met monthly at informal Black student meetings and almost every Tuesday and Thursday in a poetry class, during the spring of 1975. Matia remembered Abecca, all too well. Yet, their association had never been what one could call personal. Honestly, Abecca had hardly noticed that Matia was alive. Although Matia had marveled over the odd power of the contradiction of Abecca's plum dark complexion and cottony moss like ringlets of dark marmalade, Matia had never even exchanged words with the foreign transplant. In fact, she had never even thought of speaking to Abecca until after Abecca's unfortunate, but quite public descent from grace.

To Matia's knowledge, the fall had been caused by Abecca having had a tangled little fling with a "Fine as Wine" sort of brother from the Desire Housing Projects. The brother whose name was unknown to Abecca's classmates had been seen meeting Abecca after her classes at the Saint Charles Avenue street car stop right across the street from Gibson Hall. He had been observed while reading her poetry that he had written just for her. Some of which she had scribbled all over the cover of her poetry tablet and shared with her female classmates.

The cover of her tablet read in various shades of color:

Marmalade Plum

The dark midnight sky wraps you in mystery.

You are incredible to see.

Your grandeur uproots me.

Willow's thick mossy ringlets cascade down your back.

You parade quiet majesty.

Your golden bloom revives me.

A disagreement of marmalade plum you are.

You are a contradiction of marmalade plum.

In response to this poem, the male students became sick, while the females were caught up in the rapture of who had created it.

Nile had also been observed bestowing upon her gifts of sweet chocolate. If not lots of candy, he offered lots of himself. So, poetry and chocolate was seemingly all that was required to get the beautiful Abecca to lie to her judicious grandmother about what was keeping her out after hours.

Eventually "Mr. Fine as Wine" from the heart of the Desire abruptly stopped coming around. Shortly thereafter, the rare girl, Abecca, did too.

Even so, her absence from the university was only temporary. After a few weeks, the mysterious Abecca did return to the university. Still, it was while she was away that the details of her whereabouts circled the campus courtesy of Huey, the unofficial Black student body's spokesperson. He was a handsome, but nosey chap who for his very life could not manage to hold his tongue.

And so, on the day after Abecca was released from Charity Hospital's psychiatric ward Matia discovered her desire to speak to Abecca. Well, what Matia really discovered was the fact that she just had to ask Abecca a question. Matia was dying to know. I mean truly aching to know. Without any question, she was dying to know what would make a foreign transplant with the plum night for skin and running marmalade for hair attempt to carve even the finest of brother's initials into her wrists.

Long after Abecca had returned to school, Matia had not managed to ask Abecca what it was about the brother that had made her mutilate and almost kill herself. Still, Matia fancied what this fellow must have been like.

For Matia too had thought that she had experienced love. She too had been hurt. She had honestly cared for Candy. However, not even once after Candy's terminating the life of their friendship or even his premature death had she considered hurting herself on account of losing a fellow whom she clearly had never really had. She sometimes played with the thought that Candy had been just a mere apparition, vanishing in mid air before she could ever really get a good hold of him.

Thus, she found it hard to fathom one not wanting to live without the love of an ex-beau. *Did Abecca not know that after spiritual death there can occur life?* Matia's mind struggled trying to understand what kind of male would be capable of captivating the mind of a bright and attractive young woman in such a way.

I believe that it could have been this subconscious venture that indirectly led Matia to Nile. It was not enough for Matia to imagine what Abecca must have experienced. It was not enough for her to swear to herself that never would she be taken aback in such a way. No, Matia was dying, aching and having to know what it was like to love and perhaps be loved by Abecca's ex beau.

Nevertheless, it was the spirit of Abecca's love for Nile that drove him away from her. It had been instrumental in driving him away from Abecca and towards Matia in a roundabout way.

Abecca had put herself at Nile's complete and utter disposal. He no longer had to toil for anything that she gave him. And it is common knowledge that those things that require the most labor also, gain the greatest appreciation. This was a lesson that Abecca had never learned and so she decided that she would do most anything for Nile. With this, there was little exception.

Consequently, Nile reasoned that it was Abecca who had caused him to grow both bored and then tired of her company. This is why without even the slightest explanation their delicious little rendezvous had been brought to an abrupt end. Nile had determined in his own mind that the easiest thing for him to do would simply be to eradicate Abecca from his life.

He chose to view his actions as noble rather than cowardly. It had never occurred to him that his not taking the time to say goodbye to her might destroy whatever confidence she had left. Breaking her heart was not enough for him. Because of his cowardliness, he had to shatter her spirit too.

On the day that Abecca attempted to carve Nile's initials into her wrists, she had found him while he was in the midst of justifying his behavior. She was searching for him in the Desire Housing Development when she came upon him and his closest friend, Bill T. Washington. The two friends were sitting on the porch of Nile's apartment and listening to Stevie Wonder's voice as it poured through the window of Nile's apartment window.

Just moments before Nile spotted the lovesick Abecca walking up his courtyard, he and Bill had been having a discussion. They marveled over what they saw as the genius in Stevie's songs.

What Nile loved most about Stevie's music was that it had inspired him to develop a mission statement for his life. He wanted more than any other thing in the world to find fulfillment and the true meaning of life.

Only he did not know how to find either. He was in constant pursuit of these ideas, but did not know how they looked, smelled or tasted. All that he knew was that he wanted them.

Nile had mistakenly thought that he had finally found what he was missing in Abecca. He had learned far too quickly that he was wrong. Though breathtaking, Abecca had not turned out to be as resilient as he had imagined her to be. He had discovered that like him she was flawed. When he had decided that he no longer wanted her, he had declared her love for him as oppressive. Through his unloving eyes, she suddenly seemed too weak and unworthy of his love. He determined that she was not the one that he could rely upon for his fulfillment of understanding life's meaning.

So, he was thinking on what he viewed as his life's fulfillment at the exact moment that he spotted her entering his courtyard. Rather than run from the young woman who had running marmalade for hair and midnight plum for skin, Nile simply said goodbye to Bill. Bill exited the courtyard just as the beautiful Abecca climbed Nile's steps. She followed him into his apartment and he shut the door. Nile stared coldly into her wide-open face in silence. For several moments, he could not speak.

As the fleeting seconds passed, Nile's mind got all jammed up with the titles from the poems that he'd written for Abecca during their relationship. Without warning, he had somewhat of a delusional experience. The "Abecca inspired" poem titles found their way into the sentences in the flow of a conversation that Nile began to have with himself.

He thought he heard himself say to himself, *"Everything's Fine" "Marmalade Plum"*. Only he had not opened his mouth.

And yet, he thought that he did hear himself say out loud to himself, *"Marmalade Plum"* is *"Afraid To Lose You"* Nile and *"Trying To Say"* *"I Require Love"*. Still, as the titles of his Abecca induced poems filled his head and seemingly his consciousness, his mouth did not open. Then he heard the words, *"Never Let Me See You Cry" "Marmalade Plum"* because *"There's No Use"* in you *"Trying To Say"* *"I Require Love"* to a guy who's just not *"Here To Stay"*.

Several moments later, he had come back to reality.

"I never asked for your love," Nile explained.

He told her he no longer wanted her love and that it would be great of her to bow out gracefully. He took her heart from his pocket and tossed it onto the floor. He then, kicked her love back towards her and across his living room

floor. Then he whispered apologetically, insisting indig-
nantly, that he never ever said that he was truly *"Here To Stay"*.

"I require love," she said, weakening at her knees and failing in her attempt to repossess her injured heart. Once, she
could gather herself to some extent. She pulled herself back
up and ran sobbing into Nile's mother's potty, locking herself
inside for several moments that seemed to Nile to last eternally.

He had gone after her, you know! Failing to catch her before
the door was slammed shut and locked tight. He had gone. He
had arrived only a few seconds too late. He had pounded his
right fist against the door until it ached. Still, Abecca had neither answered Nile nor opened the bathroom door. She had
only made a series of gurgling noises that reminded Nile of a
cross between a crying newborn and a mad woman. So, the
young man who up until this ordeal had felt that he was only
guilty of failing in his search for fulfillment had been forced
to begin to come to grasp with another's desire for fulfillment.
Having to witness the aftermath of his dealings with Abecca,
Nile had been forced to kick his mother's bathroom door in.

When he did, he found Abecca in a messy heap, cringing
and shaking on the blood red, black and white tile of the bathroom floor. Only his mother's bathroom tile was not supposed
to be blood red. It was only supposed to be an agreeable pat-
tern of checkerboard black and white. Abecca had embel-
lished the decorum with the wretched act of carving Nile's
initials into her wrists with one of Nile's pitiless razor blades.

Upon his entrance to the bathroom, Abecca spun towards
him, chortling the most hideous sounds.

"Charlatan, thief," cried Abecca.

She filed this charge against him. Since, she had been
trying to figure out how to get her heart back from Nile since

the first day that he had decided to steal away with it. She had tossed and turned both mentally and physically in her wrestle with the truth. Nile neither loved nor wanted her. He had sampled at no cost what was priceless.

Now Abecca lay in a messy heap, trying to find herself amidst the bottom of Nile's pitiful pile of indifference.

"Charlatan, thief," she charged most passionately.

Could it have been that this was the charge that Nile needed to have made against him?

Perhaps, it truly was.

So, maybe Nile's epiphany took place after Nile called an ambulance. Maybe it occurred after Nile grabbed Abecca, causing her to drop the razor blade. Maybe it happen after he sat in the middle of the bloody bathroom floor applying pressure to her wrists and begging for her forgiveness. Maybe it transpired after she had been rushed to Charity hospital, stitched, and gauzed. Maybe it was after Abecca's grandmother had been called from Milan Street and had arrived cursing an apologetic Nile and ordering him to leave and stay away, declaring that Nile had been foul and putrid for her granddaughter's life. Maybe it came into being by the sheer nature of Nile's being forced to stomach the power of both Abecca's charge against him and her grandmother's accusation. Maybe it was the gravity of the two women's words, massaging Nile's brain that moved him to shed true tears and run out into a New Orleans' moonlit street.

Nile did run, you know. He did run out into a moonlit street, seeking forbearance and admitting to himself that, playing the role of a swindler & fraud, he had indeed stolen Abecca's heart, only to carelessly discard of it later. Seeing for the first time the severe truth that he was indeed a charlatan and thief who had been both foul and putrid for Abecca, he ran, still composing sentences with his poems that were ode to Abecca. He sang, *"Heaven's My Witness"*. So, *"Is Your Wrong Innocent"* because *"Marmalade Plum"* is *"Forever Damaged"* and *"Trying to Say"* *"Heaven's My Witness"*.

Without a doubt, Nile had been a fraud and a swindler. He had stolen Abecca's heart. Nile was seized by this fact. He was overcome by the fact that he had not realized that it might be wrong to take her heart, if he did not intend to hand over his own. He was further saddened by the late recognition that her heart was not for him, an uncommitted chap, to take. A cruel and abusive thief indeed was he!

He had never truly loved Abecca, but had only used her. He had never loved her because on the face of it, he did not know for sure how to love.

2

Up until the day that Abecca marred herself in response to Nile's uncaring dismissal, Nile had been living a life of lies. He had been telling himself that there was nothing wrong with the way that he handled the young women that he romanced. Nile was determined to protect his own heart. He believed his love was priceless. The danger in this belief was that he often managed to convert the young women that he met into believers as well.

Why must I insist that this was a danger?

Simply because Nile had been deceived into thinking that he had mastered being deceitful. A fraud, he had somehow managed to gain the ability to charm and resist simultaneously.

He had been trained in some of life's most bittersweet class-rooms. He had studied the methods of a father who had loved him enough to give him a name, but not enough to feed him. He had been fed at the bosom of a mother who chided him for not being a man, while unconsciously work-ing in her own favor to keep him a boy. He had wrestled for a seat at the table of a country that asked its' people to fight to protect freedoms for others that it worked viciously to deny its own. He had gleaned from a world of people who vacil-lated between being their brothers' keepers and crabs in a bucket. It was not extraordinary to say one thing and then to do another in his world. He had seen up close the two-facedness of humanity. Accordingly, he had committed to the art of winning others over without allowing himself to be won.

This tendency was most apparent in Nile's relationships with the women that he rented. He would perform the most astonishing and delectable tricks to capture a woman's heart. Once the poor woman was captured, he would retreat and refuse to engage in any further contact.

Yes, just like the "Father of Lies", he would misrepresent himself. He was a bandit who was always making off with someone else's goods because something was quite flawed in him. He lacked the strength to commit. He was cracked. He was unable to grasp the purpose of the power that he had to love. Consequently, his God given gift of charisma was distorted.

Did he understand that he was playing the part of a son of the "Father of Lies"?

No, he did not really.

Though, it was terribly sad he did not know the truth of his actions because he was not prepared to deal with the weight of it. He was abiding in untruth. He could not see a way out. Nor could he tell the difference between what he had painted as truth and truth itself. So, as it related to Abecca, the lies that Nile told had become vital to his biggest lie, the one that he told himself. The lie was that he had not done anything wrong. That he was indeed innocent. The lie was that he had not misrepresented himself and stolen something most valuable from her. He had believed this lie.

Until, the day that Abecca lay in Charity hospital, he had believed this lie. Until the day that Abecca lay despondent and bandaged due to her bad reaction to his pursuing his life's fulfillment, Nile had mistakenly believed this lie.

3

Life is never without consequence. Whether good or bad we are likely to give birth to what we conceive.

Nile had stolen and abused Abecca's heart and it produced suffering that he could see! It had led to a temporary madness. It had led to bloodshed. He had witnessed Abecca's passing madness. Affected, he had sat in Abecca's blood. Chanting, *"Heaven's My Witness"*, he had sat in her blood. Saying, *"Is Your Wrong Innocent"* because *"Marmalade Plum"* is *"Forever Damaged"* and *"Trying to Say"* *"Heaven's My Witness"*, he had her blood on his hands. He had truly heard her for the very first time crying, *"I require love"*.

Whatever the case, the day's ordeal had landed him on the front porch of his older sister, Luna, confessing all. Luna was a preacher's wife and a mother of twin boys, Alec and Alex Jr. Luna drenched her younger brother in pity. Then she washed him in her fine clothes of wisdom. He sat drunk with sorrow as she calmed his soul with gentle potent words.

After nearly an hour of listening to Luna speak, Nile made an inquiry.

"What did I do to deserve this," Nile asked.

"It's not just what you did," Whispered Luna, looking after her baby brother with sincere love. "It's what you didn't do."

What?" Nile asked.

"You didn't love," Said Luna matter-of-factly. "You didn't cherish. You did not respect. You did not protect. You did not give anything of yourself, Nile. You only took."

A new window to Nile's soul began to open. Into it, Luna poured the light of all the love that she could spare.

By the time Nile was leaving Luna's porch, he was vowing to change his life's course. In searching for his fulfillment, he decided that he must learn to give of himself fully, allowing nothing to be withheld. In order to find his life, he would have to be willing to lose it.

4

But to whom would Nile deliver his existence?

Who would be fit to stomach it?

Alex Trueman, Nile's extremely honest and likeable brother-in-law, insisted that he had the answer.

Alex and Luna never stopped explaining their grounds for maintaining an unapologetic faith in Jesus. Jesus had died for their sins, had risen from the dead and through faith had given them the power to live spanking brand new lives. He had made everything alright with God for them. He had taken the wrap for all of their sentences. He had rescued them from sin's life imprisonment.

Now, they were free from people's expectations and the mindless control of their own misguided urges. They were free. They were free and could now be in hot pursuit of their purpose.

They had learned that they could afford to trust God. After all, He is trustworthy and consistent.

God was so faithful! They had learned this. So, they were now more committed to Him than they were to themselves. They were more committed to Him than Nile had been to his own life's fulfillment.

5

After the hullabaloo with Abecca, Nile could be found almost nightly at The Trueman family's abode.

Alex, a plumber by trade, had started The New Life ministry fellowship. Alex loved Nile as if he were his own baby brother. He saw every opportunity to encourage Nile as a Godsend. Alex and Luna had spent years hoping and praying that Nile would trust Jesus with his life.

On this particular night, something extraordinary was happening. To some it would seem just another ordinary Friday night. With the exception of what was taking place on Arts Street. As Nile sat on Arts street in his big sister's home, he was determining that he was ready to attend their church fellowship, The New Life Center. So, there sat Nile, somewhat anxious and several months after Abecca had shown

Nile that she required love. There he sat on Luna's indigo floral sofa, preparing to go with the Trueman family to their church meeting and go they did.

6

A compelling congregation of high-spirited worshippers sung of Jesus' love, sincerely pleading with all who listened to consider whether they understood the full measure of Jesus' love for them.

Their words shot back and forth through Nile's head as he tried to grasp the manner of love that was being expressed. Nile wondered how Jesus' love factored into his own life.

The congregation persisted in their worship, caught up in the very atmosphere of their giving thanks to God. The people were soaring on the wings of sweet praise.

Nile sat stoically, pretending that this intense declaration of Jesus' love did not move him. This was the seventh song the worshippers had sung. Nile was enlightened. He was reflective. He was provoked even. Moved to exhale with great relief, there was a stirring in his soul.

"Not me," said Nile. "How could He love me?"

By the song's end, so moved was Nile that he had a hard time resisting the temptation to leap to his feet and plead, "Why would He love me?"

Just as he realized that this question had lit a fire inside of him, a husky ginger colored woman who was sitting in a front row pew began jumping up and down. Flapping both her arms, she looked as though she might take flight at any moment. Just as suddenly as she had started, two dignified looking women dressed in pearly white uniforms and caps, rushed to the woman's sides. They worked attentively to calm the woman.

Then, Alex stood up on a podium that faced the congregation. "Jesus loves us, y'all. It's an amazin' thing how He loves us even when we appear to be unlovable. When we can't love ourselves, Jesus loves us. When we're havin' trouble lovin' others, Jesus loves us. He'll teach us how to love each other, if we let Him. He'll be a friend, when we are deserted. He'll be a brother, when we have none. The law convicted us. Said we were all dead in our sin. We were all found guilty as charged. Then Jesus showed up. I asked Him to represent me y'all. He is my only defense. God threw out the indictments that had been filed against me and I turned my situation over to Him. Now, I'm an unbound man, free from the dominion of sin. I have been released to serve God and get to my intended end. How about you, today? Are you free to reach your intended end? Is God askin' you to give up your familiar for His best?"

Alex slipped on his reading glasses and glanced rather unassumingly at Nile.

"Turn with me please to Genesis chapter four and verses four through ten," said Alex.

"In verses four through six, we see that the enemy is successful in his attempt to persuade both Adam and Eve to both doubt and disobey God. Why? Had God given them a reason to doubt Him? Hadn't He provided for them in every way?

Alex paused and cleared his throat, while scratching his head and gazing into the congregation as if he were waiting for someone to answer his rhetorical questions.

"We discover them livin' in abundance," said Alex. "A man and woman found in a garden that could easily be described as a delightful and rich paradise. The book of Genesis describes their home as a garden. This is a fertile place where flowers, fruits, and herbs are grown. Surely, in this garden planted by God, The Garden of Eden, they wanted for nothing. According to Genesis, God even placed pleasurable trees in this garden for their satisfaction. He gave them a river to satisfy their thirst. It is clear that they were set up in a choice resort of a honeymooner's dream. Still, the devil was able to influence them to both doubt and disobey God. All because they wanted what God said would destroy them."

"Preach preacher," shouted an aged gentleman in suspenders, sitting to Nile's left.

"Later in verse seven," continued Alex, wiping sweat from his brow, "we see Adam and Eve tryin' to cover their own nakedness. They are strugglin' with the consequences of their sin, tryin' to resolve a problem, usin' unproductive measures. They are in trouble. In verse eight, we begin to see their sin further separatin' them from God. They hear God comin' and because they have not listened to Him, they are now afraid. So, they try to hide. They seek to hide their problem from the only one who can truly help them solve their problem. Then, God asks Adam a question that God already has the answer to."

"Where are you," asked God with a purpose.

"You teachin' now," shouted the aged gentlemen, encouraging Alex. "You teachin', teacher."

Nile hung onto every one of Alex's words. It was as if Nile's very life depended on the message that Alex was presenting.

Somehow, in a room of over one hundred people, Nile felt alone in the congregation. He believed that God was now speaking directly to him and he was listening.

"Alex walked to the foot of the platform and looked out into the congregation. He sat down on the platform floor's edge, allowing his legs to hang freely.

"What a question," declared Alex. "To hear the God of all creation callin' you in the middle of your day is a beautiful thing, y'all. To have the same God who formed you with purpose, speak to you in your troubles. It is beautiful, when God shows up and we are where we are supposed to be. However, what if He shows up and we are ashamed of where we are?"

Alex looked intently out into the congregation of people. For a few moments he was silent, then he asked, "What then?"

The room was still.

In verse ten we find Adam telling God, "I heard your voice and I was afraid because I was naked and so I hid."

Alex hung his head in despair, his eyes watery.

"Adam," cried Alex. "Where are you? God called out to His beloved son. But because of his disobedience, Adam was afraid of the one whom loved him most. He tried to hide his condition. Instead of runnin' to God, he ran away from Him. I've heard the spirit of God callin' me from deep within the very depths of my soul in times of trouble, sayin', 'Alex, where are you?' Don't run and hide when God calls you no matter where you are. Romans chapter three and verse thirty-three tells us, for all have sinned and come short of the glory of God. He sees you for what you are and loves you in spite of everything. You can't hide anything from God, anyway. No sense in tryin'. Only Jesus can cover you. Will you let Him do that for you? Will you accept Jesus as your Lord and Savior tonight?

Nile felt a cool gust of wind surround and almost lift him up out of his seat. Before he knew what was happenin' he was grievin' and walkin' towards the podium. When he reached the platform, he fell to his knees.

"Father," whispered Nile, prayerfully and with tears in his eyes, "I have broken your law and my sin has separated me from you. I need you Jesus to save me! I need your spirit to guide me!"

7

"To hatch" says the French word couver from which the term couvade stems. Couvade, an expectant father's sympathetic pregnancy, is the poorly understood wonder that Nile experienced as he neared the birth of the relationship that he would share with Matia. His pregnancy was of a spiritual nature. The closer that he and Bill came to Alabo Street the more birth pains Nile experienced. Struck with nausea and the pain of a cruel headache, he was due to hatch his portion of a relationship that would convert his life.

Matia was experiencing her own symptoms. She had become terribly moody, crying even at the jokes she heard that night. Her appetite had increased unbelievably. She hadn't stopped eating, since she'd had her first slice of pecan pie.

To address his condition, Nile locked himself in Patricia's hall bathroom. He pulled off his indigo blue knit top, draping it over the side of the sea green bathtub. Seconds later, he became better acquainted with the toilet, a sea green bowl. His nausea had finally gotten the best of him. When his stomach was finished with him, he took a considerable amount of time, freshening up. Afterwards, he sprayed a breath spray into his mouth and popped a couple of breath mints. He stood before the bathroom's mirror cabinet, studying his appearance. His entire body anticipated what was to come. Only Nile was unaware. There was no way for him to grasp the significance of these last fleeting moments.

He listened as strains of a Marvin Gay song, commenting on the state of the family relations in the world, seeped into the bathroom. The lyrics of the song triggered Nile's memory, leading his thoughts back to a scene from earlier that evening. It had been before Nile left to wait for his ride in the courtyard. He had been buttoning his shirt and playing a gospel record. His stomach felt funny, but he was eager about the house party that Bill had invited him to. Then, he thought he heard a man's voice in the house. The tone of voice was oddly familiar. It sounded like an older version of Nile's brother Will's voice. Something within Nile suggested that the voice belonged to Nile's father, a man whose infidelity had been chronic. Still, neither Nile nor the rest of his family had seen his father in years, so Nile quickly dismissed the thought of his father. On his way out of the house, Nile stopped by the living room to say goodbye to his mother, searching the room with hopeful eyes. Nile discovered that the voice he had heard belonged to a middle-aged Black man who was speaking on a television program that his mother was watching.

Nile laughed at himself as he considered his childlike eagerness to imagine that the voice that he had heard had been his father's voice. Nile exited the apartment. When Nile reached the spot at the end of the courtyard, where Bill was to pick him up, he considered how his father, Will Sr., had disregarded the needs of his family, selfishly electing to have an existence that did not include his wife and children.

Deep inside Nile knew that he still longed to know his biological father. He had asked God to help him forgive and pray for his father. Nile's father, a stranger to him, was a man whom Nile had never stopped loving or hoping for.

Far too many times, Nile had walked up and down Canal Street, wondering if he had unknowingly passed his father. His father could have been among the host of seasoned artisans, who travelled along the historic thoroughfare daily. Too many unions still excluded Black members. For that reason, many Black craftsmen from towns and cities throughout the state combed the streets of New Orleans looking for work. Nile's father had been no different. A skilled machinist his dark russet skin had worked against him in finding steady employment. This had added to the pressures that had driven Nile's father away from his family time and time again. His struggle to get and maintain employment had overwhelmed his self-worth. Kidding himself and betraying his family, he had argued that if he left, he would be one less mouth to feed.

Nile hoped that he would one day have the opportunity to establish a relationship with his father. It was not to say that Nile thought it would be easy. No, he knew that it would not be, because no relationship is easy. It would however be worth it. Nile was different. His heart was overflowing with love that he wanted to share with the world. Nile had it in him to forgive his father and many others who had hurt him.

Nile had experienced an amazing grace, welling up within him. This grace had been the extraordinary strength that Nile needed to love unconditionally. Never before had he been more prepared to receive his father despite the past. He coveted the opportunity to bear witness to what God had done in his life. He wanted to rise to the occasion and embrace his father as a friend with both joy and laughter.

These thoughts should have terrified Nile. For years he and his brother Will had become dreadfully comfortable, nursing their anger and bitterness. These bad feelings had become usual tenants.

Nonetheless, Nile decided that he was prepared to extend to his father the proverbial olive branch.

When if at all would the reconciliation occur?

Of this Nile was unsure!

Why had Nile been so quick to think that his mother would entertain his father in her home after having gone missing so many years ago?

Nile knew that to his mother, Mama Royal, the simplicity of being a courageous and gorgeous woman had not been enough in life. After all, it had failed to help her hold onto her husband's loyalty. So, she had decided to employ all of her idiosyncrasies in an effort to milk her life for all it was worth. This meant that she often took time to entertain the shocking. It was part of her attempt to avoid being shocked or wounded. No matter how devastated, she no longer wept, blushed or allowed her mouth to fall open in the midst of life's sudden tragedy. She simply scoffed at life's heartbreak, loading up and preparing to fire her own blows from out of the blue.

Nile imagined this was why he had considered that his mother might entertain her estranged husband. He considered that if his father had ever called, before he could ask to visit, his mother would extend a shocking invite. Nile knew it would be foolish of him to rule out this as a possibility.

Further consideration of his father, Nile decided would simply have to wait. He had plans to enjoy a New Year's Eve house party in the lower ninth ward. With confidence, Nile slipped his top back on and primped in front of the mirror. Pulling out his afro pick, he picked out his afro. When finished he slid it back into one of the back pockets of his cobalt corduroy bellbottoms. Without skipping a beat, he spun around in front of the mirror, checking himself out one last time. Then he exited the bathroom, rejoining the party.

8

The party room had become a birthing room. It was filled to capacity with new life, as there were new relationships and ideas forming everywhere. It stood jam-packed with young men and women who were soaring with a spirit of sugary excitement. They were dipping and swaying and dipping and swaying. Their jasmine, cherry, and chocolate hues, shuffled across a hard wood floor. Their souls were alive with life's greatest anticipation. They were expecting.

Nile pressed forward through the crowded room of people, sweating beads of anticipation. His heartbeat increased with each step. His breathing was heavy as he labored and push toward an opening. With great relief, he gave it one final push before finding himself out of the crowd. Before him was possibly to him the most beautiful being he had ever laid eyes on. In a more secluded area stood a beautiful young woman and that woman was Matia.

Suddenly, something of grave importance happen. Nile could feel a force pulling him toward the beautiful Matia. A bizarre sensation, it, was rather dreamlike. Driving him was an unmistakable unfailing power.

9

When Nile first found Matia, it was if he had discovered "woman" for the very first time. Of course, Nile had known his share of women, but he had never met the one that his soul longed for, Matia. So, it was at first sight that she became beyond question the apple of his eye. Her golden brown and peachy skin glowing, she made him hungry for all that life had to offer. A broad and fat button of a nose with keyholes sat amid noble cheekbones on her delicately fashioned face. Mesmerizingly, she looked right through him with cattish eyes. Her plump and full heart shaped lips were adorned in coral. Any prior knowledge that Nile had held regarding other young women became obsolete. He saw Matia and understood from the start that he had found a good thing. Something so good had he found in her that he felt at once that he could not afford to lose it.

There she stood snuggled into the cozy arched alcove of an adjoining room with her back against the wall. A wall flower, she, added to the rooms decorum by making herself a part of the hostess' greenish blue wallpaper. Adorned in a carroty peasant blouse and a form fitting chocolate midi skirt, she was to Nile quite exquisite. Her pressed sandy brown hair hung long, thick and flawless. In her, he saw a gem.

Matia had wrapped her thoughts snugly around the sport of people watching. She was people watching at the precise moment that she and Nile first met eyes. Still, she was not the only one doing the watching. If you were a young fellow from the lower ninth ward's "Back of Town", you knew who Matia Singleton was. She like her sister before her had garnered the attention of every young man in the neighborhood simply by being. This had always proven fruitless, since her father had worked to intimidate anyone who he had suspected might dare to proposition Matia. The gents of the neighborhood admired Matia from afar. Save for Nile was not a fellow from Matia's neighborhood. Furthermore, the fellows threatened by the possible wrath of Matia's father did not include Matia's coveted Candy or Abecca's ex, Nile.

As I had mentioned before, Matia was people watching at the precise moment that she and Nile first met eyes.

"It's hot in here," Nile said, drawing Matia into a conversation and entering the alcove. "Don't you think?"

Rendered speechless, Matia's tongue became heavy. Right before her stood the literal man of her dreams. Without any doubt, she knew that this was the guy that she had dreamed of shortly after Candy's death. She could not dispute it. She had not been able to forget his sweet face.

This "Man of Her Dreams" was very easy on the eyes. In fact, he was the chef's special. He was lean and chiseled into a fine muscular specimen. He looked like the sort of fellow that Sadiki would have classified as an African warrior. He sported a glorious lustrous Afro and was well over six feet tall. To boot, he had the most beautiful skin. Its undertone reminded Matia of an indigo blue.

"I said it's hot in here," said Nile, shouting over the music.

Confounded by the flesh and blood appearance of Nile, Matia remained silent.

"Somethin' wrong?" Nile asked.

Matia continued to stare, wordless.

"If you want me to go, I'll split."

Still perplexed, Matia remained silent.

"I'll book," Nile said, slowly and painfully as he turned to walk away, "if you want me to."

"No," Matia said abruptly, surprising herself, "stay."

"What?" Nile asked, struggling to hear Matia's voice over the loud music.

"You alright," Matia shouted, trying to understand the significance of this dream man walking into her waking life.

Nile relaxed a little and leaned his back against Matia's wall.

"What did I just do," Matia mumbled, under her breath.

"Did you say somethin'," asked Nile, hungry for Matia's next word.

"Huh?" said Matia, shouting. "Yeah, it is hot in here! But this New Aw-lans and it's always hot and humid. You from the ninth ward?"

"No," He said arrogantly. "Technically, I'm from the country!"

"Huh," Matia said, leaning her ear closer towards Nile's face.

"I said I'm from the country," Nile shouted.

"The country," She shouted, smirking.

"Yeah, the country!"

The song changed to a slow jam, making it easier to hear.

"The country?" she asked, rolling her eyeballs around inside of their sockets most curtly. "What you doin' here, then?"

"Didn't say I still lived in the country," said Nile. "Said, I was from the country."

"There's not much of a difference," Matia said, smiling nervously. "Is there?"

A slightly irritated Nile was about to explain with great grandeur that country folk were no less literate or capable than city folk, when Matia started talking again.

"Well," she said, "yeah, I guess there's a difference. You know like when I say that I'm from New Aw-lans, it's not the same as sayin' I'm from the ninth ward. You know, some people who aren't from here don't usually get that."

"Don't get what," asked Nile.

"They don't get that New Aw-lans is like a little kingdom in and of itself," she insisted. "We have seventeen wards and the ninth ward is our largest."

"It's true," Nile agreed. "It is geographically the largest ward, with the Upper 9th, the Lower 9th and New Orleans East."

"No other city like New Aw-lans in this whole wide world," said Matia, a little too proudly.

"Well," said Nile with some reservation. "I don't know. Everybody says that."

"Everybody says what?"

"That their city is one of a kind."

"You question the idea of New Aw-lans being a world renowned city," asked Matia, defensively.

"No," said Nile, "no, I don't. History makes that plain."

"History makes what plain?"

"That God caused New Or-lans to become rich in faith, culture, food, people and history. He's allowed her to grow to be great in the hearts of millions of people all over the world, but God has built many great cities throughout the history of the world. It's Him that causes cities to rise to greatness, allows them to crumble and if He chooses then allows them to be rebuilt even greater than they were to begin with. Sometimes, He refuses them the opportunity to ever be rebuilt at all."

"New Aw-lans is still holdin on," said Matia.

"Yeah," said Nile, "she's been through the fire, flood and storm, but she's still standing."

"You think you know a lot about great cities, huh?"

"I do," said Nile.

"Name one of the great cities that fell," said Matia, sarcastically.

"Timbuktu," said Nile matter-of-factly.

"Timbuktu?" Matia said.

"Yeah, Timbuktu," said Nile, "the Black Pearl of the Desert."

"I don't know nothing about "The Black Pearl of the Desert", but I can tell you a little somethin' about the "Black Pearl of New Aw-lans," said Matia.

"Oh, yeah?" Nile said. "Isn't that uptown around Pearl Street and Lowerline?"

"U-huh," said Matia, "Mahalia Jackson grew up around there and I can't get enough of her music."

"Mahalia Jackson?" Nile asked. "You like Mahalia? That's alright."

"Yes indeed," said Matia. "And to tell ya the truth, I forgot that there even was a Timbuktu."

"I don't know how," said Nile. "Timbuktu had one of the first universities in the world. It was a prosperous city in Africa and one of the world's greatest trading posts for salt, ivory and gold."

"Our port is important for world trade too," said Matia.

"The Port of New Orleans is one of the largest ports in America," said Nile. "It is."

Matia took a deep breath and folded her arms across her chest.

"Your turn," said Nile.

"My turn for what?" Matia said.

"Name a great city that fell."

Matia shrugged her shoulders in uncertainty.

Matia arched her eyebrows as she thought. "Ancient Rome," she said, suddenly. "Ancient Rome fell."

"That's a good one," said Nile. "What do you think made it great?"

"I don't know," said Matia. "I guess the fact that it managed to influence the entire world."

"What ya think caused it to fall?"

"I'm not sure," said Matia, shrugging her shoulders again.

"Some might disagree, but I think it was the split of the empire that caused it to fall. Everyone knows that a house divided is hopeless. It can't help but fall apart."

"Your turn," said Matia, smiling. "Name another city that fell."

"Um, Babylon," said Nile.

"Babylon," said Matia. "What in the world was great about Babylon?"

"It was once the largest city in the world," said Nile, "and I know I don't need to remind you of the Tower of Babel. It was on the border of Babylon, what we know as Iraq."

"No, you don't have to remind me of the Tower of Babel or the confusion it led too," said Matia. "Who would decide they didn't need God and try to reach Heaven on their own."

"Uh, many of us," said Nile, candidly.

"I can't tell if you a preacher or a historian," Matia said, her eyes lighting up.

"Alright, alright," said Nile, laughing nervously. "Why ya say that?"

"No way around it. You sound like a preacher who moon-lights as a history professor."

"Ya think so?" said Nile, laughing again nervously.

"Yeah, I do."

"Well, I like to read."

"And what about the preacher in you?"

"My maternal grandfather was a preacher in the country."

"Where ya from in the country?"

"Ponchatoula."

"You serious?" Matia smiled in shock. "My mama's from Ponchatoula."

"F'true," said Nile.

"Yeah," said Matia, "and when I was a little girl I use to love visitin' my grandparents farmland in Ponchatoula. My grandmother's strawberry pies were delicious and the trees draped with moss were so beautiful. All that moss reminded me of the moss in our big parks here in New Aw-lans."

"I guess all that moss is why the Choctaw named it Ponchatoula in the first place," said Nile. "They say Ponchatoula means flowin' hair in Choctaw."

"My mama's people are Montgomeries and Bryants," said Matia. "You not related to any Montgomeries or Bryants are you? We could be cousins."

"I don't think so. My daddy's people are all Hashes and Womacks," said Nile smiling, "but I'm pretty sure I've heard my mama mention some Montgomery's that she met when we lived in Ponchatoula."

"You ever miss bein' there," asked Matia.

"Not really," said Nile, "I've been livin' in the ninth ward since I was five. It's the only true home I've truly known."

"So, where you stay," she asked.

"The Desire," said Nile.

Matia nodded her head.

"I'm about to move to France Street in a few months," added Nile. "I've been helpin' my mama fix up a neglected double shotgun that she managed to save up and buy."

"Helpin' with the renovation?"

"Yeah," said Nile, "and with the repair expenses."

"Oh," said Matia, arching her eyebrows, "it's good that you can help her."

"Yeah," said Nile, "this house means a lot to her. When I was a young boy, I watched her work two and three jobs for years. This is a way to get in a better situation and have extra income."

"Where on France?" asked Matia.

"Between North Roman and North Derbigny."

"That's two blocks off North Claiborne, right?"

"Yeah, that's right."

The music got loud again.

"So," Nile shouted over the music, "you wanna go outside to watch the fireworks? It's hard to talk in here with the music."

"What?" Matia asked, nervously.

"No skin off my back if you wanna stay inside," said Nile. "If that's what you want, I'll stay."

"Excuse me. I'll be right back," Matia said, abruptly disappearing into the crowd of party guest.

10

Love at first sight seems so improbable.

Don't you think?

It knows so little, but promises everything.

Yet, what Nile had for Matia was a love at first sight. His love, born within a few short seconds, tested positive. Honestly, the poor guy was rather helpless in the matter. So, fertile was his life and ripe for new birth. And Matia, the epitome of all that he had been praying and hoping for, had implanted herself into the very wall of his existence. There she was. There was no denying her presence within his reality. And there was no denying the love that he had immediately conceived in finding her.

Now, he felt driven to go after her, find her and never lose sight of her again.

"What if she don't come back," he mumbled under his breath.

The possibility of never looking into Matia's face again seemed unbearable to him. He had decided that her face was the face that he was born to love. He went searching for her. He travelled through the same crowd of party guest that he had seen Matia walk through. He followed her trail.

"Oh, God," Matia said prayerfully as she scooped herself a cup of fruit punch at the punch bowl, carefully making sure to get as many cherries and pineapples as she could into her cup. "What was that?"

She had barely been able to stand being in Nile's presence. The stranger who had been born of her dreams had moved her in such a way. Being in his very presence had felt like coming home for the very first time.

11

Moments later, when Nile spotted Matia beside the punch bowl, he thought he saw her notice him, but pretend not to see him. She was talking to the woman that Bill had introduced as the birthday girl's mother.

"Mr. Johnny and me sorry Franklin couldn't make it," said Patricia's mother. "We miss him. You and Pat grew up together, Matia. I know it's hard to keep in touch, since she went off to school. She finished now and tryin' to get on at a firm in D.C. I hope y'all can get together before she go."

"Yeah," said Matia, smiling. "You know Pat is one of my best friends, Miss Annie. We use to be together with Binta and Shallow all the time. Then we all ended up at different high schools. Then different colleges. Patricia went to Princeton. I went to Tulane. Shallow went to Xavier. Binta decided not to go at all. I guess if Pat had stayed in the city, we'd all be just as close as ever, but time and circumstance has a way of changin' things."

"Uh-huh," said Miss Annie. "You've always been a smart one. I'm surprised some smart young man ain't swept ya off ya feet yet. Pat has a friend! Don't tell her, but he's asked Mr. Johnnie and me for our blessin' to marry her. He's goin' ask Pat at this Sunday's dinner. Sure can't see Franklin keeping ya to his self for too much longer, baby."

"Oh , Daddy said to tell y'all he said hello," said Matia.

"Tell him we said hi," said Miss Annie. "Johnnie and I would love if y'all came by for dinner. Tell Franklin there's a couple a plates with y'all names on em. You take care, baby."

"Nice seein' you Miss Annie," said Matia as Patricia's mother moseyed off into the crowd.

"Excuse me, "Nile said softly from behind Matia, after sidling up behind her.

To both their surprise, he startled her half out of her mind. She jumped, jolted by his presence. She choked on her punch and as a result, her body rejected it. Her punch came shooting out of both her mouth and her nostrils. It went all over Nile's shirt.

It was a regular horror film. Matia was beside herself with embarrassment.

She may have cried from embarrassment if it were not for the sweet smile Nile gave her. He laughed. He laughed so genuinely. His laughter made it okay for her to laugh. She relaxed.

"I'm so sorry, she cooed, attempting to dry Nile's shirt with beverage napkins. "I didn't mean to do that. Really, I didn't.

"I'm really sorry, uh," Matia began and stopped, realizing she did not know his name. "What's your name?"

"Nile," he answered, pleased with Matia's cooing and fussing over him.

"Like the river in Africa?"

"Yeah," he said, chuckling to himself, "like the river."

"Is it Nile Hash or Nile Womack?" asked Matia, taking into consideration their earlier conversation.

"Nile Hash," he said, smiling and reaching for her hands and gently taking the napkins from her. "Girl, it's just a little spilled punch."

Matia looked at Nile and felt an unexplainable longing to be near him, an absolute stranger. She had only known him in her dreams. She had rich and vivid flashes from her memory. It was ironic that she had never been happier than she was standing there with punch all over her. Ridiculously content, she smiled back into the face of this stranger who had ridden into her night like a medieval knight full of chivalry.

"I'm comin' back," she said abruptly as she turned to walk away.

"Hey," said Nile, still holding onto one of her hands. "You promise?"

"I promise," said Matia, gently pulling her hand free from Nile's hands. "Trust me. I'll be back."

Matia looked for Binta. As she walked, she carefully considered how her night had taken a turn. She had met "the Man of Her Dreams". She had prayed that tonight would be the beginning of the rest of her life. What did it all mean?

What should she do?

She truly did not know Nile from Adam. She could use some advice.

"Safiya and Franklin Singleton didn't raise no fool," she muttered to herself as she sought out Binta. She would simply ask Binta to accompany her and Nile.

Nevertheless, when she found Binta, she ofcourse was not alone, but seated next to Bill on a sofa. Matia felt like doing an about face, standing there before her two friends.

Instead, she dug up the guts to continue her endeavor and openly discuss the matter of "Nile".

"What's happenin', Matia," Bill said.

Binta just smiled and winked her eye at Matia.

"Hey Bill," said Matia, "I need a favor."

"What's goin' on?" asked Binta.

"Well," said Matia, "I met this guy named Nile."

"For real," said Bill. "That's my podna. He came here with me."

"Oh," said Matia, surprised, "well, he asked me to go out to watch the fireworks with him and since I don't know him from Adam, I thought that maybe you two could join us."

Binta stared at Matia in amazement and before she could speak, Bill was talking.

"No kiddin'," said Bill, chuckling. "My boy Nile is tryin' to rap with Matia Singleton. That's alright! I'll give ya the skinny on him, Matia. He good people. We went to high-school together at 35. Matter of fact, he goin' be with us on the way home later. He alright, Matia. If he give you any trouble just call on your big brother here, I'll set him straight. Just kiddin', he alright!"

"You sure Bill," asked Matia?

"F'sure," affirmed Bill.

"Nile's good people," said Binta. "Why? You think you might like him?"

"Like him?" said Matia, clearing her throat. "I didn't say that. I just was wonderin' if he was alright or not."

"What you think of him, Matia," asked Binta?

"Don't ask," said Matia, turning to walk away.

"Come on, called out Binta. "Tell us!"

"Y'all wouldn't believe me even if I told you," said Matia.

"Believe what," Bill and Binta asked in unison.

"See y'all later," said Matia, avoiding further questions.

Matia disappeared into the lively crowd of souls that packed the room. She could not imagine attempting to explain to Nile or anyone else that he had come to her straight from her dreams.

12

Just moments later, Nile and Matia had made their way out onto the front porch. Like Matia's front porch, the porch was concrete and rectangular. Nile and Matia sat down on the side of the porch that faced the fireworks. Three cute and rambunctious little boys sat on the steps. Older men and women sat at a picnic table, laughing and talking a few feet away.

Nile tried not to stare at Matia, but found it hard to control himself. As she locked eyes with him, a sudden gust of wind blew past them both. With the enlivening breeze came a strong sense of déjà vu. Matia noticed the gust and was suddenly mindful of the fact that an unearthly gust of wind had blown past her earlier that night. Still, the gust was refreshing and brought with it great comfort.

"What's wrong," asked Nile.

"Oh," nothing," Matia said quickly, noticing Nile's eyes even in the moonlight.

"Of all his face had to offer, she found his eyes the most precious. They were big, bright and beautiful. Miniature hurricane lanterns they were, illuminating everything they uncovered.

"You have the prettiest eyes," Matia said.

"Thank you," Nile said, chuckling.

"They are…" she started, but then stopped.

"Go on," Nile urged. "They're what?"

"They're so big and full of light," said Matia, blushing. "It's almost like they're little hurricane lamps."

"Hurricane lamps," said Nile, smiling. "I've never heard that before."

"What color are they," asked Matia.

"Hazel," said Nile. "Hazel with a green ring around them."

"Interesting," said Matia, reaching into her pocket book.

"Want some pecan candy," she asked.

"Sure," Nile said, smiling and revealing perfect teeth, "I love pecan candy, girl."

Matia noticed that he had a beautiful smile.

"I don't eat much pecan candy," she said, handing Nile a small package wrapped in wax paper. "I just make it and sell it. It's one of my family's finest recipes, but I've studied and taught myself a lot. I can make all kinds of stuff. For now, I make most of my profit off the pecan candy, though. I have three corner groceries and a lunch truck carryin' it, regularly."

"Girl, this is some good candy," insisted Nile after tasting the sweet nutty New Orleans' delicacy.

"Thank you," Matia said.

"I mean it's real good," he said. "Can I have another piece?"

"Sure," said Matia, pulling, her last piece out of her purse and giving it to Nile.

"Beauty, brains," said Nile. "and the sweetest spirit in this world."

"Huh?" asked Matia.

"You not only beautiful," said Nile, "but you industrious."

"Who asked you, anyway?" Matia said, blushing.

"I was just sayin'," said Nile.

"I know," said Matia, laughing. "I was just playin'. But seriously, one day I hope to open up my own confectionary somewhere near the French Quarter."

"Why the French Quarter?"

"Are you kiddin me?" Matia said. "The tourist, they'd give me a steady flow of customers."

"What else you make?" Nile said.

"Oh," said Matia, "besides pecan candy, I can make pralines, peanut brittle, caramels, fudge, jelly beans, candied apples, caramel popcorn balls, jellies, jams and fruit preserves too. I can also make sweetcrust and shortcrust pastries like cakes, cupcakes, muffins, scones, tarts and pies."

"Wow," said Nile, "how long you been making candies and cakes?"

"As long as I can remember," said Matia, growing distant in thought. "My mama use to sell candy in our neighborhood and both my mama and my sister started teachin' me when I was old enough to help out in the kitchen."

Images of Safiya and Sadiki making candy flashed across Matia's mind.

"You alright?" Nile said, noticing that Matia was in another world.

Matia shook off the images of her mother and sister and looked at Nile. "Yeah, I'm alright."

"How old are you?"

"I'll be twenty-three next month," she said. "And you?"

"I'm twenty four," he said. "So, you're a New Year's baby."

"No," said Matia, "Pat's a New Year's baby. My birthday isn't until January 23rd."

"F'sure?" asked Nile with enthusiasm.

"Yeah," said Matia. "When is yours?"

"August 23rd," said Nile.

"On the same day as mine," said Matia.

"That's alright!"

"You were born in summer," said Matia, smiling. Summer is nice."

"Yeah," said Nile. "It is. It' my favorite season."

"Oh, well," said Matia, "we're smack dead in the middle of my favorite season."

"Winter?"

"Yes, winter," said Matia, smiling. "What's wrong with winter?"

"It's cold for one thing," said Nile.

"Well," said Matia, "I'm a winter girl. Although, New Orleans don't usually have much of a winter. One day it's in the mid to upper 50s. The next day it's in the 70s."

"True," said Nile.

"Hey," Nile said, smiling, "I've been talkin' to you all this time and I don't even know your name."

"Really?" Matia said, giggling. "Oh, didn't I tell you?"

"No," said Nile, "you didn't."

"Matia," she said, "Matia Singleton."

"Maria?" said Nile unsure of what he'd heard.

"No, Matia," she said. "It's Maria with a T instead of an R."

"What does Matia mean?" asked Nile.

"Gift of God," said Matia.

"That's alright," said Nile, approvingly. "What school did you go to?"

"High school or college?'

"Both," said Nile.

"Well," said Matia, sighing, "at first for high school, I went to Carver and then I was accepted into a semiweekly college prep scholastics program that was being offered Uptown at Jean P. Villery."

"You didn't like Villery?"

"Well," said Matia. "It's not that. It's just that I was a cheerleader at Carver. After I joined the program at Villery, I didn't have time for cheerleading and I missed seeing my friends as much."

"I'm sure you had no trouble makin' new friends," said Nile.

"That's true," said Matia. "I did make some new friends. You'd be surprised the people you can meet on Canal Street and catchin' the RTA bus."

"What about college?" he said. "Where'd you go for college?"

"What makes you so sure that I attended college?"

"Girl, please," said Nile. "You are a college woman if I've ever seen one."

"Okay, okay," said Matia. "I'm a member of Tulane's class of 75."

"Whoa," said Nile, clearing his throat and remembering Abecca. "You're even smarter than you look."

"You think so," said Matia, laughing.

"Yeah," said Nile.

"What about you," asked Matia?

"Huh," said Nile.

"Where'd you go?"

"Oh," said Nile. "Three Five."

"Really?" said Matia. "You went to thirty-five. You're one of those McDonald 35 zealots, then."

"Come on now, girl," he joked. "Don't be jealous."

"Okay," said Matia laughing, "so, you answered my question. You are definitely a devout "35" alum."

"F'sure," said Nile.

"And after 35," asked Matia. "What did you do?"

"I took a break from school and started workin' full time as a manager at Sam's Aquarium World. I worked there all through high school. Started helpin' out when I was just a young boy."

"That pet store on St. Claude Street," asked Matia.

"No," said Nile, "I managed the one on Toulouse. It was the first shop. The one on North Rampart was the second one. We just opened the one on St. Claude about three years ago and Sam's plannin' to open one in gentilly next year. You wouldn't believe how many people are into bringin' the natural beauty of sea life into their homes."

"Really?" said Matia.

"Really," said Nile.

"You must be a real asset to the store," said Matia, "to get a chance to help run things right out of high school."

"Sam, the owner, has been like a father to me ever since...." Nile paused, realizing that he was sharing more than he had intended to.

"Go on," said Matia, softly, "ever since…"

"Since after my pops left," said Nile, drifting off into thought for a moment.

"Oh Nile," said Matia, "I'm sorry to hear about your father. I can't imagine what life would have been like without my daddy, when I was growin' up."

"Anyway, I was blessed to have good men around me even though my dad wasn't around."

"That's good," said Matia hesitantly. "I can see how it would be hard gettin' past it, though."

"Girl," insisted Nile, "I'm not studin' 'bout him. I'm fine. Besides Sam, I sometimes had my older brother, Will, and my brother-in-law, Alex. All three of them are good men. I've watched them be devoted and loving husbands and fathers."

"You said that you took a break," said Matia. "Does that mean that you thinkin' about goin' back to school."

"I already did," said Nile, clearing his throat. "I'm takin' classes at a technical institute. I'm an apprentice plumber, workin' towards gettin' my master plumber's license. I'm finishin' up my class hours and on the job trainin'. Next, I have to take the state licensing exam."

"When you have to take it," asked Matia.

"I'll take it this spring," said Nile.

"How'd you go from workin' with animals to fixin' leaky faucets?"

"Good question," Nile said, chuckling. "My brother-in-law is a certified master plumber. For years, he's been tryin' to get me interested in plumbin'. He was always teachin' me how to repair or test somethin. Now, I work with him."

"You get paid?" Matia said.

"Yeah," said Nile, "I get pay and benefits. I still work at the pet store part time. I help with inventory, trainin and closin at the shops."

"Wow," said Matia, "you're a busy man, a soon to be licensed plumber too. My dad would love to meet you."

"You think so?" asked Nile.

"Yes indeed," said Matia. "My daddy's a contractor and he's always happy to find another good plumber."

"Your dad's a contractor?" asked Nile. "That's alright!"

"Yeah, he builds like his father before him and his father before him," said Matia.

"Your great grandfather was a builder too?"

"Uh-huh," said Matia, "my great grandfather was a Free Black and one of the skilled Black artisans and craftsmen in New Orleans that was blessed to enjoy some success despite racism during his time."

"Apparently," said Nile, "your grandfather and father were blessed too. Some, people don't like to see Black men runnin' anything. Not even today."

"Yeah," said Matia, nodding her head in agreement, "I know. My daddy had the support of his family. They owned a lot of land in South Louisiana. Most of it is still in the family."

"Your daddy's a race man?" asked Nile.

"Yeah, he's been involved in the fight against racism for years. He even marched with Martin Luther King," said Matia.

"That's alright," said Nile.

"My daddy argues that to this day too many Black New Orleanians are unemployed not because they are uneducated or unqualified, but just because they are Black."

"Too many Blacks in America are unemployed just because they are Black," said Nile, "whether they are New Orleanians or not."

"Yeah" said Matia, sighing. "My daddy hates seein' anybody bein' disenfranchised regardless of color. He hates to see any person bein' deprived of their moral or legal rights. He hates injustice."

"That's part of my daddy's vision for Singleton & Company," said Matia. "He strongly believes it's his callin' to help educate and employ any serious young man who might not otherwise have an opportunity at gettin' a chance at education or decent payin' work because of his race or his bein' poor. He'll help anybody who wants help. He has a college track program for workers who are interested in higher learnin'. Every year he awards two first year scholarships to his alma mater, Dillard University. He also, encourages the guys in his programs to work their way through college."

"Wow," said Nile, "that makes me think of how the men in my life have mentored me."

"Yeah," said Matia.

"So," said Nile, teasingly, "you broke with family tradition and decided against becoming a builder, like your father before you and his father before him."

"Well," said Matia. "I've followed in my mother's footsteps mostly by fallin' in love with numbers, but dad did get me to go into the family business. I work for him."

"Oh, yeah," said Nile with surprise. "Doin' what?"

"I'm a licensed accountant for Singleton and Company. Though, I know I could be a contractor if I wanted too. I'm certainly capable."

"Who can find a virtuous woman," said Nile looking intently into Matia's eyes and quoting the King James Bible, "for her price is far above rubies. The heart of her husband doth safely trust in her, so that he shall have no need of spoil, Proverbs thirty one and verse ten."

"She will do him good and not evil," continued Matia, blushing, "all the days of her life. Proverbs thirty one and verse eleven."

"Favour is deceitful," added Nile, "and beauty is vain: but a woman that feareth the LORD, she shall be praised. Proverbs thirty one and verse thirty."

"So, you're not a preacher, but you are a Christian?" Matia said, wondering if things could get any better with Nile.

"Yeah," said Nile, "a born again, bible believing Christian.

"Catholic or protestant?"

"Protestant," said Nile.

"How about you?"

"Huh?"

"You a Christian?"

"I am," said Matia. "I'm Baptist. My daddy use to be Catholic, when he was a little boy. In college he joined the Methodist church and after he married my mama he joined her denomination and became a Baptist."

"You're different," said Nile.

"That's an old line," said Matia sarcastically, "if I ever heard one."

"It's not a line," said Nile. "It's true."

"Well," said Matia, "I know it's true. But, how would you know?"

"Hey," I'm not pullin' your leg," said Nile. "I've known many girls and women. You stand out."

"You know lots of women, huh," said Matia, raising her eyebrows. "Just how many women do you know?"

"That's not what I meant," said Nile, blushing and trying to forget Abecca. "Okay, so I do know lots of women. No, what I meant was that I use to know many women, but not anymore. I changed. God is my witness, Matia. God has taught me how to let go of my familiar for His best. And I've never met a woman I could talk to like this."

Matia was extremely touched by Nile's words, but did not want him to know.

"You're so cute," said Matia, laughing wholeheartedly.

For several moments, neither of them said a word. They just sat marveling over the explosive chemistry that they had discovered in both each other and the fireworks display. A fabulous rainbow of light illuminated the pitch-black sky. There was continual radiance, where there had previously been just darkness.

There was a temporary break in the fireworks display. Nile broke the silence.

"I'm tryin' to see if I can see the Milky Way," he said, staring up into the night sky and pushing the lingering thoughts of Abecca out of his head.

"The Milky Way," said Matia, looking up into the sky.

"Yeah," he said. "Did you know that it is a galaxy that has over one billion stars?"

"No, I didn't" she said, looking up into the sky.

"Yeah," He said, "The sun is one of its stars."

"I never really pay much attention to the stars."

"Never?"

"Nope," said Matia. "Never."

"Are you serious?"

"Well," said Matia, "not unless I'm looking for God. Sometimes, when it gets really dark, I stare up into the sky and wonder where God is exactly?"

"I guess the whole world looks for him, when life gets its' darkest."

"I guess you're right," said Matia.

"Well," said Nile, "the good news is that he is everywhere! We left him at home, joined him at the party and met him again outside on this porch."

"Oh, yeah?" Matia said. "You keep it up and I'm goin' start callin' you preacher."

"Everybody preachin' something!" said Nile. "So, watch out now!"

"Yeah," said Matia, laughing, "everybody is! That's the truth."

The fireworks started up again, exploding into the sky like rockets. Crimson, sapphire, emerald and gold lights danced across the skies. Matia and Nile watched quietly.

Nile's stomach started to bother him and he turned away from Matia. He checked out. The truth that Matia attended Tulane had made him nauseous. It was as if his past was catching up with him at the worst possible time. The probability of Matia knowing Abecca was great. Too great.

Should Nile come clean in regards to his relationship with Abecca?

And if he should, would he?

The answer seemed impossible, until Nile looked back into Matia's satisfying face. It was in this moment that Nile got a strong inclination to bear all. Before he could talk himself out of telling all of the sorted details of his fling with Abecca, he was speaking.

"Do you know a girl named Abecca Rosengarten?" Nile asked, judiciously.

"Sort of," said Matia, startled by the mention of Abecca's name.

"I knew her well," said Nile, ashamedly, "She loved me."

Much more than the possibility of Matia knowing Abecca troubled Nile. It was the possibility of his deciding he did not want to have to live without Matia and her returning the favor. It was this along with the likelihood of Nile never owning up to his past sins against Abecca. It was this along with the chance of Matia's learning of his past relationship with Abecca from someone other than him. It was this along with the likelihood of Matia being poisoned against Nile for life. These were the odds that mounted up and frightened Nile into being upfront and candied about the whole sorted drama that had unfolded over a year before Nile's having found Matia perched on a wall at Patricia's birthday party.

So, Nile did bear all. He told Matia all about his affair with Abecca, leaving out no details. He even told Matia of his brief, but potent psychosis and how it had led him to seek his fulfillment in something greater than what man had to offer.

13

Life is full of new births. It is a cycle of newborn babies. I have reasoned that spiritual death itself can be followed by a new beginning. By its very nature, it produces the kind of fertile environment that requires renewal.

Matia's life showed this concept, by virtue of the very fact that she had experienced death's residue, but continued to begin again the deliberate, scientific and sanctified dance that shaped her life.

Hearing Nile's confession of all that had happened between he and Abecca, should have made Matia flee for her very life. However, she did not flee from Nile. It was as if her prayers were being answered. She was in the eve of providence. She could not help but see that there meeting was far more than happenstance. It was ordained.

Were she and Nile mere chessmen in one of life's chess games?

Would she threaten to capture Nile's black king?

Alternatively, would Nile check her, capturing her solitary queen?

Or would Nile's pursuit end in a stalemate, a hopeless situation.

Matia became nervously excited as she listened to Nile's confession. She had an internal dialogue. This is no coincidence she told herself. Matia recalled Abecca's awaited return to school. Matia brought to mind that upon Abecca's return, she had been aching and dying to know what would make a foreign transplant with the night for skin and running marmalade plum for hair attempt to carve even the finest of brothers' initials into her wrist. She remembered being fascinated with the idea of what Abecca's fellow must have been like. She remembered trying to understand what kind of a guy would be capable of captivating the mind of a beautiful, young and clever woman in such a way. Yes, she wondered.

Matia wondered if it had been her silent, but strong desire to know Nile that had led Nile to her. For her burning, but silent meditation on him had been almost prayerful.

Perhaps, this providential meeting was indeed the answer to Matia's silent prayer.

"You know?" Matia said. "I know Bill Washington."

"You do," said Nile, caught off guard.

"Yes, I do," said Matia. "We practically grew up together. He lives in my block and is engaged to one of my best friends."

"You know Binta?" Nile said.

"She's like a sister," said Matia.

"That's alright," said Nile."

"Bill told me some interesting things about you, while you were waitin' for me at the punch bowl."

"He did?" Nile asked, nervously. "What'd he tell you?"

"It's not that important," said Matia, smiling.

"Well," said Nile seriously, "will you let me be the judge of that?"

"No," said Matia, rolling her eyes. "It's not really your business what someone else tells me in confidence, Nile."

"Oh," said Nile, nodding his head, "that's true!"

"Yes it is," said Matia, laughing.

"You know you wrong," said Nile. "Why'd you bring it up if you weren't goin' tell me?"

"Alright," said Matia, still laughing. "I'll tell you what he said."

"Alright," said Nile. "What'd he say?"

"He said that you're a low down dirty dog," said Matia, holding back her laughter.

"He said that," said Nile in disbelief. "I can't believe that. Well, maybe he doesn't believe I've really changed."

"No, Nile," said Matia, laughing. "Bill didn't say that! He said that you're good people."

"Girl," said a relieved Nile, smirking, "you really had me for a minute. I thought for sure that Bill had slipped and told you about my ten children."

"Your ten what?" asked Matia, leaving her mouth hanging open.

"Gotcha," said Nile, chuckling. "Girl, I don't have any children and I don't intend to have any until I'm married."

Matia shook her head at Nile and giggled. For the remainder of the party, Nile and Matia continued to connect. When all was said and done, they had formed a soul tie.

Turning the fact that she had discovered a treasure in Nile over in her head repeatedly, Matia was praying a prayer of penance. She knew her father would not be happy. Whilst, Nile was praying a prayer of thanks because he believed that he had found his wife.

14

Bill dropped Binta off on the corner of Charbonnet, but he did not neglect to walk his lady to her front porch and they said a long goodbye. When they were done saying their goodbyes, Binta floated up her front porch's steps.

Next, Bill proceeded to drop Shallow off a couple of houses down the street from Binta's home. Before Binta got out of Bill's car, during the brief drive home from Patricia's party back to Charbonnet, Shallow had discovered that she was sick with resentment. By the time that Bill had reached

Shallow's grandparents' Creole Cottage, Shallow was almost beside herself with envy. Between Bill and Binta's cooing over each other and Nile and Matia's shameless staring, she had had a hard time keeping her dinner down during the quick drive.

"Good riddance," said Shallow as she slid out of the back seat of Bill's burgundy Oldsmobile Cutlass, slamming the car door behind her.

"What's her problem," asked Nile.

"The million dollar question," exclaimed Bill from the front seat, chuckling under his breath. "Don't worry about her, man. She's having a bad life."

"You mean a bad day?" Nile asked.

"No," said Matia, smiling, "he mean's a bad life!"

When Bill pulled up to Matia's house, the house stood quiet and still. Like clockwork, Matia's father went to bed at nine o'clock each night. Even when he tried to stay up late, he would fall into a deep slumber on the living room sofa.

Nile walked Matia to her front door.

"Well," said Matia, "I guess this is it."

"I guess," Nile said, awkwardly.

"I had a great time, tonight," said Matia. "I'll see you again in November. Binta told me your Bill's Best man and I'm her matron of honor."

"Wait, Matia," said Nile, warmly. "I got to see you again before then."

"Nile," said Matia, sadly, "don't take this the wrong way, but it's not goin' happen."

"What's not goin' happen?" asked Nile.

"Whatever you're thinkin' about," said Matia.

"Hey, Matia," said Nile, pointedly. "Are you tellin' me that you don't want to see me again?"

"No," said Matia. "I wouldn't say that."

"Can I call on you sometime soon?" asked Nile almost pleading.

"Call on me?" Matia said. "Do you mean, come to my house to see me?"

"That's exactly what I mean," said Nile.

"What exactly are you tryin' to woo me into?" asked Matia, laughing to herself.

"Lettin' me change your name," flirted Nile, with an incredible smile.

"Lettin' you change my name?" Matia gasped, almost choking. "Are you talkin' about marriage?"

"How else, are we goin' to live happily ever after," said Nile, confidently.

"Marry me," whispered Matia, in disbelief. "Are you serious? I don't know you from Adam."

"I'm tryin' to change that," insisted Nile.

"You're crazy," whispered Matia, concerned they might wake her father.

"Would you at least think about it," asked Nile.

"Think about what?" She said. "Talkin' my daddy into lettin' you come here to see me or marryin' you?"

"My comin' here, for starters," said Nile.

"Nile," said Matia compassionately, shaking her head and smiling at Nile. "That's not goin' to happen. My daddy would take one look at you tryin' to pursue me and have a bonafide fit."

"Your father?" Nile said. "Girl, I'll do whatever ya daddy says I need to do. Just to see you again. I'll cut off my afro, change my style of clothes, do manual labor and even change your name."

"Boy," said Matia, "you are just too much. Have you been drinkin' liquor? They didn't have any liquor at Pat's party."

"I don't drink liquor," said Nile, "and I know what I'm sayin'. I mean every word."

Bill, who had been waiting patiently for Nile, killed the engine to his car.

"I've got to go, Nile," said Matia, firmly, glancing back at Bill in his car, "but give me some time to think about it and I'll stay in touch through Bill."

"So," said Nile, "I guess that answers my next question."

"What question?" asked Matia.

"Can I have your number?" Nile said.

"No, you cannot," said Matia, "but you do have my word that you'll hear from me through Bill. Franklin Singleton would hit the roof if you called this house."

"Alright," said Nile, "Alright, I know when to cut my losses. I must say that it was a pleasure meetin' you Matia Singleton. I look forward to seein' you again, soon."

"Goodnight, Nile," said Matia, pulling her keys from her pocket book.

"See you later," said Nile, turning slowly to walk away.

Nile looked back, just in time to see Matia disappear through her front door, shutting it behind her.

As Nile walked back to Bill's car, he did a three hundred and sixty degree spin and chuckled to himself.

"Matia Singleton," he whispered, "am I glad I found you."

As Nile slid back into Bill's Cutlass, Bill re-started his engine.

"Whoever said you didn't know how to beg," teased Bill.

"Whatever, man," said Nile. "You think she likes me?"

"I think so," said Bill. "She sure looks like she digs you, man."

"For real, man," said Nile giggling like a newborn.

"Hold on, man," said Bill, "just hold on. You're really gone off the deep end for her aren't you? You were beamin' in the back seat with her and you were smart enough not to try to lay one finger on her. It's a good thing you didn't too. She's like a little sister to me and I would have to set you straight."

"Of course not," said Nile, defensively. "You think I'd blow my chances with her by disrespectin' her. The word of God says it's not good for a man to touch a woman."

"That never stopped you in the past," said Bill, cynically."

"Well," said Nile, defensively, "we're not talkin' about my past."

"I hate to be the one to bust your bubble," said Bill, "but you might as well throw in the towel, now."

"Throw in the towel," said Nile in disbelief.

"That's what I said," said Bill. "You'll never be able to have Matia."

"How you figure that?"

"Her daddy is not goin' have it," said Bill. "Mr. Franklin's a mean man! And Matia's really not your type anyway."

"What you talkin' about? She's not my type? She's everything I ever hoped for!"

"No," said Bill, "believe me when I say she's not your type."

"Why you keep sayin' that? Since when did you start determinin' my type."

"Yeah, Nile," said Bill, sarcastically. "I know you and I know your type. You like them nice and easy!"

"Easy?" Nile said. "Easy as in loose?"

"That's it man," said Bill. "Matia's like my Binta. With them you don't get the milk for free."

"Bill," yelled Nile, "I keep tellin' you that I've changed. I'm different."

"Yeah," said Bill. "You keep tellin' me that, but we both know that you've had a hard time stickin' with one chick. You've broken many hearts. Now, you want me to believe that all because of this religious conversion of yours that you're ready to get serious with Matia?"

"Bill, you sure you been saved, man?" asked an aggravated Nile.

"Yeah," said Bill, chuckling, "I'm a rosary bead carrying member of the Roman Catholic Church. I'm at Mass every Sunday at Saint David's."

"You sure, man? Because you don't sound like somebody who's ever needed Jesus to save you from nothing. You sound like you've never sinned a day in your life."

"Alright," said Bill, apologetically, "alright, man! No doubt, I know the Lord and I can see your point. We've all sinned and come up short. I get it. Besides, I have my own struggles. It's a struggle keepin' my hands off Binta. I see her and I just go crazy. It's to the point where she won't trust us to go out together unless we're with other people. We need help, stayin' out of trouble she says. She's always remindin' me that the good book tells us it's not good for a man to touch a woman unless it's his own wife."

"Look, Bill," said Nile, staring at Bill, "I'll never be what I was again. I want to be a man after God's own heart! I don't even know why I keep tryin' to convince you of it. I've got to pray about all of this. I think I've found the woman I'm supposed to marry."

"Did I just hear you say marry?" asked Bill, swerving in the road and almost hitting the car next to him. "You're talkin' about life Casanova? Slow down, man. Don't you think you're movin' a little too fast?"

"No," said Nile. "I'm not movin' too fast. Matia is the woman I've been prayin' for. Don't ask me how I know? I just do! By the way, I owe you big. If you hadn't invited me to this party tonight, I'd have never met her."

"You're dead serious aren't you," said Bill, as he parked in the back of Nile's apartment.

"Should Nelson Mandela be a free man, walkin' the streets of South Africa?"

"I'll take that as a yes," said Bill.

Nile nodded his head with sweet anticipation and laughed to himself. "You should."

"If you're set on takin' this role, you've got to learn your lines and have them well rehearsed for curtain time. If you don't hit it off with Mr. Franklin, you can forget about her. The last brother that tried to get next to her was a dude named Candy. I heard he had her full attention too!"

"What happen to him?"

"He got shot," said Bill, seriously. "For all we know Mr. Franklin killed him."

"Man get on away from here with that," said Nile, pretending to be indifferent. "You're kiddin' me, right?"

"Yeah, man," said Bill, laughing, "Matia's dad didn't kill him, but somebody did."

"Well," said Nile, "I'm sorry to hear about Candy, but glad to hear that Matia's father didn't kill him."

"Only because he didn't get the chance," said Bill, with a stern look.

"Aw come on," said Nile, "the man can't be that mean."

"He can," said Bill, "and he is. Some people won't walk past his house, unless they cross to the other side of the street."

"I'm not backin' down," insisted Nile.

"Are you sure?" asked Bill.

"Not unless I know she wants me to," said Nile. "As long as she's interested, I'll be around."

"Just one thing you should know, man," said Bill.

"What's that?"

"Her mother and older sister both died a couple of years ago," said Bill, "before Candy got shot."

"F'real, man," said Nile. "What happen?"

"A bad abortion and a mother's heartache," said Bill. "It was a shame. Her mama was right as rain on a hot summer day around the ninth ward. The whole neighborhood loved her! And her sister, Sadiki, was a real brain and a stone fox to boot. The world was her oyster. Their deaths left Charbonnet Street in mournin' for a good while. I'm just tellin' you this, so you'll know. She been through boo-coo stuff these last few years. So, treat her right. And don't bring up her sister and mother either because she freaks out when she gets to thinkin' about them."

"Alright," said Nile soberly, "thanks for tellin' me, man."

Bill nodded his head and smiled.

"Congratulations," said Bill, reaching his hand out to Nile for a hand dap.

"For what?"

"For findin' the future Mrs. Nile Hash."

"Alright," said Nile, chuckling, "now, you're talkin' my language. So, I can count on you?"

"You know it, man," said Bill.

"Good, good," said Nile. "Matia said she's goin' keep in touch with me through you and Binta."

"Alright," said Bill, "sounds like a plan!"

PART FOUR
PRENATAL CARE

1

Matia lay in her bed, heavy with thoughts of her unbending father and the charming Nile. She turned her attention towards her bedroom window, which gave her a clear view of her church fellowship, Christianway Baptist Church. The fellowship was one empty lot away from Matia's home. As she gazed through her bedroom windowpane, she could see her minister, Pastor Wright, and his family arriving to Christianway Baptist for Sunday morning worship. Pastor Wright held the door to the sanctuary open as his wife and five daughters entered the church. Worship would begin in about 60 minutes and Matia was still in bed.

"Matia," said Franklin, "your oatmeal is on the table. We leave in 45 minutes."

"Okay, daddy," said Matia through her closed door, "I'm comin'."

After eating a quick breakfast, Matia and her father walked down the street to the fellowship. Matia prayed privately that the sermon this morning would give her some clarity on what to do about Nile. She was already partial to Nile and desired to get to know him better. Still, she knew that her father would see what she coveted as a blatant disloyalty. Franklin required that Matia resign herself to being devoted only to him. So, she understood that her wanting something other than what he wanted for her, even if it was not wrong, would anger him. A conflict with her father was not what she wanted. It was much more than she felt she was prepared to deal with.

As Matia and Franklin entered the vestibule, the choir members began to line up for their march into the sanctuary.

Matia sat next to Binta, while Franklin joined the rest of the deacons in the front of the church. The church had prayer and worship and then came Pastor Wright's sermon.

Pastor Wright stood to his feet and found his way to the podium.

"Good mornin' church," he said.

"Goodmornin'," the church responded.

"It certainly is good to be in the presence of the Lord on another day. It is good to experience his goodness and excellence. Amen church?"

"Amen," responded the church.

"Only a good God would go on lovin' a people who sometimes even in their best efforts fail to do good. Only an excellent God could create such a beautiful day, put a brilliant light in the sky and paint the skies a heavenly blue and white without colorin' outside of the lines. His work is perfect! So, I don't know about you all, but I'm glad to be alive this Sunday mornin'. I'm glad to be experiencin' His awesomeness."

"Amen, pastor," said a silver haired woman from the choir stand. "Amen."

"I was havin' a talk with my Father in heaven," said Pastor Wright. "I asked Him to give me somethin' to tell His people this Sunday. He answered me. The sermon this mornin' is titled, "Heart Check: Get Your Mind Right!" The openin' scripture is found in Proverbs 23:7, where Solomon was inspired by God to write, "As a man thinketh in his heart, so is he."

Pastor Wright was a stout and "coffee and cream" colored man. His hair was naturally wavy, as was his disposition sometimes. He was educated, having received a Bachelor of Arts in history from Southern University at Baton Rouge and a Bachelor of Arts in anthropology from Dillard University in New Orleans. While he had much knowledge, his wisdom outweighed his knowledge. Therefore, he knew it was best to tell the truth. Even if it hurt him, he told the truth. He loved to smile too, especially when he was talking about Jesus. Still, he had a seriousness about him that scared some out of their wits.

During his sermons, his well-intended peers often encouraged him with a nod, smile or affirming amen. There were always those with ill intentions waiting around like turkey vultures for someone's leftovers. These ones stared him down. A couple of these men wondered if they would ever have a chance to replace him as Pastor of Christianway. A few of these women, the ill-intended ones, let their imaginations run wild with shameful imaginations. They wondered if Minister Wright had truly been faithful to his wife of 35 years. If he had, they wondered if they could break his commitment. Thankfully, Pastor Wright never thought too much of what people thought of him. He was resolute to tend to his family's needs and be about the business of the Lord.

"Now, many of us were raised to believe that what went on in our minds had nothin' to do with what was goin' on in our hearts. But Proverbs 23:7, suggest otherwise. As a man thinketh in his heart, so is he, says Proverbs 23:7. Man, woman, boy or girl, what you hold in your heart or think, will influence you spiritually, mentally, emotionally and physically. So, this is to say that what you think will affect the condition of your heart. Equally, what you hide in your heart will control your thoughts church. What are you thinkin' about this mornin'? What is hidden in your heart at this very moment? Are you thinkin' about Jesus and all He has done for you? Are you thinkin' about God and how He has loved and cared for you? Are you thinkin' about your husband and what he means to you? Are you thinkin' about your wife and the gift that she is to you? If you're not guardin' your heart and thoughts, you may be thinkin' about someone else's husband or wife, but they are not for you!"

"Lord, have mercy on our souls," whimpered an aged lady as tears began to roll down her cheeks.

"Some of us are here because we had a little talk with Jesus. Some of us are here because we need to have a little talk with Jesus. Some of you are here because you want yourself a husband. Some of you want a wife. Some of your fathers or mothers made you come. Some of you want to show off your new dress or suit. Amen, church?"

"Amen," responded some of the deacons.

"I'm goin' to tell the truth and shame the devil this mornin'. I'm goin' to tell the truth and shame the devil's advocates. Some of you are at this fellowship because it's the in thing to do in your house. Others are here because you're in a situation and you don't know what to do. It's alright. It's alright this mornin' church. God wants me to tell you that He's no respecter of persons. He wants us all to get a checkup. He wants us all to make sure our minds are right. Whatever a man thinketh in his heart, so is he, church. We ought to remember that our thoughts will direct our hearts and our thoughts will guide our hearts."

Pastor Wright stepped out from behind the podium and walked out into the aisle that separated the two sides of the church.

"I once knew a man who was afraid of everything. He was afraid of heights so he would not look out of windows. He would not go for walks because he was afraid that a car might hit him. He would not swim or take boat rides because he was afraid that he might drown. He would not get married because he was afraid that his wife would leave him. He did not want to have children because he was afraid his children would die. He would not eat fish for fear that he'd choke on a bone. He would not! He would not! He would not! His long lists of "Would Nots" cost him his life. His fear had tied him up into a knot. He was stuck in his fear and unable to free himself. One day he was clingin' to a column on the second floor of a burnin' buildin'. No matter how hard the fireman tried to pry his hands, arms and legs free from the column, he fought to hold onto it. He was afraid to let go because he refused to face his fear of heights. He was afraid of havin' to jump from the second story window to safety. He was afraid of bein' thrown to safety. The doors were all blocked by ragin' fire and the window was his only way out. Still, he was afraid. So, he died clingin' to his fear. "

"Are you that man?"

Franklin experienced a burst of raspy uncontrollable coughing, drawing unwanted attention to himself at an awkward moment. Everyone, including the pastor looked at him.

"You alright, Deacon Singleton?" asked Pastor Wright.

"Excuse me church," said Franklin nodding his head in the affirmative and waving his hand for the minister to continue.

"There was a woman that lived in the house next door to my childhood home. She was consumed with anger and always feelin' bad. Her anger consumed her. She was angry with her husband if he came home early because she was caught off guard. She was angry with her husband if he came home late because it was inconsiderate. She was angry if her husband interrupted her activity with chatter. She was angry if her husband was silent. She was angry because she had no children. She was angry, after she had had children. She was angry if it rained. She was angry if it was too sunny. She was angry when she had to harvest her vegetables from her garden. She was angry when her garden was sickly and didn't produce a harvest. No matter what she was angry. Over the years, this anger caused her stature to become bowed over and her expression on her face turned into a permanent scowl. She was always sick from her anger and never able to enjoy life. Eventually, her husband left her. Her children whose births she'd cursed stopped visiting. It became hard for her to walk and so she spent less time in the rain, sun and garden. She refused to let go of her anger. Her anger turned into bitterness and hatred. Her hardened heart killed her. With hardened arteries and high blood pressure, she hated herself to death."

"Are you that woman?"

"These are true stories about people that I once knew. Their costly lesson to me was not to allow myself to live in fear or anger."

"God's lesson to us all is much greater, church. Let us consider the magnitude of our thoughts. Whether good or bad, they will influence our behavior and therefore our lives. If you are housing thoughts of envy, fear, anger, unforgiveness, lust or hatred in your heart, these feelings will produce fruit. You are feedin' your souls poison. It leads to bad decisions. It will even lead to sickness and disease. So, church, I encourage you to commit yourself to thinkin' only those things, which are beneficial. Our closin' scripture is Philippians 4:8. Philippians 4:8 in the King James bible says, Finally, brethren, whatsoever things are true, whatsoever things are honest, whatsoever things are just, whatsoever things are pure, whatsoever things are lovely, whatsoever things are of good report; if there be any virtue, and if there be any praise, think on these things."

2

Sunday, January 2, 1977
Dear Nile,

Friday night I was afraid of you. I was afraid of what being with you made me feel and think. Just talking with you was so exciting. I have tried not to think of you for the last two days, but I have not been successful. During worship this morning, the pastor preached on Proverbs 23:7. God's lesson for me was that the heart never lies. It exposes the truth. It bares our secret thoughts and feelings, Nile. I have never been one to admit too great of an interest in love, until now. My heart has given me away. Oh Nile, it has exposed even my deepest desires. I think that even Shallow, Bill and Binta could tell you were on my mind. Meeting you has been like discovering a secret doorway that has led me home.

I must admit that I think that you could very well be the man of my dreams. While, I wasn't looking for you, I can't pretend that I'm not glad you found me. I am glad, Nile. I'm just not quite sure what to do with you. My father depends on me for so much. I don't think he could handle the idea of my having designs of my own. So, you see this is why I have not been able to approach the subject of seeing you again with my father. Don't worry! I am praying about this and I have faith.

Truly Yours,

Matia

Thursday, January 6, 1977
Dear Matia,

It is late Thursday night and I just got home from playing basketball with Bill at Stallings Gym. I read the letter that you wrote me four days ago. Thank you for writing. I wasn't sure if you would really keep in touch. I'm glad you did.

Since, you were straightforward, I thought I would be too. Unlike you, I have been openly looking for love. In the past, I looked in all the wrong places. Now, that I know God, I've been looking to Him for my future. I prayed that God would help me find a wife. I don't want to scare you, but I believe that you are the answer to my prayers.

Nile

Sunday, January 9, 1977
Dear Nile,

I come from a long line of women of faith. My Grandmother Rain believed God when doctors told her that her little girl, my mama, would not live to be an adult because of a fragile heart. My mama, Safiya, determined at a young age that she would live life to the fullest. She would not just wait on death. When the doctors told daddy and her that she could never survive a pregnancy, she turned to God in faith. With their words of hopelessness still ringing in her ears, she conceived and gave birth to my sister, Sadiki. She found Sadiki's name in a book that she read once. The book was about the Ibo.

Do you know who the Ibo are, Nile? They are people from the Southeast of Nigeria. They are one of the biggest and most prominent ethnic groups in Africa. Like us here in New Orleans, they like to eat yams, but there yams are not sweet potatoes like our yams, Nile. No, their yams are real yams and they are their main crop. They are farmers and farmers function based on the notion that what they plant will grow one day. This requires faith. For them to have belief in something is to have "Sadiki".

I once asked mama if she was ever afraid, while pregnant with Sadiki. She said that to live bound by fear would be death itself. She said that for her bearing Sadiki was necessary. She simply had to have her faith! Let's do that Nile. Let's make up our minds to have faith that everything will work out for the best.

Sincerely Yours,
Matia

Thursday, January 13, 1977
Dear Matia,

It is Thursday night again and I just got home from playing basketball with Bill at Stallings. He gave me your letter and I was so happy to get another one, I could not stop smiling as I read it. All that you shared with me about the Ibo people and faith was so beautiful, but not as beautiful as you are to me. I know it has only been a couple of weeks, since we saw each other, but I really would like to see you soon.

Missing You,
Nile

Sunday, January 16, 1977
Dear Nile,

Are you familiar with chapter eleven and verse one of the Book of Hebrews? It says that faith is the substance of things hoped for, the evidence of things not seen. It is my favorite scripture, Nile, always reminding me that what I long to achieve in life will begin in my hopes and dreams if I just hold out and keep believing. Try not to doubt that everything will work out.

Sincerely Yours,
Matia

Thursday, January 20, 1977
Dear Matia,

My car keeps breaking down on me and I am looking to buy a new one. So, I've been relying on the RTA, Alex and sometimes Bill for transportation. Bill just dropped me off home after giving me a ride home from work at the aquarium shop, tonight.

I had a busy day. My last plumbing job took longer than I expected. A customer poured a whole sack of potato peelings down her brand new garbage disposal. I thought I'd snake the drain and be done, but I was wrong. I ended up having to use baking soda, vinegar, hot water, a plunger and good old fashion elbow grease. It was easy enough, but it did take me a bit longer than usual. When I was finally finished, I had to return the plumbing company's work truck. Sam's out of town. So, Alex gave me a ride to Sam's World on his way home from work because I needed to drop by Sam's Aquarium World to restock, do inventory and make the night deposit for the home store after closing. I never made it to Stallings to play ball. After Bill finished playing ball, he dropped by, handing over your precious little letter. Thank you so much. Reading your letter was like a breath of sweet fresh air after a long hard day.

Matia, I have got to be honest with you about how I'm feeling. I can't stand having to sneak you letters like we're two under age delinquents. We are both adults. I just know if I could just meet your father and explain

my intentions, he won't have a problem with
me getting to know you.

Nile

3

On the morning of Matia's 23rd birthday, Nile had the following dream:

He dreamed that he was in the custody of prison guards,
who marched him and other captives into an old church
building. While standing before the altar, Nile could see
rusty iron shackles on his wrists and ankles. He was in complete bondage.

"Release him," he heard a great voice declare from up
above him.

At once, his shackles crumbled to pieces, falling to the
floor. He walked out of the fellowship, leaving his chains
behind him. He stepped out into the light of day to find
Matia sitting in the driver's seat of a shiny new candy apple
red Mustang. Nile noticed that in the dream the surroundings outside the church fellowship were unfamiliar to him.

"Don't forget our stuff," said Matia.

Nile looked down and discovered suitcases on either side
of him. He picked up his and Matia's belongings and threw
them into the back of the Mustang. Matia asked him to drive.
As he walked towards the driver's side of the Mustang, Matia
slid over into the passenger seat. Nile started the engine and
they drove off down a dirt road into the unknown.

4

Hours later, Nile zipped up his thick tan and leather jacket and slid his hands into two of its' four pockets. He searched the cloudy sky for the sunlight and found that it had not made an appearance yet. When he walked out into the courtyard, the crisp air caused him to shiver. Wondering if he should have worn a thicker shirt, Nile started walking up the court-yard that lay before his apartment in the heart of the Desire housing Development. Hating his car for calling it quits on him for the third time, he was talking to Sam about a lead on replacing it with a new car.

"At least it's not snowin' like it was in Miami this week," Nile mumbled to himself, recalling the Miami news story he had seen a few days ago.

In spite of its usual tropical weather, snow had fallen in Miami, Florida. It had been big news in the Gulf South.

Nile turned the corner of the courtyard, coming face to face with Renaldo, a 24 year old Vietnam vet who was a disre-garded prisoner of war.

"What's up Renaldo, man," Nile said, nodding his head.

"Take cover, Nile," said the troubled Renaldo, dodging imagined gunfire. "Vietcong is everywhere. Can't you see em?"

I do not wish to argue who won the Vietnam Conflict. Let history speak for itself. In this particular instance, a pic-ture is worth more than a thousand words. Yet, if I were to say that I had a related matter of concern; it is one that exam-ines the Vietnam War's paradigm of humanity's passion for freedom. For every battle is indeed fought to conquer or preserve freedom.

If the Vietnam Conflict was fought for freedom, what freedom then did it deliver?

Yes, this is the question that was born deep within the depths of my sad observation of Renaldo. Further examination of Renaldo's war has led me to see so clearly that for the American troops and our South Vietnamese allies there simply was no comfortable receiving blanket to wrap this war's independence into. Please for the record allow me to say that I am not what one could call anti-war. I believe that there is "thank God" a time for peace, but to nail the truth on its head there does also exist a certain time for war.

Did the Communist forces embody the death of freedom? I believe so.

In their capturing of Saigon in 1975 they neglected to give birth to that basic concept of freedom that all of humanity longs for from the moment of its conception. Instead, they spawned that seed that can be most treacherous, dominion. And with their domination they worked to obliterate freedom and deconstruct the significance of its true potential. And what of South Vietnam's battle to maintain their freedom? Of this, I still say a picture's worth more than a thousand words. How many words, then? How many words would be necessary to paint a picture of the loss of land, dignity, life and soul?

And our American troops, they had survived perhaps what they thought to be their life's hardest battle only to return home and be spat on. No, they were not still in Vietnam, but many of them were still prisoners of war. They remained P.O.W.'s standing on American soil, their minds so wrought with the inner and outer conflicts of what their time in Vietnam had produced. Some of them wounded within, with internal injuries that received no acknowledgements. Where were their purple hearts to recognize their wounded minds and black-and-blue souls?

This was the very same question that Nile asked himself as he studied Renaldo moving through the courtyard. Renaldo was a former valedictorian and star athlete on his Carver high school football team. What had the Vietnam War meant for Renaldo, a young Black male trying to survive within the racial powder keg that existed in the 1970s?

Nile considered what the Vietnam War had brought into his community. He recalled that the chance to fight for their country had meant a great deal to some of the young Black men in his neighborhood. Misunderstood and underestimated, it was their opportunity to show the world what America meant to them. So, they had fallen in line and become soldiers fighting for what they and generations before them coveted most, liberty. Fighting for independence, only to return home and be reminded that their own prospects for full liberation stopped just short of their ability to justify the color of their skin.

The continuous fight to claim both one's dignity and autonomy regardless of skin color is catastrophic when neither won nor acknowledged. Renaldo had had his portion of the evidence in this truth.

While waiting at the bus stop, Nile ducked into Bertha's, a corner po-boy shop, to get a fried ham and scrambled egg po-boy. As he paid for his sandwich, the aroma of freshly baked French bread, fried ham and scrambled eggs engulfed the store. Nile inhaled deeply, taking pleasure in every moment of the mouth-watering aromatherapy that was taking place. This was the beginning of what Nile expected to be a lovely day. The only thing that would make it better would be his seeing Matia's face.

5

Charbonnet pronounced (SHAR bon EY) is an alternative of Charbonneau, descending from a minor form of the Old French *charbon* "Charcoal". The name was believably a nickname for a person with black hair or dark skin tone. I must admit that I have marveled over the story behind Charbonnet Street, Matia's Street, being so named. For the street's name worked so well at suggesting the presence of its Black inhabitants, during Matia's place in history.

Matia too had wondered about the past of her lower ninth ward neighborhood. She had combed the bookshelves and archives of her city's main library, Central Library, discovering that Charbonnet Street had been so named since at least the mid 1800s. She had learned that Alabo Street, the neighboring street that she had met Nile on and that had served as a second home to her as she had played with childhood friends had once been named Adams Street. So much had she learned, but still she felt she had so much to learn about the history of this place that God had placed her in for just a moment in time.

Who she wondered had been the many residents of Charbonnet Street? What indeed had been their fate?

Once on Charbonnet Street, Nile wondered the same thing. He did a visual study of Charbonnet; the morning sunlight had finally made its debut, revealing a brilliant blue sky.

The street, he thought, had a fascinating story to tell. It was a story of native New Orleanians and non-natives alike who had respectfully relished their resolve to christen New Orleans as their home. He had learned enough in his McDonough 35 history classes to be in love with New Orleans. He knew the astounding chronicles of New Orleans, a true cultural doorway into world history. He had studied of the diverse groups of people whose roots were deeply embedded into the city's flesh: Native Americans, the French, Creoles, Africans, Spaniards, Haitians, Jews, Greeks, Italians, and Cubans to name a few. And he like so many others believed that for good or for bad the city's story was without equal. Nile knew a colorful mix of people. People of various ancestries and hues crossed his path weekly as he worked throughout the city. Yet, it was a known fact that while many of their families had called the city home for many generations, some were only the first or second generation in their family to reside in "The Crescent City". Then there was his mother, Royal Noel Hash. Even though, Royal Noel was a native of New Orleans, she had left home after marrying William Hash, a Louisiana countrymen. Later, indigenous to New Orleans she had chosen to uproot herself from the life that she had struggled in vain to build in the Louisiana countryside. Royal left both it and her chronically adulterous and absentee husband behind in search of a better life for her family in her native city.

6

Nile paid close attention to the story that each home had to tell. He looked through the windows of colorful houses.

Attractive single and double wide shotgun houses, Creole cottages and avant-garde bungalows lined Charbonnet in shades of lemony yellow, eggshell white, sky blue, and sea green. On the right-hand side of Matia's street, heading towards the Florida Avenue levee, set a corner grocer named Henries. On the left-hand side, Matia's side, set a church fellowship. Matia's family home, a charming freshly painted and front-gabled bungalow trimmed in blue, had white bevel wood siding and a large stony concrete porch. An apron that was held up by black wrought iron brackets sheltered the porch, adjoining the bungalow's sloped roof. A black wrought iron fence that was lined with scarlet red rose bushes framed the front yard.

Returning to the fact that he believed that he was at the beginning of what he anticipated would be a lovely day, the moment of truth had arrived. As Nile climbed the steps to Matia's home, he continued in his belief that the only thing that would make the day better would be his seeing Matia's face when she answered her front door.

Nile rapped lightly on Matia's front door, but there was no answer. He rapped again a bit harder. Still, no one answered the door. He sat down on her porch and in her spot.

This moment called to my mind that moment that Candy had done the same, the circumstances in the case being quite different. In that, Nile had found Matia and desperately longed to have her hand in marriage, while Candy just longed to have her.

It still remained to be seen whether or not Matia would allow Nile to have her hand. It still remained to be seen if she could stomach the thought of it. If she wanted to stomach the thought of it.

Nile could hear the singing of a gospel choir as their voices poured through the windows of a church fellowship one lot away on the corner. Moving harmony carried Nile back to his early childhood. He could see and hear his paternal grandfather preaching at the fellowship that he had planted deep in the woods of Ponchatoula. Leading Mighty Zion Hill African Methodist Episcopal Church had been one of his grandfather's greatest joys. Memories of trailing his mother and older siblings up the dirt road that led from their old country house to the doorway of Mighty Zion Hill A.M.E. were still so fresh in his head. Tears formed in the corners of Nile's eyes as he remembered the day they buried his grandfather in the cemetery just a few feet away from the church's building.

At the tender age of five Nile could sense God calling him to follow him. Amidst the deadly turmoil of violence and divorce that his family faced, God's voice was drowned out by confusion. How amazing was it that God had not only kept him through all these years, but that God had not given up on him.

"What kind of love is this," whispered Nile, trying to make sense of God's faithfulness to him despite his unfaithfulness.

"Hey dere," said a raspy male voice, jolting Nile back into the present moment. "What ya doin' up dere, son?"

Nile looked up and saw a man heading towards him from the house across the street. The aged man, a stout fellow with wavy hair, had on a worn gold wedding band on worn copper colored hands.

"Goodmornin' sir," said Nile, smiling. "Are you Mr. Franklin?"

"Franklin, huh?" grunted the older man. "No, I'm not Franklin, son."

"Elijah," said the man, extending his hand to Nile for a handshake, "Elijah John Hero."

"Nice to meet you Mr. Hero," said Nile, setting a small purple satin gift box on the porch and shaking the elder's hand. "My name's Nile Hash."

"Ya a roofer or a framer?" said Mr. Hero.

"No, sir," said Nile, "I'm a plumber."

"Ya lookin' for work, Nile," asked Mr. Hero.

"Huh," said Nile confused.

"Work," said Elijah. "You lookin' to work for Franklin on some of his jobs or get into one a his trainin' programs?"

"Oh, no sir," said Nile. "I just need to talk to him about somethin'."

"Oh," said Mr. Hero, turning to walk away, "Dey down on the corner at the church. Dey probably be back in a few. I see people startin' to leave, now."

"The mornin' service still goin' on," said Nile, looking at his watch. "It's long after lunch."

"Yeah," said Elijah, noticing the little purple gift box next to Nile before glancing at his watch. "It is two o'clock, but sometimes dey in there till evenin'."

"Oh," said Nile.

"Son," said Elijah, whirling back towards Nile as though he'd discovered something enormous. "You look like a young man with somethin' of great consequence on ya mind. You wouldn't happen to be comin' a courtin'?"

"Comin' a courtin'," muttered Nile, laughing to himself. "Yes, sir. I guess I am."

"Lord have mercy," said Elijah, shaking his head and clapping his hands. "Franklin goin' sure enough hit the roof."

"Excuse me sir," said Nile.

"Franklin know you?" asked Mr. Hero.

"Not yet," said Nile.

"Yes indeed," said Mr. Hero. "Ya want me to stick around in case ya need some help?"

"Sir," said Nile, a little puzzled, remembering Bill's warnings.

"Ya don't know what ya gettin' yourself into," said Elijah. "Do you, son?"

"No, sir," admitted Nile, gulping. "Maybe I don't."

"Let me put my lawnmower back in my shed," said Mr. Hero, hurrying back across the street. "I'll come sit wit ya. Don't wanna miss this."

"Ok," said Nile, hesitantly.

Nile scratched his head receiving the confirmation that Bill had been right about Matia's father. Mr. Franklin did indeed seem to be a force to be reckoned with it.

Nile said a little prayer to God, concerning his spur-of-the-moment visit. He hoped he had not made a big mistake.

A screen door slammed shut. Nile looked up to see if it was Mr. Hero returning. It was not. The noise came from the Double Shotgun next door and to the right of Matia's house. Twin girls around ten were causing a hullabaloo on their front porch.

"Melinda," said the shorter girl, "ya wanna play *Miss Mary Mack?*"

"See Belinda," said the taller girl. "I told ya it wasn't that cold out here. We don't need no coats."

"Melinda, if ya take ya coat off," warned the shorter girl, "I'm goin' tell mama."

"Oh look, Belinda," said the tallest girl, pointing at Nile. "Somebody's on Matia's porch."

"Melinda, take ya hands off ya hips. You just showin' off."

"What you talkin' about Belinda? I'm not doin' no such thing. I'm goin' tell mama ya out here startin' mess with people."

"Who ya think he is, Melinda?"

"Maybe he's Matia's '*boo*'," answered Melinda.

"Oh, Matia's got a '*boo*'," sang the twins. "Matia's got a '*boo*'!"

Both of the girls looked over at Nile with playful grins on their faces, looking like they thought they had gotten away with stealing cookies from their mother's cookie jar.

Nile smiled back at them and waved.

"Oh Melinda," said the taller twin, "he waved at us."

"Let's go tell mama, Belinda," said the shorter sister. The girls ran back inside their home, giggling.

Mr. Hero caught Nile's attention as he shuffled back towards Matia's house, joining Nile on the front porch.

Before Mr. Hero could settle in his seat, Franklin and Matia returned home. Nile took a deep breath as he absorbed the sight of Franklin. All six foot four inches of Franklin were colored a ruddy yellow.

As they entered the yard, Mr. Hero patted Nile on the shoulder and rose to greet Mr. Franklin.

Nile rose to his feet, looking Matia in the eyes. He was suddenly uneasy with clammy palms. He sat back down on the porch, seeing Matia's horror. It was as plain as the nose on her face. She was disappointed.

"Good afternoon y'all," said Elijah, swiftly taking hold of the situation.

"Good afternoon," answered Franklin

"Hi, Mr. Elijah," said Matia.

"Hey dere, Franklin," said Elijah, extending his hand. "Been out there in Plaquemine's parish by ya cousin, Ferdinand, catchin' any trout or catfish, lately?"

Mr. Franklin smiled, shaking Elijah's hand.

Matia stood frozen in disbelief. She felt as if she were standing near the edge of a treacherous sea cliff. She knew what danger might be there, just a few short feet away from her. One wrong move and it could mean sure disaster.

Why was Nile here?

Had not she made it clear that her father was not ready for his visit. That she was not sure if she was ready.

"Elijah John Hero," said Franklin. "I know what you're up to. I can't go fishin' with you way out in Plaquemine's Parish this Sunday, Elijah. Today's my baby girl's birthday."

"F'true?" Elijah said, digging into his pocket and pulling out a ten dollar bill to hand to Matia. "Happy Birthday pretty little lady."

"Thank you Mr. Hero," said Matia, smiling and accepting the birthday money. She stared past her father at Nile.

"Well now Franklin," said Mr. Hero, chuckling to himself, "look like we got ourselves a brand new president."

"That's right," affirmed Franklin, walking over to his front porch and taking a seat beside Nile. "I watched President Carter's inauguration on Thursday. America's got herself a 39th president. Speaking of politics, we'll be votin' for a new mayor soon."

"Yeah," said Mr. Hero, nodding his head, "a lot a men ready to throw their hats in this here mayor's race, but I'm sure goin' hate to see Moon go."

"Uh-huh," agreed Franklin thoughtfully, "He has been a mighty fine mayor. We need more fair dealing politicians in this country. We need public servants who understand that most colored people in this country don't want more than their willin' to work for, just a fair shake at provin' that there just as capable as anybody else.

"Yeah," said Elijah, nodding his head, "that's it!"

"Who are you," Franklin asked Nile gruffly.

Oh," said Mr. Hero before Nile could speak, "excuse me. Franklin meet Nile Hash. Nile Hash meet Franklin Singleton."

Nile quickly extended his hand to Franklin with a smile.

"Pleased to meet you sir," said Nile.

Franklin shook Nile's hand and wondered at his enthusiasm.

Suddenly, Mrs. Hero came out onto the front porch of her single Shotgun house. Her royal blue and daffodil yellow housecoat shone beautifully against her brown skin in the sunlight.

"How y'all doing," she sung, waving at everyone. "Telephone Elijah. It's the cab company."

"Alright, Delilah, sugar," answered Elijah. "Tell em I'll be in."

"Alright, Elijah," said Franklin, nodding his head with understanding. "See ya later."

"I got to go to work y'all," said Elijah, patting Nile on the back and hurrying off back across Charbonnet Street.

"Aren't you goin' with him," said Franklin assuredly with an icy look.

"Uh, no sir," said Nile. "I'm a friend of Matia's."

Mr. Singleton glared at Nile and began to express great amusement.

Standing before her father, Matia shook her head in utter disbelief. She was silently mouthing the word no, when Franklin frowned at her, requiring an explanation.

"Is that so, Matia?"

"Yes, daddy," said Matia, clearing her throat and shaking off her nerves.

"Oh, it is," said Franklin, turning towards Nile with an eye of inspection. "A friend, huh."

"Yes, sir," said Nile quickly. "And it is an honor to finally get to meet you sir. Matia's told me so many great things about you."

Franklin studied Nile, noticing that his hands looked like a laborers. They reminded him of what his hands had once looked like before he'd moved totally into supplying labor and overseeing staffs.

"Matia," said Franklin. "Why haven't I ever heard anything about Nile?"

"Oh," said Matia, "I just met Nile at the end of last year. Bill and he are good friends. We talked at Pat's birthday party. I wasn't expectin' him today."

"Is that so," said Franklin, looking over at Nile again.

"Uh, yes, sir," said Nile, grasping the position that he had put Matia in. "Matia had mentioned that today was her birthday and I wanted to wish her a happy birthday and give her a gift."

"I see," said Franklin, nodding his head with awareness.

"Do you want him to stay," asked Franklin.

"Yes," said Matia too quickly, "that would be nice."

"Go ahead then, and invite your birthday guest in," said Franklin. "He here way ahead of ya other guest. So, maybe he can be of some help".

"Welcome," said Matia, smiling at Nile.

"Thank you," said Nile.

"You cook?" asked Franklin.

"Sir?" asked Nile.

"Can you cook?" said Franklin stressing the last word. "Don't tell me you one of them young fellas that thinks cookin' is just for women?"

"Oh, no," said Nile. "No sir, I can cook. My mama taught me how!"

"Good," said Franklin. "Dinner's at six and I could use some help in the kitchen. You can start by washin' up at the kitchen sink. Then, you can cut up the seasonin' and peel the potatoes."

"Yes, sir," Nile said.

Nile held his head up high, happy to be of assistance. Now, he would have the coveted opportunity to impress Matia's father that he so longed for.

Mr. Franklin ascended his front porch's steps with Matia right behind him. As she opened her front door, she looked back over her shoulders at Nile. She had come full circle. The death of her relationship with Candy, a bloody and fertile matter, having given birth to her start with Nile.

"Don't just stand there," said Matia. "Come on in!"

"Alright," said Nile.

Just moments later, Nile stood alone in the living room, talking with Franklin.

"Nile," said Mr. Franklin. "Ever had stuffed redfish?"

"No, sir," said Nile.

"Well, then you're in for a treat. Matia loves my stuffed redfish. I stuff it with a crabmeat dressin'. She likes potato salad and dirty rice too. So, that's what we're goin' to be cookin' this evenin' for her birthday.

"That's alright with you?" asked Franklin.

"Yes, sir," said Nile, "sounds dynamite. Thanks again for invitin' me to stay."

"Well, son," said Franklin. "I've never been one to turn someone away when I have plenty to offer."

"Yes, sir," said Nile, finally relaxing and regretting the misgivings that he had allowed himself to have concerning Matia's father.

"Right this way," said Franklin turning to walk away and motioning for Nile to follow him.

Franklin stopped abruptly and grabbed Nile by his shoulder.

"Just one more thing," said Mr. Franklin.

"Sir?" asked Nile.

"Just know that the plenty that I'm offerin' does not include my daughter," said Franklin rather pointedly.

"Yes sir," said Nile deflated.

7

Rummaging through her dresser drawers for a change of clothes with visions of Nile and her father heavy on her mind, Matia thought about the man her father used to be. Her father had always been dignified, but he had once also been full of joy. He took full advantage of his marriage, doting over her mother, Safiya, and bestowing upon her every kindness that he could envision in his mind's eye. What's more, no good thing did he deny his daughters the pleasure of experiencing

Was it shocking to her? This change in her father was not. She knew that it had arrived with the death of Sadiki and that it had become a permanent resident with the death of her mother, Safiya.

He, an honorable man, had lost his eldest child to "The Ways of The World". Sadiki often called that which was wrong right and that which was right wrong. Driven by a hunger that no one but Jesus could satisfy, she had lived dangerously. He had only been able to stand by and watch, while Sadiki's barefaced addiction, an acquired taste for sin, had led her to an abrupt and untimely death after a botched abortion. Father unknown and pregnancy disdained, Franklin believed that the absolute horror of losing their eldest daughter, whom they had affectionately called "Faith" had killed his beloved Safiya too. Franklin had been forced to dig the same untimely hole for Safiya that he had been forced to dig seven months earlier for Sadiki.

"The world would not take his Matia, too," he often declared.

He had made it clear to anyone who would listen. He would not just stand by and allow some sweet talking Casanova to steal Matia's life right out from underneath her.

Or, was it from underneath him?

Despite his bullying ways, Matia had great compassion for her father.

He required compassion. He was in danger of losing all of himself to hatred and resentment. He was becoming quite proficient at loathing life. He had lost his faith to live. Though he could not admit it, he was quite angry with God.

Why was Franklin angry?

Had not God allowed him to lose both his first love and first born?

This had stupefied him, a man who considered himself intelligent. The day after Safiya died, Franklin shook his fist at God in anger, cried out to God for understanding and groveled at God's feet for mercy all before the sun had set.

As time went on he completed only part of his journey to his healing place, backpedaling to a place of fear. He clung to Matia, his human life preserver. He chased away thoughts of packing up his life and moving. He fought off ideas of beginning again with another. At any rate, to stay in New Orleans was his heart's desire. To salvage whatever he had left of his life with Safiya was his only foreseeable future.

After hurricane Betsy, Franklin toyed with the idea of moving the family West to California or East to South Carolina. Safiya hit the roof, protesting any move from her beloved city. Franklin sulked pointing out that Safiya's lack of support for a move wounded him.

Driven to explain herself, she sat very close to Franklin on their living room loveseat and attempted to make plain her position.

"In a world that denies both its livin' and its dead," she had said softly. "I'd rather be in a place that knows how to celebrate life and death. No other place I'd rather be, Franklin."

Franklin was reminded that trying to separate Safiya from New Orleans was futile. Hurricane Betsy had not been fit to persuade her into parting with New Orleans for good. The hurricane took their home and even some of their loved ones. Still, Safiya was resolute in wanting to stay. Standing amidst the remains of what once had been her home, she said, "There are three kinds of New Orleanians worth mentionin', Franklin. There are the ones that are born and die here, the ones who arrive and refuse to leave, and the lovesick ones who dream of returnin. I'm the second."

Still, there came a time when Safiya grew disgusted with her beloved city. Right before her death she'd colored New Orleans seductive and accused her of sometimes having the sort of brazen ways that could shame the walking dead back into their graves. Greif stricken over her eldest daughter's death, Safiya had bitterly blamed the city for Sadiki's troubles.

"Always remember to be a lady, Matia," she'd pleaded just days before her death. "Keep your skirt down and your teeth to ya self."

Safiya had told Matia that she should never be the kind of woman who left her porch's screen door unlocked at night for stray men to come and go, as they pleased. Just to lead them astray; she had said that too often her adored city was the kind of mesmerizing woman who left her wooden shutters ajar while changing her colorful garments just to woo the dead weight lust of the "World's Peeping Toms".

Franklin had just stared at Safiya, his spitfire who had born faith. She was undeniably striking in her own right. A brilliant mind she had for numbers. Unsung, she was his business' spine. She had been the driving force behind the financial side of his company's success. Plus, a sweetness to good for words seeped through every fiber of her being. She could not help but love. Then on top of all of this, her indigo blue skin forever commanded his admiration. It was more than beautiful. The way that it glowed and mirrored beauty's light boggled the mind. So beautiful was she both inside and out. So, beautiful was she.

So, what did it matter that she talked a little bit out of the side of her neck? God had fashioned her for him and God had led him to her. For better and for worse they had vowed to be one. He had loved her. He would always love her.

8

Franklin and Nile walked through the living room. Wall to wall pine hardwood floors spread across the room. Natural light flooded the interior of the home from windows that lined an outer wall on its left. To the right of the living room was a large room. A sign hung on the door that read Singleton and Company. The door was halfway open and Nile could see inside of the room. Stocked full with 2 mission style desks, 4 wooden bookshelves and 4 large metal file cabinets, it looked to be a busy home office. A wide archway formed a passageway to a large adjoining dining room. The dining room led to an arched door, the entryway to the kitchen.

Franklin and Nile exited the dining room, entering the kitchen.

Its' walls were painted a buttery yellow. The wooden cabinetry was painted white. A forty-inch wide Wedgewood stove with one oven, two broilers, four gas burners, one griddle, one storage drawer, and a folding utility shelf set on the wall adjacent to the kitchen door. The stove covered in a lemony yellow porcelain enamel steel and nickel plated trim stood on dainty cabriole feet, giving it the look of a piece of furniture.

The men washed up and started dinner. Franklin began seasoning and sautéing various meats, while Nile cut up fresh seasoning and peeled potatoes.

"Your home is beautiful sir," said Nile.

"Thank you, son" said Franklin. "I built this house for my family after hurricane Betsy."

"That's right," said Nile. "When we were talkin' about my work, Matia did mention that you were a builder."

"Businessman, philanthropist, contractor and skilled draftsman," said Franklin. "Studied at Gilbert Academy and Dillard University. Learned everything else I know from my father, who was an original member of The Manhood."

"You mean The Gilbert Academy that use to be on St. Charles Avenue in the 1930s," said Nile, "one of the first private school's for Blacks in the city."

"That's right," said Franklin. "I'm surprised you've heard of it."

"Some of my teachers at 35 always talked about Gilbert Academy. They said that before McDonough 35 and Booker

T. Washington, there was Gilbert Academy, educatin' Blacks in the country at a time when Blacks were still havin' to fight for the right to breathe."

"Yes," said Franklin.

"That's alright," said Nile. "I see where Matia gets her drive."

Franklin turned red in the face because of the pleasure he took in hearing Nile's flattery.

"But the Manhood," said Nile, "what's that?"

"Yeah," said Franklin, matter-of-factly, "The Manhood Alliance of American Contractors & Engineers. The Manhood let Blacks and Whites into their union during segregation. They even had a Black president from New Orleans for a time. His name was L. T. Guillory. My father knew Guillory personally."

"Are you a member," asked Nile.

"Use to be," said Franklin. "Joined and was an active member with my father for a while before he died. The alliance shutdown, though. There was too much pressure from those who opposed integration to keep out Blacks."

"Sin," said Nile.

"If that's a new word for racism," said Franklin, "then sin it is! It wasn't that long ago that I couldn't get a good meal at some places on Canal Street simply because I was a Black man. Some places in this world we still aren't welcome. We have to work twice as hard just to get the opportunities that the other fella has, but we are up for the job."

"Yes, sir," said Nile, nodding his head.

Franklin smiled.

"The house," said Nile. "It's a California Bungalow isn't it?"

"Yeah," said Franklin, "I'm surprised you know that. It's my version of a Bungalow. We had a shotgun before Betsy. It was beautiful, but Betsy destroyed our house. After Betsy, my wife and my daughters went to visit some of my cousins in California, while I worked on gettin' my business and our livin' conditions right again. My wife wrote me, sayin' that she loved California, but she said New Orleans was her first love and would not be betrayed. She talked like that. Real colorful like. I decided I would bring a little bit of what she saw in California here by buildin' her a bungalow. At the time weren't too many bungalows on Charbonnet, but they were all over Gentilly and mid-city. I chose bevel siding for the outside wall and a stone composite concrete for the porch. Safiya took one look at the high ceilings, sloped roof, wrought iron columns and roof apron and smiled."

"That's alright," said Nile, nodding his head in awe. "If you don't mind my sayin' so, your work is beautiful."

"Thank you."

"You're welcome."

"So, what is your work," asked Franklin.

"I'm an apprentice plumber," said Nile, clearing his throat. "I'll be finishin' up my trainin' this spring. Plumbin' is a fine gig, but I love carin' for fish and settin' up their aquariums. I help run a fish pet shop chain."

"A pet shop?" Franklin said, shaking his head at Nile in disapproval. "That's more of a waste of your time than the plumbin'."

"Sir?" asked Nile.

"A man needs a solid education during these unstable times. Now, becomin' a master plumber is a good honest livin', but a graduate of 35 could do a lot better. You should have greater ambitions. After all, you were prepared for college. Isn't that right?"

"Yes, sir," said Nile. "I was."

"And why didn't you go?' asked Franklin, arching his eyebrows in judgment.

"I'm not sure sir," said Nile. "I guess, I honestly did not want to at the time."

"Well," said Franklin in disappointment, "that settles it then. The boy didn't want to. So, to hell with it, then. "

"Sir?" asked Nile in surprise.

"Everyone isn't meant to be educated. Some people can just barely be trained to accomplish the mundane. Those of us who are scholarly enough to stomach excelling in education should do just that. Our communities are dependin' on us to rise up out of mediocrity and open up the doors of opportunity."

"I love learnin', sir," said Nile. "I do. My head is always in a book. I guess you could say I'm optimistic though, because I believe that with enough support anyone can excel in education. I think it's just a matter of puttin' your finger on what a person's particular talent is."

"If you love learnin', why choose plumbin'? Granted, you'd have yourself a niche in the community. Aren't enough properly trained and licensed plumbers in our community. I know plenty of people who are always lookin' for good plumbers. I could use one myself. Whose workin' with you?"

"My brother-in-law, Alex Trueman," said Nile chuckling, at the erroneous contradiction in even the most accomplished carpenter showing disdain for plumbing.

"Oh, Trueman," said Franklin, "I've heard of him. He's that young minister over in Gentilly whose tryin' to get involved in politics. I met him at some NAACP meetings a while back. I hear he does quality plumber's work."

"Yes, sir," said Nile.

"Does he work outside Orleans parish?" asked Franklin. "I get plenty of jobs in Plaquemines, St. Bernard, Jefferson, Lafourche, St. Charles and John the Baptist too."

"I believe so," said Nile, "but I only do jobs for him in the city. I could ask him."

"Do that," said Franklin, rinsing his hands and leaving the kitchen.

Franklin returned rather quickly and handed Nile a business card.

"If you don't mind," said Franklin. "Give him my business card. I'd like to meet him and see if we can do business. My plumber started doin' shoddy work. I'm lookin' to replace him."

"Oh, no sir," said Nile. "I don't mind. I'll give it to him."

"You should go back to school, Nile," said Franklin abruptly. "Study business or better yet, philosophy."

"Philosophy?" asked Nile his eyes big with wonder.

"Certainly," said Franklin, "you seem like a philosopher. Like a thinker. You could become a professor. Write world changing books. You'd enjoy it and lots of colleges and universities could use someone like you."

"I should have been an architect or studied political science," said Franklin, full of regret. "My father wanted me to, but I studied business and went into carpentry, instead. Got involved in the boycotts and strikes of the Civil Rights Movement. Still today, I'm an active member of the NAACP and the Southern Christian Leadership Conference. You have to stay active in the political and social work of our day."

"Do you know Bill?" asked Nile. "He's a good friend of mine."

"Yeah," said Franklin, "he's a great young fellow. Now, he's somebody to watch. I think he's doin' great things to help bring his father's business up to date."

"But he's a mechanic, sir?" said Nile arching his eyebrows. "Isn't that a problem for you?"

"Yes," said Franklin, "I know Bill's no academic, but he's not over by my house, tryin' to talk to my daughter either."

Nile laughed to himself, nodding his head in agreement.

"Isn't that right?"

"Yes, sir," said Nile, "that's right."

"How long have you known Bill?" Franklin asked Nile as he returned to his cooking.

"Since our high school days at 35," said Nile.

"I do like Bill just fine," said Franklin. "The way he's stepped up to the plate by helpin' his father with his auto shop is somethin' worth mentionin'. The shop was on the verge of failin' after Bill Sr. had his stroke. Your friend Bill breathed life into that place. Bill Sr. knows it too. They're makin' money hand over fist. That fellow, a freshly licensed mechanic whose been groomed for auto work his whole life, is full of clever ideas for that shop. Any man would be proud to have a son willin' to follow in his footsteps. I can't help but admire him for it."

"Yes sir," said Nile listening intently.

"My Matia, said Franklin. "She's no son. She's a girl through and through."

"Yes, sir," said Nile nodding his head with poise and respect.

"Still," said Franklin, "any man would be honored to have her for a daughter. She keeps excellent books and leaves my financial affairs in pristine order. And she's full of great marketin' ideas too. I don't know what I'd do without her."

"And as a wife, sir," added Nile boldly.

"What," said Franklin taken aback. Franklin arched his eyebrows and cleared his throat as though he were trying to get rid of something that was threatening to poison him.

"Any man would be honored to have her as his wife," stressed Nile. "She is incredible."

"Incredible, huh?" Franklin grunted.

"Yes, sir," affirmed Nile.

"I don't know how incredible she is," said Franklin sarcastically. "She can sure be stubborn."

"Is she stubborn," said Nile, "or strong-minded, sir?

"Reach me the cayenne pepper out of that cabinet on your left, son," directed Franklin.

Nile hurried to the cabinet.

"So, you think there's a difference between a stubborn and strong-minded woman, huh?"

"Yes, sir," said Nile as he went to the cabinet and retrieved the cayenne.

"So," said Franklin, as he slit open red fish and stuffed it, "do you know Jesus?"

"Yes, sir," quickly answered Nile. "I do."

"Good," said Franklin. "Good."

"Got any children," asked Franklin?

"No sir," Nile said, "no children sir."

"How about drugs?" Franklin asked.

"Sir?" asked Nile, puzzled.

"Do you fool around with drugs?" asked Franklin.

"Oh," said Nile, "No. No drugs, sir."

With question after question, the grilling of Nile continued in between the seasoning, and roasting that proceeded supper being served.

By the time that the rest of the dinner guest arrived, Nile too felt as if he had been well cooked.

9

Later, during dinner, Nile set a satin box covered in royal purple on the dinner table closely beside his plate. No one appeared to notice.

Nile spoke of Matia's respect for her father, "Matia says you have a vision for franchisin' the disenfranchised. If only more of those who have achieved some success would have a heart for givin' somethin' back. America would be better off."

"You sound like my kind a fella," said Franklin approvingly. "So, tell me. Do you recognize the need for our finest to educate themselves and lead the way for the future?"

"Education is the key to our success as a community," said Shallow.

"That's right dear," said Franklin, smiling at Shallow approvingly. "It is. Matia, you should take notes as this young lady speaks."

Franklin reached out for the platter of redfish, getting a serving.

Matia laughed to herself.

"So," said Matia, being messy, "Do you agree, Nile? Is education the key?"

"Not education alone," said Nile as he reached for a piece of hot buttered French bread.

Everyone's eyes were on Nile. Though, they all remained silent.

"So," said Franklin, "You don't agree that colored people along with the rest of the world need the freedom to exercise and enjoy their rights? And that learning is the only way to obtain this freedom?"

"No sir," said Nile.

"No sir what?" asked Franklin.

"No sir, I don't disagree that gettin' knowledge is important."

"Alright then," said Franklin, "I'm right. You agree that education is the key."

"No sir," said Nile, "I didn't say that."

"What are you sayin' then?" asked Franklin.

"I believe that the integrity of a man has to come first," said Nile. "He must be willin' to see his flaws. He has to be ready to admit to them. Then, he has to be open to change and growth."

Matia smiled, her eyes beaming with approval.

Franklin rolled his eyes at Matia and grimaced.

"It would really be somethin' if the whole world understood that different does not always mean better or worse," said Nile, drinking some sweet tea, "but that sometimes different just means different. God is no respecter of persons. He values us all."

"Please, pass the tea," said Binta, addressing Shallow.

Shallow reached Binta the tea.

"I agree with that," said Matia slicing into her redfish and crab dressing.

"What's that?" said Franklin, startled that he was losing face with Matia.

"What Nile just said," said Matia, "I agree with him."

"Wow, Nile," said Shallow wiping her mouth with a napkin, "I never considered that my education alone might not be enough or that it might be an error of judgment to automatically take an educated person for one of character."

"Uh-huh," said Franklin, chuckling, "I told you, Nile. You a philosopher. A philosopher in need of a soapbox. Better go back to college and get yourself a soapbox, son."

"Sounds like he already has one to me," said Matia, winking her eye at Nile.

Everyone laughed.

"So, Nile," said Franklin, "you disagree that it is detrimental to encourage people to settle for trades?"

"Yes sir," said Nile, "education in the area of trades with self-suffiency in mind is priceless. America needs producers to continue to lead and thrive."

"Without a good solid education, a man or woman is at a disadvantage in this world," said Franklin. "There's no way around it."

Bill reached for the bread bowl, clearing his throat.

"Without moral integrity, all of the education in the world will not be enough to help America get and keep prosperity. I mean true prosperity and success is not just measured by what a man owns or the titles that he holds."

"Yeah," said Matia, "and havin' all the education in the world can't give mankind the moral compass that is needed to keep us from destroyin' ourselves from within or even each other. Education is vital, but surely it is not enough."

Uncomfortable with the fact that Matia was agreeing with Nile again, Franklin abruptly changed the subject.

"How's dinner?" said Franklin. "Is everyone enjoyin' it?"

Everyone was quick to praise the meal. Bill was intense in his eating, gobbling down large spoons of potato salad and not hesitating to get second and third helpings.

He ate as if eating for his former McDonough 35 high-school football team. Franklin ate calmly and with great dignity. But then, he did everything with great dignity. He would never fail to play the part of dignitary as he sat at the head of his very own table.

The room grew quiet from a pause in conversation. All that could be heard was the chiming of silverware as it hit china dinner plates. It was dinner party music in its most primitive state.

Transfixed, Nile stared at Matia. Sitting close to him, she was making her own music. Mental improvisations of Jazz filled Nile's head. Matia mesmerized him without even trying. She wore a flower choker, an off the shoulder peasant blouse and flared jeans. The canary yellow blouse that she had slipped on complimented her skin beautifully. She made him think of a songbird. So petite and exotic, she sat perched gracefully at her end of the table, singing a song that only he could hear.

"So," said Matia, noticing the satin covered box on the table, "what do you have in that box."

"Oh," said Nile, picking up the purple satin box, "you mean your box."

"My box," said Matia

"Yes," said Nile, reaching Matia the box, "it's just a little somethin' I picked up on Canal Street for your birthday."

"Nile, you shouldn't have," insisted Matia as she accepted the box.

"But he did, '*sha*'," added Shallow. "So, open the box so we can see what it is."

Matia smiled and removed the lid of the little box. She carefully removed its contents, a14k gold ring.

"It's beautiful," said Binta.

Speaking in disbelief, Matia repeated that Nile shouldn't have bought her a gift, "We just met. I can't accept a ring from you, especially not one like this."

Matia held the flower-cut diamond and garnet leaf ring in her hand as if she were afraid she might break it.

"Why not?" asked Shallow, rolling her eyes.

"Oh, yes you can," said Binta, rushing over to Matia and Shallow's end of the table to get a closer look at the ring.

"That's dynamite man," said Bill. "How much did that one set you back? Did they let you finance it?"

"Bill," said Binta, "you shouldn't ask."

"It had to be a pretty penny, '*sha*'," said Shallow, "especially with that three karat diamond flower."

"Yeah, man," said Bill, trying to be messy, "looks like an engagement ring to me."

"Nile I really shouldn't take this ring," said Matia. "You might wake up one day and expect somethin' in return for it."

"It's just a birthday present," said Binta quickly. "Right, Nile?"

"It's whatever Matia wants it to be," said Nile.

Matia turned red and stared at her new ring in silence.

"So," said Franklin, "a plumber can afford a garnet and diamond ring these days."

"Daddy," said Matia disapprovingly.

"That's alright," said Nile laughing and shaking his head. "A garnet and diamond ring and more, sir."

Franklin was exasperated. His face reddened and he stood up abruptly, "I'll get your birthday cake," he said. He cleared the table and disappeared into the kitchen.

"Did I do something wrong?" asked Nile, looking at Matia.

"You mean other than bein' born?" said Matia, laughing to herself. "Don't worry about it. Daddy's bark is a lot worse than his bite."

"Well," said Binta, feeling a little bad for not having brought a gift, "don't forget Shallow and me goin' treat you to lunch at Burger Orleans tomorrow. I feel bad that I didn't buy you somethin' this year."

"Oh, girl," Matia said to Binta, "I wasn't expectin' nothin' besides our annual lunch at Burger Orleans."

"Count me out again this year y'all," said Shallow, apologetically. "I already started my rotations for pharmacy school."

"Aw, '*boo*'," said Binta. "We goin' miss you."

"You don't have to work tomorrow?" Nile asked Matia.

"All of Singleton & Co.'s employees get their birthdays off with pay," said Matia. "So, since mine fell on a weekend, I'm off this Monday."

"That's alright," said Nile. "It's nice of your father to give his workers their birthdays off with pay."

"I'd say you're the nice one," said Matia, smiling at Nile. "bearin' unexpected gifts. You sure do know how to make a girl feel special." She blushed. Nile was looking at her. He noticed that he could see himself in her eyes. He was brand new. He was a newborn learning so much for the very first time. His face flushed.

Franklin walked back into the dining room, carrying Matia's cake. The cake, a delicate shade of white trimmed in orange and yellow smelled like a confectionary, fragrant with hints of vanilla and lemon. He sat the cake on the table in front of Matia.

"Thank you daddy, said Matia. "It looks and smells delicious."

"I'm glad you like it," said Franklin.

"You can even smell the lemon fillin'," said Binta.

"I know," said Matia, "it's my favorite fillin'."

Everyone sung the birthday song to Matia. When they had finished, Franklin nodded his head at Matia.

"Go on and blow out your candles," said Franklin.

"Don't forget to make a wish," said Binta.

Matia smiled and took a deep breath, taking in the delicious aroma and joyous moments. She closed her eyes, images of her and Nile smiling and talking still fresh in her head. She made her wish and blew out both her candles.

"What did you wish for, 'sha'?" asked Shallow.

"I wished Nile would stay and watch *Roots* with us." said Matia.

"Well," said Nile. "I did plan on tryin' to make it to the night service at the fellowship. But the way buses run on Sundays, I'd be lucky to catch even the end of service."

"You should stay and watch it, man," said Bill. "That is if Mr. Franklin, don't mind."

Everyone looked up at Franklin who had been silent.

"Who's askin' to stay?" said Franklin. "Not the plumber."

"Oh, daddy," mumbled Matia shaking her head.

"That's alright," said Nile to Matia. "It's not the extent of what I am, but I am a plumber. I'm not ashamed of it. There's nothing wrong with it."

"Now you're talkin' like the philosopher again," said Franklin. "I like the philosopher. He can stay."

10

Later, the dinner guest settled into the living room to watch *Roots*, the movie based on Alex Haley's book, *Roots: The Saga of an American Family*. The room was a long spacious room, thirty by twenty. From the ceiling a decorative crystal chandelier hung. The room was dressed with wood paneling and floral antique furniture was covered in thick plastic. There was a vermillion floral sofa, a magenta and dark yellow love-seat along with two gold upholstered side chairs. Dark yellow drapes hung at the windows.

For awhile the dinner party talked about the movie. The cast was a magnificent parade of who's who in the late '70s' Black Hollywood.

"I hope it's not a disappointment," said Shallow.

"It's a movie about slavery, Shallow," said Bill. "What you expectin'?"

"No," said Nile. "If it's like the book, it'll be hard, but worth watchin'."

"You read the book?" asked Franklin.

"Yes, sir," said Nile, nodding his head at Matia's father, "three times."

"They say John Amos, Ben Vereen, and Le Var Burton in it," said Bill, settling into a side chair beside Binta who was sitting on the sofa with her two girlfriends. Shallow sat in the middle and Matia at the other end of the floral couch.

"Louis Gossette Jr. too," said Nile, sitting in a side chair at the other end of the sofa, next to Matia.

Mr. Franklin sat in the loveseat opposite Nile's chair, pretending not to be paying close attention to his every move.

"Leslie Uggams, Olivia Cole and Roxie Walker in it too," said Binta.

"Todd Bridges too," said Matia.

"Cicely Tyson in it too," said Binta.

"Who's not in it?" said Shallow sarcastically.

"Thank you Shallow," said Franklin arching his eyebrows. "You took the words right out of my mouth."

"I don't know y'all," said Bill, "but I hear some are worried about the TV ratings for the movi*e."*

"I wonder if people will even tune in to watch it." Binta said.

"America goin' watch it," said Nile

"How long is this movie supposed to be?" Shallow asked.

"Eight nights long," said Bill.

"F'true," said Binta.

"Yeah," said Matia, "and some nights are two hours long and others are one."

"How long it's goin' be tonight?" asked Binta.

"I'm not sure which it is," said Matia, glancing at her father. "Daddy you know?"

"Two hours tonight," said Franklin.

"Don't worry about gettin' home, Nile," said Bill. "I gotcha."

"Thanks man," said Nile, "I'll be glad when I get my new set of wheels. Havin' to catch the bus is crampin' my style."

"Right on, man," said Bill, nodding his head.

11

After the movie, Matia said goodnight to her birthday guests and father. She was forced to. For it had occurred to her that it was her time of the month and she suddenly was not feeling so well.

"Are you goin' to be alright," asked Binta, giving Matia a friendly hug.

"Yeah, *'sha',*" said Shallow. "Anything we can do to help ya feel better?"

"Thank y'all," said Matia. "but the first day is always the worst. I just need to lay me down."

"Here," said Shallow sliding a twenty dollar bill into Matia's hand. "Get yourself something nice for your birthday. I was goin pin it on your shirt, but I forgot to bring a safety pin."

"Big spender," said Bill, playfully.

"Oh, Shallow," said Matia, "you don't have to give me nothing."

"I know, *'sha',*" said Shallow, "but I want to. Go on and get ya rest."

When the rest of the guest were on their way out, Franklin pulled Nile by the arm, asking to have a private word with him.

"I don't want you to come back around here," said Franklin.

"Why not?" asked Nile confused.

"Because I don't want you too," said Franklin.

"What about what Matia wants?"

"She don't know what she wants," said Franklin, irritated. "She's just a child."

"I would think that at twenty three she's old enough to know," said Nile.

"Well," said Franklin, "you would think wrong."

"Do you mind if I ask her myself?" asked Nile.

"Does "Fats" Domino love New Orleans?" asked Franklin.

Nile grimaced with understanding and nodded his head.

"I do mind, son," said Franklin.   "Besides, you're a plumber. You have nothing to offer her."

"That's not true."

"Just leave her alone," said Franklin.

"I don't know if I should do that, sir," said Nile.   "Not unless, she wants me to."

"You'll ruin her life," said Franklin.

"No, sir," said Nile offended, "she wouldn't let me."

"What?" asked Franklin.

"I don't think you give her enough credit," said Nile. "She would never allow anyone to ruin her life."

"Go," said Franklin, glaring angrily at Nile, "and don't come back."

"Alright sir," said Nile turning to leave, "please tell her I hope she feels better.

"Shut the door behind you," said Franklin, ignoring Nile's request.

12

That night Matia dreamed that she swam in the Mississippi River, near its French Quarter shore. She saw herself at a distance enclosed in darkness. She wondered how she was staying afloat. It was an unmistakable fact that she could not swim. She simply could not. She had always been terrified of water. Afraid of being overwhelmed by the current. Afraid of seeing herself go under.

A red cardinal and pearl white riverboat paddled pass her, its paddlewheel churning the water like smooth cream. Its polished wooden outer decks were trimmed with shiny brass railings. Through large windows, Matia could see that the inner rooms were lavish with a Victorian elegance. Soft ceiling lights illuminated the otherwise dark scene. At one of the windows, Sadiki appeared, her face pressed against the glass pane and her eyes loud with abandonment. On deck Franklin and Safiya so in love, danced an unearthly dance as a brass band played. Trumpets, sousaphones, trombones and saxophones all coupled together with liberating sounds of percussion.

Matia focused her attention on her sister and cried out to her. "Sadiki! Where you been?" The fog thickened for a moment and when it cleared, Sadiki had disappeared. Matia cried out in horror at Sadiki's utter and complete desertion of her. She called out her sister's name repeatedly, hoping and praying that she might reappear in the empty window. But this was all in vain because Sadiki was gone for good.

Matia's eyes were red and her arms and legs grew tired. Her head bobbed in and out of the water. She heard a familiar voice call out to her from behind. As she turned, she saw Nile. He was near the rocky edge of the shore, beckoning her with open arms. The riverfront's mouth opened and prepared to swallow her. Matia's limbs moved slower. Her head went under once. She was gone for a couple of seconds, before resurfacing. She went under a second time, her resurfacing again seeming rather unlikely. Within seconds, she felt someone take hold of her and lift her head up out of the water. Somehow, she knew it was Nile supporting her, though she could not see him. Holding her, he swam her safely back to the shore.

13

Matia slept in the morning after her birthday. When she finally awoke, she remembered her dream, trying to hold onto every single detail of it. She wanted to keep it. Did not want to lose it, but had to retain it until she understood it. She sat in bed flipping through her bible and dissecting her dream's characters and signs for meaning. The prophetic and instructive language that she believed God sometimes used in dreams was quite real to her. However, too often dreams were misunderstood.

The phone in the living room rang. Matia slid out of bed and made her way to the telephone.

"Hello," said Matia, groggily.

"Matia, it's eleven thirty," said Binta. "You sound like you still in bed."

"I was still in bed."

"Hey '*boo*', you gotta get up," said Binta. "You ready to go to Burger Orleans."

"It's still mornin'," said Matia.

"By the time we get there it'll be after twelve," said Binta.

"Okay," said Matia. "Give me thirty minutes. I'll be down there by you by then."

"Alright," said Binta.

"Alright," said Matia, before hanging up the telephone.

14

As Matia stepped outside onto her front porch, she took a deep breath. It was sunny outside. The cool air was unusually dry and crisp. The sky shone bright and clear blue. She quickly walked to Binta's house on the corner.

They arrived at Burger Orleans at twenty minutes after twelve, Matia noticed, glancing at her watch. They walked up to the order window. Binta ordered a shrimp po-boy and a cold drink. Matia ordered a cheeseburger, fries and cold drink. They sat at a picnic table outside of the sandwich shop and on the corner of St. Claude Ave. and Alabo Street, talking.

"You watchin' *Roots* again tonight?" asked Matia.

"Yeah," said Binta. "I'm goin' watch it with my mama and daddy."

"They watched it last night?" asked Matia.

"U-huh," said Binta, "they watched it."

"I wonder how many people saw it last night," said Matia.

"I was watchin' channel four news," said Binta, "and they said over twenty eight million households watched the movie last night."

"I wonder what people thought about it."

"I went to sleep cryin'," said Binta.

"You did Binta?" asked Matia.

"Yeah, girl," said Binta. "It was just so sad to see innocent people happy and mindin their own business, just to suddenly have their lives stolen from them. Made me sick to my stomach."

"It made me mad," said Matia. "To think that someone could consider the life of another human being as so dispensable is just too much."

"I know," said Binta.

"I couldn't believe it when I heard your name," said Matia.

"I know," said Binta, "isn't that something?"

"Where'd your parents get your name?"

"On my daddy's side of the family most everybody's Haitian Creole," said Binta. "Most of them came here from Haiti. It was my mama who named me after her great-great-grandmother," said Binta. "They always told me that she was a West African. I wish I knew more about my African roots."

"Me too," said Matia. "I know one of my great grand-fathers was a free Black. I've heard stories of a great-great grandmother who was an African princess. I have even heard stories of a great-great-grandmother whom they say was bought by an Irishman down in the Quarter. And one of my great great-great-grandfathers was said to be a Black Frenchmen. But nobody seems sure of any of the stories. So, I can only imagine. I wonder if any of my African ances-tors come from West Africa like yours, Binta. Maybe we related."

"Could be," said Binta, smiling. "I did a history project my senior year at St. Mary's and found out that Louisiana Africans came from many different places. Though, many did come from West Africa and South-Central Africa too."

"How's it all make you feel, Matia," said Binta, "not knowin' for sure your ancestry."

"Frustrated sometimes," said Matia. "I remember takin' a class at Villery and the teacher had us do a genealogy analy-sis. The teacher and most of the students who were not Black could go back many generations. They had definite names of all of these grandparents along with captions explainin' what parts of the world their ancestors immigrated from and what they did for a living. Most of their family's real last names and histories' were there for them to dig up, if they wanted to. The studies done by most of the Black students in the class were limited of course by the harsh realities of history. I could barely go back three generations with many of my facts. After that, the information was ambiguous, incomplete or just unavailable. That cow teacher gave me a C for a grade and criticized me for leavin' too many holes in my family history. She said I should have gone further back into my family history and provided more information."

"You didn't tell her that you didn't have any more information available to you?" asked Binta.

"I tried," said Matia, "but the more I talked to that woman the more I just wanted to choke her. It was like tryin' to explain bein' Black in this world to someone who wasn't. They just can't understand no matter how much talkin' you do."

"So, what did you do?"

"I was goin' go to the head of the program and make a formal complaint about the bias in the goal of the project," said Matia.

"Did you?"

"No," said Matia. "I didn't."

Finished eating, the two friends threw away their trash.

The sky still dry, bright and blue, it began to rumble with loud thunder.

"Want somethin' sweet?" asked Binta, smoothing out the folds in her knit top.

"For real, Binta?" said Matia, rubbing her lower belly. "You still have room for more?"

"Yeah, I got room," said Binta, smiling.

Matia smiled. "Alright, I'll have somethin' sweet."

"I wish Mrs. Smith was sellin' frozen cups this month," said Binta.

"She probably not," said Matia. "It's not warm enough, yet."

"It's in the sixties," said Binta.

"Just for a couple of days," said Matia.

"Well, I'll settle for some ice cream. How about you?"

"Alright, if you insist," said Matia, laughing, "but let's walk while we eat it. I think I smell rain in the air."

"You and me too," agreed Binta.

After standing in line several minutes, Matia ordered a chocolate ice cream cone and Binta ordered a vanilla cone. Then, eating their ice cream cones, they walked to the corner of St. Claude Avenue and Alabo Street. After the traffic stopped, they crossed over the South bound side of Saint Claude Avenue, reaching the neutral ground just as it started drizzling rain.

Within the next few short moments, they watched a life pass from this world over into the next. There was a blood curdling screech. It all happen so quickly. All they and several others could do was watch as a little brown boy no more than three or four years old darted out into the North bound side of the street, his mother looking after him in shock and screaming nonstop at the top of her lungs for him to come back. It happen so quickly. The boy relented and stopped dead in the middle of the road. In a matter of a few short seconds, it happen. His mother and bystanders began to run towards him frantically and then bang. It happen so suddenly. A candy apple sports car appeared out of nowhere, hitting the young boy and sending him flying up into the air some several feet before the boy came tumbling back down, landing on the hood of the Ferrari and rolling off onto the side of the road. The driver, a twentyish White male, sped off, leaving the scene post haste and not even staying to see if the child was alive or dead. The boy had survived.

"I'm sorry mama," the little boy gurgled as his eyes fluttered and blood flowed from his mouth and nose.

He had survived, briefly, but while waiting only a short while for an ambulance to arrive, he had given up his ghost. His spirit had passed on, leaving this world behind. And leaving his mother shrieking the most deafening sound Matia had ever heard come out of a human being. The short and thin dark chocolate colored woman knelt over her child with her face tilted back and up towards the sky's face and its teardrops of rain, sounding her voice like a siren for all of heaven to hear. And the siren, it said, "This could not and should not be happening."

Matia saw a wedding band on the woman's hand and wondered how she would possibly be able to say to her husband, "Our son is dead".

Matia looked down, she had crushed her ice cream cone in her hand. Ice cream melted all over her hands and dripped down onto the grassy median.

Matia and Binta walked home in silence. Once home, Matia washed her hands, changed into dry clothes and lay in her bed crying.

"Are our lives so expendable?" she mumbled to herself, echoing her earlier words regarding American slavery and trying to understand why the driver had not stopped.

He must have been too afraid to stop, she reasoned.

How else could she give explanation for his abandonment?

At the moment that the driver sped off Matia received a painful confirmation regarding fear. It was revealed to her, the sheer coldness, cruelty and insanity produced by fear's nature.

PART FIVE

THREAT OF ABORTION

1

The following Saturday Matia moved her record player into the dining room, while she did the laundry. Leaving the back door open, she invited her two favorite queens, Mahalia and Aretha to keep her company. As the music flowed through the kitchen screen door, Matia thought of Nile.

"I wonder where he is," Matia said staring up into the sky, wondering how she could approach the subject of Nile with her father without starting a disagreement.

Matia was moved as Aretha's voice flowed from the record player, washing over her soul and taking the edge off her worries.

Matia was in love with music. She had a thing about Aretha and Mahalia's music especially. Their voices more than ever, spoke softly to Matia, exposing her heart's greatest desires. When Matia played them on her record player, she professed her undying love for God and testified of her long-ing to understand more fully love and its part in heartache. Mahalia delivered a velvety message with her contralto voice, securing Matia's spirit and soul. While presenting a voice so supreme, Aretha's music grabbed hold of Matia, refusing to let her go. It gave her no other option, but to believe in love's command. Queen Mahalia and Queen Aretha sung and Matia, their loyal subject, listened as stories of love and sorrow, right and wrong and heaven and earth filled the air. She took notes as the melodic stories that were etched at the very heart of a woman's utter love for man were told. She paid attention to the lyrical testifying of stirring stories that were meant to help redeem the human soul by testifying of God's love for mankind. In the two women's music, Matia could celebrate the nature that existed at the very core of her very own being. Matia the worshipping praying spirit and Matia the feeling desiring body, they were one, working out her soul's salvation.

She flocked regularly to the record stores on Caffin Avenue and Canal Street along with her friends, buying up Aretha and Mahalia albums and playing them on her bedroom record player. Sometimes, she was just a young saint who longed to reach up into the sky and touch the hand of God. Other times the saint longed to be the mesmerized girl who was unashamedly in love with love.

"I love music," she had said to her father after buying her newest record player. "As long as it exists, I'll have no need for wine." Franklin had given her a talking to. He had grumbled over what he called both her having her mother's peculiar ways and her incessant need to play her music every night after dinner, almost like clockwork.

As I already mentioned, it was Aretha's voice that Matia listened to as she did the wash. She put a load of clothes into the dryer on the back patio and walked out to the backyard to hang the sheets and blankets on the clotheslines. Almost done with the laundry, she heard the lawnmower start in the front yard. Her father had returned home, while she was out back washing. She was picking up her clothesbasket to make her way back towards the house, when she heard the lawnmower stop. She strained to hear what her father was saying as he spoke harshly with someone. Unable to hear, she walked quietly up the side alleyway of her house. When she reached the side of her front porch, all she could do was gasp. Franklin towered over Nile, demanding an explanation for his being there.

"I'll ask you again," said Franklin. "What are you doin' here?"

"I'm here to talk with you and Matia, sir," said Nile apprehensively.

"But I told you not to come around here, no more."

"Yes, sir," said Nile, "but I was hopin' that you might reconsider, if you got to know me a little better. I'm willin' to prove my intentions are good."

"Hell no, I won't reconsider. This is my property and I want you off it."

Nile was stoic. He stared wordlessly and with a blank face.

"Fool," said Franklin, "I know how to get rid of you."

Franklin turned and went into his house, his eyes bulging and temples twitching.

"Daddy," said Matia, rushing from the side of the house. "What you goin' do?"

Franklin was gone, both literally and figuratively. So, he could not respond. He was seeing the color red. He was seeing death.

2

If Nile had obeyed Franklin's request to stay away from his home, all would have been right in Franklin's world. But all would not have been right on Nile's planet without any hope of the beautiful Matia joining him in his life's journey. While he knew that Franklin wanted him to stop calling on Matia, he believed that she felt altogether different about the situation. After turning the matter over in his head several times, he had made up his mind that he would return to her home at least once more to learn of her true heart's desire.

But in Nile's returning to Franklin and Matia's front door, after being cautioned to stay away, he had gone way too far for Franklin. Nile arrived, requesting to speak with Matia and was met with Franklin's total outrage. To illustrate just how outraged Franklin was, he, the dutiful father of Matia, got his hunting rifle from the top shelf of his bedroom closet. After getting hold of this said rifle, he marched back out to his front yard and pointed the rifle towards Nile's chest. Ironically it was not Franklin, but Nile who was arrested. Nile was arrested, not by police, but by disbelief. The sheer absurdity in the situation seized him and held him as a short-term prisoner.

Shouting furiously, Franklin threatened to shoot Nile if he did not leave postehaste. But Nile was arrested by shock, remember. Frozen stiff, he could not move one inch of his body.

"You willin' to die for her," said Franklin, matter-of-factly and holding his rifle steady for all the neighbors to see. And see they did. Everyone in the block had begun to come out onto their porches to witness the spectacle that was taking place on Charbonnet.

Nile with his heart still set on Matia did not budge from his resolution of creating a life with Matia.

"Daddy don't," said Matia, carefully stepping in between Franklin and Nile.

Painfully disturbed by the thought of Matia's standing in harm's way, Nile slid his body back in front of Matia's petite frame.

The saving grace of course was not Matia's intervention alone, but the fact that Franklin knew and believed wholeheartedly the ten commandments.

Deep within Exodus, Franklin had read and believed that he should not kill. Understood in its fullest context, he recognized that it meant that God did not approve of men going around killing each other gratuitously, spilling innocent blood. The stage was set. His charge, as a agent of God, was to preserve human life and not take it.

How ridiculous that Franklin would even justify his behavior long enough to allow himself to partake in such foolishness, it was sheer madness.

Franklin understood that he had no true justification for his act of violence. So, he lowered his gun and retreated penitently back inside his home with his daughter thoughtfully on his heels.

Binta rushed past Nile and up Matia's front steps. Knocking at the screen door for Matia, until the door was opened to her.

Bill grabbed Nile, pulling him from the property of the Singleton residence.

"Fool that you are" said Bill, walking away from the house and across the street with Nile, "you almost got both yourself and her killed."

Nile regained his motor skills and looked back to see the whole block of neighbors, staring back at him. He had given Charbonnet Street something juicy and succulent to talk about for many years to come.

3

Some of us believe that it is critically wrong to kill a tree, dog, whale or cow. People would sacrifice their very own lives for the preservation of an endangered plant or animal, stressing that it is wrong to destroy deliberately that which is living.

Why then do people agree so easily to kill each other?

Why do we just sit by and watch apathetically the slaughtering of humanity?

I have wondered about this.

Upon further observation of humanity, I see a history of our adjusting human value in order to justify our unjustifiable behavior. In my mind's eye, I can see very clearly along ages of history's hallways. I see babies, children, men and women both young and old. Disillusioned, they line centuries of neglected corridors, waiting and hoping that someone will at last pick them up as their cause. Sadly, they are reduced to wait in vain while humanity runs to the rescue of the next dying rainforest or endangered whale. "One day," they say, "someone will care whether or not we are being killed all the day long. Someday, humanity will recognize and care that she herself is an endangered species."

4

The next night, Matia sat on the top step of her front porch, gazing into the blue-black vastness that was the sky. The night was slightly cool with a brisk breeze in the air. She followed a star with her eyes; it seemed to be beaming almost attempting to communicate with her. She watched the wind dance across the ground, rearranging the fallen leaves that covered the lawn. A lovely night, it was filled with the music of wind whistling through treetops and beating methodically against rooftops. Her eyes watered at the simple beauty demonstrated in a night like this one. She wondered why all of life could not be simplistic and beautiful. A fleeting vision of Nile flashed across her mind. The whistling wind grew louder and transformed. Matia looked up to see Nile strolling up her walkway.

"What are you doin' here?" Matia whispered nervously.

"I had to talk to you," said Nile, "especially after yesterday."

"You shouldn't have come back so soon," Matia whispered. "You know I still haven't gotten daddy to come around."

"I can't help myself," said Nile, smiling.

"Clearly," said Matia in agreement.

"Just give me a few minutes and I'll go," said Nile.

Matia jumped up and motioned for Nile to follow her to the alleyway on the left hand side of her house. When they had both reached the back porch, Matia sighed a sigh of relief and turned to face Nile, looking him dead in the eyes.

"Okay," said Matia, "tell me what's so important."

"Well," began Nile.

"I mean," interrupted Matia, "important enough to almost get us both killed and my father carried off to jail."

"Do you believe in love at first sight?" Asked Nile, with tenderness.

Matia looked at him and shook her head in wonder.

"You are as serious as a heart attack, aren't you?"

"F'sure," said Nile. "I am."

"Why do you ask?" said Matia, batting her eyes with a faint smile. "Are you here to tell me that you took one look at me and it was love at first sight?"

"I am," said Nile. "I laid my eyes on you and knew instantly that you were the one."

"Which one?" said Matia, sarcastically. "The one for the night?"

"The one my heart longs for," said Nile.

"I don't believe you," said Matia, blushing and laughing to herself.

"Please do," said Nile. "I'm very serious."

"And what if I did choose to believe you?" said Matia. "What then?"

"Then, I'd ask you if you feel the same way about me."

"And what if I said I did?" said Matia. "What would you say, then?"

"Let's you and me get married."

"What about my father, Nile?"

"What about him?"

"We'd have to get his blessin' in order for me to have peace about leavin' him."

"Alright," said Nile, "but it does seem to me that at your age you're old enough to make up your own mind about this."

"I am," said Matia, cutting her eyes with a grin. "and I've made up my mind that you are goin' to have to get his blessing."

"Alright, alright" said Nile, delighted, "whatever it takes!"

"Nile?" said Matia.

"Yes?"

"I keep tryin' to convince myself that I don't want you around, but in my heart I know I want you to stay. I want you to stay with me."

"Me too," said Nile. "I keep thinkin' back over what my life was like before I found you, Matia, and I don't want to go back. I mean not if I have a choice."

"Honestly?"

"Yes, honestly," said Nile.

"You're like a dream come true," said Matia with tears. "I can't lie. But my father needs me and I can't bear the thought of me leavin' him."

Nile was silent and thoughtful.

"How after everything he's done for me can I just leave him all alone in this empty house with all of its ghosts?"

"How can you?" said Nile, backing down from his pursuit of Matia and being careful not to ask about the ghosts.

"How can I?" she said again conflicted by the contradiction in her own desires.

"You shouldn't leave him if you don't want to."

"No?"

"No," said Nile.

"I don't want to stay here for the rest of my life," said Matia, "but I don't know how to go."

"You can't do both," said Nile. "You can't stay and leave."

"You know they use to tend to that garden together," said Matia, pointing to a kitchen garden that lay a few feet away from them. "It use to seem to make them stronger, the time that they spent together workin' in it."

"What happen?"

"She died," said Matia, "and I started helpin' him with it."

"Maybe it's time for you to envision plantin' and tendin' to your own garden."

"Maybe it is," said Matia, smiling. "Will you help me?"

"If you want me to."

"Maybe I do," said Matia, "when the season's right. Let's try to be patient and give my father some more time to come around."

PART SIX

QUICKENING

1

"Go ahead and say it," said Franklin.

Matia poured over the account books and receipts that were scattered all over her desk, pretending her father was not in the room.

"Where is that invoice," she said to herself, scratching her head.

"You're going to ignore your own father?"

"I'm not ignoring you."

"Then answer me."

"You didn't ask a question."

"Say what's on your mind."

"I have nothing to say, daddy."

"You've been sayin' that for days. You're givin' me the silent treatment."

"I have nothing to say," said Matia, refusing to look up at her father.

"You've been cryin' and playin' that Aretha Franklin and refusin to eat the meals I fix you."

"I haven't had an appetite and I play Mahalia too."

"It's because of him," said Franklin. "Because of what I did?"

Matia set her pen down on her desk and looked up at her father broodingly.

"Yes, I hate what you did," said Matia. "I really do. It makes me sick just to think about it."

"He's alright," said Franklin. "I was just tryin' to scare him off."

"I'm the one you scared," said Matia, "and every time I bring him up you tune me out. You won't even let me talk to you about my feelings for him."

"He's no good for you," said Franklin.

Matia returned to sorting invoices and crunching numbers, hoping her father would leave her office.

"What about Jacobs," asked Franklin.

"What about him?" asked Matia.

"He's comin' by soon," said Franklin. "He's building a big pretty house out in New Orleans East for him and his future wife."

"Jacobs is engaged?" asked Matia surprised.

"Not yet," said Franklin. "He wants to have his career, house and car ready, when he finds his bride. So, he can offer her the American dream."

"That's interesting," said Matia, frowning.

"Why?" asked Franklin. "What's wrong with it?"

"I didn't say anything was wrong with it," said Matia.

"Not with your mouth, you didn't," said Franklin. "but with your face you said a lot."

"Oh, it's nothing," said Matia. "It's just that I think that it would be nice to help design the house that my husband was building for us, if it was at all possible. To know that the window seat was on a particular wall because it faced a special tree or view that reminded us of the park we loved to walk in. Or something like that."

"You're foolish," said Franklin. "You can't possibly have a problem with a man wanting to have a big house to take his future bride home to?"

"I didn't say that I had a problem with it," said Matia.

"You'd live in a Manuel's hot tamale cart if that Nile asked you to," said Franklin angrily.

"You're probably right," said Matia, giggling.

"That's what worries me," said Franklin.

"Here's that invoice," sang Matia, jumping up from her desk and walking to the file cabinets.

"If you came to our lunch meeting today," said Franklin. "You could get to know Jacobs better. You might find you like him. He already told me how much he likes you."

"You are the one partnerin' with the architect," said Matia, "not me."

"Don't be like that," said Franklin. "Terrence Jacobs is a nice young fellow and comes from a good seventh ward family. I went to school with his father at Gilbert Academy."

"I know daddy. Terrance is a great talent and the city's fortunate to have his work. I have nothing against him."

"If you really got to know him better, you'd really like him."

"I don't want to know him anymore than I already do," said Matia, sitting back at her desk.

"You have a problem with Singleton becoming Singleton Jacobs?" asked Franklin.

"No," said Matia, "no problem here. As long as you know I'm not interested in becoming a Singleton Jacobs."

"So," said Franklin, "you don't approve of our business merger."

"I'm happy you found someone to invest in your dream, daddy."

"But it's not your dream," said Franklin. "Isn't that what you're sayin?"

"No, it's not my dream, daddy," said Matia. "It's never been my dream."

"It's a poor shame. You know your mother loved Singleton & Co. She helped me get and keep it off the ground."

"Mama, loved you," said Matia. "She did. She really loved you and loving your dream was a part of her loving you."

"And I loved her. Still do."

"I know, daddy. I know."

"You're makin' a mistake by not givin' Jacobs a chance."

"He's very materialistic," said Matia. "Has more stuff than he knows what to do with. And from what I can tell he doesn't know the difference."

"Doesn't know the difference between what?"

"He doesn't know if the stuff belongs to Terrence Jacobs or if Terrence Jacobs belongs to the stuff. Take away his family name and money and what else is there?"

"What?" said Franklin annoyed. "He's affluent, educated and many a young woman in New Orleans would be happy to have him."

"Good," said Matia, "then, he won't miss me."

"Your foolish," said Franklin.

"How is it that since Nile has came into the picture, you suddenly want to play matchmaker?"

"It's not because of Nile," said Franklin, irritated, "that I like Jacobs."

"Oh no," said Matia, "well, you've never suggested anyone before."

"If you marry an educated man," said Franklin, "you'll live better."

"Nile is educated."

"Oh yeah?" Franklin said, sarcastically. "Where did the plumber get his degree of higher learning?"

"Oh, daddy," said Matia. "What makes the architect worth more than the plumber? It certainly isn't the money. Plumbers make a good living. And Nile is so much more than a plumber. Plumbing is just one of the things that he does."

The front office door chimed. Jacobs entered the cozy receptionist's area of Singleton & Company.

"In here Jacobs," said Franklin standing in the office doorway and motioning for Jacobs to join him in Matia's office.

The white olive colored Jacobs entered the room, grinned at Matia, showing off his dimples. He was very tall like Franklin. Built very nicely and dressed even nicer in a tailored navy business suit. His black wavy hair was combed back. He was a young Billy Dee dipped in white chocolate.

Matia sat still, trying not to notice Terrance noticing her or his Billy Dee charm.

"Hey there, Matia," said Jacobs, almost eating her up with his prolonged glare.

"Hey, Terrance," said Matia nicely, but staring coolly into the pages of her accounting books.

"So," said Franklin. "You're not goin' change your mind about joinin' us for lunch? We're goin' to Dooky Chase."

"No, sir," said Matia as her stomach growled, resisting any interest that she might have in white chocolate. "You can bring me back a shrimp poboy if you don't mind, though."

"You don't listen to your father," said Franklin, grabbing his car keys.

"It's not you that I'm not listenin' to," said Matia, teasingly.

"No?" asked Franklin. "Who then?"

"The architect," said Matia laughing.

2

"I'm in love, you say to me," said Samuel Friedman, as he sat down to enjoy a supper of matzah lasagna with Nile.

"Yeah," said Nile, awaiting his surrogate father's blessing, "I'm in love."

Samuel asked, shaking his head in uncertainty, "what means this?"

"It means that I'm ready to get married because I found the one that my heart longs for."

"This girl," said Samuel, lifting a fork of lasagna to his face, "you will marry her? When Abecca Rosengarten you did not marry?"

Nile paused for a moment with sadness in his eyes. Then, nodding his head, he reached across the table to get another serving of lasagna.

"Yeah, Sam," answered Nile in sincerity, "for the first time, I'm truly in love. Her name is Matia Singleton. She's a good Christian girl. Just like you always say Ms. Eliza was. The kind you always said I should find. You'll like her. Watch! You'll like her."

"You compare her with my Liza," said Samuel, "my blessed angel sent from Heaven up above. What kind of a girl is she that you must compare her with my Liza?"

"Dynomite," said Nile.

"She must be someone special," said Samuel, his pasty white skin slightly flushed, "if you compare her with my Liza. I knew Elizabeth T. Waters was special the very first time I stood next to her and looked into her sweet dark brown face at that streetcar stop on Saint Charles Avenue. She wouldn't have anything to do with me at first. Had difficulty gettin' past the fact that I was standin' in white skin, while she was standin' in brown. Looked me up and down before she would even speak to me, she did. And after I'd spent months tryin' to impress her with my impeccable Hebrew, fancy dinners and pendin' Tulane business degree, she still didn't want to agree to havin' any part of a future with me. 'We have enough troubles in this world without marryin' them,' she said worriedly. But her mind I changed. She learned that I believed that Jesus is the Messiah and suddenly she was impressed. Then and only then, would she let me talk her into becoming Mrs. Samuel N. Friedman. Seems like only yesterday, she lay helpless in our marriage bed, wastin' away, while that ugly monster Lupus took everything that ever mattered to us away."

Samuel's face sagged and his eyes darkened, causing him to look dismal. Then his eyes lit up with a question.

"Does she have Lupus, this girl?"

"No," said Nile, "or at least, I don't think so."

"Well," said Samuel. "How can you say no, if you don't know. You should ask her. Not that you shouldn't marry her if she does. You just ought to know."

"Okay, okay," said Nile, "I'll ask her."

"Why is this the first I've heard of this Matia?" asked Samuel.

"I just met her a couple of months ago."

"Just met her?" asked Samuel.

"Yeah," said Nile, "at a birthday party that I went to with Bill. She's beautiful Sam. I was created to love her. No other woman like her on the face of the Earth."

"Does her mama like you?"

"Her mother passed away."

"Sorry," said Sam, "my mama I knew only in the womb. I know how it feels to be motherless.

"Yeah," said Nile, sadly.

"And what of her father?" asked Samuel. "What does he think of your sudden love for his little girl?"

"He's comin' around," said Nile.

"Comin' around you say," said Samuel. "This means he's not happy. You leave her alone then!"

"What," said Nile in disbelief.

"You heard me," said Samuel.

"But if he could just get to know me," said Nile.

"Better to leave this girl alone than to cause a rift between her and her father."

"I'm not causin' a rift."

"If not why do you look so worried?" Samuel said.

"I don't know Sam," said Nile. "I just don't know what I'll do if I can't be with her."

"Is she of age?" asked Sam.

"She's twenty- three."

"Has this girl agreed to marry you?" Samuel said.

"I," started Nile, frowning.

"Well," said Samuel, "has she or not?"

"I think so," answered Nile.

"What did she say when you got down on bended knee and asked her," asked Samuel.

"I haven't officially asked her," said Nile, "but I've told her my intentions and she says yes maybe, eventually."

"Maybe, eventually," said Samuel.

"Maybe, eventually," said Nile.

"This is no good," said Samuel. "Does she want to marry you or not? This you should know. Samuel N. Friedman may not know all there is to know about love, but I do know that it is not right to be talkin about marryin' a girl when you do not have her permission."

"I know," said Nile. "She says she's interested, but needs more time for her father. I'll talk to Alex about it tomorrow after church. I could use his advice."

"Get to know her father," said Samuel. "Let him get to know you. If he's worth his salt, he'll learn to like you. It's hard not to."

"I hope your right," said Nile.

"Have you thought about what I asked you?"

"About becomin' a partner in Sam's Aquarium World?"

"Yes," said Sam, "about becomin' a partner."

"Do you really think I'm ready?"

"I know it."

"I don't have a whole lot of cash to work with, Sam."

"I know it, but it's what you do with what you do have that matters. Great vision, discipline, valuable skills and work ethic, you have, Nile. Besides, after you get your masters plumbin' license, you'll have more money to invest. You could take over one of the stores, then, if you want to."

"Alright," said Nile, "I want to. I want to. I'll start savin' more."

"Vainburg says you can have his son's 1972 Chevy Malibu for one thousand. It's royal blue, your favorite color."

"I'm sure that's not what he said."

"What means this?" asked Samuel.

"I mean that you and I both know that Maurice Vainburg would never sell anything personal of his to me."

"Maurice is a blind man," said Samuel. "He can't see that Black is beautiful! That you are beautiful! He can't see that God lives in all colors!"

"To you I'm beautiful," said Nile. "To you all people are beautiful, but not to Vainburg. People like him think the color Black is something dirty, something that needs to be washed off the face of the earth."

"You're my son," said Samuel, pounding his chest. "Eliza and I would've adopted you, but your mother, Royal, would have died first. Before we knew you were even breathin', she had legitimate papers on you and years of blood, sweat and tears. What do I have, but covetousness and good intentions?"

"Mama don't mind you," said Nile. "She appreciates you for takin' an interest in me back then. I was on the edge of getting' into trouble with my daddy gone and Will so busy."

"Eliza couldn't have loved you anymore if she had given birth to you herself," said Samuel tearing up a little.

"I know, Sam," said Nile. "I know."

Samuel blew his nose on a napkin and began clearing the dinner table.

"Maurice's Chevy is in mint condition. He brought it by yesterday and we took a spin in it."

"How does it drive," asked Nile, helping clear the table.

"Smooth," said Samuel. "Real nice."

"Smooth huh," said Nile.

"Why's he gettin' rid of it, then," asked Nile.

"I'll explain," said Sam. "Maurice and his wife, Odessa, are movin' back to New York next month," said Samuel. "A hard time they've had, since their son, Leonard, got killed in Vietnam. Maurice is prayin' to God that goin' back home to Brooklyn will bring his Odessa back to life."

"Why didn't you ever go back to stay?" asked Nile.

"Back where?" asked Sam. "To Brooklyn?"

"Yeah," said Nile. "I mean it is New York. All the world is captivated with New York."

"I was born in New York," said Sam, "but my poppa was born and raised in New Orleans like his poppa before him and his poppa before him. The story, I already told you. Poppa met my dear sweet mama at the City College of New York. They married. She died in childbirth. Years later, he died still grief-stricken. I moved back here to this house to live with my grandfather, my only living relative who would have me. This house has been in my family for generations. I brought the only wife I've ever known home to this house. This is as close to home as I get to get on this earth."

"Still," said Nile, "it must a took a lot a guts, leavin' everything you knew behind for good."

"What guts? Thirteen years and a hungry orphan I was until my grandfather took me in. Besides, I already told you. With my parents dead there was nothin' left for me there, but ghosts."

Nile looked at Sam long and hard and then patted him on the right shoulder.

"Tell Maurice I'll take the Chevy," said Nile. "Ridin' the RTA bus is growin' old."

"Good," said Samuel. "I'll tell him we'll take it."

3

Later that evening, the Louisa bus arrived and Nile loaded the half-empty bus anxious to get home. As Nile paid his bus fare, he stood facing the rest of the passengers. There were ten passengers, already on board the bus. Besides the regular bus driver, Frank, there were three whispering young women sitting in the first three seats to Nile's right; they were in hospital scrubs. After them and facing Nile, sat candy stripers, two unassuming teenage girls in red and white peppermint striped jumpers with gathered skirts and pockets. They were quietly reading an Ebony magazine. Across from the candy stripers and on Nile's left, sat a tired looking middle-aged cook. He wore a white cook's coat and checkerboard slacks. Behind the cook sat two luminous faced and Black nuns dressed in habits and holding small black bags in their hands. They were of the flock of The Sisters of The Holy Family. At the back of the bus, facing Nile sat a very tall and muscular man who was dressed as a woman; he was dressed in a banana colored headscarf, red tie top with ruffled shoulders, red tiered skirt, red earrings and heels. He looked to be in a perpetual daze; as if he had received a shock and had never been able to recover.

"Kim and Natasha," said one of the young women in scrubs to the other two, while pointing towards Nile. "There go a real man, right there."

She batted her doe like eyes and offered Nile a delightful smile.

The other two young women laughed to themselves.

"Yeah, you right Lathalia," said one of the other women, running her fingers through her long straight hair, "cause there is a difference."

The cook yawned, putting his head down and revealing a shiny dark brown bald spot at the top of his head.

The candy stripers neither batted and eye nor flinched an inch.

"That thing right there is too sweet for his own good, Lathalia," said another one of the young women, snickering and showing her dimples and pearly white teeth. "He wrong for all that rouge and red lipstick. He look a mess."

One of the nuns scolded the young women, urging them to hush.

Nile turned his head just in time to see the man masquerading as a woman, rising and snapping his long fingers at the young women. The color of his olive black skin standing out against his costume, he looked a lot like Miss Chiquita, the banana.

"I'm not playin' wit y'all," said the costumed man. He spoke with a strong lisp. "I'll cut ya if ya keep talkin' bout me. Ya hear me? I'll cut ya."

"Alright na," said the bus driver. "I'll throw y'all all off my bus."

"We not scared of you, Miss Chiquita," said one of the young women.

"Say y'all," said Nile firmly, "leave the man alone before somebody gets hurt."

"He ain't no man," said one of the women in scrubs. "He don't know what a man is!"

"He a man," disagreed Nile, with resolve. "Something's made him want to forget, but he still a man."

4

Nile entered the Desire neighborhood. He had a sudden feeling of nausea. Yes, at any moment he was certain he might be sick. Though, he had walked several blocks since exiting the Desire bus, he could still see the flamboyantly painted man, his makeup clownish. The cook, bus-driver, women in scrubs, candy stripers and nuns were in Nile's line of vision too. Collectively, they were a patchwork mirror of something revealing to Nile. Their presence etched in his mind's eye, they had all climbed off the bus with Nile without leaving their seats and they were following him home.

Nile drifted along the sidewalk, saying a silent prayer.

Out of the blue, a slinky man walked carefully out of the darkness that surrounded Nile. The man passed by watchfully, but swiftly, glancing back over his shoulders almost rhythmically. When the glancing man went by, he strode right past Nile as if he were invisible. Moments later, there were two other men running pass Nile. The second man to pass Nile ran past him, shouting after the first man who had passed.

"We can't let you go, Eli," he called out.

The glancing man who was walking up ahead of them took flight.

"This kind of livin' not for me," said the glancing man as he disappeared around the corner of one of the stately elevated brick red tenements. "I need to be free."

"Guess we goin' have to help him change his mind," said a pipe carrying third man.

Nile's presence was so obscure to the third man that he almost trampled Nile as he ran pass him indifferent to his existence.

Then in a flash of an eye, they were all gone. All three men disappeared into the dark of night. A quiet stillness returned as if nothing had occurred. Nile listened for a cry for help or the hint of commotion, but heard nothing. The three men were gone just as suddenly as they had appeared.

Slowly but surely, images of the masquerading man crept back into Nile's mind. The images took on a new single form, drawing Nile's attention. He struggled to see what there was to see in the apparition. Eventually, Nile saw clearly in the masquerading man exist the image of his own father clothed in deception.

Who had his father masqueraded as in order to work up the audacity to abandon his responsibilities as both a husband and a father? What lie had he told himself in order to stomach his gross miscarriage of justice? What had caused Will Sr. to forget that he was a man and that a real man was characterized by his endeavors to take care of his own?

Nile examined himself. He had made a commitment to God and self to improve. He was improving every single day. Still, was he capable of forgetting himself and masquerading too? He wondered. What would stop him from forgetting the man that was within?

Suddenly, out of the darkness behind him came a soft voice.

"Got a light?" said the still male voice.

Startled, Nile turned a bit on the defensive side.

"Sorry, man," said Nile, looking back, "no light here. I don't smoke."

But at first glance, it appeared that nothing was there but dark empty space. Then, Nile looked down and discovered a regal Harlequin Great Dane, staring up at him, hauntingly. Nile attempted to shake off what he had heard; it was only a dog.

As Nile turned back around to continue walking, he heard the voice again.

"You do, man. You got a light. I can see it shining from inside you."

Dazed, Nile spun around in the mysterious darkness, expecting to see his unlikely canine messenger once more, but saw only majestic dark shadows falling from tall arresting brick structures. Closing in on him like an invisible fiend, his fear confounded him. With this Nile took off running up the courtyard. He took off, not stopping until he had safely reached the reassuring confines of his own bedroom in his mother's apartment.

In his sleep that night, Nile wrestled with himself, struggling with the man that he hoped he would never be again and the man that he hoped to become. Running through his mind were the words of the book of John 8:12. All night long, he could hear Jesus saying, "I am the light of the world: he that followeth me shall not walk in darkness, but shall have the light of life."

PART SEVEN

BABYDROP

1

One can never see with the naked eye a baby developing in a mother's womb. It is a mystery. Not even the physician with all the world's technology can change the fact that mankind waits with baited breath, hoping and praying while the unborn baby's development is hidden behind a curtain. Yes, even if we've heard the most positive report regarding our baby's condition, we wait and hope that when that long awaited moment of delivery comes, all will be well with our baby.

This is what Nile was going through. Though he waited and prayed, he longed to know what was going to happen between Matia and him. Pregnant with a vision of them having a life together, he wanted to know that in the end all would be well.

2

Sitting stuffed into the corner of Alex and Luna's sofa, Nile had waited to talk with his-brother-in-law, while thinking about Matia.

What if Matia's father never came around?

The sizzling of chicken in the kitchen married with childish laughter as his sister Luna hummed a hymn and prepared chicken Fricassee, her sons playing football in the back yard with their Gentilly neighborhood friends. This was the life, thought Nile, good memories, a beautiful family and a home that they could call their own. This was what he and Matia could make for themselves, a life together. How many people lived and died without realizing their dreams and finding someone to share them with?

"So," asked Alex after Nile explained his situation with Franklin, "You prayed about this?"

"Yes," said Nile, "I prayed.

"Well," said Alex, "you can't dishonor her wishes. If she wants you to give her some time to make peace with her father, then you should."

"But what if he never comes around?" asked Nile.

"Then, he never comes around," said Alex. "You can't force this thing. It's clear that her relationship with her father is a priority for her."

"You're killin' me, man," said Nile.

"Look Nile," said Alex, placing his left hand on Nile's right shoulder. "Can't you trust God with this?"

"Yes," said Nile, "I can trust God with anything."

"Alright then," said Alex, "I'm not tellin' you to do nothing. I'm tellin' you to watch and pray. I can't tell you what'll happen, but I can tell you this from experience. God will work it out."

"But Alex," said Nile.

"Yes," said Alex.

"What if Matia's father's never okay with me?"

"I'll say it again," said Alex. "If you say that you can trust God, then trust God with Matia and her father."

3

"Matia and Nile sittin' up under the sassafras tree," Binta sang like a schoolgirl, rocking her porch swing back and forth. "I bet they goin' get married."

"That's not how the song goes," said Matia, shaking her head in disbelief at Binta and chuckling.

Suddenly, Binta's front screen door opened. Binta's parents, Mr. & Mrs. Baptiste, exited their house. They were dressed up and on their way out for the evening.

Happy to see her parents, Binta smiled.

"Y'all look some nice," said Binta.

"Thank you, baby girl," said Mr. Baptiste, patting Binta on the shoulder as he passed her on his way down the porch's steps.

"Uh, huh, real classy," said Shallow.

"Maybe if you did somethin' with that hair of yours, you'd look half decent too, Binta," said Mrs. Baptiste, as she followed her husband to their Chevy Station Wagon. "Maybe y'all can talk Binta into straitening her hair for her wedding. She won't listen to me."

"My afro's alright, mama," said Binta, pleasantly. "I'm goin' pull it up into one great big puff for the wedding."

"Alright, huh?" Mrs. Baptiste said as she climbed into the passenger side of her station wagon. "That's what ya mouth say."

Binta looked unmoved by her mother's harsh remarks.

"Have a good time y'all," said Binta, waving goodbye.

"Thank you, sugar," said Mr. Baptiste before driving off.

"Binta," said Shallow, rolling her eyes, "she don't work on your nerves with all her criticism."

"Oh, mama's just bein' mama," said Binta. "I don't let her bother me."

"You sure?" said Matia.

"Yeah," said Binta, "or least I don't think I do."

"I don't know, '*sha*'," said Shallow, shaking her head in disagreement.

Binta was silent.

The three friends sat quietly on Binta's front porch, eating Hubig's fried lemon pies and enjoying the evening weather. The warm delightful March air was breezy, but laced with a touch of humidity. From the porch you could see some of the bustle happening on Charbonnet Street and North Claiborne Avenue. Vehicles and bodies moved through the lower ninth ward, travelling. Charbonnet Street was mostly calm with the occasional horn honk of motorist or hushed conversation of passersby.

Shallow at the thought of losing another friend to marriage was troubled. What would it mean for her? She might be all alone.

"Binta you crazy," said Shallow, "Matia not about to get married."

"Stranger things have happen," said Binta.

"Like what '*sha*'?" asked Shallow.

"Like you lovin' home economics in high school," said Matia, laughing with Binta.

"I ain't studdin' bout y'all," said Shallow. "I'm fire and ice all at once. Y'all don't understand the complex woman that I am."

"You're right we don't," said Binta, poking her tongue out at Shallow.

"I understand ya, '*boo*'," said Matia.

"Alright '*sha*'," said Shallow.

"So," said Binta. "How ya goin' tell ya daddy that ya fallin' in love with Nile?"

"Who said I was fallin' in love," asked Matia.

"'*Sha*', please," said Shallow, "even I can see that boy got ya nose wide open. You, so in love."

"Yeah, Sweet T," said Binta pointing at her own nose, "nose wide open."

The fishy plumbing philosopher, Nile Hash, had indeed worked and theorized his way into Matia's heart. No force had been needed. He had shown up, tapping steadily at her heart's door, until she had relented and allowed him to come in. Now that he was inside, he had heeded her advice and given her the time that she hoped to use to change her father's mind about Nile. But where was he, she wondered, privately hoping for one of his letters or impromptu visits. It had been at least a month since she had received a word from him.

"He's different," said Matia, taking the last bite of her lemon pie. "He's gentle and kind. He gets me. He listens and hears me, but most of all when I'm near him I feel like I'm home."

"Yeah," said Binta, "well I hear from Bill that he use to be a real Casanova, but all that's changed since...."

"Since what?" asked Shallow.

"Since, Matia's got his nose open wider than he has hers," said Binta.

"I don't know '*sha*'," said Shallow. "Once a Casanova, always a Casanova."

"Well," said Binta, "nothing wrong with him bein' a Casanova as long as she the only one he's proposin' to be a Casanova with."

The young woman with her nose wide open smiled at the woman who was so in love with Bill and the girl who was unapologetically in love with not being in love. The sun was setting into a violet orange haze on the canvas of a New Orleans' skyline.

Down the street, Franklin, angrily stomped out onto his front porch and stared Matia down. He called out her name rabidly like a dog gone mad.

She looked back at him, perhaps a sheep being led to the slaughter.

"I gotta go, y'all," she said slipping off Binta's porch and leaving her two friends behind.

They had their misgivings about Matia leaving, but watched in silence as Matia walked quickly to her home, entering it.

4

"What's wrong?" Matia asked.

Tense, Matia shut the door behind her, locking it. Startled to find her father behind the door, towering over her in outrage, she stepped back a little to the left of him and towards the loveseat.

"Tell me who gave Nile Hash permission to call my house."

"Not me," said Matia, defensively.

"You're lyin' to me," said Franklin.

"When have I ever lied to you, daddy?" Matia said.

"But he just called here," said Franklin.

"That doesn't mean I gave him our number," said Matia. "Although, I wish I had."

"What," said Franklin.

"I miss him," said Matia, nervously.

"Have you seen him since your birthday?" asked Franklin.

"Yes, I have," said Matia.

"So, you have been deceiving me?"

"No," said Matia, "I have not."

"But you have," said Franklin. "You heard me tell him I didn't want to see him again."

"Yes, daddy," said Matia, "and you haven't."

"What?" Franklin said.

"You know," said Matia matter-of-factly, "you never asked me if I wanted to see Nile."

"Well," said Franklin. "Do you?"

"Yes, daddy," said Matia. "You know that I do. I think that I've tried to make it pretty clear to you that I do want to see him. "

Franklin sighed and shook his head in distress.

"Daddy, I've trusted you all my life to look after me and I've tried hard to make choices that are in line with the morals that you and mama raised me with. Don't you think I'm old and mature enough to recognize God's will and make up my own mind concerning choosin' the guy I want to spend the rest of my life with."

"Impossible," said Franklin, his voice cracking in light of his daughter's frankness with him. "You can't possibly know!"

Matia exhaled noisily.

"Besides, you don't have time for him."

"I don't know if we can say that I honestly don't have time."

"We can't?" said Franklin, his voice cracking again and his eyebrows arching in response to Matia's candor.

"No," said Matia, "I have nothing but time. Besides you seem to think I have time for Jacobs."

"What about your friends," said Franklin, ignoring Matia's mentioning Jacobs. "You forget that you spend time with them."

"No," said Matia, "I didn't forget about them."

"Well, then," said Franklin.

"Since Binta got engaged," said Matia, "she's almost always with Bill and I guess Shallow's working most of the time because I hardly get to see her."

"Matia," said Franklin, "you are twenty three and too young to be thinking about getting' married."

"I am twenty three daddy and old enough to conduct your financial affairs and help you run both this house and Singleton & Co."

"Of all the people in the world," said Franklin, "you go and pick a plumber?"

"Maybe he picked me."

"Then," said Franklin, pointing at Matia, "after he picked you, you picked him."

"It's a shame ya know. I can see it all over your face every time you speak of him. You care for him."

"Why is my interest in Nile such a shame?" Matia said. "What makes him so unworthy of your approval?"

"Matia, he's a plumber for goodness sake."

"He's a God-fearing and hard workin' man."

"He's still a plumber."

"Is that all that you have against him?"

"What more do I need?"

"Would you rather if I picked someone like Jacobs, your beloved architect?"

"I would rather if you picked no one," said Franklin, "but if you had to pick someone, Jacobs might do for me."

"Jacobs might do for you?"

"Yes," said Franklin.

"What about me?"

"What about you?"

"You want me to be all alone then?" asked Matia. "Or with someone I don't love?"

"I love you," shouted Franklin, rather pathetically, "besides you're not alone. You have me. And when I'm gone, you'll be well taken care of."

"And lonely," said Matia.

"Many women are alone and not lonely."

"Yes, daddy," said Matia, "the ones who are alone because they chose to be alone."

"Nothing's wrong with being alone," said Franklin.

"No?" asked Matia.

"No," said Franklin.

"Then why don't you want to be alone?" said Matia unintentionally with the words slipping from her lips before she could catch them.

Franklin cursed under his breath his eyes large with amazement. Feeling a little as if he had been kicked in the teeth, he sunk down into the sofa. Somehow, when he wasn't looking, he had lost his little girl's heart. She no longer was entrusting him with it and had decided to give it away.

"I'm sorry, daddy," said Matia, taking steps towards her father.

Franklin waved her away from him, rejecting her attempt at reconciliation.

"I still don't think you're ready," said Franklin, rebounding. "What do you know about him? I'm afraid of what you don't know and how it might hurt you."

"Your fear, daddy," said Matia, sitting next to her father on the sofa, "it is what hurts me. It locks me up and blocks off almost every path that leads to life."

"And?" asked Franklin angrily. "A faithful daughter would be thankful for a father who cares."

"I am daddy," said Matia. "For your love and care, I am thankful, but you don't have to be afraid of me havin' my own desires. Don't you trust what you've instilled in me?"

"You sound like him," said Franklin.

"What you mean, daddy?"

"I mean he said the same thing to me his first night at this house."

"He did. Why?"

"I told him that night that if he didn't leave you alone, he was goin' ruin your life. He said that you'd never allow anyone to ruin your life."

Matia's head began to spin. In the midst of this all too common conversation with Franklin, she experienced a discerning leap in her understanding.

"Nile was wrong, daddy."

"I knew he was."

"Please forgive me for sayin' this, but until recently I think I was content to allow you to choose my life if I thought it would save yours. But not anymore. The kind of loyalty you require belongs to no one but, God."

Refusing to hear Matia, Franklin stared silently at a picture of Sadiki and cursed himself for not being able to convince Matia that she was making a mistake. He was a man who was losing his illusion of control.

This loss posed a serious problem for Franklin. For since the death of his wife and oldest daughter, Franklin had grown to believe that his having control was essential to his survival. This lie encouraged a violent rage in him. For Franklin rage was not customary, but still the same violent.

Rising, Matia started towards her room. As she walked, the telephone rang.

"It's him again," said Franklin, nodding his head at the ringing phone. "I told him to call back in an hour."

"You did?"

"Yes," said Franklin with hateful regret, "I thought I could talk some sense into you. That I could convince you to tell him that he was wasting his time."

"Oh, daddy," said Matia shaking her head, her face dismal.

Franklin stood to his feet and walked to the dining room table. Staring at Matia, he picked up the telephone receiver and stretched out his arm, reaching the phone out towards Matia.

"Go ahead, Matia," said Franklin, irritably, "tell him he's wastin his time."

"Daddy," said Matia, almost apologetically. "You know I can't do that."

"Tell him," Franklin insisted almost begging.

"I can't lie," said Matia firmly.

"Yes," said Franklin, angrily, "you can."

Nile could hear it all. Franklin's hounding demands and Matia's quiet, but strong refusals. Sick to his stomach, it was all starting to make sense to him. Franklin was furious and gnashing his teeth at Matia. He could see it all in his mind's eye. He could have kicked himself for calling and trying to reason with Matia's father. His heart pounding with regret, he could have kicked himself for causing her any trouble at all. He grabbed his car keys and raced out of his house.

Matia shook her head in disagreement.

"Why not?" asked Franklin.

"Because he's not wastin' his time," said Matia. "I'm fallin' in love with him."

As if the wind had been knocked out of him, Franklin struggled for breath and stumbled back a few steps, before regaining his composure.

"But you are supposed to love me, don't you see," said Franklin, the blood draining from his face. With this, he slammed the telephone down onto the dining room floor, bashing it wide open.

"Daddy, you broke the telephone," said Matia, shaking her head in disbelief.

For a few moments, Matia stood in shock, staring at the broken phone. Then she bent over and began to pick up the telephone's broken pieces, sitting them carefully on the dining room table.

"What is happening to you?" Matia asked, as she withdrew to her bedroom without waiting for a response to her question.

Franklin did not attempt to answer her question. Honestly, he could not. He was resorting to committing the lowly act of bullying. He could see that now. What he was doing was something that he had always abhorred in the worst way. Had not he worked most of his life to insure the rights and freedom of others. His ancestors and brothers had fought for freedom. They had fought in movements and wars to garner freedom. He had joined in the political, social, and spiritual battles of his day. It was what his ideals were built on. Yet, he had resorted to this. This he realized meant that he understandably should abhor himself because for him there was no separating the wrongdoer from the wrong.

So, he ignored her question, pretending initially not to care. But he did care. So he tread softly to Matia's closed bedroom door and leaned his head against it, waiting for her to play a song for them. Something sad or moving. Something soothing to lull him off to sleep as he tried to forget the night's quarrel, was what he coveted. But no song was played. Lamenting took the place of music. Matia wept deeply. And Franklin wept repentantly at the thought of having made her weep, quietly begging her forgiveness.

5

There was a hard knock at the front door. Right away, Franklin felt a sudden rush of anxiety.

Had the neighbors heard him arguing with Matia? Had his lost of control brought more shame on his household? His eyes were red with worry.

As he walked into the living room with heavy reluctant steps, he wiped the tears from his eyes. The knocks persisted.

"Alright, alright," shouted Franklin, clearing his throat and bracing himself, "I'm comin'."

Franklin could see a little through a narrow opening in his living room window's curtains. A blue car had parked in front of his house. He unlocked and opened his front door, finding himself standing face to face with Nile.

Having heard the knocks at the door and curious about their late night visitor, Matia returned to the living room, stopping near the sofa.

Nile stood sandwiched between the screen door and Franklin.

They stood so close, glaring into each other's eyes. They could hear each other breathing and sense each other's tension.

Nile was waiting to see what his next move would have to be. He was expecting Franklin to take a swing at him or even worse, but this encounter was unavoidable. Nile had been driven to come to Matia's defense if she needed one. He simply needed to know that she was alright.

Franklin inhaled deeply, taking in the full breadth of the situation. Here before him stood his problem.

But was Nile truly his problem?

Staring silently at Nile, Franklin thought back to his days of youth. He had spent his days and nights studying and working to get himself established. Saving up his earnings, he had labored and planned for the birth of Singleton & Co. He had ignored his father's urging to study law and political science. He had rejected his father's offer to support him financially in architectural or political pursuits. Instead, he had gotten involved in the sit ins and demonstrations of the civil rights movement, almost getting himself killed on more than one occasion. But Saturday nights had been his to do as he pleased. He had done some things of which he was now ashamed. He had always been the kind of man who was willing to go to extreme lengths to get what he wanted.

Franklin's mind searched to find a vision of the night that he had first met Safiya. Back to Cellestine's Place, a dinner club, near North Claiborne and Franklin Avenue that was never short on okra gumbo, stuffed mirliton, potato salad or fried catfish. There had been plenty of fun, dancing and good food to be had at Cellestine's Place. From sunset to sunrise the jazz musicians played. It was there in the midst of the arresting and eclectic vibrato of a soprano saxophone, that he had discovered the young and sassy Safiya.

"Franklin," said Adellaydi, the wife of Franklin's best friend, Antoine, "this here is Safiya, my younger sister."

Franklin had turned around and found his future staring him in the face. Safiya Montgomery. As cool, refreshing and tall as a glass of fresh ice water, she was to him. Franklin spent the whole night trying to get Safiya to answer two questions. Are *you taken? And where are you staying?*

Safiya smiled and talked to Franklin for hours before sharing that she was just visiting her older sister and returning to Ponchatoula after the church meeting the next day. Franklin had fallen head over heels. The following day, he had shown up at Antoine and Adellaydi's house right after church and proposed to Safiya on the spot. Safiya had turned him down, explaining that she was already engaged to be married.

"Whatever he's spent on you," said Franklin, promoting himself, "tell him I'll pay him back. Whatever he's claiming he can give you, tell him I will give you more. Tell him if he loves you, he'll let you go."

To his surprise, Safiya had laughed and given him her fiancée's full name and address. Her only words had been short, but to the point.

"Tell him yourself."

Franklin had begged Safiya to move to New Orleans and marry him and she had left without making any promises. Seven months later, after having fended off Safiya's fiancée and paying several visits to Ponchatoula, Franklin received a blessing from Safiya's parents. In the end, Safiya had agreed to both return to New Orleans and marry Franklin.

Adellaydi and Antoine exchanged their life in New Orleans for one in Chicago. While Safiya and Franklin gave up the lives that they had, in order to build a new life together; two became one, believing in the promises of love.

"Good evening sir," said Nile, forcing Franklin back into the present. "Is everything alright?"

"Everything's fine," said Franklin, talking to himself, "just fine."

Matia nodded, assuring Nile that all was fine.

"Alright," said Nile, looking past Franklin and nodding at Matia, "I guess I'll be goin, then."

In this moment Franklin saw Nile for the first time. He truly saw Nile for what he was and this helped Franklin to see who he had himself become.

Nile had come to Matia's defense. He was determined to know that Matia was alright.

Who then was Matia in need of protection from?

Franklin glanced back at his daughter and into her hurting eyes, realizing that it was him. Matia was in need of protection from him, perhaps. Maybe. And if the need for her protection had arrived, Nile had shown up to assure that she had whatever aid he could provide.

Suddenly, Franklin recognized that Nile had already taken his place in Matia's life in a round a bout way. He was the man of Matia's dreams. Gone was his little baby girl, hanging onto his every word and waiting at the front door for him to return home from a long day's work. His job was done. He had helped train his little girl and she had grown into a capable woman. Nile was to be his replacement and so very much more. Franklin stepped to the side and whole-heartedly welcomed Nile into his home.

"Where you think you goin, son?" said Franklin. "You just got here. Come on in."

"Yes, sir," said Nile, entering the house and stopping just short of the front door.

"Don't just stand there," said Franklin, shutting the front door. "Go on over there and talk to my daughter. Can't you see, she's waitin' on you."

Franklin watched as Matia stood anxiously, anticipating Nile's next movement. On her face was the look of surren-der. She was relinquishing her heart. Nile had chosen her. He had submitted to the rules of loving her. And in return she had decided to choose him. She did not comprehend the full scope of what role he would play in her life. She could not. But whatever the role, he had joined her on life's stage and she had joined him.

Franklin locked the door.

"I'll make y'all some sweet tea to go along with a couple of slices of the buttermilk lemon pound cake Matia baked yesterday," said Franklin, walking towards his kitchen.

As he walked, he peered back over his shoulder, looking back into his living room. Matia and Nile stood, greeting each other. The moments were enormously pregnant with wonder and hope.

Caught up in a vision from his past, Franklin watched himself open his arms and he saw Safiya burying her head into his chest. He heard Matia whisper Nile's name and the illusion ended.

"Oh, Nile," Matia said.

"Yes?" asked Nile.

"I can't believe you're here."

"Where else would I be?" asked Nile, staring deeply into Matia's eyes.

6

In no time, Nile and Matia's courtship developed into a formal engagement. Their relationship took shape, repositioning itself. No one who observed Matia and Nile could honestly say that the two young people were not pregnant with hope. A rare bond, their relationship seemed something out of this world.

As Matia sat on Binta's porch swing, she beamed filled with new life and hope. Her relationship with Nile, a new babe, was growing and stretching her.

"Y'all goin' walk with me across the street to Mrs. Smith's. I want a grape frozen cup," said Binta.

"You shouldn't get a frozen cup, Binta," said Shallow.

"Why shouldn't I?" Binta asked.

"Your lips and tongue are goin' be all purple and crazy lookin'," said Shallow.

"Oh yeah," said Binta, "I forgot about that."

"What we goin' see at the movies again," asked Matia.

"Star Wars," said Binta.

"Which movie theater," asked Matia.

"The Plaza," said Shallow.

"Why we not goin' to the Saenger Theatre?" Binta asked. "I love the Saenger. It's so pretty in there."

"We always want to go to the Saenger," said Shallow, "and we always go to Canal Street. I don't intend to spend my first Saturday off in over a month, drivin' around Canal Street lookin' for a parking spot. It's easier to park at the Plaza and it's free."

"It is, Binta," said Matia.

"That's true," said Binta, "It is. What time does the show start?"

"The one we're tryin' to make starts at two thirty," said Shallow. "So we have more than an hour."

"Yeah," said Binta. "We're makin' good time."

"Who's drivin' with who," asked Shallow, "cause we all can't go together."

"Nile is pickin' up Bill," said Matia. "So, I guess that means, he and Binta are ridin' with us."

"Yeah," said Binta, "Bill stomped his big toe at the auto shop. He thought it was fractured, but it's not. He's been tryin' to give it a break."

"You drivin', Shallow?" asked Matia.

"I would drive my Beetle," said Shallow, "but Lexy just got a brand new Trans Am. And I love that car."

"Oh," said Matia, "the new Trans Am. Nile loves that car. Is it a black and gold one?"

"Yeah, 'sha'," said Shallow, "it's black and gold."

"I thought Lexington just graduated from law school," said Binta.

"And?" Shallow frowned.

"How can he afford to get a new car," asked Binta.

"His parents," said Shallow. "How else? They help him a lot, while he's gettin' established."

"That's real nice," said Matia.

"I know," said Shallow, "But girl if you think that's somethin', you wouldn't believe his parent's brand new Cadillac. It's gold on pearl white with gold leather interior. And it has an 8 track player and beautiful wood grain trim."

"My daddy wouldn't give up his Cadillac for nothing," said Matia. "My mama hand-picked that car."

"Y'all know I like the finer things in life," said Shallow, "and I intend to have them all in my own name. The next thing on my list is a Cadillac."

"You still plannin' on gettin' your masters degree?" Matia asked.

"You know it, *'sha'*," said Shallow.

"I know I'm dippin' in ya Kool-Aid Shallow," said Binta, "but Lexington must really be diggin' you to pass up his scholarship offer to Howard Law School and go to Loyola just so he could stay close to you."

"He went to a good law school," said Shallow, "and besides stayin' home was his choice."

"I didn't say, he didn't go to a good school," said Binta. "It's just that you said yourself that he wanted to go to D.C. and D.C. is an exciting place to be."

So, is New Orleans," said Shallow, "and that's where he wanted to be. Closer to home."

"More like closer to you," said Binta. "Although, one would have a hard time understandin' why. I know I do!"

"Aw *'sha'*," said Shallow, looking at Matia, "this cow is workin' on my nerves already and we haven't even left yet."

"You just mad cause I'm tellin' the truth," said Binta. "That brother got it bad for you. He's in love and wants to get married, Shallow."

"I like Lexy," said Shallow, "but you know I'm not thinkin' about gettin' married."

"Well," said Binta, "you need to tell him then."

"I have," said Shallow.

"What did he say?" asked Matia.

"He says I just need more time," said Shallow.

"Is that true?" said Matia.

"Is what true?" asked Shallow.

"Is it true that time is all you need to warm up to the idea of gettin' married?" asked Matia.

"I don't know y'all," said Shallow. "Lexy is real nice, but I don't know if I can ever see myself bein' somebody's wife."

"You need to tell him that, then," said Binta, "and stop lettin' him think he has a chance with you, if he don't. Besides, it's not right to always have him spendin' money on you and buyin' you expensive stuff and you don't even love him and want to be with him."

"You are trippin'," said Shallow. "It's not like what you're sayin' at all."

"Oh," said Binta, "so, you're not usin' him for his money?"

Shallow fought the urge to try defend herself in anger. Instead, she just shook her head in frustration.

"No 'sha', I'm not," said Shallow calmly.

"Binta," said Matia disapprovingly, "you need to mind your business and stop bein' so messy."

"She can talk, 'sha'," said Shallow. "People got to say what's on their minds. Besides, it's no skin off my back. Lexy is my best friend, after y'all. The only thing that's wrong with him is that he's a male and thinks I'm supposed to be his wife."

"Nothing wrong with that, huh Matia?" asked Binta.

"Nope," said Matia, giggling, "and if you don't mind my sayin' so. You and Lexington don't look at each other like I look at any of my girl friends."

"Nope," said Binta, "and he wants marriage. Stop running from it. It's bound to happen."

"Why do you have to use that word like a weapon, Binta?" asked Shallow.

"What are you talkin' about," asked Binta.

"You beat me over the head with marriage all the time," said Shallow. "Like it's some sort of life sentence to prison that I have to serve."

"Girl," said Binta, "I don't know what you're talkin about. I don't beat you up with nothin'."

"You do," said Shallow.

"Do I, Matia?" asked Binta.

"You do," said Matia. "I don't think you mean to, but you do have a way of makin' marriage sound like an obligation rather than a choice or a blessing."

"See," said Shallow, poking her tongue out at Binta jokingly. "I told you."

"Well," said Binta unamused. "Shallow is always makin' me feel like a loser for wantin' to get married in the first place. It's like her life is worth more than mine just because she's been to college."

"I'm sorry, 'sha'," said Shallow. Wrapping her right arm around Binta's shoulders. "You know you my girl. It's just that you've been designing clothes for us since middle school.

You're such a talented seamstress and you've got brains too. You could've done anything you wanted with your life."

"I am doin' what I want with my life," said Binta. "I'm marryin' the man I love."

"F'sure," said Shallow. "I can see that you are. Maybe if my daddy had loved my mama enough to marry her, I would see things differently."

"Did he ever explain why he didn't marry her?" asked Matia.

"I've never even spoken to the man," said Shallow. "I guess I never knew him."

"Aw, *'boo'*," said Binta, "so you never found out why?"

"Oh, I know why," said Shallow.

"Why?" Binta said.

"My grandmother, Genevieve," said Shallow. "She hated my mama cuz she was light skinned and half Creole. She spit on us the only day my mama ever took me over there to see my daddy 'n' em."

Binta and Matia both gasped.

"When you were just a baby?" Matia asked.

"Yeah," said Shallow, "that was it for my mama. I heard her say once before she died that she walked away from my daddy that day, leavin' all her regrets behind her."

"People in this world so sick," said Binta. "Either they goin' hate you cuz you too Black or they goin' hate you because you too white."

"You think so?" Matia said. "I've always thought they hate you because you too Black or because you're not Black enough."

"That's the same thing, isn't it?" Binta said.

"Maybe it is," said Matia. "It depends on whose doin' the hatin'. My daddy mama, Grandmother Delia, swore Sadiki wasn't his baby until the day she died because Sadiki was dark skinned," said Matia. "It broke Sadiki's heart. Had her always searchin' for somethin' to fix what wasn't really broken."

"Sick," said Binta.

"And sad," said Matia. "She made my sister feel like an outcast in her own family. That's why my mama never could stand my paternal grandmother."

"What I wanna know is how we can get mad at other folk for not lovin' us, when we still strugglin' tryin' to learn to love ourselves?" Binta said.

"You right, Binta," said Shallow.

"Maybe the problem is people don't really love God," said Matia. "I mean if we did wouldn't we want to love each other and ourselves? You couldn't tell me you loved me all the day-long and then kill yourself tryin' to hurt my children. If you hatin' my child, you hatin' me."

"That's it," said Shallow.

"No room for God and hatred in the same heart," said Binta.

"Why can't people see it?" asked Shallow.

"Maybe because sometimes people are blind to the need for freedom unless it's their own freedom their fightin' for," said Binta.

"That sounds hopeless," said Matia.

"I know," said Shallow, "but from what I can tell people try to build and fasten' their freedom on other people's backs even if they have to use chains of oppression."

There was a period of silence.

"What ended up happenin' with your grandmother, Shallow?" said Matia. "Ya daddy's mama, I mean. She ever came around?"

"Not to this day," said Shallow. "My daddy died in Vietnam without ever acknowledging that I was his. He wouldn't even give me his last name. When I was a baby he said I didn't even look nothin' like him. Truth is I don't. I look just like my mama except I'm darker. After my mama passed from Lupus nobody from my paternal side of the family even checked on me to see if I was alright."

"That's so terrible," said Matia. "She didn't just cheat you out of havin' ya paternal family in ya life, but she cheated herself out of havin' a granddaughter."

"Aw, 'boo'," said Binta.

"It's alright," said Shallow, "but now maybe y'all can see why when ya'll goin' on about how much y'all parents loved each other, I'm not that impressed. Maybe at some point both my parents loved each other at the same time. But I'm livin' proof that sometimes love just isn't enough."

"Shallow," said Matia. "Where there is real love, there is the place that you will also find commitment. My mama use to always say that real love gives birth to faithfulness."

"Real love, huh?" Shallow said. "I don't think I could believe it even if I saw it."

7

After the movie was over, the young couples went to dinner. They settled at Cher Jambalaya's, a candlelit Creole café that specialized in New Orleans' cuisine. The owner, Lexy's uncle, had invited them as his dinner guest in honor of Lexy's graduation.

The three couples snuggled into a dimly lit corner booth of the restaurant at a table for six.

"So," said Nile, smiling, "not too much longer before the big day.

Everyone smiled.

"What day is that," asked Lexington.

"Bill and Binta's weddin' day," said Matia.

Lexy looked at Shallow, who avoided eye contact with him.

"Why didn't you tell me they were gettin' married?" Lexington asked.

"I didn't tell you," said Shallow, looking guilty. "I thought I did. You sho I didn't?"

"I'm sho," said Lexington.

"Shallow," said Binta, "are you sho you didn't tell him on purpose?"

"Binta," said Matia dissaproovingly.

"Well," said Binta, "you know she gets all nervous every time he try to talk to her about marriage."

"Alright, Binta," said Shallow. "That's enough."

"So," said Lexington approvingly, "you been talkin' about me."

Lexington smiled and laughed to himself.

"You must be so proud," said Lexington to Bill, "to get to walk down the aisle with the woman of your dreams. And she's beautiful, man. Just beautiful."

"Thanks man," said Bill, nodding his head at Lexington.

"Seriously," said Lexington, glancing at Shallow before finishing his statement. "I envy you. Not every man is so lucky as to win the hand of the woman that he adores."

"A woman is not a prize to be won," snapped Shallow.

"Shallow," said Lexington, "I wasn't implyin' that a woman was a prize."

"But every time," started Shallow.

"Did Shallow forget to tell you about Nile and Matia too," asked Binta, deliberating cutting Shallow's sentence short. "They'll be getting' married soon too."

"Whoa," said Matia, "we haven't even picked a date yet."

"How about a Winter weddin'," said Binta. "Y'all could get married with us and we could have a double weddin'."

"A double weddin'," said Shallow. "I didn't volunteer to plan no double weddin. Dealin' with y'all two and y'all families is already too much. Everybody's an expert on how this weddin' should happen. Now, you want to add more people to the show."

"No," said Matia, "you don't have to worry about it. We're not havin a winter weddin'. Matter of fact, while we appreciate the offer, that wouldn't work with our plans."

"Oh yeah," said Bill, looking at Nile, "and what plans are those? You never told me nothin' about ya weddin' plans bruh."

"Our plans are whatever Matia tells me they are," said Nile, laughing. "I'm just responsible for pickin' up my tux and getting' to the weddin' on time."

"That's right," said Matia, winking at Nile.

"But seriously," said Shallow. "What are your plans, *"sha"*?"

"Well," said Matia, "we've picked Alex and Luna's back-yard garden for the location. Luna's garden is a prize winning garden. It's just beautiful."

"Okay," said Shallow, "we have a good location. What about a good date?"

"I know," said Matia. "We could do it around this time next year, in the Spring. It would be perfect, Nile. I love it."

"A spring weddin', huh," said Nile. "If that's what you want, it works for me."

"Oh," said Matia. "I can't wait to get started with the plannin'. We have so much to decide."

"Okay, okay," said Shallow, "no beggin' necessary, I'll help you plan your weddin'."

"What?" Binta said. "They didn't ask you for your help."

"Oh, come on y'all," said Shallow to Matia and Nile. "Let me plan it."

"Ofcourse you can," said Matia, glancing at Nile for his opinion.

"Yeah," sure," said Nile, agreeing with Matia.

"We can use all the help we can get, girl," said Matia.

"Alright, 'sha', " said Shallow, "y'all just write down what you want and let me know the budget and then we can get started."

"Don't you think it's a little early," said Lexington. "I mean y'all have a whole year."

"Oh, no," said Shallow, "weddings take time to plan. Binta and I are still busy gettin things done and we've been workin on her weddin' for almost a year in a half."

"A year in a half," said Nile, looking at Bill.

"Don't look at me," said Bill. "I'm not plannin' a thing. Just doin what I'm told, because I don't want to upset this pretty little lady. You dig."

"I'm diggin' it, bruh," said Nile, laughing.

"Yeah," said Lexington, "me too. I wish I could get y'all cute little weddin' planner to plan her own weddin."

"Don't start, Lexy," said Shallow.

"I wouldn't be surprised if you two were next," said Binta, winking her eye at Shallow.

"Don't count on it," said Shallow, "I'm goin' make him wait until we're a ripe old age and nobody else wants him."

"And for a moment, we all thought she was human," said Bill.

Everyone laughed.

"Seriously, though," said Bill, "you're a real glutton for punishment foolin' around with Shallow."

"Oh," she's alright with me," said Lexington, elbowing Shallow gently. "She's just playin' hard to get."

"Yeah," said Nile, shaking his head in disbelief, "real hard."

"I'm not studin' bout y'all," said Shallow.

"Look, Lexington man," said Bill. "I've got a little sister who's real sharp and as cute as a button. She'll be a sophomore at Dillard in the Fall."

"Bill," said Shallow, "you wrong for that."

"What?" Bill said. "I'm just tryin' to help a brotha out. The man wants a wife and you clearly not interested."

"Binta," said Shallow. "Aren't you goin' say somethin' to your fiancée?"

"Alright *'boo'*, I will," said Binta. "Good job, baby. Somebody's got to help Lexington get out, while he still has a chance."

"Thank you, foxy," said Bill.

"That's what I'm talkin about," said Lexington, slapping the table, "appreciation."

Everyone laughed, including Shallow. While she was not totally comfortable with the line of conversation, she could not help but see the humor in it. She was having a good time.

"Y'all go ahead on and laugh," said Shallow. "One day I might surprise all of y'all."

"I hope so," said Lexington, using his eyes to flirt with Shallow.

"I just got the greatest idea," said Binta.

"What," said Matia and Shallow in unison.

"Well," said Binta, "Matia, you helped me work on my weddin gown. The least I can do is return the favor by helpin you. I'll design the gown of your dreams."

"Alright," said Matia, "sounds good to me."

8

When the waiter arrived with everyone's orders, they were famished.

"Four mint ice teas, two strawberry lemonades, two giant seafood platters," said the waiter as he began placing dishes on the table. "French bread, two okra gumbos, large potato salad, and six side orders of jambalaya."

"Thank you, Eddie," said Lexington, noting the waiter's name on his nametag.

"No problem, bruh," said Eddie, the waiter. "Just holla if you need me, I'll be around."

"Man this food looks and smells good," said Bill, as everyone started digging into their dinner.

"It really does," said Shallow as she put fried shrimp, oysters and catfish onto her plate.

"Yeah," said Lexington, "My uncle Andre really hit the nail on the head with this place. He use to be a waiter at Dooky Chase when he was in school at Xavier. Even when he was in college he always had his mind on runnin' his own restaurant."

"All I could think about was eatin', the whole time we were at the movies," said Shallow."

"I thought I heard ya stomach growlin'," said Lexington.

"At least it was just her stomach and not her," said Bill, laughing.

Everyone joined in the laughter except Shallow who put her fist up in a threatening manner.

"I wish Jaws 2 was out," said Nile.

"You didn't enjoy Star Wars?" asked Matia.

"No, it was good," said Nile.

"Jaws," said Binta, dissaproovingly, "I can't stand sharks."

"Have you ever seen a shark before?" asked Nile.

"No," said Binta. "Have you?"

"Yeah," said Nile. "All sharks aren't bad. It's just the man eaters that attack swimmers and boats. Whale sharks and basking sharks are harmless, though. They eat tiny plants and animals that are too small for us to even see."

"Man eaters," said Matia, "why do they have to call them that?"

"Could it be because they eat people," said Shallow, sarcastically."

"No," said Matia, rolling her eyes at Shallow, "I mean don't they have another name?"

"Yeah," said Nile, "White sharks."

"Excuse me?" Binta said, "but can we change the subject."

"Oh, sorry," said Nile.

"Hey, man," said Lexington, "you sure know a lot about sharks."

"Oh," said Nile, nodding, "I love fish. I've been studyin' and carin for them since I was a kid."

"Caring for them?" Lexington said.

"At Sam's Aquarium World," said Nile.

"No kiddin'," said Lexington, smiling with recognition.

"Yeah," said Nile, "you've been there?"

"I've been to the one on Toulouse Street a few times with my older brother, Maris," said Lexington.

"Maris Savoie?" suggested Nile.

"Yeah, Maris Marcellus Savoie," said Lexington, laughing. "He's a trip, but he the only brother I got."

"Yeah, man," said Nile, "Maris lives at Sam's Aquarium World."

"Don't I know it," said Lexington. "His house is full of aquariums. Drives my sister-in-law, Evon, crazy."

"I thought you looked familiar," said Nile. "Y'all two favor each other."

"Yeah, everybody says that," said Lexington.

"How he doin'?" Nile asked. "Haven't seen him in a while."

"He's tryin' to cut back on the time he spends at the pet shop and takin' care of fish."

"Why?" Nile asked.

"Evon says, he spends too much time foolin' around with the fish and not enough time foolin around with her," said Lexington, chuckling.

"Sounds kind of fishy to me," said Bill. "What man in his right mind would rather spend his time with a cold fish, when he's got a beautiful wife waitin' at home to be with him?"

"Now that's a good question," said Nile, smiling at Matia, "but you goin' have to ask Maris because I don't think I'll ever have that problem."

9

Winter arrived with its usual festive holiday spirit, ushering in Binta and Bill's long awaited and enchanting wedding day.

When the wedding ceremony was over and the reception had begun, the wedding party and guests found themselves to be a willing audience situated in wonderfully plush surroundings.

Virgil Baptiste, Binta's father, stood at his end of a beautifully adorned wedding banquet table preparing to give a toast. His sable black and silver hair as thick as his waistline, his spirit was full from the events of the day.

"I'm not goin' talk too long, y'all," said Binta's father, Virgil, chuckling and winking his eye at his wife, Rosalie. "Rosalie said she goin' leave me if I talk too much."

"Oh, Virgil," whispered Rosalie, turning red in the face, "I didn't say that."

"I know baby," said Virgil. "I'm just kiddin' y'all. Rosalie, didn't say that. Seriously, y'all, since I'm the head of my family, I think it's time I be honest about how we truly felt about Bill marryin' our baby girl, Binta."

Everyone in the reception hall was quiet, especially those in the wedding party.

Bill stirred in his chair nervously, glancing at Binta with concern.

Binta shrugged her shoulders and smiled, patting Bill on the shoulder, reassuringly.

"Now Bill Washington," said Binta's father, "Bill, Bill, Bill. I think of the first time I saw you over at Washington's Auto Repair on Franklin Avenue, when you were just a little boy. I said to myself, look at him, he's probably goin' grow up to be a mechanic just like his daddy. I pray my little baby, Binta, don't grow up and marry no mechanic."

The wedding guests all laughed.

Glancing at Bill, Virgil smiled. "Then," he said. "Bill grew up to be big y'all. He's just so big. I remember goin' to the shop to pick my car up when Bill was still in highschool and askin' myself why did he have to be so big. Whenever, I look up and see him walkin' towards me it's like I see a linebacker comin' straight at me."

"That's right, Virgil," said Mr. William, Bill's father. "He's a big boy. He'll make ya eat ya lunch."

Everyone laughed again.

"I know you proud of em, William," said Virgil, laughing to himself. "It's a true blessin' when a man can be proud of his son. But to tell ya the truth, I always saw my Binta marryin' somebody important, somebody like a dignitary, ambassador, composer, scientist or somethin'. Can y'all imagine how I felt when I realized Bill Washington was goin' be the

one she married? He's no dignitary. He's no ambassador.
He's no composer or scientist. He's none of that."

"Watch it, Virgil," said Mr. William, arching his eyebrows.
Virgil smiled at Bill's father.

"But let me tell y'all what I've learned he is," said Virgil.

"Tell us what ya learned," said Mr. William.

"I learned that Bill is a real man," said Virgil. "Y'all know
what I'm talkin' about. Bill is a man's man. He's not afraid
of hard work and he is a man of his word. Ya know if ya spend
a lil bit of time with the young fella, ya find out some things
about him. I've spent some time with him. I've learned that
Bill is lovin', happy, calm, patient, carin', respectable, loyal,
measured and kind. He is a man of integrity. Now, I can't
say f'sure that Bill will never decide to become a dignitary,
ambassador, composer, or scientist. Honestly, y'all, today, I
can honestly say that I couldn't care less. He don't ever have
to do any of that to be worthy to me. What matters to me is
that my daughter has married a man of integrity and I know
from experience y'all that they make the best husbands."

"Aw," the wedding guests resounded in unison.

"Oh, and mechanics too," said Virgil. "Men of integrity
make the best mechanics too!"

Everyone laughed.

Bill thanked his father-in-law and wiped the tears from
Binta's eyes.

Binta's mother, Rosalie, stood to her feet.

"This is for you Binta comin' from the true person in
charge of the Baptiste household," said Rosalie, before blowing a kiss to her husband, Virgil. "If ya wake up one day
and ya find what appears to be a stranger glued to ya sofa,
watchin' ya television, makin' a mess of ya house, eatin' up

all ya food without even sayin' thank you and even sleepin' in the bed next to ya at night, don't get scared and jump up and call the police. It's just ya husband, the man ya said ya wanted to spend the rest of ya life with."

The wedding guest laughed.

"Ya tellin' the truth yeah, Rosalie," yelled out one of the female wedding guest.

Rosalie laughed and then began to cry. "Now, this is for both of y'all. We often ask God for somethin' only to receive it and not recognize it once we got it. In order to have joy in marriage we have to be willin' to see things through God's eyes. They always look better from His perspective."

"Aw, mama," said Binta, getting emotional.

"I know I don't always do the best job of showin' it, but I love ya Binta," said Rosalie, blowing Binta a kiss and re-taking her seat. "No better daughter on this Earth."

After everyone settled down a little, Bill's father, William Washington, stood to his feet, commanding everyone's attention with his tremendous height and size.

"I'm not goin' talk to long y'all," said Mr. William, breaking up with emotion. "I'm goin' keep it short and sweet. But y'all got ta know, I love this young man right here. I love my son."

"Take ya time, pops," said Bill. "Take ya time."

William Washington cleared his throat and pointed at his son and shook his head with great pleasure and approval. He pulled a handkerchief from his tuxedo pocket and patted his eyes damp eyes dry.

"Alright," said Mr. William. "Here we go, y'all. It really don't matter what kind of desire for food y'all two young people got, as long as y'all make sure to always save it for home. Eat at home y'all. Eat at home!"

As Mr. William took his seat, his wife Isabelle stood up.

"Congratulations to the best son in the world and thank you for blessin' me with such a beautiful daughter-in-law."

"Thank you, mama," said Bill.

"Congratulations y'all," Nile said, when Bill was finished speaking. "You know you truly have somethin' special, when two people really know each other like y'all two do and still want to love each other in spite of it. Keep on lovin' and keep bein' blessed!"

As Nile took his seat, Matia and Shallow stood up at the same time.

"You go," said Matia, sitting back down.

"No, you go, 'sha', " said Shallow, sitting.

"Somebody need ta go," said Rosalie.

Matia stood back up. "I use to look at you guys and think that y'all made havin' a relationship look so easy. The admiration and respect that you have always shown each other is inspirational. It's the stuff that story books are made out of. Congratulations y'all."

Shallow cleared her throat and stood up as soon as Matia was done.

"Like Matia," said Shallow, "I must say that y'all don't make fallin' in love and gettin' married look too painful. Okay, enough of that mushy stuff. Binta, I want to remind you how important it is in marriage to split everything with Bill. I'm talkin' about the dish washin', gumbo cookin', porch sweepin' and the diaper changin', 'sha'. Don't forget to share that."

"That's a good one, Shallow," said Rosalie, laughing and nodding her head."

"Don't worry Shallow," said Binta. "I'm all for sharing with Bill."

"Me too, baby," said Bill. "I'm all for sharing with you too."

10

Later, when the reception was nearing its end, Bill & Binta who had been dancing the night away re-joined their friends at the wedding party table. The six young people sat around a pearl white and cranberry winter theme decorated table, laughing and chatting.

"I have two extra tickets to the Super Bowl in New Orleans on January the fifteenth," said Lexington. "My uncle bought tickets for the employees at the law office and two of the guys will be out of town on business. Y'all interested."

"F'sure," said Nile. "That's good of you man. You alright!"

"Count me in," said Bill. "I can't wait to see the Broncos beat the Cowboys' butts in the Superdome!"

"What?" Nile said.   "Man, the Cowboys got Roger Staubach, Harvey Martin, Tony Dorsett and Randy White."

"Man the Broncos got the Orange Crush Defense," said Bill.

"But the Cowboys defense is dynomite too, na," said Nile.

"And don't forget the Cowboys have Billy Joe Dupree from West Monroe," said Lexington."

"Dupree from Monroe, Louisiana?" Bill said.

"Yeah," said Lexington, "when it comes to blocking and pass receiving, they don't get no better."

"Yeah," said Nile.

"I heard Southern at Baton Rouge's band is playing in the pregame show," said Bill.

"For the Super Bowl?" Binta said.

"Yeah, for the Super Bowl," said Bill, "It would a been somethin' else if they could have had Grambling and Southern do a battle of the bands for the Super Bowl. Would a blew America away."

"We missed the Bayou Classic this year," said Binta, pouting.

"It won't happen again," said Bill, kissing Binta's nose.

"I can't wait to get you alone on that cruise ship Mrs. Washington," said Bill.

"That's right," said Shallow. "Y'all goin' on an International cruise."

"That's alright," said Lexington.

"When y'all set sail?" Nile said.

"We leave for Miami early tomorrow mornin'," said Bill. "but we don't board our ship until tomorrow night."

"I'm so happy for y'all, man," said Lexington, smiling.

"Lexington," said Nile. "You comin' to me and Matia weddin' too, right?"

"F'sure, man," said Lexington, "f'sure."

Because he desired to be alone with Shallow to talk, Lexington asked Shallow to dance with him.

"Dance with me, Shallow Flowers," said Lexington to Shallow who for once had nothing to say.

Lexington stood to his feet and offered Shallow his hand. She took his hand and stood. The two of them moved out onto the dance floor, joining the other dancers as the DJ began to play a love song by Heatwave. As the love song began to play, Lexington and Shallow both softened in each other's arms. Their bodies appeared to be made for each other. To look at them was to witness a completed work of art. "A gentleman and his lady" would have been an appropriate title. Lexington was lean and noticeably attractive. And he only had eyes for Shallow. He did not really look at her. What he did was more like take her in. They danced smoothly as one, anticipating each other's moves.

The song ended and there was a hiatus in the music. Lexington marveled over Shallow's face, delicate with beauty and firm with unbending pride. Her course black hair was pulled back from her face and up into a braided knot at the crown of her head.

Lexington gently brushed her right cheek with his hand.

"When are you goin' to marry me and make me the happiest man on Earth?" Lexington asked, almost whispering.

"Lexy, please," said Shallow, trying to brush off the question, "not now. Your goin' ruin the night."

"Nobody's tryin' to ruin the night," said Lexington, still holding Shallow close.

"This song always makes me think of you," said Shallow. She looked up into Lexington's face and smiled.

"Really," said Lexington doubtfully.

"Come on, 'sha'," said Shallow gently, "you know how I feel about you."

"And you know how I feel about you," said Lexington. "That's why I can't understand why you won't marry me."

"Lexy," said Shallow sighing and pulling away from him, "stop this."

"I'm sorry, Shallow," said Lexington. "I can't stop wantin' you."

"Yes, you can," said Shallow.

"No, I can't," said Lexington again. "I have everything I've ever wanted, except for someone to share it all with."

"You can share it with me without us gettin' married," said Shallow.

"No, Shallow," said Lexington. "I'm tired of comin' home to an empty apartment and spendin' my nights alone. I want a wife. Now, I've asked you to do me the honor of being that wife. That's what I want. It's what I wanted yesterday. It's what I want today and it's what I'll still be wantin' tomorrow.

"Next, you'll be wantin' children," said Shallow.

"And?" asked Lexington. "What's so wrong with that?"

Shallow cursed under her breath and walked off the dance floor, leaving Lexington to dance alone. Lexington followed her, calling out her name.

When he caught up with her, she had already rejoined their friends at the table.

"Shallow, we still need to talk about this," said Lexington, gently touching Shallow's shoulder. "It's not goin' away."

"What about you then," said Shallow. "Will you go way, cause ya workin' on my nerves?"

Everyone at the table stopped talking and laughing upon hearing the hullabaloo that was going on between Lexington and Shallow. All eyes were on them.

"Is that what you want," said Lexington in frustration. "You ain't sayin' nothin'. I can make that happen."

"Tell her man," said Bill. "A man can only take so much."

Binta patted Bill on the thigh and shook her head at him with a disapproving look.

"Well, *'sha'*," said Shallow, nodding her head towards the door, "nobody's stoppin' ya."

"Shallow, don't," said Matia, attempting to calm her friend.

"No, Matia," said Lexington. "What she says is true. There's nothin' here for me. Nothin' to stop me from walkin' away and never lookin' back. I don't know why it's takin' so long for me to see it."

Lexington stood to his feet and nodded his head at Bill and Binta.

"Thank y'all so much for havin me at y'all weddin," said Lexington, his voice cracking slightly.

As Lexington turned to walk away, Shallow grabbed him gently by the arm.

"Lexy," she said, "let's not make somethin' out of nothin'. You don't have to go."

"Why should I stay?"

"Can't we talk about this tomorrow?"

"The tomorrow that I hope for will never come with you," said Lexington, gently removing Shallow's hand from his arm.

As Lexington walked away, Shallow jumped up from the table.

"Lexy," screamed Shallow angrily.

"Shallow, let him go," said Matia rushing to Shallow's side and trying to calm her down again.

"No," Shallow said. "He can't just walk out on me like this."

"It's alright," said Matia, "you can catch a ride back to Charbonnet with me and Nile."

"No, 'sha'," said Shallow. "It's not alright. He can't just leave me. Nobody leaves me."

"Well," said Bill, sarcastically, "he just did."

"Bill," said Binta, "not now."

"I'm sorry baby," said Bill, "but your friend don't make no sense. She told the man to leave. Then, she got mad because he left."

"I'm not goin' let him do this to me," said Shallow, going after Lexington.

"Shallow," yelled Matia as she watched her friend disappear through the exit door.

Immediately, Shallow spotted Lexington getting into his car. Without thinking, she slipped out of her heels and ran towards his car, throwing her shoes at and hitting his front windshield.

"You want to leave me, Lexy," said Shallow. "Then go. I knew I couldn't trust you to stay anyway."

"What?" Lexington yelled as he jumped out of his car and slammed the car door. "Stay for what. You just said in there that you don't want me. What's wrong with you?"

That was it. Those were the words that Shallow had been asking herself her whole life. *What was so wrong with her that even her own father did not want her? What was so wrong with her that her father had not thought twice about turning his back on her, his own flesh and blood?*

"Don't say that to me," cried Shallow, almost doubling over in emotionally induced pain. "Don't you say something's wrong with me. I knew you would leave me, just like him. I knew you would do me just like my daddy."

"What," asked Lexington, grabbing Shallow by the arms and trying to help her stand upright again. "What are you talking about?"

"I hate you, Lexington," said Shallow. "I hate you so much."

Suddenly, the veil was pulled back. The truth was no longer concealed from Lexington. He could see so clearly, what he had not been able to distinguish before. Shallow had not been fighting him for all this time, but her father. And Lexington, innocent of the crime that had been committed, had been chosen to serve her father's sentence in his stead. Why? Simply put, Shallow knew deep down inside that Lexy did love her. And terrified of believing in that love only to lose it, Shallow would not allow herself to believe in it.

"I am not your father," insisted Lexington, grabbing Shallow gently by the shoulders. "I am not that man who would love and then leave you. If you would just let me love you, I will stay. I will stay until the day I die."

"No," said Shallow, still crying, "I'm sorry, Lexy, but I don't know how."

"Let me teach you," Lexy said, reaching one last time for her love.

Shallow pulled away from Lexington, shaking her head in rejection to his offer of love. She took deliberate steps backward, trembling in fear.

Lexington hung his head in defeat as he climbed back into his car. As Shallow turned to walk away, Lexington sped off.

Matia who had been watching at a distance, joined Shallow in the parking lot.

"What you goin' do now?" asked Matia.

"I'm goin' find my shoes and put em back on," said Shallow, trying to smile.

Matia stood at arm's length of her friend.

"I think he's really gone for good this time," whispered Shallow.

Matia nodded her head in agreement and reached out to her friend. Shallow rested her head on Matia's shoulder.

"You know, *'sha'*?" Shallow said with optimism.

"Huh?" Matia said.

"It's a good thing I didn't love him," said Shallow.

"It's a good thing," said Matia, questioning the words as they came from her mouth.

11

On his first day at the law office, Lexington had seen her sitting at the small desk right outside of what was to be his office. Celeste was short, thick and shapely. Her caramel face framed two big innocent eyes and she had a calming velvety voice. She was filled with a relentless enthusiasm for life. She said anything was possible! She believed everything was worth a try! And so at the time that Lexington was struggling to forget about Shallow, he grew fond of Celeste. Nile, Maris and Bill all insisted that he would have been crazy not to. After all, he had been looking for a wife. And she, Celeste, warm-hearted, eager to please and gentle could be that wife.

Rehearsing the turn of events that created the fabric of his life, Lexington knocked at Shallow's front door.

"I'm comin'," said Shallow.

Lexington knocked on the door again.

"What are you doin' here," asked Shallow, opening her front door with a glint of delight in her tone. "It's been months."

The last several months had given Shallow a lot to think about. She had nagging regrets. And she wondered if perhaps now she could work up the nerve to admit to Lexington that she did love and want to be with him. Perhaps, now she could ask him to teach her how to accept and give the love that he had been offering. Maybe God was giving her another chance at love. Perhaps now she was ready to learn how to.

"I had something to tell you," said Lexington. "Thought I owed it to you to make sure you heard it from me and not somebody else."

"Come on in then, 'sha'," said Shallow, disheartened by his last words.

Lexington walked into the living room, his tall frame complimenting Shallow's petite stature. He was relieved to find that they were alone in the house.

"Ya maw-maw 'n' em, gone?"

"Yeah," said Shallow, "maw-maw and paw-paw went ta make grocery."

Lexington nodded.

"You're lookin' good," he said still standing.

"Aw, thank you, 'sha'," said Shallow, sitting down on her grandmother's antique sofa, which was covered in plastic. "You too."

"Thanks," said Lexington. "I don't know how though with all the business lunches and dinners I been havin'."

"Sit down," said Shallow. "Matia and Binta told me you keep in touch with Nile and Bill."

"Yeah," said Lexington, joining her on the sofa, "we all went to the Super Bowl together, when it was in town at the

Superdome last January. I play a little basketball with them at Stallings and Nile's talked me into buyin' two big fish tanks for my apartment. He's helping me set them up, now. Their expensive!"

"What's happenin', Lexy?" asked Shallow, abruptly. "What don't you want me to hear from somebody else?"

Lexington sat facing her. He cleared his throat before responding.

"I met somebody," said Lexington.

Shallow shrugged her shoulders.

"And?" said Shallow, taking a deep breath and trying to appear unaffected.

"Seems like we both want the same things out of life," said Lexington. "She knows all about my unrequited love for you. She jokes that she's goin' make me forget I ever knew you."

"What's her name?" said Shallow.

"Celeste," said Lexington. "I've known her for a couple of years, really. She's a paralegal at my uncle's law firm and a close friend of the family. When I joined the firm at the end of last year, she was assigned to work with me. And well you know how things happen."

"Yeah, I guess I do," said Shallow still trying to look indifferent.

"I've asked her to marry me," blurted out Lexington.

Shallow coughed, choking on her saliva.

"Wow, Lexy," said Shallow. "Married. When?"

"Next year, in October," said Lexington.

"I haven't told Nile or Bill yet," said Lexy. "Honestly, those guys and I have gotten pretty close over the last year. I'm plannin on askin them both to be in the weddin."

"Really?" Shallow asked, laughing bitterly. "Am I invited too, *'sha'*?"

"If you want to come," said Lexington, suddenly breathing heavily. "I mean if we're nothin' else we're still friends, right? You know that I'd still walk on water for you if you'd just let me."

"Lexy," said Shallow, grasping for her pride and turning her face away from Lexington."

She stood up.

"Don't, Lexy," said Shallow. "Don't say somethin' you'll just regret later."

Lexington stood up and gently turned Shallow's face towards his.

"Alright, alright," said Lexington. "I'm sorry."

Shallow could not speak. She could only cry.

"I don't know what's wrong with me, Lexy?" she said, burying her head into Lexington's chest. "I should be happy for you. If anyone deserves to be happy, it is you."

"Nothing's wrong with you," said Lexington, holding Shallow as if his very life depended on it. "Some fruit just take a little longer to ripen than others, that's all. One day you'll be ready and I'll curse the guy who's blessed to have you."

12

That night Shallow cried so hard and long that, she became dehydrated. She grew sick from sorrow, eating at her bones. No foresight, her vision failed her as she struggled to find herself in her bathroom mirror. She could not. When her sight began to clear, the Shallow that she had always imagined herself to be was not the woman staring back at her. The woman staring back at her was someone who had lost in the game of love. Only Shallow had determined a long time ago that she would never lose in the game of love. She would never lose because she would never play. She would never play because she would never love. Too bad she had not learned that romance is not a fair sport.

The misunderstanding had begun for her as a young girl. Shallow had begun to label men as the enemy, as the adversary who was plotting for her destruction. She had never been able to bring herself to forgive her father for denying her. And he indifferent to her existence, had never given her the chance to express her lack of respect or anger towards him. So, she looked for her father, the unreliable man, in every man and usually after much scrutinizing found him. She had never understood that some mothers leave their little boys too. Or that each man was different, thought different and moved to the beat of his own drum. She expected each man to fail. And ofcourse since perfection is a myth for us mere humans, no man had proven to disappoint her. Each had made his share of mistakes. Consequently, she was blind to anything that most men did right. Matia made the case that in this way Shallow was impossible to please.

When Shallow finally fell to sleep on the night that she learned of Lexington's engagement, her sleep was interrupted by a recurring dream that she had been having ever since her mother's death. She dreamed she was a child of about seven and in a bubble that was floating through what she somehow knew was a Vietnam war zone. Bombs were exploding all around her. The bodies of dead men were scattered throughout the land she hovered over. Gunfire zipped past her, sometimes bouncing off the bubble that protected her from the combat that surrounded her.

"There is your father," said a ubiquitous voice.

Shallow looked down and saw Antoine, the man who was said to be her father, injured and laying in a bushy grassy area. He was surrounded by dead men.

"Daddy," said Shallow, "it's me Shallow, your little girl. I found you."

As her father looked up, he grimaced.

"I don't know you," he said.

With this the bubble Shallow was in began to float away from her father, leaving him behind to die in his denial. And why not? There was nothing left to be said. Shallow could not repudiate his statement. She could not claim to know him. Honestly, she did not know the man. She did not and never would know this man that had walked away from her as a child denying his paternity.

The scene of the nightmare switched to Shallow still as a young child, leaning against the outside of her mother's locked bedroom door and listening with her ear to the door in terror. A chaotic clatter of crashing and thrashing was coming from inside the room. The noise of glass breaking and bloodcurdling screams could be heard, as Shallow's mother thrashed around her bedroom in unimaginable pain. The turmoil echoed throughout the rest of the quiet still house.

"Help me," screamed Shallow's mother, Jean Marie, as she struggled to manage her pain. "Mama please help me. Oh no, not again! Please no! Please stop! Oh, my Father in heaven!"

"Hold on Jean Marie," said Adelaide, tenderly as she tried to calm and secure her daughter. "Try not to move about so, *'sha'*. I called an ambulance. Just hold on, na *'sha'*. We goin' get ya to Charity. They goin' help us stop this Lupus from eatin' you alive. They goin' help take away ya pain like they always do."

"It's hurtin' me mama," screeched Shallow's mother, desperately. "It's killin' me. Oh, God make it stop. Don't let it kill me, mama! Please, please, make it stop! Somebody make it stop!"

Shallow lay prostrate with her face to the floor crying out to God.

"Please God," she begged on her mother's behalf, repeating her mother's sentiments, "if you can hear me make it stop and this time make it stop for good!"

The scene of the dream switched to a silver hearse driving off into eternity, carrying the body of Shallow's mother, Jean Marie, away forever.

13

The next morning while Matia was getting ready for church fellowship, her father called her to the telephone.

"Something's wrong with Shallow," said Franklin as he handed Matia the telephone.

Matia heard Shallow's grandmother, Adelaide Celestin Flowers, speaking at the other end of the telephone line. She was calling for help on Shallow's behalf. Apparently, Shallow, dejected, refused to eat or speak. Shallow's grandmother was terribly worried. Regrettably, she could not entirely ascertain what the trouble was with Shallow and had been unable to console her granddaughter. Moments after Matia hung up her telephone she was telling her father goodbye and rushing down the street to Shallow's aid.

When she arrived, Binta was already there beating on Shallow's bedroom door. After several moments of pleading with Shallow in an effort to gain entry into her room, Shallow let Binta and Matia in.

"Aw, *'boo'*," said Binta, noticing Shallow's puffy face and red and baggy eyes, "you look a mess."

"Binta," snapped Matia.

"I'm sorry, *'boo'*," said Binta to Shallow, covering her mouth.

The two of them sat at the foot of Shallow's bed and listened as Shallow recounted the details of her visit from Lexington.

"I'm sorry I didn't tell you about Celeste," said Matia.

Binta was silent.

"What could you say?" said Shallow.

"Maybe, Lexington's seein' somebody," said Matia.

"It wouldn't have hurt any less comin' from you, *'sha'*," said Shallow.

"Why you so quiet, Binta?" asked Matia.

"Don't want ta say the wrong thing," Binta mumbled.

"Go on and say I told you so," Shallow said to Binta, sniffling. "You were right about me."

Binta went to Shallow's side and put her hand on her shoulder. "No *'boo'*, I wasn't right about you. I thought you were too selfish to love anybody but yourself. I was wrong. I can see that now. You love, but you are just too afraid to show it."

"How can I?" said Shallow. "How can I protect my heart and open it up too. That's too much of a risk."

"If it's the right person it's more of an investment than a risk," said Matia.

"You forget my name's Shallow," she said. "My mama gave me this name so I would be too insincere and mean to make the mistake of lovin' anybody the way she loved my daddy."

"But becomin' a slave to fear and hate won't protect you, Shallow," said Matia. "People were created to love."

"You always talkin' about how much God loves us, Matia," said Shallow.

"That's because He does," said Matia.

"If He loves me so much," said Shallow in a state of unmistakable impairment, "how could he take both my daddy and mama away from me before I was even old enough to really get to know them."

Matia was quiet with loving eyes and a patient heart.

"Can you help me understand why a loving God would do that?" Shallow asked.

"He did not do it," said Matia.

"Ah, but He allowed it," said Shallow.

Matia nodded her head in agreement. "Yes, He did."

"What did I do to deserve it?" Shallow pleaded.

Matia was silent and hung her head in sadness.

"Who are we really to question God?" Binta said, gently squeezing one of Shallow's hands. "Not that He forbids our askin' Him questions or anything like that, He want us to seek Him. But in the overall scheme of life, He knows what's best. He was here when our ancestors were born and when they passed away. He will still be here, when we long gone. He knows the beginnin' and the end."

"Binta's right," said Matia, "but we're human. Sometimes, we can't help but want to know why God allows what He allows. We don't know like He knows what tomorrow will bring or even his purpose in it. We can't see everything he's protected us from or see everything He's preparin' for us. Our limited picture of this life is a lot like the ant's, compared to God's never-ending and unlimited view."

"How am I supposed to make sense out of my life, if I can't understand it?" Shallow said.

Matia gently grabbed Shallow by her free hand.

"I hear you, Shallow," said Matia. "Really, I do. I felt the same way when mama and Sadiki died. I felt like God had forgotten me too."

"And?" Shallow said.

"And I lived long enough to see that He had not," said Matia. "I held onto my faith in Him or maybe it was Him holding onto me. All I know is after too many dark days; I looked up and saw His glory shinin' down on me so brightly. His grace came floodin' into my life's lowest valley, when I was just about ready to give up. A stream of His sweet love flowed straight to me, liftin' and strengthenin' me."

There was a gentle knock at the door.

"Shallow?" said Shallow's grandmother peeking into Shallow's bedroom.

"Yeah, maw-maw?" said Shallow.

"Ya feelin' better na huh, *'sha'*?" Adelaide said.

"Yeah," said Shallow, "a little bit."

"That's good, *'sha'*," said Adelaide. "Rain can't last forever. Sooner or later the sun goin' shine again."

"I know maw-maw," said Shallow.

"Thank y'all for comin' by to check on her for me," said Adelaide. "I'm always tellin' her she's blessed to have y'all two. "That's f'sure. Y'all goin' be able to stay a while, huh?"

"Yes, mam," said Matia and Binta in unison.

"Thank y'all, ya hear?" Adelaide said.

"Thank you for callin' us," said Binta.

"Ya welcome, baby," said Adelaide.

"How's ya appetite, *'sha'*?" Adelaide said to Shallow. "You ain't eat nothin' for dinner last night or for breakfast this mornin'."

"I'm a little hungry," said Shallow.

"We goin' for a little while, *'sha'*. Ya paw-paw's goin' drop me off at Saint David's for Mass on his way to men's day at his church. We goin' have a shrimp and crab boil for y'all when we get back. They got some glazed donuts, orange juice and milk in the kitchen if y'all get hungry."

Adelaide gently shut Shallow's bedroom door.

"I love your grandmother," said Matia.

"She's the nicest woman," said Binta.

"I know," said Shallow. "No other people like my maw-maw and paw-paw on this earth. It's a funny thing. When I was a little girl, I use to think they were angels keepin' watch over me."

PART EIGHT

FALSE LABOR

1

"So," said Alex, resting on his back porch, "what I want to stress in my pre-marriage counselin' with you two is that a marriage is not a contract. The Judeo-Christian teachin' is that it is a covenant relationship between a man, woman and God. It can be easy enough to tear up a business contract and walk away for any number of reasons without havin' generational repercussions. But in divorce, the tearin' will always hurt and forever change all involved, even the children. I'm not sayin' that adultery or abuse never give people good reason for divorce. Unfortunately, sometimes out can be the only right direction to go in. What I am saying though, is that God makes it clear that He hates divorce. So, I know what I said. What do you hear me sayin'?"

"You just said a lot, Alex," said Nile, smiling.

"Seriously, brother," said Alex. "What am I sayin'?"

"Okay, okay," said Nile, "I think your main point is that we need to really consider whether or not we are prepared to marry for life."

"Alright," said Alex.

"And that if we have any doubts about whether or not we can see ourselves bein' together for life, "said Matia, "then we need to address those doubts before getting' married."

"Yeah, yeah," said Alex, "I'm goin' be completely honest with y'all. I don't want to see y'all get married, if y'all not goin' stay married. What's the point? I'd rather see y'all go on about y'all business. Nile fixin' leaky faucets and feedin' fish and you, Matia, countin' money and makin' candy. I would rather see that than see y'all playin' house without bein' in it to win it. I'm talkin' about for the long haul. But what I want don't mean a thing. What matters is what God wants and what you two want. Now, I believe that I'm on God's side in this. He don't want to see you two destroy each other. He'd rather see you two strengthen each other."

"We're in this for the long haul, Alex," said Nile. "You know we are."

"I know you are sayin' that you are today, said Alex, "but what about three or seven years from now? Life gets hard. Unimagined challenges come our way. We wake up sometimes and find ourselves facin' things that we never knew were even possible. I'm talkin' about stressors like undesired change, physical changes, sickness, financial troubles, death, unemployment, challenges with children, other relatives and friends."

"We can face anything," said Matia, "as long as we have God."

"You've said a mouthful, sister-in-law," said Alex. "With God's help anything is possible, but we have to actually believe that we can ask God for help. So, often we do what we want to do, even if we know it is not right and then we try to blame God for the fallout. *Why'd God let this happen to me?* But the funny thing about God is that he's not fickle like us when it comes to forgiveness. While we have to face the consequences of our mistakes in life, God is always there waitin' for us to turn to him. He's more faithful than a mother. So, we can always change our minds and turn away from the wrong thing and He will help us find the right thing."

"So, what does bein' a wife mean to you, Matia?" asked Alex.

"It means lovin' and helpin' my husband," said Matia. "It means supportin' his leadership."

"Alright," said Alex, nodding in agreement, "but don't forget that he's goin' to need to know your heart too. He's goin' need you to tell him those things that only a wife can discern and he's goin' need your help to manage y'all life together. So, often when we see a man we forget that we are seein' the woman in his life too and vice versa. That's right! Now, I need Luna. God Bless her, but I need God more and I would have to learn to live without her if God took her before me. But I am so thankful to have her in my life because I would not be the man that I am today without her. When I feel all alone in this world, I'm reminded that I have her and she understands me in a way that no one else does. You know what I'm sayin' Nile?"

"Yeah," said Nile, glancing at Matia, "I think I do."

"Now, Nile," said Alex. "Your turn."

"Huh," said Nile.

"How would you define your role as a husband?" asked Alex.

"To protect, lead and provide," said Nile.

"Okay," said Alex, "that's right. Leading, providing, protecting are all part of your callin' as a husband. You are also expected to love Matia as Jesus Christ loved the church."

"How did Jesus love the church?" asked Alex, looking at Nile.

"He gave his life for her," said Nile.

"Exactly," said Alex. "A lot of men get stuck on the idea of bein' in charge, but don't want the servin' that comes with marriage. Yes, you are called to lead, but you are also called to love your wife. Love her not because she looks good, cooks good or brings home a lot of bacon. Love her because it is the most powerful thing that you can do for her, your children or yourself, after lovin' God. Help her, pray for her and encourage her to be her best. Don't just let her pour into you without seein' to it that she's gettin' what she needs too. Pour into her. Marriage is a commitment to take care of each other, it's a two way street."

The back door opened and a weary looking Luna and the twins appeared in the doorway.

"Hey, Uncle Nile and Auntie Matia," shouted the two animated boys. They playfully tackled Nile before giving Matia a quick hug. Then, they disappeared back into the house.

"Hey y'all, I'm so sorry I'm late," said Luna. "The boy's baseball practice ran late this evenin'. Let me get settled and I'll be right with y'all."

"Take your time, baby," said Alex. "I peeled those shrimp you asked me to peel."

"Oh good, thank you," said Luna brushing her glossy honeyed auburn hair out of her face and giving Alex a light kiss before turning to leave her back porch.

"Alright, na," said Nile, jokingly to his brother-in-law, "that's how y'all got those two little boys in the house."

"That's my wife," said Alex, "the apple of my eye. Ain't no way I'm about to turn down one of her kisses."

Nile and Matia laughed.

"We were goin' make seafood gumbo for y'all tonight," said Alex, "but Luna look tired and we not even finish talkin' yet. I'm a see if she want me to make a run down Chef Highway to We never Close for some po-boys, when we finish."

"Did I hear somebody say po-boys," said Luna, quickly returning to the back veranda.

"You move fast," said Matia, smiling.

"Thank you," said Luna smiling, "now what's this about po-boys?"

"I can see you tired, baby," said Alex. "Nile and me goin' make a quick run to the East to get dinner, when we get finished talkin'."

"I can still make the gumbo, y'all," said Luna."

"Don't worry about it" said Nile. "You don't have to cook no gumbo for us."

"I know I don't have to," said Luna. "I want to."

"If we can have a rain check, we'd be happy to come back to get some gumbo, big sis."

"It's a deal," said Luna. "I'll have some ready for Sunday."

"We'll be here," said Nile, glancing at Matia for reassurance.

"Yeah," said Matia, "count me in."

"Alright then, y'all," said Alex. "Where were we?"

"Marriage is a commitment to take care of each other," said Matia.

"Yeah," said Alex, smiling. "Anything you want to add to that, Luna?"

"Focusing on what we need to know as wives," said Luna. "I'm goin' tell you somethin' that it took me a little while to learn."

Matia nodded and took a deep breath.

"Your husband is not your little boy," said Luna, laughing.

"And you are not marryin' your mama, Nile," said Alex, grinning.

Everyone laughed.

"Seriously, though," said Luna. "Women are particular and we get impatient when things are not lookin' or happenin' a certain way. I've seen so many women hollerin' and screamin' at their husbands, demandin' that they do this or do that instead of talkin' to the man. It's a two way street. We can't holler at them like we half crazy and then turn around and say that there is something wrong with them hollerin' at us. It's poison for our relationship. No man wants to climb into bed at night with someone who reminds him of his scoldin' mama. If we treat them like our rebellious little boys, then they'll see us as their overbearin' mamas. And you do realize that most boys grow up and leave their mothers' houses one day."

Matia nodded and laughed.

"Oh," said Luna, "and prayer. Instead of gettin' on the phone with other people about y'all issues, pray. Pray without ceasin' for your husband and your marriage. You will have an influence over your husband that supersedes most. So, don't take your influence for granted. Use it wisely and never try to use it to try to supersede God's will."

"Anything you want to say?" asked Luna.

"No," said Matia, "I'm just listenin' and digestin'."

"Earlier," said Alex, "you said that bein' a wife meant helpin' and supportin'."

"Yeah," said Matia, "I did."

"So," said Alex, "what happens if he wants you to do or agree to do something that you don't want to do?"

"I don't know," said Matia, nervously. "That's a good question."

"It's comin'," said Alex. "Happens with me and Luna all the time."

"It does," said Nile, surprised.

"Yeah," said Alex, laughin, "you grew up with Luna. You should know better than most that she's goin' speak her mind."

"Yeah," said Nile, laughing, "I should."

Luna shook her head in agreement and laughed.

"Y'all know I'm Mama Royal's daughter," said Luna, smiling.

Everyone laughed again.

"So," said Matia, "what y'all do when y'all disagree?"

"First, I'll tell you what we've promised not to do," said Luna. "We try not to fight, but disagreements goin' happen. It's natural. We disagree, but we don't yell and act a fool because that kind of foolishness can turn into something bad. Oh, and we never decide to have our disagreements in front of the children, even if it means goin' into the bedroom and turning on some music. We never let it get violent. And we never try to force the other person to do what we want them to do."

"What do you do, then?" asked Nile, looking at Alex.

"I do the same thing she does when she's tryin' to get me to see something," said Alex. "I pray. I talk to her, but if she's sayin' no to somethin' and I'm askin' her to say yes, I can't do anything, but talk to my daddy about it. I might go for a walk. Might take a drive. I figure, if I'm tryin' to do what God wants me to do then He'll tell her. If after all that she's still not agreeing with me, then it's a rap and it wasn't meant to be. I can't make her do anything. For better or for worse, I need her cooperation and she needs mine. One thing you both must understand, is that God has not called us to dominate one another. It is not our right to try to force another human being to do anything. God does not force us to do anything. He gives us a choice."

2

In the average man's lifetime, he finds that he belongs to no less than two women. He belongs first and foremost to his devoted mother and then God willing and finally to his faithful wife. This is a concept that Nile had never really given much thought to until the moment came for him to confess to his mother that he no longer belonged to her. Yes, God had smiled on him and the time had come for him to have a wife. This is what he was explaining to his mother when she tripped over the tangled telephone cord, accidently knocking the phone to the floor and breaking their line of communication. When he had said all that he had to say about Matia and his plans for their future together his mother spoke:

Lord have mercy! We need to talk about this! Did you just say you gettin' married? Oh Nile! My poor son. My poor poor son. Did you fool around and get yourself in trouble with this girl? If she pregnant, how you know it's yours? No. You say she's not pregnant. Well, if she's not pregnant, why marry her then? Why would you be talkin' about marryin' her? I hope not cause she's pretty. Pretty girls come a dime a dozen. Are you sure you not makin' a big mistake? What's that you say? You know you not? You sound pretty sure of yourself. Could you be movin' too fast? What you say? You say you don't think so? Well, I do! I think so. I think you're makin' a huge mistake. Look at your brother,

Will. He married that spoiled rich girl, Queenie. What?
You say you like Queenie and she's a good wife. Well, you
like everybody! Which is why I think you probably movin'
too fast with this girl. You're too young to be gettin' married. You're too young to really know what you want out of
life. She is too. What you say? Wisdom's not held in reserve
just for the older folks and you seen plenty of old folk who
ain't got no sense. Well, la di da! Young people always think
they so in love. Till they go and get married, then they find
out the hard way that people aren't who they seem. What if
that happens to you, Nile? What if you wake up one mornin'
after marryin' this girl, thinkin' you then made the biggest
mistake of your life? What then? Your entire life would be
ruined. What you say? You say the biggest mistake of your
life would be in not marryin' her? I disagree. Besides if she
was all that you'd a brought her to meet me by now. What
you say? You didn't want me to scare her off? If I could, then
it would show that she not the one. I don't like your tone of
voice son. Wait! Where you goin'? You say you leavin'? Why
you look so angry, son. Don't leave like this. I'm sorry, if it
seems like I'm tryin' to rain on your parade. Mama Royal
just tryin' to look out for you, son. What's that? I then went
and made you late for your little rendezvous. What ? You not
goin' even say goodbye to your mama? No! Nile Hash, I'm
your mother. What's that you say? Goodbye, to you too, son.
Wait! Don't go yet. Sit back down and talk to your mother.
I just got a marvelous idea. Y'all can rent the other side of
my double at a cut rate. What's that? Am I sure I want to
do that? Ofcourse, I'm sure. It would be good to have y'all
in the shotgun next door. It'll give me a chance to make
sure my baby boy is alright. You know you always been my

favorite. Always have been able to count on you. Let me do this for you, please! So, what do you think? You're right, it's not such a bad idea. It's not a bad idea at all. Let me know after you tell her what we decided. We good, right? Oh, good son. We never fight. I'd hate to see somebody ruin' our relationship. Come give Mama Royal a hug. Alright, hope I didn't make you too late for your engagement.

3

"Matia," said Binta, "you got to calm down. I'm sure Nile is alright."

"But he's almost two hours late and nobody's answerin' his phone," said Matia as she peered out Binta's parent's livin' room window.

"Girl," said Binta, "I can tell you not use to dealin' with men because they are very rarely on time."

"My daddy's always on time," said Matia matter-of-factly.

"Well," said Binta, "Nile is not your daddy. Besides, Bill always runnin' late. He'll probably be late, when it come time for him to pick me up from over here by mama tonight."

"You sure y'all don't want to come to Pontchartrain Beach with us?"

"Bill is helpin' his daddy fix somethin' at the shop," said Binta. "I thought we'd be workin' on your weddin' gown until the minute Nile came to pick you up, but beading the bodice took a lot less time than I thought it would."

Matia retook her seat on the antique sofa beside an end table that held the telephone. She picked up the telephone receiver and dialed Nile's home number.

"Still no answer," said Matia.

"Call his sister," said Binta.

"I already called, Luna," said Matia. "She hasn't heard from him either."

"Stop, worryin' Matia," said Binta. "We prayed and now we just need to wait. I'm sure he'll turn up. Let's talk about somethin' else."

"Like what?"

"Like what's goin' on in the city," said Binta. "You heard about that receptionist that got killed durin' that beauty salon robbery?"

"No," said Matia frowning. "When did it happen?"

"March ninth," said Binta. "The robber ordered all twenty-five people inside to get down on the floor. Can you imagine? I don't know what the world's comin' to! I would have been beside myself f'sure."

"Is this suppose to help calm me down?"

"I guess not," said Binta.

"Let's go sit on the front porch," said Matia, making her way towards the front door. "I could use some fresh air."

"Alright," said Binta on Matia's heels.

The two friends had barely gotten settled in their seats on the porch, when Nile drove up.

"See," said Binta, "I told you everything was alright."

Matia stood up and walked quickly down the porch steps.

"How you doin', Nile," said Binta, waving at Nile.

"I'm good and you," said Nile forcing a smile as he made his way into the front yard.

"I'm alright," said Binta. "Just waitin' on Bill to get off from work."

"Nile, where were you?" asked Matia, softly. "You alright? You look like you upset about something."

"I'm goin' see y'all later," said Binta, reentering the house.

"Yeah," said Nile, lying, "I'm alright."

"What happen?"

"Nothin'," said Nile with a blasé attitude.

"Nothing?" Matia said.

"Nothin'," said Nile in annoyance.

"I've been waitin' on you for two hours," said a hurt Matia, folding her arms. "I was worried sick."

"I don't know why," said Nile, still irritated from his earlier conversation with his mother. "I'm a grown man."

"You could a called or somethin', Nile."

"I could have," said Nile, regretting his every word, "but I didn't."

Matia looked at Nile in disbelief.

"You must be drunk," Matia said, putting great emphasis on the word drunk, "talkin' to me like this."

Nile hung his head in frustration with himself. Pride and anger influenced him to resist his desire to apologize.

"I don't drink," said Nile.

"You sure?" asked Matia.

"The phone wasn't workin'," said Nile. "So, I couldn't call. Let's just go to Pontchartrain Beach!"

"Are you serious?"

"Serious about what?"

"Serious about worryin' me half to death by comin' here two hours late and with a bad attitude?"

"Nobody has an attitude," said Nile. "and you shouldn't a been worried."

"I didn't know if you were dead or alive."

"Dead or alive?" said Nile. "Girl please, I been takin' care of myself for years. I don't need nobody worryin' about me."

"I can't believe you're not even sorry about havin' me waitin' on you Nile."

"Matia," shouted Nile, "can't you just drop it. I'm here now, but I don't have to be!"

Matia looked at Nile as though he had lost all of his mind and some of hers too. She cocked her head to the side and examined his behavior while considering the facts. What was happening here? He had her waiting on him for hours and had arrived without an explanation or apology. Who had he mistaken her for? Who did he think he was, getting her all excited about spending the day with him at Pontchartrain Beach and making her believe that she had a reserved seat for life in the center of his world? Undoubtedly, he was mistaken in showing up with a nasty attitude, one that she had not been privy to before today. Who was he really? She had to wonder. Was this the true Nile Hash? Was this uncaring, selfish, bad-tempered fraud the guy that she was signing on to be with for life?

"No, Nile. You're right. You don't have to be here. You think I need you? Well, I don't. I don't need you or your nasty attitude."

As Matia spit out her last words, a pain began to swell up inside of her chest and she began to cry. She struggled to find more words and her heart began to feel like it were a swelling balloon. At any moment it would burst. The pain was swelling. It was growing, but had nowhere to go.

Nile looked at Matia and saw what he had done. He had hurt the one who his heart longed for. He had begun to erect a shallow wall between them. He had left his mother's home heated with frustration only to come to Charbonnet Street and risk the best thing that had happen to him since Jesus.

"I'm sorry," said Nile, gently grabbing Matia by her shoulders. "Really, I am."

"You should be," said Matia stiff with an unforgiveness.

"Come on Matia," said Nile, smiling. "I was a fool to trip on you like that. Will you forgive me? Please!"

Matia softened at the sight of Nile's sweet smile.

"I'll forgive you this time," said Matia. "You goin' tell me what happen?"

"It was just a little confusion with mama, that's all!"

"Confusion about what?"

"Nothin', Matia," said Nile. "It don't matter, now. I handled it."

"It does matter to me," said Matia, unfolding her arms and gently taking Nile's hands into her own, "because it mattered enough to you to upset you."

"I told her about the engagement," said Nile.

"You finally told her," said Matia, "good. What did she say?"

"She had some reservations about us gettin' married."

"Why?"

"She's only tryin' to be a good mother."

"We waited too long to tell her," said Matia. "She probably feels hurt."

"I know my mama, Matia," said Nile, "and we did ourselves a favor by waitin' to tell her."

"Why you say that?"

"More time would've just left room for more song and dance."

"Well," said Matia, "at least I'll finally get to meet her next week at Sam's engagement dinner."

"Yeah," said Nile, wrapping his arms around Matia and giving her a tender hug, "It'll all work out."

They left the yard, closing the gate behind them.

"Oh," said Nile as he opened the passenger side door of his car for Matia, "I sort of agreed that we would rent out the vacant side of her double."

"You didn't?" said Matia.

"Yeah, I did."

"Why would you do that without talkin' to me first?"

"I didn't think you'd have a problem with my findin' us a place."

"What?" said Matia. "We've been lookin' at places for over a month, tryin' to find something that we both liked. We agreed we wouldn't pick a place until we found one we agreed on."

"My point exactly," said Nile. "So, I found somethin' that we both can grow to like at a good price."

"What's the price?"

"I don't know."

"Huh?"

"Mama didn't say."

"So, how do you know we got a good price?"

"Because it's my mama and so whatever the price it'll be alright."

"Oh, I see how it's going to be."

"What does that mean?"

"What?"

"What do you mean you see how it's goin' be?"

"Nothin', Nile."

"Yeah, you meant somethin'."

"Alright, you're right," said Matia. "I did mean somethin' by it."

"I knew you did," said Nile.

"I meant that where you and your mama are concerned I'm going to be a third wheel."

"That's not true."

"It's not?"

"No, it's not."

"Then, how else could you explain choosin' our first home with her instead of me.

"Aw, girl," said Nile, "come on. I didn't choose my mama's place. It was her idea."

"Okay," said Matia, fuming, "I stand corrected. It won't be you and your mama runnin' our lives. It'll just be your mama."

"She's only tryin' to help."

"With all due respect for your mother, she's only tryin' to run our lives."

"Here you go again," said Nile, stepping back from his car and Matia. "Makin' somethin' out of nothin'. First, it was me and now it's my mama."

"So," said Matia, "you really didn't think somethin' was wrong with you standin' me up for two hours?"

"Matia, stop this," said Nile, "and you need to watch what you say about my mama."

"What is that suppose to mean?" said Matia. "I'm really not tryin' to disrespect your mother, Nile. I wouldn't do that. I just can't see myself leavin' my father's house and then havin' to move into your mother's house. I didn't agree to that."

"If you can actually manage to allow yourself to leave your father's house," said Nile.

"What?"

"You heard me."

"What do you mean by that?"

"I mean you act like you can't bear the thought of leavin' your father's home," said Nile. "I have to wonder if you will be with me while you're heart is still over here tryin' to handle what's goin' on with him on Charbonnet Street."

"Don't bring my daddy into this, Nile," said Matia. "He would've never left me waitin' on him like you did today."

"He's already in it," said Nile, "and while I have all the respect in the world for him, I don't plan on havin' him controllin' my every move in life. As you just so eloquently put it, I didn't agree to that."

"My daddy, has shown you nothing, but respect since we've been officially engaged," said Matia. "You're in no danger of havin' him run your life."

"You think so," said Nile.

"I know so," said Matia. "He respects marriage."

"Honestly, I was worried more about you than him," said Nile.

"What do you mean by that?"

"I mean if your father is a problem in our marriage it'll be because of you and not him," said Nile. "It'll be because you couldn't leave and cleave."

"And what about your mama?" said Matia. "Are you going to leave her and cleave?"

"Mama Royal won't cause no problems."

"I got news for you," said Matia, slamming the passenger door of the car without getting in the car. "She already has."

"I mean it Matia," said Nile, walking toward the driver's side of his car and pulling his car keys from his pocket. "I'm not goin' listen to you talk about my mama."

"I'm not talkin' bad about her," said Matia. "I'm just speaking the truth. You're goin' to have to tell her you made a mistake by agreein' to rent her shotgun without us talkin' about it first."

"No I'm not," said Nile, turning back towards Matia. "It won't hurt us to help her out by rentin' her place."

"Yes, it will too," said Matia. "If you are going to let her run our lives now, I won't stand a chance if we move under her roof."

"I asked you to stop with all the negative stuff about my mama."

"Are you going to say everything I say about your mama is negative even if it's true?"

"This is a waste of time," said Nile. "Are you gettin' in the car or do you want to keep arguing over our pendin' wedding plans?"

"What?" said Matia. "What do you mean by pending?"

"Pendin'," said Nile, "as in possible."

"Oh," said Matia, "so, one conversation with your mother and now our plans aren't definite."

"You know," said Nile, "maybe mama was right about our marriage. Maybe this is a mistake."

"A mistake," said Matia in shock. "What are you sayin', Nile?"

"You heard me?" said Nile. "Maybe we are rushin' into this a little too soon. I mean, I've gone out of my way to get along with your father, but you can't do this one thing for me to work things out with my mama. Honestly Matia, if you have a problem with my mama, then you have a problem with me."

"No," said Matia beside herself, "I can see now that I don't have a problem with your mama, Nile Hash."

"Good," said Nile, "let's go and get somethin' to eat because I'm starvin'."

"But I do have a problem with you," said Matia, holding back her tears and walking away from Nile and his car. "And if you're goin' to insist on stayin' your mama's little boy, you cannot be my husband."

"Matia," shouted Nile as Matia headed home.

Matia did not respond, but instead sped up her pace walking.

Binta stuck her head out her parent's front door.

"Matia where are you goin'," yelled Nile once more as Matia went up her front steps.

"Everything alright out here?" asked Binta, pretending she didn't already know the answer to her question.

Matia slammed her front door.

"It is what it is," said Nile with pain in his expression.

"Maybe you should go after her," said Binta, apprehensively.

"No," said Nile, obeying his pride, "I shouldn't!"

"Bill on his way," said Binta, extending an olive branch on Matia's behalf. "You could talk to him, if you need to talk. Maybe, he could help."

Nile looked at Binta, thoughtfully and appreciatively.

"No," said Nile, turning back towards his car, "I don't need to talk to anybody."

"You sho, Nile," said Binta, quickly descending the front porch's steps.

"Yeah," said Nile as he slid into the driver's seat of his car.

"But you do, Nile," said Binta almost running towards Nile's car and shouting as Nile started his car's engine. "You probably do need to talk."

With this, Nile sped off, leaving Binta standing alone in the remains of the bad scene that both he and Matia had just created.

4

Matia was so disturbed. She had believed that in Nile she had found a faithful and constant friend, only to learn that even their relationship had its own vulnerabilities. Surprised she was indeed and more than that she was heartbroken. She was so devastated that as she and Nile prepared to cross the very threshold that would lead them into a life joined together as one, Nile would dare invite another woman to go across their threshold with them. Even if the other woman was only his mother, Nile's behavior had thrown up a red flag that caused Matia to question his love for her. He had already begun to forget that they had proposed to commit themselves to each other and that their devotion to each other was supposed to be second only to their commitment to God. He had omitted their plans and intentions also. Replaced them with his obligation to fulfill his intentions towards another. Matia had left him standing in what at the time she had seen as his misguided good intentions. She had marched home, beside herself and had sought refuge in her bedroom, arguing her case against Nile before her just God. After pleading her case, she knelt beside her bed crying. Then, she turned on her record player. Somewhere between Aretha's crooning and Mahalia's praising, Matia had repented of her anger towards her intended, Nile.

After all, what had Nile really been guilty of?

Staring her so clearly in the face was the revelation that all Nile really had been guilty of doing was attempting to honor his mother in the same limitless way that Matia had struggled in vain to honor her father since the deaths of her mother and sister.

Nile was doing the wrong thing for all of the right reasons. It had not occurred to him that relationships with mother's or even fathers for that matter sometimes required restrictions, respectable boundaries that insured everyone's safety.

So, their own little romance and squabble aside, Matia could understand why Nile had caved into his hardworking and beloved mother's bullying. He loved his dear mother and did not want to let her down. To put it more bluntly, he could not bear the thought of failing his mother as did his father, Will Sr.

Hence, what would it cost Matia to help her well-intentioned young man in his efforts to love his mother? What would it cost her, really? Some hopes. Some dreams. Maybe it would cost her a whole lot of comfort and a little tiny bit of dignity.

Whatever the cost, Matia decided that she would work up the strength to pay the cost. She would be willing to pay a precious fee to continue to taste the sweet pleasure of her merger with Nile. She loved him that much. She loved him enough to sacrifice on his behalf. She imagined herself climbing into life's vehicle with Nile. A willing passenger, she was eager to share her life's ride with him. Without ceasing, she prayed a silent prayer that God would forever remain their driver.

5

Nile drove throughout the city for over an hour, struggling to regain his composure. His head ached as he replayed the events of his day, the latter events causing him the greatest amount of anguish. *Why was Matia so opposed to their living next door to his mother? Why was his mother so threatened by Matia's existence? Would he be forced to choose between the two women whom he loved most?*

Piano music poured from his car's speakers as Andre Crouch & The Disciples sang out in a chorus on an AM gospel station that Nile was listening to. Nile noticed that Danniebelle Hall's voice was sincere and heartfelt as she sung.

At Napoleon Avenue and South Claiborne, Nile noticed that his Malibu was running close to empty. He pulled into the parking lot of a corner gas station to get fuel, replaying the unpleasant words that he and Matia had exchanged over and over again in his troubled mind. *Maybe mama was right about our marriage! Maybe this is a mistake! Maybe we are rushing into things. As long as you are Mama Royal's little boy, you can't be my husband.* The words ricocheted through his head like ammunition, causing him great pain. Why had he allowed himself to think or say those words? He was sick with regret and as he further considered Matia's last words he realized she was right. How could he expect her to leave and cleave, if he was not willing to also?

Still, his realization aside, so many words had been said. So many unnecessary hurtful words that could not be taken back. The deed had been done. He had put his foot in his mouth and had no idea how to get it out. Less than two months before his wedding day, he had suggested to his bride to be that their wedding was a mistake. He had allowed her to believe that he was not convinced that he wanted her, when nothing could have been further from the truth. Nile pounded his steering wheel and rested his head on it. If only he could go back and fix it all. If only he could make it like it had been, when he'd first awoke, a day filled with delicious promise and anticipation for sweet moments with the woman he loved. God only knew how Matia had left their argument viewing his careless and hurtful behavior.

As Nile slid out of the driver's seat of his car, he felt the weight of the world on his shoulders. He walked up to the payment window and paid for his gas. On his way back to his car, a car full of young women drove past him, honking it's horn. Nile looked right through the car as if it were an apparition. Suddenly feeling lonely, Nile longed for Matia's presence and regretted not having her with him. He could have sworn he had caught a whiff of Matia's scent, a light fusion of fresh grapefruit and mango. When he had nearly reached his car, he heard someone call out his name. He was moving almost in a state of unconsciousness, he turned almost expecting to see Matia, but it was not Matia. As he turned, he recognized at once that it was Abecca, exiting the car full of young women that had just passed him.

"That don't look like the future Mrs. Hash to me," said Nile to himself.

Abecca waved demurely as she strutted mercilessly his way.

"Abecca?" said Nile, frowning in disbelief. He was now suddenly forced back into reality, questioning the biting irony in his running into Abecca on such a night as this one.

Why must he be tested so? He wondered. Then, he grieved over what he worried he might have lost with his precious Matia.

"Hello, Nile," said Abecca, offering a tempting smile.

"You look good," he started to say, but decided not to.

Honestly, he did notice that Abecca looked good. Perhaps, better than good. The girl that he had seen as having night for skin and running marmalade for hair looked just as painfully beautiful as ever. Her beauty remained both impenetrable and flawless. Powerful it was. As Abecca moved towards him in a short red mini dress, revealing her long bare legs, he felt noticeably uneasy with Matia still steadily on his mind.

"It's good to see you," said Abecca, closing the distance between them.

"Good to see you too," said Nile as he hurriedly rushed to pump his gas. He was unable to say what he was really thinking, that perhaps the devil himself had dressed her in tempting scarlet and deposited her in a car full of young women to torment him at this very gas station and on this very night.

Abecca reached out and gently touched Nile's forearm, squeezing it gently.

"I miss you," she said, softly.

Hearing Matia screaming, "I don't need you," Nile took steady deliberate steps back and away from Abecca.

"I owe you an apology," said Nile, clearing his throat.

Abecca was quiet, but thoughtful as she considered Nile's words.

"For what?" She said.

"You were right to call me a charlatan and a thief," said Nile. "I misled you. I took what was not mine. I stole from you."

"But I could be yours," said Abecca, closing in on Nile.

"But you're not," said Nile matter-of-factly.

"Still, I could be," said Abecca, "and you could be mine."

"I'm engaged."

"What?" said Abecca, surprised. "To who?"

"Someone, I met in the ninth ward."

Abecca sighed and shrugged her shoulders. "C'est la vie!"

"What?"

"Such is life," said Abecca. "Life is sometimes harsh but one must accept it."

"It's true," said Nile.

"When's the grand event?" asked Abecca with a strained labored smile.

"In two months," said Nile.

"How ironic," Abecca said. I'll be leaving the Paris of The South for Paris, France in two months. My parents have finally sent for me. They said something about my father having secured a well paying appointment for me. Here's to life's many birthing pangs."

"Yeah, birthing pangs," mumbled Nile, deep in thought, "and the opportunity for growth that they offer us."

Before Abecca realized what was happening, Nile was closing his gas cap and jumping back into his car.

"Have a safe trip home," said Nile as his car sped out of the parking lot.

"Adieu," said Abecca, bidding Nile a definitive and final farewell.

As he drove, he looked in his rear view mirror and saw that like a mirage Abecca had already disappeared back into the car full of women.

6

"You said what?" asked Luna, after Nile told her and Alex the sorted details of his squabble with Matia.

"I know," said Nile. "You don't have to tell me."

"What did you do after she left?" asked Alex.

"I got in my car and drove off," said Nile.

"Nile," said Alex, resting his head in his hands, "you shouldn't have left. You should have gone after her."

"You really just left things like that with her," said Luna, shaking her head in bewilderment.

"I know," said Nile ashamedly.

"Man," said Alex, "you know we love you, but wrong is wrong. You got to be willin' to let Mama Royal be mad at you, if you're goin' to stand a chance at stayin' married."

"Well," said Nile, "I don't think she'd marry me now if I was the last brother on Earth."

"Boy," said Luna, swinging at Nile playfully, "y'all goin' work this out. Especially after you explain to her just how wrong you were."

"How do I deal with her attitude about mama?"

"What attitude?" asked Luna.

"What did she say that was wrong?" asked Alex. "Sounds to me like she called it like it is. You've got to help Mama Royal cut those apron strings, if you're serious about havin' a wife."

"How do you suppose I do that?" asked Nile. "I mean, I want to do it, but how?"

"You just start cuttin'," said Alex. "You may want to start with tellin' Mama Royal that y'all not movin' into her place."

Nile sighed and shook his head.

"I'll get some scissors and show you how to if you need me to," said Luna, teasingly.

"You enjoyin' this a little too much, Luna," said Nile.

"I'm sorry," said Luna smiling warmly. "It's just so refreshin' to see you truly givin' of yourself, lovin'."

"Mama goin' hate me," said Nile chuckling.

"Join the club," said Luna, laughing. "Just kiddin', mama will be alright. She just needs a little time and a lot of fervent prayer."

"Therefore a man shall leave his father and mother and shall cleave to his wife," said Alex. "God told you what to do in Genesis Chapter Two and Verse Twenty-four."

"I can't believe she just left me standin' there callin' after her," said Nile, chuckling to himself. "Didn't know she had that kind of nerve."

"You'll learn soon enough that most women have plenty of nerve," said Alex.

"Serves you right, makin' her feel like an intruder in her own relationship," said Luna. "You not marryin' mama, Nile. You marryin' Matia. And you knew mama was wrong. Admit it, you just scared of her."

"I'm not scared of nobody, girl," said Nile.

"Oh, you not, huh?' said Luna.

"Alright," said Nile, suddenly serious, "maybe just a little bit. She can get kind of scary sometimes. Like she might kill you or somethin'."

"Yeah," said Luna, laughing, "don't I know it? She got a pretty mean right hook too."

Alex shook his head in amazement.

"Y'all crazy yeah," said Alex.

"Seriously, though," said Luna. "Mama will be mama, but she won't try to meddle in your marriage if she knows you won't let her."

"Well," said Alex, "you better get back over to Charbonnet street before it gets too late. You've got some beggin' to do."

"I don't know how," said Nile, proudly.

"You do it like this," said Alex, falling on his knees before Luna. "Luna baby, please, please, please!"

"Alright brother-in-law you can stop your beggin'," said Nile. "I get it."

All three of them laughed as Nile grabbed his keys from Alex and Luna's coffee table and headed out the front door.

"Nile," yelled Luna, rushing to her screen door, "remember one of the quickest ways to a girl from New Orleans' heart is good food. And get her some candy too, mama's boy!"

"You wrong for that," said Nile. "Y'all pray for me."

"Alright," said Luna, "but don't forget to pray for yourself."

7

When Franklin heard a car pull up outside of his house, he was relieved. Since Nile and Matia had officially announced their engagement, Franklin had grown to like Nile and looked forward to having their often lengthy discussions. Franklin set the book that he was reading, Billy Graham's *Angels: God's Secret Agents* down on the coffee table. After looking through the slightly parted curtains in his front living room window, Franklin was pleased to see that the visitor was indeed Nile. It was hard to ignore the joy that Franklin was having in his new acceptance of having Nile for a son. Thankful to see that Nile had not stayed away, Franklin opened his front door and spoke to Nile as he walked up the front steps.

"What took you so long to get here," said Franklin, looking at his wristwatch. "Y'all had y'all little argument hours ago."

"You were expectin' me?" asked Nile.

"Oh, yeah," said Franklin, chuckling to himself.

Nile entered the Singleton house with some hesitancy, unsure of where he stood. He was carrying two Burger Orleans' bags and a K & B Drugstore bag.

"So you made her mad?" said Franklin.

"Yes, sir," said Nile, handing Franklin one of the bags from Burger Orleans. "I bought you your favorite, a shrimp po-boy."

"Thank you son," said Franklin, peeping into the bag.

"Is she coming out?" asked Nile.

"Who Matia?" said Franklin, shrugging his shoulders. "She might. She's been in that room for hours, playing that record player of hers. First it was Mahalia stirring our souls and now as you can hear it is Aretha. I heard what you did."

"You did," said Nile, swallowing.

Franklin walked into the dining room and placed his food on the table. Then, he entered the hallway and knocked on Matia's bedroom door.

"Matia," shouted Franklin over Aretha's voice, winking his eye at Nile, "your fiancée's here."

Matia was silent.

"Well," said Franklin, reentering the dining room and sitting down at the head of his table, "I told her you were here."

"Yes, sir," said Nile, nodding.

"What's that in the other bags," asked Franklin.

"I got her a cheeseburger, some French fries and all the Watchamacallits they had left in K & B."

"You know my daughter," said Franklin.

"Matia," shouted Franklin from his seat in the dining room, "Nile got you your favorite from Burger Orleans and Watchamacallits too."

The music stopped, but still there was no sign of Matia.

"Give her some time," said Franklin. "She'll be out."

"You hate me, sir?"

"Hate you?" said Franklin. "Oh no, son. For what? You didn't do nothing that most men your age haven't done."

"No, sir?" asked Nile, surprised.

"No," said Franklin. "You got food in that bag for you too?"

"Yes, sir," said Nile.

"Well, have yourself a seat and eat."

"Thank you, sir," said Nile, grabbing a seat and ripping the paper wrapping off his catfish po-boy as if he were starving.

"No, son," said Franklin. "Most men end up having the "Mama Fight" with their fiancées or wives, eventually. I sure did."

"You, sir?" asked Nile.

"Yes indeed," said Franklin.

"So, Matia told you about our argument?"

"Oh, no," said Franklin. "Did I say that?"

"Yes, sir," said Nile. "You said you heard about it."

"No," said Franklin, "she told the four walls that make up her room. I just overheard it. She's been talkin' to God and fussin' about you all evening."

"I love your daughter Mr. Franklin," said Nile. "I do."

"Sure you do," said Franklin. "Just cause you two had the "Mama Fight" I'm not goin' doubt you love my daughter."

"What do you mean by the "Mama Fight" sir?"

"Oh, you know well what I mean," said Franklin. "My mama wanted to kill Safiya and Safiya wouldn't admit it, but there was a time when she thought about gettin' rid of my mama."

"I don't understand it sir," said Nile. "How can the two women who love you most make you so miserable?"

"Well, now son," said Franklin. "You're lookin' at it all wrong."

"I am?" sighed Nile, staring at Franklin.

"Yeah," said Franklin with great animation, "yes, indeed. The day you found Matia and decided you wanted to spend the rest of your life bein' married to her was the beginnin' of something new. Something new for all of us, your mama included. She fears losin' her son. But marriage requires change, you understand. Now, you goin' love and honor your mother for life, but Matia's suppose to have a place in your life unlike any other woman's."

"But I only have one mother," said Nile.

"True," said Franklin, "but if you intend to only have one wife, you goin' have to make certain that she feels second to none but God."

"I can do that," said Nile, taking a deep breath.

"It's no different from what Matia had to learn to do with me. I'm her father, but my role is changin' now that she's marryin' you."

"I love her, sir," said Nile. "It's just that I'm new to all this. I've never had to try to be transparent with another person like this."

Franklin nodded his head in agreement.

"What you know about gardenin' son?" asked Franklin.

"A little," said Nile.

"A marriage is like a garden," said Franklin.

"Oh, yeah?"

"Yes, yes," said Franklin, "you've got to remember to water it. And you have got to take time to feed it or it will die. Sometimes, no matter how much you water and feed it, you still goin' have to weed it. Like pest, people and situations show up, workin' to choke the life out of your relationship. It's the funniest thing how you can be workin' hard at havin' a healthy marriage only to have somebody try to dump the critters from their own backyard into yours."

"I never knew how much wisdom could exist in somethin' as simple as gardening."

"Yes, yes," said Franklin, nodding his head. "Another thing to remember is that just like there are no two gardens that are the same, there are no two marriages that are the same either. We try to nourish our garden or marriage with exactly what we see other people feedin' theirs with. Some of what our grandparents, parents and friends fed their marriages will not work for us. We make our first mistake by failin' to take the time to learn our relationship and find out what our marriage needs to grow. There will always be certain needs for each of our situations. This uniqueness is part of what makes each of our marriages beautiful. Sometimes, in a garden you have to work for a good while before you see the results you hoped for. Marriage can be like this. If you make up your mind to work at it, during the difficult seasons and refuse to give up, somethin' beautiful is sure to bloom. Safiya and me had some beautiful years. With her, I had a love that was so sweet. I should have a cavity!"

They heard a door open in the hall. Matia entered the dining room. Without speaking, she sat close to Nile, slid her food from the bag, and began to eat.

"Well," said Franklin, leaving his dining room table, "I'm goin' go in my home office and look over some plans, I'm workin' on.

Nile nodded his head.

"Oh, and Nile," said Franklin.

"Yes, sir?" Nile said.

"You probably know that I offered to pay for Matia to get her masters in business," said Franklin, "but she's not interested right now."

"Yes, sir?"

"For the record," said Franklin, "the same offer is available to you. We're goin' be family now and if you ever decide to go back to school, I want you to know I'll pay for it."

"I couldn't let you do that, sir," said Nile.

"Yes, you can," said Franklin. "If you can't see me doin' it for you, look at it as me doin' it for my daughter. No obligation to take the offer, just want you to know it's available if you ever want to take it."

Nile jumped to his feet and shook Mr. Franklin's hand. "Thank you, sir."

"Alright," said Franklin as he disappeared into his home office, "let me know if y'all need me."

"We will," said Nile, sitting back down beside Matia as the office door closed.

Matia looked into Nile's eyes, searchingly.

"I was wrong," said Nile, staring intently into Matia's eyes. "There's no excuse for the things I said and did."

"No," said Matia, "I was wrong. It wouldn't be the end of the world for me to do this for you, if it means that much to you. It won't kill me."

"No, no," said Nile, "In life there will be plenty of times when we'll need to make sacrifices to do what is right. This is not one of them. You were right. This was our decision to make. I was wrong. I shouldn't of tried to make the decision without you."

"It's okay with me, though. We can go on and rent your mama's place."

"Is that what you really want, Matia?"

"Honestly?"

"What else?"

"Not really."

"I know it's not. And if it won't work for you, then it won't work for me."

"Oh, Nile," said Matia. "It's been a long day."

"I know," said Nile. "I'm sorry."

"I'm sorry too, Nile," said Matia. "And even though, I didn't like the way you said it, some of what you said was true. You gave me a lot to think about."

"Please forgive me," said Nile.

"You're forgiven," said Matia, gently touching Nile's nose.

"I'll let mama know that we want to keep lookin' for our own place."

"You don't have to do that, Nile," said Matia. "If you really want to live in your mom's place, I'll live there."

"No," said Nile. "That's not what we said we wanted. So, that's not what we're goin' to do. We'll keep prayin' and lookin'."

"Thank you," said Matia, smiling.

"You are welcome," said Nile.

Nile smiled nervously and handed Matia a sheet of lavender stationary.

"What's this?" Matia said.

"A poem I wrote for our engagement dinner. After acting a fool earlier, I thought it would be more appropriate to give it to you tonight."

"You didn't have to do that, Nile."

"No, after what I said, I want to make my feelings crystal clear. I need to. Please, read it."

Matia took a deep breath and read the poem out loud. She read:

Sound Called Love

We are two colliding at the heart of love's vibration,

Too amazed to not stay.

Unable to consider running away,

We resonate musical notes of tenderness.

Our elation keeps us listening for more

In this sound called love.

My audible range gets so hazy,

From just the thought of losing you.

My heart gets so loud

With all of the beating it does for you

Please let me dwell with you perpetually

In this sound called love.

I am searching heaven's skies

For any reason not to stay,

When I recognize I already know.

I know I have found rest in you.

I know I have uncovered my residence in you.

In this sound called love.

It is clear that I am yours.

No one else could have me now.

It is true; I am yours.

No one else would matter now.

It is so surreal to feel,

What I feel for you

In this sound called love.

Every moment of each day

I pray to God that you will stay

Here with me,

Loving me

In this sound called love.

One hundred years may slip away.

Our love a melodic jubilee,

As pungent as pure sassafras,

A bond as beautiful as

The jazz musician's brass,

In this sound called love

"Oh, Nile," said Matia, swept away with emotion, "it's beautiful. I couldn't possibly love it more."

"No," said Nile, "you're the one that's beautiful and I can't wait to marry you and take you home with me."

8

New Orleans is a city built on ancient elaborate stratums of history. Layer after magnificent layer of time sits on a foundation that thrives below sea level.

If you study the past landscape of Nile and Matia's particular story, what might you find at its' origins? How does the historical topography of this romance set in New Orleans truly begin?

Could it be that some of the seed for this story came into being before 1000 BC with Native Americans living in the area and creating a route between their Bayouk Choupique, what we now call Bayou St. John, and the Mississippi River?

Can we trace some of its life's beginning to the Chitimacha being raided and enslaved by Jean-Baptiste Bienville and the French Mississippi Company upon the land that the French took and christened La Nouvelle-Orléans? Was there any seed in this story that may have been conceived in the distinctive forty-one year reign of Spain? Maybe its beginnings are somewhere within the delicate folds of the history of Native American and African relationships in Louisiana, villages and legacies that were formed as two groups of people fought to survive. Are there any traces of the Haitian patriot who even in death defeated Napoleon Bonaparte, Toussaint Louverture, or his mark on history in this story? Did Louverture's leading hundreds of thousands of enslaved people in Saint-Domingue into dogged revolts for their independence and triggering several thousands of Haitians to flee to New Orleans have any DNA in the origin of this romantic tale? Perhaps the fragments of its formation might be found in the enactment of France's Code Noir or Black Code, which took apart piece by piece the God given rights of countless African men, women and children and ordered all Jews out of France's colonies. Are there seeds of conception in the countless stories of Africans whose backs were feasted upon and whose wombs were exploited to bank untold wealth? Maybe its beginnings took form in what during the city's early history was the main neighborhood of "The Free People of Color", Faubourg Tremé, and its' Congo Square or "Place de Negres", where many Creoles of Color and enslaved men and women bought, sold, sang, danced, played instruments and captivated all with their storytelling? Can any of the beginnings of this story be traced back to the Louisiana Purchase, when Creoles of color were dispossessed of their rights, property, and fundamental freedoms, after New Orleanians started transforming into Americans and Americans started being converted into New Orleanians?

Or are the roots of my tale, Nile and Matia's love story, embedded deep within the city's largest geographical region, the New Orleans Ninth Ward?

In the 1800s before the Industrial Canal was dredged through the Ninth Ward, severing it into two separate bodies there was little distinction between the two massive masses of land. They were one body joined together. Maybe the true roots of this romance can be found in the Ninth Ward where the descendants of Native Americans, Europeans and Africans came to settle their very lives. Conceivably, it is here that the romance's objets d'art or artifacts can be unearthed.

Or credibly the story's foundation is in all of these events. Quite believably, the matter that made up the environment that gave birth to the very layers of Matia and Nile's story exists truly in all of these people, happenings and so much more.

9

After taking off from work to enjoy a leisurely day of shopping for her wedding day, Matia exited Krauss' Department Store and walked down Canal Street, gazing up and down the wide and busy thoroughfare as if she might miss something of great consequence if she failed to pay close attention. She still had fresh images of the St. Charles Streetcar in her mind from earlier in the day. As she had headed to Krauss with the Mississippi River at her back, she had stared at the streetcar. The streetcar conductor had nodded his head at her and rung his bell at pedestrians as he had driven by. Spilling from the streetcar's open windows, were the various heads and limbs of several of its' colorful passengers, along with their excited chatter and contagious laughter. The knocking and humming of the army green streetcar with blood red trimming had charged down Canal Street's median on its' metal tracks just briefly before turning back onto Saint Charles Avenue.

The day, still sunny like Sunday morning in spite of it nearing its end, seemed sacred to Matia, in light of her upcoming nuptials. In her arms, she held a large Krauss' Department Store package of white taffeta and Chantilly lace. The lace had been special ordered months earlier, when she and Binta had searched through the delicate materials, looking for the fabrics that would be the last of what they needed to complete Matia's wedding gown.

Matia turned the corner of Canal Street and N. Rampart Street. Trying not to upset her empty stomach, she struggled to ignore the mouthwatering aromas coming from the Woolworth's Diner across the street. She would be eating soon enough, she thought as she maneuvered her way through heavy bus passenger traffic, leaving the crowded and bustling corner sidewalk behind her. She strolled down North Rampart and past The New Orleans' Saenger Theatre reading signs that announced that it would be closing for renovations. At the corner of North Rampart and Iberville, she crossed the street daydreaming of the Saenger Theatre's velvet red curtains, deep dark blue ceiling and it's numerous twinkling stars.

Matia's heart delighted as she prepared herself to meet the rest of the guest at what was to be a private engagement dinner for her and Nile. Sam had invited both the betrothed and their parents to his Creole Townhouse in the French Quarter for an evening of delicacies and human amusement. As Matia turned onto Toulouse Street she quickly jumped out of the way of a little boy who was rushing past her.

"Excuse, me lady," said the boy, holding onto the shoe-strings of a pair of worn tap shoes that were dangling from his shoulders.

His brown limbs pumped hard as he dashed across the street, yelling for the bus to wait for him. Matia smiled as the bus stopped for the boy, giving him a chance to load it.

As she looked up the street, she spotted her father's 1974 silver Cadillac and Nile's royal blue Chevy Malibu parked on the side of the street in front of Sam's World. She took a deep breath as she approached the front door of the storefront. Sam's townhouse sat on the property line. The two-story stucco townhouse had a sharply slanted roof, side-gabled, with roof dormers. Sam made his home primarily on the top floor of the townhouse.

"Here I go," Matia said under her breath as she pushed the door open.

10

Upon Matia's arrival, the dinner party headed straightway up the stairs to Sam's dining room. The dining room, previously three smaller rooms, ran parallel to an open-air upstairs porch to its right. Matia, distracted by the beauty of Mama Royal, almost stumbled, while going up the stairs.

Mama Royal's skin was a lovely shade of golden apricot. Her hair a fiery red, hung down her back in long and wavy locks of hair. She wore a pink chiffon scarf in her hair. And she was unarguably an unusually beautiful woman. Wearing a lime green midi skirt with a pink satin blouse, she stood tall and shapely. Her curvy form, was the perfect natural hourglass. Something about the way she carried herself screamed, "Adore me, I'm a star!"

Matia wondered how Nile's father had managed to walk away from Mama Royal in all of her splendid glory. She was what some men dreamed of. And was it not every woman's dream from youth to capture the world as a witness to her undeniable beauty? Mama Royal was proof that "beauty" a man did not keep. Matia marveled over exactly how many extraordinarily beautiful females had probably cried themselves to sleep in their lifetimes simply because they had discovered that while most men can be captured by beauty they are incapable of being faithful to it.

"Make yourselves at home," said Sam, pointing towards his dining room. "Dinner will be ready shortly."

Upon everyone settling into the dining room, Sam and Nile disappeared back down the stairs. Franklin sat on a settee that was against the wall and mama Royal joined him.

After several moments of silence, Franklin stood and walked over to the glass paned French doors and looked out onto the porch walkway.

"Where'd the men disappear to?" asked Franklin.

"They downstairs in the kitchen," said Mama Royal, looking around the large room.

"That's right, that's right," said Franklin to himself, while examining the house, "the kitchen would have originally been downstairs."

"It's supposed to rain and get cool tonight," said Mama Royal. "Sam probably thought it would be more comfortable inside."

"So," said Nile's mother, smiling, "you're Matia."

"Yes, mam," said Matia, a little nervously.

"Well," said Mama Royal, "don't just stand there. Come on over here and give Mama Royal a big hug."

Matia gave Mama Royal a friendly hug.

"And you're the man responsible for the young woman that's done bewitched my poor son," said Mama Royal, laughing playfully.

"Bewitched?" Franklin said disapprovingly. "I don't know about that. Ain't no witches livin' in my house. Besides, I had to do everything but shoot the boy in my efforts to keep him away and I almost did just that."

Franklin returned his attention to exploring the house's design.

"What?" asked Mama Royal, the smile fading from her face.

"Mama Royal," interrupted Matia, "Nile told me you were lovely, but I had no idea how lovely."

"Matia," said Mama Royal, eating up the compliment, "compliments will get you everywhere with me, dear."

"No," said Matia, "I mean it. You are gorgeous. Isn't she daddy?"

"Huh?" Franklin asked distracted, who was staring down into the courtyard. "Yeah, you right baby. She's one beautiful cottage."

Mama Royal smirked.

"I wish I had my camera," said Franklin. "I'd ask Sam if I could take some pictures of the interior and exterior."

Matia shook her head in disbelief.

"I'm talkin' about Nile's mama, daddy," said Matia. "You'd have to know my daddy, he's in love with the history of New Orleans' architecture."

"That's alright honey," said Mama Royal, standing and walking over to Franklin. "Something's already then caught this man's eye and Mama Royal been around long enough to know that there's no use in tryin' to tear a man away from his first love. You must be into the art of buildin' construction. The style and fashion of it all gets you excited, huh?"

"Oh, yes," said Franklin, pulling a business card from his wallet and handing it to Mama Royal. "I am. Singleton & Co. soon to be Singleton & Jacobs does it all. We plan, design and build. A true builder understands that there is history all around us in every single characteristic of a structure."

"I have a double shotgun that Nile just finished helpin' me get into livin' condition," said Mama Royal. "I could use some advice on what else I could do to improve it."

"Is it still in its original condition?" asked Franklin.

"Whatcha mean by original?" asked Mama Royal. "It's was pretty run down, when I bought it."

"Is it a true shotgun double or has it been altered?" asked Franklin.

"I'm not totally sure." said Mama Royal. "I think so."

"Are the rooms arranged in a single row, without hallways?" asked Franklin.

"Yes," said Mama Royal.

"Is the livin' room at the front, with bedrooms and a kitchen behind?" asked Franklin.

"Uh, huh," said Mama Royal nodding her head.

"It still has high ceilings and a long pitched roof?" asked Franklin.

"Yeah," Mama Royal said.

"Uh, huh," said Franklin, "give me a call on Monday and I'll have my secretary set up a time for me to come and take a look at it."

"Will do," said Mama Royal pleased. "I'm glad I finally got to meet you and your lovely daughter."

"Pleased to meet you too," said Franklin, turning away from the French Doors.

"Franklin, sugar," said Mama Royal. "From what I can tell, the pleasure is truly all mine. Nile has made a fine choice in a future bride. Just fine."

"Thank you, Ms. Hash," said Matia.

"No, no, no, sugar," Nile's mother said, "Call me Mama Royal!"

"Okay," said Matia.

"A 1830s Creole Townhouse," said Franklin, "this is a fine house. Let's see. It's two floors. So, that's what? About Eighteen hundred square feet of inside living space."

Matia shrugged her shoulders, "I guess."

"Like the shotgun, these townhouses are some of the oldest buildings in New Orleans too," said Franklin, looking out of the French doors that led to the long narrow gallery porch, "admired for their balconies, courtyards, and walkways. Beautiful! Just beautiful! Safiya would have loved this house!"

"Who's Safiya?" asked Mama Royal.

"My mama," said Matia. "She passed away three years ago."

"Oh, I'm sorry to hear that," said Mama Royal.

Matia nodded in appreciation.

"Who's the Black woman on all the pictures?" asked Franklin retaking his seat on the love seat.

"That's Mrs. Elizabeth," said Matia. "Sam's late wife."

"Oh, really," said Franklin. "Sam was married to a Black woman."

"Yeah," said Mama Royal. "One of the sweetest creatures God ever did make. She was so kind to Nile. Loved him like a son. You know I sometimes worked two and three jobs tryin' to save for somethin' better. I was worried sick about Nile after my oldest son got married and joined the Navy. Sam and Elizabeth were like answered prayer. They gave him somethin' constructive and safe to do with his free time."

"Life never ceases to amaze me," said Franklin. "Just when you think you got it all figured out, life goes and throws you a curve ball."

"Lil girl," said Mama Royal sizing Matia up, "you've got a serious pair of hips on you. They what my mama, Bertha, use to call good birthin' hips f'sure."

"Good birthin' hips," echoed Nile, winking at Matia and grinning as he reentered the dining room from downstairs. "Sam has mint tea and Moselle white wine and he wants to know which each of you would prefer."

"Water will do for me," said Franklin. "Wine makes a fool of a man."

"A little bit of wine is alright every now and then," rebutted Mama Royal, waving her hand. "Tell him I'll have a little Moselle."

"Tea for me please," said Matia, rising to help Nile. "Y'all need any help down there."

"No, mam," said Nile as he headed back towards the stairs, "you just sit your pretty self down and let me take care of you. Y'all drinks are on the way."

There was a long break in the conversation and the room was filled with silence for a few moments. Then, Franklin broke the silence.

"Now," said Franklin sitting at the dining room table, "about all this talk about birthin' hips. The last thing on Matia's mind is having babies. "

"I don't know if I'd say that it's the last thing on my mind," said Matia.

"Well," said Mama Royal, "it should be. Don't want my son bitin' off more than he can chew, like that daughter of mine."

"What about your daughter?" asked Nile as he returned with the drinks.

"What about her?" asked Mama Royal. "I'll tell you. Since, she went and married that Alex, she's lost all her ambition for life."

"What?" asked Nile. "That's not true. Luna is full of life and very happy livin' hers."

"At least somebody gets to be happy," said Mama Royal. "All I know is I busted my butt workin' two and three jobs so that y'all could have more than I did. So y'all could be successful."

"And you got what you wanted," said Nile. "We all three happy and havin' success in the areas that we've chosen to seek it in."

"She still a disappointment," said Mama Royal.

"Why would you say that?" asked a frustrated Nile.

"She got married and started havin' babies instead of graduatin' from college," said Mama Royal. "That's why."

"She got married after doin' missionary work in Africa for two years," said Nile. "It's not like she didn't know what she wanted."

"Luna was a missionary?" asked Matia.

"Yeah," said Nile, "that's how she met Alex. They were both in InterVarsity Christian Fellowship at U.N.O too."

"Speakin' of knowin' what you want," said Franklin. "Nile, I was just tellin' your mother that Matia knows what she wants. And she don't want no children anytime soon."

"Is that what Matia said?" asked Nile.

"Well, no," said Franklin, "I'm sayin' it."

"Well, you never know then," said Nile, glancing at Matia.

Matia sipped some of her mint tea.

"Oh, I know," said Franklin shortly.

"Honest to God," said Sam, returning to the dining room with a platter of hot bagels, cream cheese and thinly sliced tomatoes. "I wish my Eliza and me could have kept at least one of our little babies, but every time she would conceive, the baby she would lose. Three babies it took from us, that ugly monster, Lupus."

"Oh, your late wife had Lupus," said Franklin. "I'm sorry."

"I never run out of tears," said Sam.

Matia's head began to ache, thinking on tears and babies. In her nomadic mind, she could see millions of infants at life's door, preparing for their opening to be born only to be denied entry into this life. Thinking of how she had never run out of tears, Images of Matia's sister, Sadiki, and her mother, Safiya, filled Matia's head. Absent from the night's festivities, they were the two dinner guest that she begrudged not seeing sitting at the table.

How could they be here with her one day and gone the very next?

Matia still found it hard to conceive that they were gone.

"I need to get some air," said Matia, getting up from the table.

She exited the dining room's French doors, which led her out onto the open-air porch that overlooked the courtyard. She strolled down the narrow length of the azolea until she was out of the viewing sight of the rest of the party. Sitting in a worn wooden rocker, she stared up into the star lit night. As she stared, she could hear a jazz band playing somewhere in the French Quarter. Spirited, unpredictable and intensifying sounds and rhythms filled the air of the Vieux Carre. She could hear Sadiki's startling words all over again, just as if Sadiki were still alive.

"I can't let my daddy find out about the baby," Sadiki had whispered into the telephone receiver. "He would never forgive me for bringin' shame on this family. I got ta do somethin' and I've got to do it fast."

Two days before Sadiki's death Matia had overheard Sadiki's secret. Baby-*Daddy-Never-Forgive-Family- Shame.* The six words ran together like a string of merciless music in her head, repeating in redundant cycles. Baby-*Daddy-Never- Forgive-Family- Shame.* Still, Matia had neither reached out to Sadiki nor informed their mother that Sadiki was in need of help.

Why had Matia kept silent?

She did not know. Honestly, she had no logical explanation for her inaction.

Perhaps, it was the inconspicuous resident procrastination or even his cousin indecision that led her to drag her feet with acting.

Which way should she go, which way should she go with the information she had unwittingly gathered? This was her question. And when Matia failed to answer the question in a timely manner, she was faced with the unforgiving reality that time can be indifferent in that it simply does not stand still for anything.

Oh yes, reality did come and it hit her hard, bringing that leech of a vagabond, condemnation, along with it. Condemnation had never relented in its severe attacks of Matia. It had gripped her savagely by the feet and crippled her walk. Little did she know that condemnation was the very same parasite that had moved in on the sorrowing pregnant Sadiki, choking her self-worth from her and leading her to act desperately, when in truth she was not desperate. She was merely in need of the assurance of her salvation's power and unconditional love's provision.

11

Who is he that condemneth? It is Christ that died, yea rather, that is risen again, who is even at the right hand of God, who also maketh intercession for us.

Romans 8:34

What does it mean to condemn?

In Old French it is known as condemner. To condemn or to damn is not merely to criticize, blame or attack, but to judge also. Its bearing is made most clear to me in its secular Greek origin, katakrino. Katakrino means to pass a sentence against after judging. In other words to katakrino is to inflict punishment.

Did Jesus wish to inflict punishment on the secret harboring Matia or even the unwed and pregnant Sadiki for that matter?

Everything, that it is true about Him says no. Jesus did not come to condemn the world, but to save the world. And the two sisters both believed in Him and His saving grace, having been set free. Only they did not fully understand this truth . They were not listening to the pleading words of Jesus; instead they had tuned their ears solely to the channels of condemnation.

It bears a resemblance to the caged bird that also happens to be blind. Having lost its' sight, the bird can never envision the opportunity for freedom even if the door to the birdcage has been ripped from its' hinges, leaving the bird no more imprisoned than the free flowing air of the sky.

12

Matia sobbed quietly into her hands, very nearly losing herself in despair. The cool brisk night air worked to rouse her senses and lift her spirit. The French doors opened and Nile walked out onto the azolea. As he walked towards her on the narrow porch, she struggled to pull herself together.

"You alright?" whispered Nile, as he sat down on a saddle stool beside her.

"Oh," said Matia sniffling, "I'm alright. It's just such a pretty night and with the music it seems like something out of a movie. So, romantic."

"Yeah, something's in the air," said Nile inhaling deeply.

"Bein' here with you celebratin' startin' our new life together." said Matia. "I might as well be cruisin' down the Nile in Africa. I'm so glad and wound up by it all."

"You've got me pretty excited too," said Nile, making eyes at Matia.

"Stop that," said Matia, giggling.

Nile laughed and took a long deep breath of the night air.

"There's a real nice breeze," said Nile. "A cold front must be coming through."

"Yeah," said Matia, staring off into the distance.

"You want a talk about it?" asked Nile.

"About what?"

"Whatever has you out here on this porch, cryin'."

"I'm not cryin'," said Matia.

"Girl, please," said Nile.

"Alright," said Matia, "maybe I was cryin' a little."

"About what," said Nile. "You havin' second thoughts? You don't want to marry me?"

"Nile, no. My sadness has nothing to do with you."

"Then who?"

"My sister," said Matia, suddenly aware of the fact that she had never discussed the death of her sister or mother with Nile.

"Really?" asked Nile, bracing himself. "What about her?"

"I'm sorry," said Matia, looking down, "I know I never told you about it."

"Never told me what?" asked Nile gently lifting Matia's face by her chin.

"Sadiki, my older sister, died after havin a botched up abortion," she said.

"Bill told me," said Nile, sadly.

"The doctor had a home office over on St. Maurice Street. He was doing abortions in a building behind his house. Sadiki wasn't his first victim, but she probably was his last. She didn't die until after she'd made it back home. She realized something was wrong because she was having heavy bleeding, but still hesitated to tell my mama what was goin on. Finally, when it was too little too late to help her, she went to my parent's room and spent the last few moments of her life, telling my parents about the abortion as she lay dying in my mother's arms on the floor."

Nile held Matia's hands as she spoke.

"It broke mama's heart," said Matia. "And the sorrow that filled my mama's heart on the night that Sadiki died eventually claimed mama's life too."

"I'm so sorry, Matia," said Nile. "So, sorry for what you and your father must have gone through."

"It just hardened daddy's heart," said Matia. "By the time he realized what had happened, Sadiki was dead. He's been blaming God for reducing him to a mere witness as his first born slipped away from him and out of this world, taking his wife with her."

Nile wiped tears from Matia's face with a handkerchief that he had pulled from his pocket.

"The only good thing to come out of the whole miserable situation was the arrest of the doctor," said Matia. "Sadiki did manage to tell us his name. During a police investigation, they received a tip that he had bodies under his house. They dug up his yard and found the remains of several babies, young girls and grown women. Makes me shiver just to think of it."

"Maybe tonight you shouldn't think of it," said Nile, "even though it must be hard to be celebratin your future without two of the people that you love most being here to share it with you."

"I'm getting' married in a couple of months and they should be here," said Matia, standing to her feet and grasping the wooden porch railing as if she might fall over it. "And I can't help but feel like it's my fault."

"Your fault," said Nile, shaking his head in disbelief. "Why?"

"Because I knew," said Matia. "I knew she was pregnant and I didn't do a thing about."

"How did you find out?"

"I overheard Sadiki on the telephone."

"At the time were you even sure of what you heard?" asked Nile, shaking his head in doubt. "I doubt it. How could you have been? And even if you did know that your sister was keeping this secret, it does not make you responsible for all that happen. Maybe you made a mistake by not telling, but you didn't kill nobody."

Matia looked at Nile as if unconvinced.

"He hath not dealt with us after our sins; nor rewarded us according to our iniquities," said Nile. "For as the heaven is high above the earth, *so* great is his mercy toward them that fear him. Psalm one hundred three verses ten through twelve."

"As far as the east is from the west, *so* far hath he removed our transgressions from us. Psalm one hundred three verse thirteen." said Matia, smiling faintly."

An echo of glorious laughter came from inside of the dining room.

"You know you are good for me," said Matia.

"I'd better be," said Nile, kissing Matia gently on the chin.

"And I'm not the only one," said Matia, blushing.

"No?" asked Nile.

"No," said Matia "I think my daddy's finally got the son he thought he'd never have."

"You think?"

"I know," said Matia smiling.

13

Nile and Matia reentered the dining room, taking their seats at the dinner table.

"How long before the food's ready, Sam?" asked Mama Royal.

"Not long," said Sam. "This meal you will love. I promise."

"Well," said Franklin, "we'll see about that. Love is a mighty strong word now Sam."

"Yeah, Sam," said Mama Royal, "now, you know I love you for lookin' out for my baby, but I'm a southern girl with a particular palette. I can't just eat no anything."

"I will give you what you can't resist," said Sam. "I'm a good cook, this I know. Restaurants don't interest me. Interest me good food and laughter. It reminds me of my Liza. We had what anyone would need in this life and more."

"Yeah," said Franklin. "I noticed the picture of your wife. She was a beautiful woman, if you don't mind my sayin' so."

"Oh no," said Sam, "say so. Say so, my friend. It is true. Liza was gorgeous."

"So," said Mama Royal, consciously interrupting the conversation, "what's on the menu for tonight?"

"Well," said Sam, "to start we have these bagels with cream cheese and tomatoes. "Try some."

Nile picked up the platter and began to pass it around the table.

"Then we'll have stuffed cabbage and beef brisket for the main course," said Sam, getting a bagel. "We'll follow that up with Apple Cake for the dessert."

"Now, what's stuffed cabbage, Sam?" asked Mama Royal, spreading cream cheese on her bagel. "I love boiled cabbage, but I never had it stuffed."

"It's cabbage leaves stuffed with sweet and sour meatballs," said Sam.

"Sounds delicious," said Matia.

"I love a good beef brisket," said Franklin. "My wife, Safiya, use to cook it on Thursdays."

"She did," said Matia, thinking, "every Thursday. She sure did."

"So, do you eat strictly uh, what do they call it?" asked Franklin. "I forget the word."

"Kosher?" asked Matia.

"Yes, that's right," said Franklin, "kosher."

"I try to, but not out of necessity, bein' that I'm messi-anic," said Sam, "but out of respect for my culture. You do realize that much of what I eat is not entirely unique to my culture?"

"Really?" asked Mama Royal.

"Yes," said Sam, "my recipes are a mixture of cookin' from the places that my people have lived throughout the centuries and dietary laws shape the recipes very much."

"Yeah," said Mama Royal, "history sure has a way of leavin' its mark on people. Colored people have grown accustomed to eatin' certain foods mostly because of slavery and how they ancestors had to make miracles out of what little they had to eat despite all their unbelievably hard work. My daddy, Jesse James, use to tell us that his grandmother use to tell of how she and other enslaved men and women were rationed a half pound of pork every day along with a little rice. She said they use to catch seafood and animals to supplement their own diets, whenever they could manage to get hold of the time to. People don't realize how much food was used to control and punish enslaved colored people, since the folk runnin' slavery couldn't afford to accept slaves becoming self-sufficient."

It was quiet for several moments.

"One thing hasn't changed since slavery," said Nile.

"What's that?" Franklin asked.

"In Louisiana we still eat rice with everything."

Everyone laughed.

"It's true," said Sam.

"So," said Franklin, "you say you're messianic?"

"Yes," said Sam.

"What does that mean?" asked Mama Royal.

"It means a lot," said Sam, "but I think you'll understand best if I say that it means I'm a Jew who believes that Jesus is the Messiah."

"If that don't beat all," said Franklin. "A Jewish Christian."

"The very first Christians, Jews they were," said Sam.

"Yes," said Matia, "they were."

"That's right," said Franklin, " and so was Jesus."

"Well, now y'all," said Mama Royal, "we've covered food and religion. Let's talk politics."

"Let's talk," said Franklin.

"Politics are just another one of man's games," said Nile.

"According to you," said Sam, shaking his head disagreeably.

"What you don't believe in the political system, son?" asked Franklin.

"Oh, I believe," said Nile. "I believe that most politicians play a good game and we the people often lose it."

"But you do vote, Nile," said Matia.

"Yeah, I vote," said Nile. "I always do. I voted for Morial. Every now and then, someone special comes along in history that has the heart to make a crucial difference and they do. I think he will."

"What y'all two think about our new mayor?" asked Mama Royal, addressing Franklin and Sam.

"Who Morial?" asked Franklin.

"Yeah, Morial," asked Mama Royal.

"He beat Councilman DiRosa by sixty-two hundred votes during the elections last October," said Sam. "Remarkable, you got to admit."

"Yeah," said Franklin, "Dutch was president of our local chapter of the NAACP in the sixties. It's real good to see him, the first person of color to hold the office of mayor in New Orleans' history, win this election!"

"Yeah," said Nile, "he sure will be makin' history on May first. To tell the truth he's already made history."

"Oh, just think Nile," said Matia. "The weekend before the mayor's inauguration, we will be makin' our own history."

14

After dinner, Sam led his guest through the upstairs gallery to his sitting room.

"That was tasty," said Matia.

"Yeah, Sam," said Franklin, "you'll have to give me your brisket recipe. I never could get mine anywhere near as good as Safiya use to make hers."

"It was my Liza's," said Sam. "If you'd like, I'll write it down for you before you leave."

"Thank you Sam," said Franklin, patting Sam on the back. "That's fine of you."

"It's nothing," said Sam.

Sam went over to his record player and put a record on to play.

A gong banged, resonating beautifully. Then a saxophone echoed, backed by the subtle flow of cascading cymbals. A bass violin joined in. A congregation of sounds met and parted repeatedly. Highs and lows both bowed to and retreated from each other. Everyone in the sitting room was suddenly elevated to a higher level.

"That's *Coltrane*," said Franklin, awed.

"You're familiar with this, then?" asked Sam.

"I'd know this album was playin' even if I was deaf," said Franklin. "I believe it will be remembered as one of the greatest jazz albums ever."

"My Liza was in love with this album concerning the subject of love," said Sam.

"Just what kind of love is worth the trouble, anyway?" protested Mama Royal, bitterly.

"Agape love maybe," said Nile, smiling, "the unselfish love of God."

"A love most unadulterated," said Sam, nodding in agreement.

Mama Royal smiled, bopping her head and tapping her fingers on the coffee table.

"Yes," said Sam, "I think Jazz is a fitting acclaim to God."

"Really?" asked Franklin. "I don't know. I do think I hear a struggle with the significance of the human existence in most Jazz."

Sam nodded. "Yes, me too and I'm reminded that we are all recipients of God's kindness, lost and searching to find the only truth that'll ever matter to any of us."

"I think the way some people use their gifts is a form of worship," said Franklin.

"It could be," said Sam. "We all want to worship God once we see Him."

"If we are truly blessed to recognize Him," said Franklin, thinking over the last couple of years of his life. "Yes, then we want to thank Him. Sam, I think somehow I lost sight of

Him for a little while. Sometimes you can be so busy looking back at what you've lost, you can't begin to see what's staring you in the face."

"Yes," said Sam, "I know it."

"Listen to the overture of percussion," said Sam. "This was Eliza's favorite part."

"Um, that's nice Sam," said Mama Royal snapping her fingers and rocking.

"Yes, it is," said Matia, staring out of the glass panes of the French doors.

It was now raining outside. Matia's soul soaring to a new level, she was feeling revived. Sanctified raindrops washed her cares away, helping to cleanse her thoughts of any fear.

"I'd like to make a request," said Nile, taking Matia by the hands.

"Yes?" Sam asked.

"Play Pops' singin' his love song to New Orleans," said Nile. "I'd like to dance with my future bride. She my New Orleans made flesh because when I'm with her, I'm always home."

Matia turned red and smiled.

"You mean, Louis?" asked Sam.

"Yeah," said Nile. "Play Satchmo for me, Sam."

"Of course, of course," said Sam. "I'll play him."

When Coltrane was finished, Sam played Louis Armstrong.

Nile and Matia moved towards each other, becoming one. As they held onto each other dancing, they became love.

"I first heard this song in a movie," said Mama Royal.

"Yes, that's right," said Sam.

"Louis played his trumpet," said Mama Royal, shimmying and laughing softly, "and Billie sung."

"Take a look at those two," said Sam, staring at Nile and Matia dancing as if they were alone in the room. "What I'd give to go back and have just one moment like that with my Liza."

Franklin nodded in agreement and sighed, remembering Safiya's smile.

"They don't look like they have a care in this world," said Mama Royal.

"Not one," said Sam, smiling.

"I'm glad I finally came around with those two," said Franklin.

As the song neared its end, Sam moved over towards the record player. After removing the needle, he addressed his guest.

"Well, I'm glad dinner has been a success," said Sam, "but as the unofficial adopted father of the groom, I have something else up my sleeve."

"What's that Sam?" asked Nile, barely able to tear his eyes off Matia.

Sam took a wooden and rectangular box from a cherry curio with glass shelves. Pensively, he moved to the middle of the room and began to speak.

"Fifteen years ago my wife, Liza, and I lost our third son to a miscarriage. Eliza had been terribly sad and no matter how much I tried, I could not console her. After a few weeks of tryin' to be strong for her, I blew my top and flew out of here enraged, shakin' my fist at God. My God, He who never fails, was listenin' and as I walked through the Quarter, I cried out to Him. 'Why,' I asked, 'Why not even one little son for

Liza and me to love and teach the ways of God?' after that I walked for over two hours. Finally, I crossed Bourbon Street. And as I crossed, I saw three little boys, street tap dancers they were, arguing over their share of the money that they'd collected from persons walkin' by as they danced. 'Equally,' reasoned the tallest boy, 'We split the money equally,' then he patted the angriest boy on the shoulder. After observin' them for several moments, I continued along my way, walkin' down Toulouse Street. Look at him, a healthy and honest boy. Would it be too much to bless my Liza and me with such a boy? I felt wretched and full of despair that evening. I was secretly prayin' that if God would not hear my prayer, he could at least open up the ground and let it swallow me live. But then the most unlikely thing happen. As I prayerfully asked why not a boy like this for me over and over again, I heard a still voice from within me. It was almost like a thought that I knew I did not have. Someone else was thinkin' or speakin' to me. 'Sam, why not you and Elizabeth?' said the still voice, 'Why can't you love and teach such a boy as this?' Instantly, I was turnin' around and runnin' back towards Bourbon Street, praying I was not too late. As I approached the street, I could see the tallest boy countin' out money to the other two boys. As I neared them, the taller of the boys, Nile, swung his tap shoes over his shoulders and turned to walk my way."

"You asked me if I liked fish," said Nile.

"And you said if it was battered well and fried," said Sam to Nile.

Sam refocused his attention back on the rest of his guest.

"Then I offered Nile a job workin' in our fish shop on Toulouse, helpin' Liza, while I got our second shop up and runnin' on North Rampart Street. After a few moments of discussin' the particulars, Nile had himself a new situation and I had myself, a son."

Touched deeply, Franklin hung his head back and visualized what he'd just heard. Perhaps, he and Sam were more alike than different.

"What a sweet sweet story," said Matia, gently touching Nile's arm.

Mama Royal wiped tears from her eyes and nodded in private agreement with Matia.

Sam cleared his throat and wiped the sweat from his brow with a handkerchief that he'd pulled from his pants' pocket.

"It has always been said that Liza loved Nile like a son. But what is true is that Elizabeth loved Nile with the love that she had stowed away for three sons. Liza knew that she had not given birth to Nile and she admired Royal as Nile's only birth mother, but in the end both Royal and Liza agreed that God had brought Nile into the lives of the Friedman's for the betterment of everyone involved. When Liza went to be with God she left somethin' in her last will and testament on Nile's behalf."

Mama Royal gasped and sat up straight.

"What?" Nile said in disbelief. "She already gave me so much in the way she loved and accepted me. I don't need nothin' else."

"Please," Sam said to Nile, "listen. For years you remember you accompanied me to North Rampart Street in the upper ninth ward?"

"Yes," said Nile, "in Bywater."

"We went to Liza's Single-Plus-Sidehall Shotgun to do repairs," said Sam. "It was the first ever property she considered and bought."

"What's a Single-Plus Sidehall?" said Matia.

"It's a double shotgun," said Franklin with excitement, "but one side is a single shotgun and the other side is a side-hall shotgun with an interior hallway or exterior porch. So, that you can have private access to each room."

"Yes," said Sam, "and this single plus sidehall cottage is your inheritance from Elizabeth, Nile. She wanted you to receive it upon your takin' a bride or on your twenty fifth birthday, whichever came first."

Still in disbelief, Nile stared at Sam, shaking his head in uncertainty.

"How incredibly thoughtful," said Matia.

"A house?" Nile asked.

"That's nice," said Franklin.

"Yes," said Sam, smiling, "and I must say that it is a very lovely house that is in mint condition. Nile has helped me see to that over the years."

"You're serious Sam?" asked Mama Royal. "Elizabeth went and left Nile a whole house?"

"Yes," said Sam, "and even more than that it is a double and provides opportunity for extra income. The kind of extra income a young family just startin' out could use."

"Yes indeed," said Franklin, rising and walking over to Nile to shake his hand. "Congratulations son, you are now a property owner. That means you have collateral, an asset, and some financial security to start out with."

Franklin walked over to Sam and shook his hand, before returning to his seat.

"I can't take Ms. Eliza's house," blurted out Nile.

"What?" asked Sam.

"You can't?" said Franklin, the smile quickly fading from his face.

"Why you can't?" Mama Royal said.

"Ms. Liza's given me so much already," said Nile. "I don't know if I feel right about takin' her house."

Matia held onto Nile's arm, showing him her support.

"Maybe you and Matia ought to talk about this before you turn it down, son," said Mama Royal, "since y'all been havin' trouble makin' up y'all minds about a home."

"Good idea," said Franklin. "Matia, why don't you talk to the boy about this."

"There is nothin' to talk about," said Sam, opening the box and removing its' contents. "The house is yours. It says so in this will. Here in my hands is the deed."

"Sam," said Nile, apologetically. "Try to understand…"

No, Nile," interrupted Sam, "it is you who must try to understand. The husband is expected to provide a home for his wife. If you don't want to live there, so be it. The house is a gift and comes with no strings. It is your house. Rent it. Sell it. Give it away, if you'd like. Just please don't say that you will not accept it because Liza left it in pure love for you."

Nile stood up and walked over to Sam.

"Sam?" Nile said.

"For you to reject this gift," said Sam slapping his chest with an open hand and watery eyes, "is to reject both Elizabeth's love and her last wishes."

"Sam," said Nile.

"The only thing that I should hear from you is…"

"Thank you," said Nile, interrupting Sam and hugging him, "thank you, Sam."

PART NINE

BIRTH

1

The smell of paint was strong in the North Rampart Sidehall Shotgun house. Matia spun around in the living room of what would soon be her new home, trying not to breathe in the paint fumes as her eyes drank in the glorious colors that she and Nile were washing the walls with. Almost dizzy from both excitement and the fresh scent of paint, Matia crept outside to the front steps of the double. The evening sun was setting, stretching a lavender and mango tinted canvass across the city's skyline. Matia leaned against the ornament and black wrought iron fence railing. Slowly, she slid down it and took a seat on the concrete porch steps.

Unexpectedly, the front door across the street opened. A man and woman appeared in the doorway of a double shotgun house that had been converted into a single family home. The ebony woman noticeably attractive and in her prime embraced the white olive colored man. Middle-aged and handsome, the man was dressed rather conservatively. They kissed briefly before the man slid into the driver's seat of his sports car and drove off. He did however take the time to glance at Matia, offering her a quick but friendly wave. The ebony colored woman slammed her door and a moment later was peeking at Matia through a front window. Matia smiled and waved only to have the woman roll her eyes and close her curtain.

"Marylyn's always like dat, 'sha'," said a voice from behind. "She thinks every woman who see Mario want him because he's Italian. Mario's no Don Juan, though."

Almost startled, Matia turned to her right and looked up to see a pregnant young woman standing in the doorway of the single shotgun next door. Her dark sable hair hung in tiered layers framing her rosy white face.

"Oh," said Matia, "I didn't know anyone was standin' there."

"Don't mind me," said the woman. "I'm always standin' in a doorway and watchin' what's goin' on."

"Oh," said Matia laughing, "at least you're honest."

"My name's Adele Olivier," said the woman.

"How you doin' Adele," said Matia.

"Oh, good," said Adele.

Matia nodded and smiled.

"What you?" Adele asked mater-of-factly.

"What?" Matia said, frowning slightly.

"What are you?" Adele repeated.

"What you mean?"

"I mean, you Creole or somethin'?"

"No," said Matia, "not to my knowledge."

"What are you, then?" Adele said.

"I'm Black," Matia said, with poise.

"Aw, *'sha'*," Adele said. "I figured you was a mutt like the rest of us in this world. You know I've always believed that most of us was a mixture of this or dat."

"You're probably right about most people bein' a mixture of this or that," said Matia, "but what I know for sure is that I'm Black."

"My mother's Italian, German and Irish and my father's Cajun French just like my husband, Paul. Paul and me moved to New Orleans about three in half years ago when my Paul came to town to study mathematics at the university."

"Oh, yeah, which university is that?" Matia said, standing up and turning to face Adele.

"UNO," said Adele.

"Matia nodded her head in recognition. "Oh, UNO."

"Y'all must be the new tenants the old man been gettin' the sidehall shotgun double ready for," said Adele, rubbing her belly. "I wish he'd a asked us if we wanted to rent it. I had my mind on rentin' it since day one and dat's for true."

"Oh, we're not rentin'," said Matia. "We're the new owners."

"For true?" Adele said stony-faced, shooting a sideways glance at the Sidehall.

Matia was about to speak, when Adele started up again.

"You tellin' me the old man went and sold the sidehall double without tellin' anybody?" Adele said coming back to life. "It's been empty since we moved onto North Rampart Street. Seemed like every few months he had somebody remodelin' somethin'."

Matia was about to explain that they had not purchased the sidehall double and that it had been an inheritance, when she decided against it. Considering that telling Adele would be like putting an advertisement in *The Times Picayune*, Matia continued listening in silence.

"Well, it's a mystery how the old man kept that from me. He don't hardly like to tell any of his business. Dat's a drawback for me. If you want to know what's happenin' on our block, I'm the one to talk to, dat is for true. Marilyn and Mario been livin' across the street for two years. They don't get too many visitors on account of both their families' havin' a problem with their mixed marriage. On the right of Marylyn and Mario's house from where we're standin' are the Dorsey sisters, they two Black widows both gettin' on in

age. The oldest one of them is sickly and the younger one
takes care of her. Dey make the prettiest quilts I ever did
see. They sell em too at one hundred dollars a pop. They
real nice people. Though, every time I try to bring them a
pot of some of my food they pretend they too sick to eat any
of it. I don't think they trust my cookin'. To the Dorsey sister's right is Leon. I can't figure if he's Black, White, Cuban
or somethin' in between, but I can tell ya he's got more
women comin' in and out of dat house of his than the law
should allow. Sometimes, two or three on the same day. To
Marilyn and Mario's left are Mr. and Mrs. Bordelon. They
Irish and own that double shotgun to their left and on the
corner. They usually rent it out to students from the university. He from Saint Bernard Parish and is uncommonly
kind for a man. His wife is not from Louisiana and she think
she's better than us "Backward Louisiana Folk", if you know
what I mean. She also thinks she owns our block just cuz
her husband's family has a good bit of money and has been
in the house for over eighty years. On our side of the street
and to your right is Mr. Dupree. He Cajun like my Paul and
me. He's a real nice old man too. Talks up a storm and
always askin' me what I cooked. Next to him and on the
corner is Ms. Camellia. She's afraid of White men, pigeons,
children, Black people, music and police sirens, poor thing.
Don't know much more about her, except she loves to eat
my duck and andouille jambalaya and shrimp risotto. To
the left of us is Koolaid and Tasha. Koolaid is Korean and
Tasha's Black. They have the two cutest little baby girls and
dat's for true. On the corner to our left are Mr. Jack and
his wife, Marshmallow. And just like the English nursery
rhyme, he don't look like he eat nothin' fattenin' and his

wife don't look like she ever stops eatin' it. I don't know for sure what they are, though they do have strong English features."

"And his name is really Jack?" Matia said in disbelief.

"Oh no," said Adele, "Mr. Jack's not his real name. I just call him dat. His real name is Mr. Bacon. He's about six feet tall and looks like the wind could knock him down without even tryin' and his wife, Sugar, is real plump, white and round like a jumbo marshmallow."

Matia shook her head and laughed at Adele's animation.

"Hey, 'sha'," said Adele. "What you think about President Carter postponin' them makin' dat neutron bomb? I was just watchin' channel six news and they were talkin' about it."

"I'm not too sure what the world needs right now is another bomb, Adele," said Matia. "But what do I know about it?"

"It kills me how we'll spend millions of dollars on figurin' out ways to kill people, but always say we can't afford to save the life of one who's on the breadline."

"It's the human condition," said Matia. "People invest in what they value. It just so happens that we don't happen to value ourselves very much."

"Noel, one of my fellow parishioners down at Saint Cecilia's, says it's because of sin."

"Yeah," said Matia, "all some of us know how to do is sin. But everybody sin, Adele, that's why the world needs the Savior."

Adele nodded in agreement.

"I'd rather be dead to sinnin', than livin' and dyin' in it," said Matia.

"Me too, *'sha',*" said Adele. "Like Solomon said in Ecclesiastics nine and four, I'd choose the life of a livin' dog over dat of a dead lion any day."

Matia laughed and shook her head in amusement.

Adele smiled.

"I like you," said Matia.

"Me too, *'sha',*" said Adele. "I like me too and I like you!"

Adele frowned and rubbed her belly. "My baby, he just kicked me."

"Oh, it's a boy! How many months is he?" Matia said, glancing at Adele's belly.

"Seven," said Adele, still rubbing her belly.

"You're carryin' your baby well," said Matia.

"Thank ya, *'sha'.*"

"Well," said Matia. "I'm glad to meet you, Adele."

"Hey, you never told me your name," said Adele.

"I'm Matia Singleton."

"Nice to meet you, Matia," said Adele. "You got any babies?"

"Not yet," said Matia. "We're gettin' married next weekend, though."

"Oh, congratulations," said Adele.

"Thank you," said Matia.

"Excuse me, Matia," said Nile, sticking his head out of the front door. "I think we're finished paintin' for today. You want to go grab somethin' to eat?"

"Sounds good to me," said Matia.

"How you doin'?" said Nile to Adele.

"Oh, I'm alright," said Adele, smiling and still rubbing her stomach.

"Oh, Nile," said Matia, turning towards Nile, "Adele and her husband, Paul, live next door."

"I've seen you before with the old man," said Adele.

"The old man's like a father to me," said Nile. "His name's Friedman."

"Oh," said Adele, mumbling to herself, "Now, why didn't I know that?"

Nile shrugged his shoulders. "I don't know."

Matia giggled.

"I guess I'll go on and lock up, then," said Nile to Matia.

"Alright," said Matia smiling, "I'm goin' say goodnight, Adele. Take care of that precious little baby boy of yours and his mama."

"Goodnight, *'sha',*" said Adele. "Time for me to go make do do. That's get some sleep in case you don't know."

Matia smiled. "Yeah, I know."

An orange Chevy Impala packed full of colorful women and men drove past slowly, honking and parking across the street. Afro-Cuban rumba music, laughter and a mixture of Spanish and English poured from the car's windows.

"How ya doin' Leon," shouted Adele, waving curtly at the driver of the Impala.

"That's Leon and his friends," said Adele to Matia in passing before she shut her front door.

Matia waved too and with a west wind to her back reentered the sidehall, leaving the many shades of color and the echo of the rumba that filled the street behind her.

Leon and his friends climbed out of his Impala, stirring like captivating musical notes and floating up the front stairs of his Shotgun, disappearing inside.

2

"What's happenin' y'all," said Bill sidling up beside Nile and his older brother, Will, and Lexington and his older brother Maris, catching them off guard.

Everyone greeted Bill.

"I wasn't too sure you'd choose us over Binta tonight," said Nile, laughing and dapping Bill off almost mechanically.

"You know I almost didn't," said Bill, laughing. "Married life is suitin' me fine."

"What's up Bill, man," said Will. "Long time no see. You look taller, man."

"How ya doin', Will," said Bill. "I probably did get taller since you saw me"

"Where everybody at?" Maris said, looking at his sport's watch. "I'm ready to play some basketball."

"Alex and some of the guys from our men's bible study are on their way," said Nile.

"Who's playin' on our team?" Bill said.

"It's you, Will, me, Lexington and Maris against Alex, Khalil, Mac, Leroy and August," said Nile.

"Men's bible study," said Maris under his breath.

"Yeah," said Lexington, "that's what he said."

"Didn't I just meet August for the first time?" Bill asked.

"Yeah," said Nile, "he came with Alex and Khalil to help us move furniture into my house on North Rampart last week."

"Oh, that's right," said Bill. "He's the cat with the bad Mustang."

"Yeah," said Nile, laughing, "that's August."

"Alright my brothers," said Alex, as he approached Nile and the rest of the guys. "For those who don't know this here is August, Khalil, Mac and Leroy."

"What's happenin' everybody," said Bill, nodding.

"How y'all doin'," said Will, Lexington and Maris in unison.

"Alright," said Leroy, nodding his head.

Khalil, August and Mac nodded their heads in recognition.

"What's goin' on August my man," said Nile, nodding at August.

"Nothing much," said August dapping off Nile.

Nile dapped off all of the new arrivals. "Appreciate y'all all makin' it."

"What's happenin', podna," said Bill, nodding at August. "You remember me don't ya?"

"That's right," said August. "I remember meetin' you man. You're the mechanic whose married to a queen named Binta."

Alex laughed.

"This brother never stops talkin' about his woman," said Nile.

"That's a good thing," insisted Alex.

"Yeah you right," said Bill to Alex, nodding his head.

"I'm so glad y'all came out for my celebration for my big day tomorrow."

"Man," Maris declared looking grimly, "I never miss a funeral."

"What you talkin' about Maris?" Lexington said. "Nobody died. I told ya Nile's gettin' married."

"Like I said I'm here because I never miss a funeral," said Maris. "Get ready to say goodbye to the Nile we all once knew and loved."

Everyone laughed.

"There's some truth to that," said Alex, smiling. "Marriage does bring about some change, good change."

"Alright, alright," interjected Bill bouncing his basketball, "enough with the salutations. I thought we came to play some basketball."

"No need in rushin'," said Alex, chuckling. "You just rushin' yourself into a good old-fashioned butt whippin'."

"We'll see old man," said Bill laughing. "We'll see."

"Old man?" Nile said. "You heard that Alex. Just cuz you got seven years on him, he called you a old man."

"I better make him eat those words, huh, brother-in-law," said Alex, smiling.

"You better at least make him wish he could," said Will, laughing.

"Alright now preacher," said Bill, jokingly. "Don't go askin' God for any special favors because then the cards will be stacked against me and that wouldn't be fair."

"God never said He was fair," said Alex, smiling.

3

"That was a good ball game," said Lexington as he shut his car door.

"Yeah," said Bill, walking from his truck over to Lexington, "especially since we whipped the good reverend's butt."

"The good reverend nearly whipped our butts," said Lexington.

"The good reverend?" Maris said as the three men approached Alex and Luna's house. "What reverend?"

"That reverend," said Bill, pointing at Alex who was unlocking his front door with Mac, Will, August, Khalil and Leroy not far behind him.

Nile was walking towards Bill.

"What?" Maris yelled. "You didn't tell me the bachelor party was goin' be at no preacher's house."

"Who said it was a bachelor party?" Nile said. "It's a celebration."

"Yeah," said Lexington, "and don't worry. Alex is alright! He don't bite."

"Still," said Maris, "a preacher!"

"What you afraid of?" Bill asked. "You got somethin' against ministers?"

"No," said Lexington laughing, "he's got somethin' against anyone who might have somethin' against him doin' wrong."

"Oh, alright," said Bill, laughing.

4

"How are the children?" Will asked Alex. "I haven't seen my nephews in over three years. I can't wait to see how big they've gotten."

"Has it been that long?" Alex asked.

"Yeah, brother-in-law," said Will. "It's been that long, since I've seen my nephews. With me servin' at sea so much, I've missed a lot of what was goin' on at home with Queenie in D.C. and all y'all back here in New Orleans."

"The boys are just fine," said Alex. "They just made ten last month. They both still playin' the saxophone and I help coach their baseball team. They've both got strong pitching arms."

"Man, that's alright," said Will. "I honestly haven't been able to spend as much time as I'd like to with my children. I'm lookin' forward to servin' on base instead of at sea this year. It'll be good for the children, Queenie and me. It can be hard on the family, my bein' away for long periods of time."

"I know," said Alex thoughtfully. "I know."

"This food smells good," said Will, grabbing a breast and wing to put on his plate. "I see my baby sister still can cook."

"Yeah," said Leroy, "my wife hasn't cooked a good hot meal in over a week. Talkin' bout she too tired and can I go get her a hot sausage poboy."

"Hey, Leroy, man," said Nile. "Your wife, Ella, is eight in half months pregnant!"

"I know," said Leroy. "You'd think she'd be hungry enough to get in the kitchen and cook."

"What I think is that you need to get your butt in the kitchen and fix your pregnant wife a hot sausage sandwich, if she needs ya too," said Alex.

Leroy grunted. "You think so, Alex?"

Alex nodded. "I think so."

Nile sat at Alex and Luna's dining room table with his friends and Alex, eating and talking. Luna who was visiting Mama Royal with the boys had baked two seven up cakes, a sweet potato pie and a pan of macaroni and cheese. She had also fried some chicken, whipped up some potato salad and thrown together a cucumber, tomato, and lettuce salad. Nile was keyed up and looked intently out of the dining room window into the garden, anticipating the joy that his wedding day would bring.

"Are you scared?" Maris said.

"Scared?" Nile said. "No way, man!"

"I was scared as Hell," said Maris, remembering he was in the home of a preacher as the words slid out of his mouth. "Oh, sorry."

"It's alright Maris," said Alex. "Hell is a word worth mentioning. Was your fear of marriage equal to your fear of Hell?"

"Yes, indeed," said Maris. "Still is! You haven't experienced the likes of Hell until you've had to face my wife Evon after comin' home four hours late from work."

"If you brought your behind home after work sometime, everything with Evon would be alright," said Lexington, disapprovingly.

"You my brother," said Maris to Lexington. "You suppose to be on my side."

"You not even on your own side, Maris," said Lexington, laughing. "Besides Evon's a good woman. She's stood by you. You should treat her right."

"Well," said Maris, "at least Evon never had my nose wide open like Shallow had yours."

"Had?" said Bill, sarcastically.

"Whoa," said Nile, chuckling. "Y'all goin' spoil my celebration."

"Who's Shallow?" Alex said.

"You met her Alex," said Nile. "She's our wedding planner, one of Matia's closest friends."

"The taller one," said Alex.

"Yeah, yeah," said Bill, "my baby Binta's the shorter one."

"Yeah," said Nile, "short and pregnant with twins."

"That's right," said Alex. "Congratulations are in order here, Bill. I know you excited about becomin' a father!"

"Excited and scared half to death," said Bill, laughing.

Everyone laughed out loud.

"Just be thankful you not married to Shallow," said Maris.

"Oh, yeah," said Alex, questioningly, "Shallow seems like she can hold her on."

"Her own and mine's too," said Lexington. "That's part of what I love about her. I always wanted to be the one to help her carry her load in life."

"I thought Nile said you were gettin' married to someone named Celeste," said Alex, scratching his head.

Maris cleared his throat and started laughing. "He is!"

"I am," said Lexington in agreement as he bit into a leg of chicken.

"But you just said you're in love with Matia's friend, Shallow?" Khalil said.

"Yeah," said Lexington, "but it's not as bad as it sounds, y'all."

"How bad is bad?" Alex said.

"Shallow isn't interested in marryin' me," said Lexington clearing his throat, nervously, "and Celeste who knows all about Shallow is both in love with me and willin' to spend her life with me."

"Oh," said Alex, arching his eyebrows.

"You understand now," Lexington said.

Alex smiled shrewdly.

"I understand," said Alex. "You willin' to allow Celeste to mess up her life by settlin' for less than she deserves."

"Huh?" said Lexington. "I didn't say that, Alex."

"You did," said Khalil. "You said ya love Shallow, but ya marryin' Celeste cuz ya can't have Shallow. That means ya just usin' Celeste and would drop her like a hot potato if ya could have Shallow."

"Celeste don't mind how I feel," said Lexington.

"Ah, my brother," said Leroy, "but you should."

"Why should he?" Bill said. "Don't the brother deserve a chance at happiness?"

"We all do," said Alex, "but at what cost? Nobody should be willin' to build their hopes and dreams on someone else's pile of misfortunes. Anybody who understands women will tell you that even if Celeste says she don't mind you not lovin' her today, she will tomorrow. Why shouldn't she mind? What you're suggestin' is imbalanced. It won't work. One day she'll wake up bitter and blame you for ruinin' her life."

"Nile?" said Lexington. "What do you think?"

"I don't know Lex man," said Nile. "I didn't realize you were still in love with Shallow. I thought you're proposal to Celeste meant you'd finally gotten over Shallow."

"I hoped it would do the trick," said Lexington, "but no cigar! I do care very deeply for Celeste, though. With time, I believe I could grow to love her."

"When's your weddin'?" Leroy said.

"In October," said Lexington.

"Y'all gettin' any marriage counseling," Alex said. "Who's performin' the ceremony?"

"We're plannin' on havin' the weddin' at the Saint Louis Cathedral," said Lexington, "but we are supposed to start meetin' with my priest over at Corpus Christi Church soon."

"I can't tell you what to do, man," said Alex, "but if I were you, I would talk with my priest about all of this."

"I'll do that, Alex," said Lexington. "I've been so busy thinkin' about my own feelings, I never considered how all this might affect Celeste if I can't get past my past with Shallow. I wouldn't want to hurt Celeste."

"Alright," said Maris, "since we're discussin' women, maybe somebody can tell me what to do about a woman who always wants to know where I'm goin' or where I've been."

"That's a easy one," said August, laughing.

"It is man?" Maris said.

"Yeah," said August.

"What's the answer?" Maris said.

"Tell her," said August.

"Tell her what?" Maris said, looking around the table confused.

"Tell your wife where you goin' and where you been, man," said Nile, laughing.

"What?" Maris said. "Why would I do that?"

"Why wouldn't you?" asked August.

"This brother must have a busload of skeletons he hidin," said Leroy.

"Busloads," said Lexington said. "They not goin' all fit into just one bus."

Everyone laughed.

Alex hung his head and shook it.

Maris sunk into his seat, feeling slightly ashamed for the first time in a long time about his infidelity.

"Any married men want to encourage Nile by sharing why they got married with the groom?" Alex said, looking around the room.

"Don't look at me," said Mac. "I'm single."

The room grew silent.

"I'll go first," said Alex. "I got married because I found the woman that was that missin' part of me. I was standin' there lookin' into her pretty brown eyes, listenin' to her sweet voice, enjoyin' her refreshin' spirit and thinkin' Luna, Luna, Luna. That's a name I won't be forgettin' ever."

"That's some real greetin' card jive right there," said Bill.

Alex expressed amusement.

"You think you can do better?" Alex said.

"I know I can," said Bill, laughing.

"Alright," said Alex, "let's hear it."

"Alright, Nile man," said Bill. "I never told this to nobody. So, you can never say you didn't know I love you man. The day I met Binta I was still a young knucklehead, I was so blown away I was clumsy. I made a fool out of myself. She thought I was an idiot and didn't want to have a thing to do with me. I went home and that night I cried like a baby because I thought I'd never have a chance with her. My father sat me down and told me how to win her heart. I knew after that night that if I didn't marry her someday, I'd be cryin' to my grave."

Alex smiled.

"I got ya," said Bill.

"Yeah," said Alex, "you got me. That was a good story."

"He did get ya," said Leroy.

Impressed with his company, Maris stared silently, listening intently to the other men talking.

"What advice did your daddy give you about Binta?" Nile asked Bill.

"He told me to always be genuine and tell her the truth. And he told me to always treat her fine and with the utmost respect."

Nile nodded.

"How about you, Will?" Nile said.

"That's easy," said Will. "I knew Queenie was my wife because she told me she was."

"Really?" said Alex, laughing.

"Really brother-in-law," said Will, "besides y'all don't know Queenie like I do. She can be real convincing."

All of the men laughed.

"How about you, Leroy?" Nile said.

"Me and my old lady been together a long time, y'all," said Leroy, "and the one thing that comes to my mind when I think about why I married her is simple. I believe that there's a longin' in most men for "the woman", the one who understands them for who they are and is willin' to stay anyway. When a man finds that woman that longin' overpowers him."

"Is that what happen to you, Leroy?"

"Yes, indeed," said Leroy chuckling.

"What about you Maris," said Lexington laughing. "Tell us why you got married."

Maris was quiet. He thoughtfully gazed out of the dining room window into the garden.

"Maris, man?" Lexington said. "You alright?"

Maris looked at Lexington and the rest of the men at the dining room table. He had an apparent look of intense understanding on his face. He smiled to himself as he thought back and turned towards Lexington, his head tilted to the side slightly and his face beamed.

"I guess it's like Leroy said," said Maris, thoughtfully. "I was just about to hit rock bottom. I hadn't been as successful in college or the business world as I'd hoped. My career just wasn't goin' as planned. My parents had given up on me and what my mother calls "Maris' Trifling Ways". Then, I met Evon. It was like she breathed life back into me. Believed in me. Helped me reestablish my career. Helped me mend relations with my folks. Made a home for me and gave me my two beautiful boys. I guess I married her cuz she was a better friend to me than I was to myself."

"Wow," said Khalil. "Can I meet your wife? I mean, does she have a sister? For real, podna, cuz the streets aren't flowin' with too many sisters like her. "

"Yeah you right," said Bill, nodding his head.

"That was beautiful, man," said Lexington, hugging Maris, playfully.

"Man, get off me," said Maris, playfully shoving Lexington away.

"May I suggest you get my sister-in-law some flowers and candy on your way home and apologize to her for actin' like a damn fool for the last three years," said Lexington.

"Yeah," said Leroy, "and if you really been actin' a fool, you might want to get a babysitter and pick up a Stylistics' album if you don't already have one at home."

"The Stylistics, yeah," said Bill, nodding his head in agreement.

"I will," said Maris, with watery eyes. "I'm goin' do all that! Thank y'all for invitin' me here tonight. There's somethin' about y'all that makes me want to be a better husband and father. I guess I can see why Lexington's been hangin' out with Nile and Bill so much. Y'all mind if I come to y'all next men's meetin'?"

"Ofcourse not man," said Nile, "you're always welcome."

Maris smiled and breathed a sigh of relief. "I don't hang with too many fellas who actually think a wife is a good thing."

"Well," said Alex, "you might want to reconsider who you're hanging with."

"That's alright, Maris," said Lexington, slapping Maris on the back. "You goin' make Evon day."

"I know I'm not married or engaged," said Khalil suddenly, "but can I get some feedback on why I'm thinkin' about marryin' every woman I meet?"

"F'sure," said Leroy.

"Y'all sure?" Khalil said.

"Talk to us, Khalil," said Alex, nodding his head and drinking a can of Pineapple Big Shot cold drink.

"Alright," said Khalil. "Every time I see a sister I'm thinkin' about gettin' married cuz this celibacy thing is killin' me. Now I made a commitment to God to restrain myself until I'm married because let's face it. Anything else would be me siftin' somebody else's cane sugar. Can you dig it?"

"Yeah," said Alex, sitting his "cold drink" can down on the table.

"So," said Khalil, "it's alright if I pull a "Lexington" and just grab the first fox I see who's interested and ask her to marry me, then?"

"Hey, man," said Lexington defensively.

The room full of men exploded into a chorus of laughter.

Nile shook his head, while chuckling.

"Exercise some self control, brother," said Leroy, smiling.

"That's what I've been tryin' to do," said Khalil.

"Khalil, brother," said Alex, "sexual intimacy is just part of the equation. You can't just marry a woman because you want to have sex. Marriage is as much about what you are willin' to give of yourself as it is about what you are expectin' to get. You have to be ready to give of yourself in ways that go far beyond anything you've ever experienced. Until you're prepared to do that you don't even qualify for the position of husband."

"Yeah," said Khalil, nodding his head, "I know, Alex. I can dig it."

"What you do, Nile?" Khalil said.

"Huh?' said Nile, caught off guard.

"What you do to keep your hands off Matia until y'all married," said Khalil.

"Oh, I pray a lot. I take cold showers. I lift weights. I play ball. Oh, and I write."

"All of that, huh?" Khalil said, frowning skeptically.

"Not all of that all the time," said Nile. "I do what I need to do to get me through. The wait won't be forever."

"Yeah you right," said Bill, "matter of fact your wait will be over tomorrow!"

5

You are cordially invited to witness

the Holy Union of

Matia Singleton

And

Nile Hash

in the Truman Family Garden

on Saturday, the twenty-ninth of April,

nineteen hundred seventy eight

at one o'clock in the afternoon

A banquet reception will follow.

On the morning of the day that Matia married Nile, her father brought her breakfast in bed. She awoke feeling rather nauseous. She had experienced some stomach cramping and felt like vomiting though she had no physical reason to do so. It was confusing, causing her to question whether or not she should take her passing sickness as a sign from God.

But if it were a sign, what did it mean? Did it mean that she was doubting her decision to marry Nile? No, it did not. And after discussing her nausea with her father, she had ruled all doubt out as a possibility. She did however, agree that the sickness was the result of her having bad nerves, the nerves the result of her realizing the finality of her making a commitment to join her life to another's. Would she be any good at marriage and motherhood? She hoped and prayed the answer was yes.

As she ate her breakfast in bed, she considered the fact that this would be her last breakfast before becoming Mrs. Nile Hash. The breakfast, a meal of yellow hominy grits, scrambled eggs, sausage patties and homemade butter-milk biscuits with orange juice hushed the turmoil in her stomach.

A few hours later, she sat in front of her bedroom vanity fussing over her hair with Binta and Shallow.

"How does the French Braid look in the back?" asked Matia, sticking a bobby pin in the back of her hair.

"Oh, Matia," said Binta, gently brushing the back of Matia's hair, "it's beautiful."

"You did a nice job feathering the front too, Binta."

"Thank you, boo," said Binta.

"And my wedding dress is the prettiest I've ever seen."

"I know, huh," said Binta, laughing. "It's even prettier than the one I made for myself. Your daddy spent some money on pearls and lace, honey."

"I know, he did," said Matia.

"Bill was so impressed with your dress, Matia. He said I did a beautiful job. He liked it even more than my wedding gown. People always askin me if I'll design a gown for them. Bill thinks I should start a home business, designing ball and wedding gowns. I told him I'd start workin on some of my ideas on paper, but for now my mind's mostly on getting myself and the house ready for these two babies in my stomach. Once they're here and I'm settled with them, I might start takin on a client every now and then. We'll see. Bill thinks I could get a lot of business."

"Yes indeed with all the balls and weddings that go on in New Orleans," said Shallow. "Aw *'sha'*, I'm so excited for you."

"Yeah," said Matia, "and thank you too Shallow. Thanks for sharin' your managin' and plannin' skills with Nile and me. Havin' you help plan the wedding has made this entire wedding flow smoothly. I don't know what we would have done without your help."

"It was my pleasure helpin, *'sha',*" said Shallow. "I loved plannin it. I loved plannin Binta's too. I might as well get this wedding plannin stuff out of my system, since I probably never will be plannin my own."

"What you talkin' about?" said Binta. "We got two down and one to go. When the right guy comes along, you'll be next!"

"I don't think so, *'sha',*" said Shallow. "Though, I'm startin' to understand why marriage can be good, I still don't see myself as the marryin' type. Marriage requires too much compromise. And havin' to discuss what I'm doin' with somebody else sounds crazy to me."

"Not to me," said Binta.

"No?" asked Shallow.

"Not to me either," said Matia. "Sounds like marriage."

6

On the eve of Matia's wedding day, before she had sat facing her own reflection in her bedroom vanity and fussing over her hair with her two friends, Matia dreamed that while sleeping, she heard someone call her name.   When she opened her eyes, still dreaming, she saw that her childhood bedroom on Charbonnet was flooded with brilliantly piercing light.   Out of the light walked an angel that she believed to be the archangel Michael.   Matia discerned that the angel in her room was Michael after overhearing a conversation that Michael was having with an angel he called Gabriel. Gabriel called the angel standing in Matia's room by the name Michael.   Each time Matia attempted to look directly at Michael she was overcome by the piercing light that radiated from him.   Golden like the sun, Michael was unbearable to look upon for any extended period of time.

"Get your things," he said.

Quickly, Matia climbed out of her bed and began packing her belongings in her suitcase.   As she packed her life into a red rectangular case, she felt no fear, but instead an extraordinary sense of peace unlike any she had ever known. When Matia had finished packing her belongings, Michael took her by the hand and they walked through her bedroom wall and out into the middle of a bustling colorful street. Alive with music, laughter and conversation, the road was wide.   There were people pregnant with life.   They were eating, drinking, dancing, singing, buying, and selling.   As they walked Michael and Matia approached a fork in the road.   As many people took the wider street, Michael led Matia up the narrower road.   Shortly thereafter Michael stopped in front of a quaint little bistro.

"In here," said Michael, leading the way into the café.

Once inside, he led Matia to a booth with velvet seats and a brass dining table that was set for three and dressed with a feast fit for royalty. After urging Matia to have a seat and dine, he vanished. She set her suitcase beside her seat, taking in all that was around her with eyes wide open and wondering who if anyone would be joining her at the table that had been prepared for her. As Matia slid into the booth, she noticed that she was suddenly heavy with child. Holding her belly, she wondered at the life that was now within her.

7

"Time to go get married," said Nile under his breath as he put on his tuxedo in Alex and Luna's bedroom.

In just a matter of minutes, Matia would be his wife. Most of whom he held dear was just outside of Alex and Luna's house. In moments, Matia would be his wife. They had prepared a home for themselves, a place in which their future could dwell and grow. And Nile finally would be the beautiful Matia's and she, his beloved, would be his.

As Nile stepped out onto the back porch, he felt that he was receiving a heavenly glimpse of paradise. The sun shone brightly. The garden seemed more beautiful than usual; it was generous in size, one hundred by sixty, Nile had measured once. A very large live oak stood in the middle of the garden and its wide trunk was wrapped in an enormous lavender and chiffon bow. Nile heard the penetrating and clear whistle that was a bird song over the excited, but hushed conversations of the wedding guest. A vividly red colored male Cardinal flew from the bird feeder and up into the oak tree. In the live oak he joined and fed a female Cardinal whose red coloring was much more delicate than his.

The orange trees overwhelmed Nile with spring's sweet fragrance of orange blossoms. The crape myrtles and camellias were in full bloom with white, purple and pink crinkled and rose-shaped flowers. Honeysuckle and blue wisteria vines lavishly draped the garden gates and sung their own praises to the Daylilies, Lemon Rose Geranium, Royal Lavender and purple majesty that lined the gravel walkways that spread about the garden.

The last of the wedding guest to arrive began to take their seats in white wooden folding chairs that set on opposite sides of the center aisle. Shallow roamed the garden, making certain everyone and everything was in its proper place.

"There he is," said Will, Nile's older brother, dapping off Nile and giving him a quick hug.

"Thank you so much for comin' here all the way from D.C.," said Nile. "Thank you for bein' here, man."

"Are you kiddin' me little brother?" said Will. "Queenie, the kids and me wouldn't miss this for the world."

Alex Jr. and Alec, Luna and Alex's sons, began to warm up on their saxophones.

"You ready, little brother?" asked Will, hugging and dapping off Nile.

"I was born ready, big brother," said Nile.

"Alright now," said Will, patting Nile on the shoulder, "I'm goin' get back to my spot before that feisty weddin' planner of yours starts in on me for being out of place."

Moments later the wedding procession began. Alex Jr. began and performed a wedding march solo on alto saxophone. When the entire wedding party had marched down the aisle, Nile and Matia found their selves side by side. Alec then, joined in on soprano saxophone and the two brothers did a duet with varying cadences. In the moment, so moved was Matia that she struggled to hold herself together.

Alex, Nile and Matia stood underneath the live oak tree. Alex stood before the bride and groom, holding his bible open.

"Ephesians Chapter Five and twenty through twenty-one reads," said Alex, gently flipping the pages to his bible. "Give thanks always for all things to God the Father in the name of our Lord Jesus Christ, submitting to one another in the fear of God. Ephesians chapter five and verse thirty-one reads, for this cause shall a man leave his father and mother, and shall be joined unto his wife, and they two shall be one flesh."

"Please join me in witnessing the exchange of the vows that Nile and Matia have worked so hard to prepare for each other," said Alex.

Nile and Matia turned towards each other.

"My love," Matia said, "God fashioned me for you as only He would do. No other man could do what you do. My heart, how you wash me with the cooling waters of God's Word. A fresh field of flowers, your devotion, causes my soul to smile. Your smile fills my spirit with laughter. On today, I dazzle beautifully for you, a crown fit for no one, but you. I vow to reflect faithfulness with you. I will honor you. I will support you. To you I surrender my love. I will follow and walk beside you. I will be faithful to cherish you through treacherous weather if you are unable to see our way. May my words to you be like soft kisses chocolate and sweet. May our embrace be a fragrant rapture of exotic sandalwood and fresh jasmine, golden."

"Matia," said Nile, "I take you as my bride and I call you wife. May we triumph together in perfect unity. I vow to protect you. I vow to provide for you. I vow to honor you. I vow to lead you in integrity. I will comfort you. I will love you. I will hold you with willing arms, in your times of weakness as well as your times of strength. I will forsake all others and be true to you all the days of our lives. I will long to know your love in every sense; to see its many shades, to taste its golden honey, to listen for its delicate melody and to stroke its richest textures. May your kisses be all the intoxication that my soul desires."

There was a brief pause in silence. The wedding guests blushed with embarrassment at the vividly striking language of Matia and Nile's vows.

"Amen," said Alex, smiling. "I think these two are ready for marriage and all that it promises. How about y'all?"

Everyone remained silent.

"Don't y'all go getting' all religious on me now," said Alex. "God made marriage and the marriage bed. Maybe if husbands and wives spent more time lovin' and less time fightin' more of us would stay together. After all, lovin' each other is what a husband and wife are supposed to do in more ways than one. Amen!"

"Amen," Luna said, blushing.

"Thank you, baby," said Alex, smiling at Luna.

The wedding guest all laughed.

"Please stand for the presentation of the wedding bands," said Alex.

The guest all stood as Nile and Matia exchanged rings and spoke together in agreement.

"As I've chosen you, I choose too this ring to symbolize my undying commitment to love you. With you, I will stay.

With you, I will go. I will remain faithfully yours," said Nile and Matia in perfect harmony.

"On today, April 29, 1978 in the year of our Lord Jesus Christ and by the power vested in me by the state of Louisiana as a minister of the gospel, I do hereby pronounce you husband and wife. Mark 10:9 affirms, 'What therefore God hath joined together, let not man put asunder.' Let us pray. May our prayer for Nile and Matia Hash, be that they never cease to show charity's undeserved and undying love to each other. I Corinthians 13: 4-7 exclaims, 'Charity suffereth long, *and* is kind; charity envieth not; charity vaunteth not itself, is not puffed up, Doth not behave itself unseemly, seeketh not her own, is not easily provoked, thinketh no evil; Rejoiceth not in iniquity, but rejoiceth in the truth; Beareth all things, believeth all things, hopeth all things, endureth all things.' May this be their manner of love, Lord. Amen. Nile, you may now kiss your bride."

8

On their wedding night, Matia and Nile shared tender kiss after tender kiss. The two in love made a love that was most precious and fragrant with the pleasure of contentment. They did not merely lay with each other. They climbed inside each other. They became one flesh, reaching, finding, sharing and holding onto their delight for dear life. There was no thought for tomorrow. There was only the intense longing that they shared for the full realization of each other's long awaited love. Thirsty, they drank themselves silly with the joy of finally drinking from the cup of love's sweet nectar.

It all began with Nile returning to their bedroom to find Matia standing on their marriage bed, a queen sized bed draped in alluring crimson velvet. Dressed in a red satin negligee, Matia stood in the middle of a crimson sea of seduction singing and swaying her hips from side to side. She was finally going to understand fully what it meant to be loved body, soul and mind. Aretha sang out from the record player, giving them a private audience. Matia listened to Aretha's words and imagined that she was prepared to go just about anywhere Nile was man enough to take her. The soft lustrous bedspread was their flying carpet. The moment they were both aboard it, they would take off, exploring new and exotic foreign lands together.

When their carpet ride was over, Matia and Nile lay within the sanctuary of each other's sacred love. They lay having conceived what is known in the Swahili language as life. They lay having conceived their daughter, Asha.

Watch for the sequel

To

Birthing Pangs